Lela May Wight grew up with seven brothers and sisters. Yes, it was noisy, and she often found escape in romance books. She still does, but now she gets to write them too! She hopes to offer readers the same escapism when the world is a little too loud. Lela May lives in the UK, with her two sons and her very own hero, who never complains about her book addiction—he buys her more books! Check out what she's up to at lelamaywight.com.

Canadian **Dani Collins** knew in high school that she wanted to write romance for a living. Twenty-five years later, after marrying her high school sweetheart, having two kids with him, working at several generic office jobs and submitting countless manuscripts, she got The Call. Her first Mills & Boon novel won the Reviewers' Choice Award for Best First in Series from *RT Book Reviews*. She now works in her own office, writing romance.

This is **Lela May Wight**'s debut book for Mills & Boon Modern.

We hope that you enjoy it!

Also by Dani Collins

Her Impossible Baby Bombshell
One Snowbound New Year's Night
Cinderella for the Miami Playboy

The Secret Sisters miniseries

Married for One Reason Only
Manhattan's Most Scandalous Reunion

Discover more at millsandboon.co.uk.

HIS DESERT BRIDE BY DEMAND

LELA MAY WIGHT

INNOCENT IN HER ENEMY'S BED

DANI COLLINS

MILLS & BOON

First published in Great Britain 2022
by Mills & Boon, an imprint of HarperCollins*Publishers* Ltd,
1 London Bridge Street, London, SE1 9GF

www.harpercollins.co.uk

HarperCollins*Publishers*
1st Floor, Watermarque Building,
Ringsend Road, Dublin 4, Ireland

His Desert Bride by Demand © 2022 Lela May Wight

Innocent in Her Enemy's Bed © 2022 Dani Collins

ISBN: 978-0-263-30092-5

07/22

MIX
Paper from
responsible sources
FSC™ C007454

HIS DESERT BRIDE
BY DEMAND

LELA MAY WIGHT

MILLS & BOON

Matthew, this one's for you.
Thank you for pushing me to dream, and dream big.
I love you.

A big thank you to my family. My baby girl Lisa!
Thank you for being my cheerleader.
Mom, thank you for encouraging my love of words.
Kim, Lou, Luke, Ste and Josh, thank you
for encouraging me to run at my writing goals
until I surpassed them.

Martin, Teresa, Amy and Joe,
thank you for believing in me.

My beautiful boys,
thank you for believing in Mommy
and for giving me the time to write my a, b, cs.

Frankie, thank you for your support and friendship
when the crows of doubt were ever present.

Shell, thank you for your friendship
when I was a newbie to the wonders of social media
and the romance book community.

Gwessie, thank you for sharing your joy of books
with me. Ride those unicorns hard, lovely lady.
The romance book community misses you dearly.

And last but not least, my editor Charlotte.
Thank you for seeing the potential in my voice
and for making me a better writer.

PROLOGUE

THE BASTARD WAS DEAD.

Ripping free the report, Akeem crushed it and threw it across the room. And there, on a rug made from silk, lay a discarded account of Damien Hegarty's life and death, all summed up in a few paragraphs on expensive paper.

He almost chuckled. The man who'd called him a monster—*worse*—was dead, and this would be the closest Damien would ever get to opulence.

Relief should be the feeling easing the tension from Akeem's shoulders. But it wasn't.

*S*he would lose *everything*.

Akeem Abd al-Uzza, Crown Prince of Taliedaa, looked down again at the document he'd thought destroyed and his heart boomed in his ribcage.

There she was. A single photograph.

Charlotte.

He traced his finger along the outline of the woman in the picture. He remembered everything. Every minor detail of her softness against his rough. Oh, how he'd been obsessed by every blemish, every minor mark shadowing the golden tones of her flesh.

She had besotted him with her kindness.

'Kindness!' he sneered, and the word stung his lips.

Akeem raked unsteady fingers through his hair. Lust

stormed through him, dredging up long-forgotten memories and stirring him in ways unexpected. *Undesired.*

The freckles above her right breast, and how he'd joined them together with his tongue before taking her nipple into his mouth. How she'd cried out his name—*his* name—as his hand explored her body for the first time the night before she'd rejected him. Thrown him away as if he was nothing.

He pushed back out of his chair to stalk to the window that revealed views of the ancient city below and the rolling deserts beyond.

It never lessened. The lurch in his gut as he looked down over the city. It would be his. It *was* his. He closed his eyes. He, the forgotten orphan heir, was the ruler, up on high in the palace in the mountains.

Why, for the love of all he had overcome, could he not leave the past alone?

Leave *her* alone?

Charlotte Hegarty had hurt him. She'd crushed all that was innocent within him. And yet, after almost a decade, he still wanted her.

Wildly.

Two weeks and he'd be officially named King. He had a limited amount of freedom left before the weight of the crown kept him firmly away from the past. *Away from her.* Away from his need to rub in her face all she'd thrown away to live a life of drudgery.

For one last time before he was King he would claim his revenge. It was the very personal act of a man, not a king, but it wasn't an opportunity he was going to miss.

Holding the past by the hand, he'd show it—and *her*—that there was no place in his world for either of them.

CHAPTER ONE

CHARLOTTE HEGARTY OPENED her palm and released the damp earth. Thud by thud it fell onto her father's coffin, deep brown against a beech veneer, and she felt...*nothing*. Numb. Completely empty.

Her flimsy ballet flats sank into the mossy ground as she turned her back on the grave and on the empty scene behind her. Empty all but for her and the vicar.

No one had bothered to show up. Not even his drinking buddies. *Friends* who were only ever there when the drinks were flowing... She took another step, and another, hating the feel of her too-thin blazer and the starched white shirt chafing against her skin. But she kept moving. Away from the past, from the hopes and dreams she'd laid at his feet. Time after time he'd squashed them, choosing the bottle over her. And in the end the bottle had won. It had taken him and any hope that one day he would turn around and *see* her.

His daughter.

The wake loomed in her mind, as big and dark as the large black ornate gates coming into view. She still hoped someone would remember him. Grieve for him. But there was no free bar at the wake. Only memories. Only pain. Only regrets. His friends didn't do real, did they? They didn't want to see the real-world consequences of their lifestyle.

She'd remember him for them.

Her last act as a dutiful daughter. She'd walk to the pub across the road, where she'd been given the back room for free, and pretend to eat the little triangle sandwiches filled with fish paste and cucumber. And then it would be over.

On heavy feet, she closed in on the wooden double doors in desperate need of paint, and opened them with unnecessary force.

She froze. Every atom of her being was suspended as her heart stopped pumping blood to her vital organs.

She'd conjured a ghost.

'Akeem?' His name left her gaping mouth before she'd processed…*him.* She took a step forward. 'You're here—it's you.'

'Here and in the flesh, Charlotte,' he confirmed, lazing back against the bar.

Her eyes locked on his mouth, to those full brown lips making each syllable of her name sound *wrong.* Just the way he'd made her feel nine years ago, when he'd reminded her of exactly who she was. Charlotte Hegarty, unworthy of unconditional love. The daughter of an alcoholic, living in the roughest end of London, surviving a poverty-stricken life and barely functioning as a normal sixteen-year-old should…

Bitterness swept through her and it made her ache. Deep in her core.

Her name shouldn't be in his mouth or in his mind.

He shouldn't be here.

But he was.

She unfurled herself, squaring her shoulders, and locked her gaze on his. How appropriate, on the day when there was nothing left to fight for but herself, that he'd show up.

'Why are you here?'

She asked the question she'd spent countless nights rehearsing this very scene with him. But in her solo rehearsals she'd been the definition of cool indifference as he'd begged her forgiveness. The forgiveness she was going to pretend there was no need for and send him on his way.

But she'd never expected it to actually happen—and definitely not today.

Akeem shrugged, one broad, black-sheathed shoulder dipping to expose the pure breadth and size of him. 'To offer my condolences.'

Indignant rage curled her toes. 'Still telling lies, Akeem?' she accused, before the words had time to linger in her mouth. He'd lied his way into her bed and then left her behind without so much as a note.

His movements effortless, he pushed free from the age-stained bar. He was six feet plus of sheer male presence, closing in on her, and he was daring to smile. Full, gleaming white teeth in a sea of a short-cropped black beard.

'I never lied to you.'

The memory was vivid—visceral. It pulled her gaze back to his mouth, and to the last lie he'd spoken to her while climbing out of her bedroom window. He'd pressed a kiss to her swollen lips before sliding down to the porch roof with promises of tomorrow and for ever.

That lie had hurt the most.

'Whatever helps you sleep at night,' she countered, marvelling at the levelness of her tone.

'Sleep is for the dead.'

His long, lithe legs crossed the wooden floor and she couldn't breathe. His hair was thick and pushed to the side, as though he'd recently dragged his fingers through it.

He was breathtaking.

'I'm very much alive, and I never sleep.' He stopped, statue-still, in front of her.

Heat bloomed in her cheeks, down her throat, to spread out over her chest and deeper—*lower*. Her body recognised him before she could tell it not to. And she didn't like it. Not one bit. Because it was terrifying. This effect he had on her by simply being in the same airspace, stealing the air she needed to survive when he simply inhaled it.

'It must exhaust you, avoiding the demons haunting your bed.'

She planted her feet, readying herself to fight against a lifetime of remembering to keep quiet and do what had to be done. *Don't argue, don't fight—just to get on with it.* She'd been readying herself for this confrontation for nine long years. And she hated confrontation. But here it was.

Her moment.

His mouth flared into life. Not a grin, but a tilt of those sensuous lips as he leaned in. A hair's breadth away from her mouth, he whispered, 'My stamina has yet to be a concern.'

The air hissed from her lips. She knew what he was doing. He was intent on reminding her how she'd shared his bed. He had slept *then*. Wrapped around her like a second skin.

'What you do in your bed has nothing to do with me,' she said, Because it didn't—not any more. 'But you're not welcome here.'

'Am I not?'

His features were unmoved—a vision of innocence. But she knew better.

'No.' She moved her head from side to side in small, quick flicks. 'My father wouldn't have wanted you here, nor your condolences.'

'My condolences are for you,' he corrected, 'not him.'

'I'm surprised you have anything for *me*, let alone that you think of me,' she countered, and prepared herself for the bit she'd practised the most. The biggest and best lie. 'Because I don't think of you at all.'

If she'd felt nothing at the graveside she was feeling *everything* now. Her sixteen-year-old self was bursting out, reminding her twenty-five-year-old counterpart that it had unfinished business.

And here he was—*the unfinished business*—now undoing the top two pearl buttons at his neck. Slowly, he revealed his bronze throat, thick and pulsing inside the crisp white collar of his shirt.

He didn't respond. He simply watched her for a beat too long. His eyes searching hers. And a magnetic pull urged her to close the distance between them, to step inside the earthy scent of wood and sand and touch him.

The words had been easy, but what she hadn't expected was the primitive reaction her body was having to him. *This* wasn't part of the script. But she wouldn't show it! She wouldn't break on the outside, even if her insides were melting.

'I think of you often, *qalbi*,' he admitted, his voice low and soft, and she felt it like a physical caress on her cheek. 'I think of the life you chose.'

'The life I *chose*?' she repeated, and she hated the crack in her voice. It had been nine years. She couldn't blame him entirely that she'd stayed where he'd left her. But she did.

She pulled her lower lip between her teeth.

She blamed him for everything.

He nodded, his dark head dipping only once. 'This pitiful existence you call a life.'

'*What?*'

She stepped back then. Only slightly, but enough to give

her room to strike him. Squarely, on that beautifully chiselled chin of his.

She knew how pitiful her life was, but— 'You have no right to judge my life,' she said, finishing her thought out loud.

'Don't I? You could have been anything. *Anything*,' he stressed. 'Instead you continued to nurse a man who belittled you at every chance he got for another decade.'

She blinked hard and fast. 'I…'

She could have been anything?

'I'm twenty-five,' she reminded him, 'not dead.'

But his words curdled in her gut, despite her feigned confidence. She didn't know what her life might have looked like now. She knew nothing apart from the all-consuming fact that she had no one and nothing to call her own.

'Tell me it's not true and regale me with your exciting plans now you are free. Are you still drawing?'

She gasped. *Drawing?* He remembered. He remembered the one part of herself that had allowed her freedom. Her pencil had been her ticket to adventure. *Her escape.* And she'd given it up. Her drawing. Her art. Her one talent. Because her dad had called her drawings stupid, a waste of time when she should have been caring for him. He'd destroyed all her work. Crushed her dreams. And she'd let him because she'd felt selfish, taking those precious moments to draw and dream for herself.

How could she have taken time for herself when her dad had needed her help to survive? How could she have chased her foolish dream of becoming a portrait artist when her reality had been so heavy?

'Are you still chasing your dreams?' Akeem continued, and she swallowed the memory of what she'd lost. What her dad had taken from her. Not only her art, but her identity.

Because the only thing that had defined who she was—not a daughter, not a carer—had been her art.

But quickly she had let her dreams go as if they'd never existed—what would have been the point of holding on to them?

She zeroed in on his face. On the man determined to make her remember. To make her regret.

His eyes, intense, were moving over her face. 'Or have you been wasting your life filling those empty whisky bottles with cold tea to fool your drunken father? Have you been wasting your life, *qalbi*, trying to save a man who did not want to be saved?'

He raised his hand, those long, elegant fingers moving towards her cheek. She backed up, one step at a time. He was too close. *Too intimate.*

But his questions spoke to her at her deepest level of consciousness. Because she hadn't done—still wasn't doing—any of the things they'd whispered about late at night, hidden in her bedroom…those dreams and hopes of being…*more.*

Her insides twisted and snaked around her lungs.

Her dad had needed her when no one else had, even if he'd never recognised her sacrifice. Her time. Her art… He'd never seen that it was her keeping him alive and forgetting to live her own life. Never acknowledged how she'd managed their minimal income by getting to the bank before he did to withdraw their welfare benefit money before he spent it on whisky so they couldn't eat. He'd never seen her visiting food banks when she'd been too late and her father had taken the money before she had.

She'd made things work on a frayed string of hope and prayer, and not once had he thanked her. The daughter who had become the parent instead of the child. Who had worked in temporary jobs from catering, to retail, to office cleaning as soon as she had been old enough to get a job.

She'd worked in one meaningless job after another... She'd stood still for nine years. Exactly where Akeem had left her...

Her chest heaved.

She hadn't had a choice!

'I did what I had to,' she said, feeling the past snarling between them. 'I stood by my father as a daughter should.' She exhaled heavily, felt the cheap cotton of her shirt loosening on her chest. 'He was all I had left.'

'No,' he corrected, his voice laced with steel. 'Your father was all you *allowed* yourself to have.'

'Stop!' she demanded breathlessly.

She didn't want to hear this—any of it. This wasn't how it was supposed to go. *This wasn't it!* Why wasn't he on his knees, begging her forgiveness for leaving her behind?

'Are you the woman you wanted to be, Charlotte?' he asked, ignoring her.

She'd dared to believe she could be someone else once—that life had more to offer her than being her father's keeper—and Akeem had smashed those notions to smithereens. She had no clue who she was now, or what she was going to do. But she wouldn't admit that to him. It was hard enough to admit to herself that caring for her father had become her life.

'Stop,' she said again.

She rubbed forcibly at her exposed collarbone. She hated him. Hated what he'd done to her. Akeem had made her question everything. Not only question why he'd broken his promise to take her with him, but question herself on who she was and what she could never be. *And he still was!*

'Stop it, whatever this is, and leave.'

'But I've only just arrived.'

She glared at him. 'I didn't ask you to come.'

'You'd rather mourn alone—' he spread his hands wide, arching a thick dark brow '—in a room like this?'

'How graceful of you to remind me.' She smiled unkindly. 'But you have no right to tell me how to grieve.'

'All you should feel is relief.' His nostrils flared, but she watched him shutter the exasperation glazing his eyes. 'But you're right,' he conceded. 'I have no right to tell you how to grieve, or where, because I am not sorry he is dead. But I am sorry you have lost your father, Charlotte,' he continued, keeping his voice low and firm. 'I know you loved him for reasons I'll—'

'This is not the time.'

'What better time is there?' he asked.

She watched the white shirt and black jacket becoming taut over his shoulders, hinting at the hard and muscular body beneath. The body she'd once coveted so wantonly.

Letting out a harsh breath, she uncurled her hands and scrubbed them across her face. It was time to end this.

'What do you want?'

He closed in, removing the space she'd created between them. 'It's not what I want that matters. It's what I have that you need, Lottie.'

'What is it that I *need*, Akeem?' she echoed back at him. His use of the name he'd used to call her by was doing things to her insides she didn't want to recognise.

'You need me.'

'*You?*' she whispered, disgusted that her body was having such a visceral reaction to his statement.

'Yes.' He smiled, his brown eyes burning black. '*Me*. Akeem Abd al-Uzza.' His voice, deep and proud, oozed masculinity. *Power.*

'Not Akeem Ali?' she asked.

'Abd al-Uzza is my father's name.'

'Your dad's? But your mum—'

She closed her eyes. It didn't matter. She didn't want to know. He'd given up his name just as he'd given her up. Abandoned them both as if they meant nothing.

Forcing herself to chuckle, she tilted her head. 'Akeem Ali—' she shrugged '—or Abd al-Uzza, I don't want you here, and I certainly don't need you.'

'Today is the beginning of the rest of your life. What better way to start that new life than with a night of pleasure in my arms, surrounded by opulence?'

'You want to take me to bed?' she spluttered.

'Yes. You will spend one night in my bed—one night of extreme pleasure.'

'Why?'

'Call it what you will—*closure*...' he stretched the word.

'Closure?' Her heart hammered. 'You came here uninvited because you thought I'd sleep with you one last time for *closure*?' Her eyes widened, and she hooked a brow. 'How very arrogant of you.'

'Does my arrogance surprise you when I can see your pulse pounding wildly beside the hollow of your throat?'

'Yes.' She nodded. 'The boy I knew would ask—never demand.'

Unbidden, memory claimed her. The swipe of tentative fingers across her naked hipbone. The press of his mouth behind her ear as he asked if she liked his hand there...did she want him to bring her pleasure with his fingers?

She shuddered. Her Akeem had been gentle, caring—never demanding. The Akeem she had known was not this man standing in front of her.

'I am not the boy you remember.' His voice was silk. Seductive. 'The pleasure you will experience in my arms will be unlike any you've known before or after me.'

He raised his hand and applied pressure to the frantic

beating at her throat. It took everything she had in her arsenal not to react to his touch and to remain indifferent. But she wasn't indifferent. She'd only ever known *him*. All she could do was watch—feel all the things she shouldn't be feeling.

She hated him, didn't she?

'Should I put my mouth here, so you may understand the power of attraction still between us?'

'No!' she shrieked, unable to breathe or to think about anything but her disloyal body. It tingled from the intensity of his gaze—his touch. And she wanted to step into his embrace.

What was wrong with her? It was the day of her father's funeral. She was on the edge. And here was Akeem, magnifying her overwrought emotions to fever-pitch. She couldn't stand it. His ability to still affect her. He would not trick her into forgetting what he'd done. How he'd abandoned her.

'No,' she said again, 'my bed is off-limits to you.'

'It's not *your* bed I want you in,' he corrected. 'It's mine.'

'Whatever bed,' she huffed, knowing he'd purposely missed her point. 'I won't be in it with you,' she declared, and hoped she meant it. 'You're the one that needs this.' She waved her hands. 'Not me. Otherwise you wouldn't be here.'

'You need to close the door on the past as much as I do,' Akeem concluded, and moved his thumb up the taut lines of her throat. With his forefinger beneath her chin, he tilted her head. 'Take a chance and come to bed with me.'

Temptation teased through her, and the knot in her abdomen was an acknowledgment of the desire she felt. She didn't need his mouth on her skin to understand that whatever was still between them was powerful—more than it had been nine years ago. But it was different—stronger. An older kind of yearning… It was lust, she recognised. *Desire.*

She was a fool.

'No,' she whispered, and his hands fell away to his side. 'I can't.'

'Fear stopped you when you were a girl, and now you are a woman—' his eyes swept over her '—you're still scared.'

'How so?' she asked, because he'd been the one to run away. He'd been the one who was afraid.

'What do you have to lose?' he asked, and she bit back the immediate response clinging to the inside of her mouth. *Nothing.*

'You have no job, no family, no money, and soon you'll be homeless. Do you wish to remain exactly where you have always been until they forcibly evict you from everything you know? Your house? Your home?'

'How do you know that?'

'It is easy to imagine the life you have led.' His lips thinned, and silently he held her gaze.

Of course he knew everything. He was a man of means now. She recognised it in every stitch of his handmade suit. He knew she hadn't moved forward. To him, she was still the same girl he'd known. Scared, and alone, and thrust into a system she had been frightened would take her away from her dad.

She'd always kept her mouth shut. As her dad had taught her. Outsiders didn't matter. Outsiders didn't count. And she had told no one anything—not even the police who'd hammered on the door because the school hadn't been able to contact her dad for three days and they'd had concerns for her welfare. They'd found her dad barely conscious. The social services team had delivered her to a children's home, and still she'd remained silent. But she had told Akeem.

Eight weeks, they'd told her. An interim care order. If in eight weeks her dad could prove he was well enough to take care of her, she could go home. For those eight weeks it had been her and him. Akeem and Charlotte.

He'd been her first and only friend. She'd opened up for the first time in her life—because he'd offered her something she'd never had. Friendship.

But she wasn't that girl any more. She didn't want to be. Because *that* girl had given everything to her father until there had been nothing left for her.

A recklessness she'd never known before pulsated through her. Urging her to throw caution to the wind and admit that his touch on her body was welcome and she wanted more. *Much more.* Because when had she ever been selfish? Or allowed herself to behave any way rather than steadfastly, working out the pros and cons first?

Once was the simple answer. Once when she'd packed her suitcase, ready to run away with Akeem, and he'd gone without her…

She had nothing to lose by spending the night with him. Only pleasure—however fleeting.

Every muscle in her body strained as she moved towards him and stood on tiptoe.

'One night?' she hissed and waited, nose to nose, eye to eye, for him to respond—like a boxer squaring off against an opponent before a fight, just as her dad had done in his youth.

The only time her father had fought for anything it had been for those few trophies on the mantelpiece at home. He'd never fought for her. For their family. The only things he'd taken pride in had been his boxing achievements. And what did *she* have to be proud of? A few awards for her portraits from secondary school? An unconditional place to study for a diploma at college she'd never taken up because she'd had to get a job instead? She'd had to take care of her dad…

'Yes.' Akeem agreed, his eyes hungry, his breathing shallow. 'One night.'

It was desire. That was all. Right now, she needed to connect, and she was reacting to the havoc of the day and to the storm of emotions he was evoking inside her. The indulgence of being impulsive was equally as exciting as it was frightening, but she was surrendering to it. To a spontaneity she'd never been allowed to have.

Until now.

Her hands had made their way to the solid wall of his chest. The fabric of his shirt was cushioning her fingers. She pushed away and stepped out of his embrace.

'Let's get it over with,' she said, trying on for size the indifference she wanted to project. But she wasn't indifferent. She was excited. Scared. Slick in places she shouldn't be.

His eyes narrowed. 'As you wish. But we will not "get it over with". It will be long and gratifying.'

Tingles shot through her. 'One night and one night only. Then we part ways. Nothing changes. We'll be the same as we are now. A distant memory in each other's life.'

'Yes,' he agreed, his beautiful face carved in granite.

Charlotte hesitated. He was lying. *Again.* Or was she? Because it would change everything. It would change *her.* But wasn't that what she wanted? To be completely brand-new and forging forward into a shiny future, not beholden to the past?

'No more thinking, Charlotte,' he said, his voice gruff, and he extended his arm. 'Take my hand.'

With bated breath, she did.

Blindly, she followed him. Took his hand, without pause and without question. To be deposited neatly into a waiting car.

She looked at him, folded against the leather interior, seemingly oblivious to her presence, and her traitorous heart did a double beat. Her hand still burned. Her palm still radiated the heat of their hands' union. And her mouth… oh, her mouth…it throbbed with the memory of his lips so close to hers.

Her heart threatening to explode, she looked away from him. Sweat beaded her palms and she smoothed them down her black pencil skirt. There was a ladder in her tights. A run where thigh met knee. She pulled at it. She didn't belong here, with her cheap skirt and ninety-nine pence tights.

This wasn't how a woman should look on her way to a hotel to be seduced.

She turned to the window. The scene beyond was a whizzing blur.

Her clothes didn't matter. She wanted this. She wanted *him*.

Keeping her back to him, she felt the warmth of his breath hit her nape before he moved his mouth to her ear.

'So tense…'

A soft but firm finger traced the outline of her spine, and she shivered as a heavy sensation dragged through her in its wake.

'I have every intention of easing this tension.'

She hadn't been touched in almost a decade. She didn't need to ask what he meant. Of course there'd been dates. She'd worked in endless jobs, and meeting people hadn't been the problem. But she'd never connected with them, never wanted them, because their lips hadn't been *his* lips.

They hadn't given her *this*. Whatever this was still burning hotly between them.

Arching her neck, she leaned into him and closed her eyes. One night—that was all—and his hands would be everywhere… On her—in her. They'd be naked and anonymous in some swanky London hotel. She *needed* this. He was right. She needed *him*.

The car slowed to an almost-crawl. Or was she slowing down? She didn't seem to be breathing—just *feeling*.

'Does it scare you?' she asked.

He pressed his chest against her back. Strength surged from him. Solid and all-consuming confidence.

'Does what scare me?'

She twirled in his embrace, splaying her hand against his seemingly impenetrable chest, keeping him at bay, although every instinct told her to pull him in. Grab him by the lapels and pull him in. Closer.

'This energy between us?'

'What I feel is excitement,' he admitted, 'not fear.'

'Me too,' she whispered truthfully. 'But it's been nearly ten years.' She grappled with her tongue. 'We are strangers, and yet...'

'We are *strangers*?'

'How can we not be? I was only sixteen when we met at St John's Children's—'

'I was nearly eighteen.' His eyes widened. 'We were both innocents, finding solace in each other.'

'But the trajectory of our lives since then has been...' She wanted to say *different*, but it didn't feel right.

He vibrated luxury. The suit caressing his body. The car. He'd moved on to bigger and better things and she—

She shook her head and looked at her hand touching his chest. Crashing into this flesh and muscle nine years ago at the children's home had opened a whole new world for her. They'd become each other's secret. They'd been each other's escape.

Akeem had offered her companionable silence in a world that had refused to be quiet, offered her comfort in the endless task of worrying about her dad by just letting her be still with him. They'd sat watching TV in the communal lounge, or talking in the garden, and she'd offered him a reprieve too, from the care system he'd been so eager to escape, by listening to his dreams. He'd wanted to build. That had been his dream. To go from labouring on a renovation site to building skyscrapers in the sky.

She'd never imagined that nearly a decade later this was where she'd be. A stranger to him.

Her fingers moved of the own volition. Testing the firmness—the *realness*—of him.

She'd wanted a family to call her own…a career that fulfilled her fanciful dream of becoming a portrait artist… And then the one person who'd believed in her dreams had vanished and so had they. Her dreams. Vanished as soon as she'd dared to believe they were possible.

Charlotte encircled the pearl button in the middle of his shirt with the pad of her thumb. Lifting her gaze, she eyed him cautiously, the pink tip of her tongue poking through her mouth to moisten her lower lip.

Akeem had made her *believe*.

She swallowed—hard. He'd made her believe in lots of falsities. Her breath caught and she pushed a finger inside the buttonhole. Her finger met a fine fuzz of hair. And heat.

But this was real.

This want.

'You know me,' he declared. 'You still want me and you are looking for a way to justify your desire. The connection still between us should dispel any shame attached to spending the night with me.'

She gasped, unable to contradict his pinpoint accuracy over her tumultuous emotions. Could he read her so easily? Could he *see* her?

'We are *not* strangers,' he continued. 'Your body knows mine.' He placed the pad of his thumb on her top lip and instinctively she opened her mouth to accept him. He pulled his hand away and reached for hers, placed it on the hard length of him beneath his trousers. 'And my body knows yours.'

She couldn't move. The heat of him mesmerised her. The hardness. The open conviction with which he wanted her.

'There is no shame or guilt to be found here, *qalbi*,' he promised, 'only pleasure.'

She didn't answer. Couldn't. And the silence stretched, palpable with the heaviness between them.

'We've arrived,' he informed her, nodding towards the window.

And before she'd caught her breath he was opening the door on her side and offering her his hand. She stepped out to join him.

Planes.

They were everywhere she looked. Small ones, big ones, and some bigger still.

She rounded on him. 'Where's the hotel?'

'There was never a hotel.'

'Then where—?' A plane in the distance took flight, and she watched as it ascended into the skies. How had they got to an airport?

Her heart hammering, she turned her eyes on him. 'You said one night?'

'Yes,' he confirmed. 'For one night I mean to have you in my bed. There is no trickery at play. No deception.' His voice was low. Gruff. '*My bed.* Not one anyone else has enjoyed, and one where only my body knows the dips and springs.'

'Sounds like you need a new mattress!'

A sting of heat worked its way from her chest to slash across her cheeks. She was reacting to him. Her traitorous body had hardened and softened in places she'd forgotten could melt with the mere sound of his voice.

'I need *you, qalbi*,' he contradicted. 'And I mean to have you in my bed. In my desert kingdom.'

'What?' Her heart hiccuped. '*Your* desert kingdom?'

'I am Crown Prince Akeem Abd al-Uzza, son of the late King Saleem Abd al-Uzza and soon to be named King of Taliedaa.'

'*How?*' Her mouth gaped as she reeled from his announcement. 'When your birth father contacted you on your eighteenth birthday I thought—'

'You thought wrong. It was not my parent who contacted me. It was my father's senior aide, who'd been watching over me my entire life. Waiting.'

'Waiting for what?' Anger replaced her shock. 'To see how much life could kick you?'

She knew how much life had kicked them both. And he was saying someone could have saved him from that. But hadn't.

'Your first thought is how it was unfair to *me*?' Thick brows arched over coolly observant eyes. 'And not what *you* could have become?'

'What *I* could have become? It's not about me...' she dismissed easily, with a wave of her wrist. 'He left you—*a child*—alone to fend for yourself when you are of *royal blood*? You're a *prince*—' she pressed a trembling hand to her chest '—and they let you be tossed from children's home to foster home to children's home again because they were...*waiting*?'

'Spare me your pity, Charlotte. I do not need or want it.'

'It's not pity I'm feeling.' And it wasn't. It was hot rage, with a cooling dose of empathy.

Red lines shadowed his high cheekbones. 'Then do not look at me with those eyes.'

'They're the only eyes I've got.' She shook her head.

'Why did they—*he*,' she corrected, 'wait so long after your mother died?'

'My mother was of no consequence to the crown.'

'Wasn't she a secret royal, too?'

'No.' The response was dry—husked. 'My mother was a plaything of my father's—a commoner working in the palace. She left my father's kingdom the minute she discovered she was pregnant for fear of being ostracised.' Harshness contorted his face. '*Her* death changed nothing.'

The confession was low and deep. She could see how much it had cost him to admit that.

Confusion narrowed her eyes. 'What about you? Why did they leave you in the care system until your eighteenth birthday?'

'Kings do not trouble themselves with their bastard sons unless they are a security risk or they suddenly need them.'

He hadn't said *want* and that chafed at her skin.

Had they both been unwanted by their fathers?

'Which were you?'

'I was—I *am*,' he emphasised, 'the only heir by blood to the Taliedaaen throne.'

His voice was toneless. Not proud. Not...*anything*. Her eyes flicked across his features. Vacant.

A heaviness expanded in her core. 'Why didn't you tell me?'

'Would it have made a difference?' he asked. 'I told you the truth. My birth family got in contact and wanted to meet me. Would the rest of it have mattered?' His eyes, black and granite, held hers.

'Of course not.' The denial was hot in her mouth. 'But we were planning to elope—'

'You promised yourself to a boy with callused hands. A boy who worked from dawn till dusk in manual labour to learn his trade.' His face was unreadable, a mask of emptiness. 'You did not promise yourself to an orphan prince raised in poverty, who would one day be a king. You wanted the man and not the crown. There was no need to tell you.'

'Is that why it was such a rush? Your plan to meet my dad? To tell him we were leaving, with or without his consent? Because you weren't only leaving London, you were leaving England altogether? Is that why you left—' She cut herself off and trapped the last words in her mouth.

Without me?

'When I suggested we run away together—run away from a system that had cared for neither of us and away from your father—I was taking us to a bedsit with the leaving care grant they'd offer me on my eighteenth birthday. But that day I was going home. To my country. It was that day or never. Because I was leaving and I wasn't coming back.'

We? Us?

'And you chose never?' she asked quietly, his choice of words making her gut churn.

'*I* didn't choose. But I'm here now.'

She wanted to push. Wanted him to say to her face that she hadn't been enough. That she hadn't been princess material and he'd forged on without her. But the words clung to her throat.

That was *why* he'd left her behind. He'd abandoned her because he'd believed she wasn't capable or worthy of his new life. He'd known the daughter of an alcoholic would never be accepted by royalty. *By his family.* Or anyone, really.

She was unlovable—destined to fail. Just as her dad had reminded her every time she'd got something wrong. No, more often than that—every time she'd breathed too loudly, spoken too confidently.

Her chest ached for the girl she'd been. The girl who'd

poured all her simple hopes and dreams into his ear. Believing he was accepting her as she was. For *who* she was.

'I can't go to Taliedaa,' she said, ignoring the past nagging at her in the bitter depths of her memories. She wanted to close the door on the past—not wrench it open! 'I don't want to go to a world where you're a crown prince and I'm...*me*.' She looked down at the splintering fabric on her knee. 'I have ladders in my tights. I can't possibly get on a plane.'

His gaze locked on hers. 'Then take them off.'

She gasped. 'I...' Exhaling heavily, she shrugged. 'I can't.'

And she couldn't. Because she might take off her tights, but she couldn't take off her skin. She couldn't shrug off who she was. And she couldn't change who he was now.

'Where will you go, *qalbi*?' he asked. 'Back to the same little house where we became lovers?'

'Once hardly makes us lovers,' she responded stiffly.

'I stand corrected,' he said placatingly, and there were those teeth again. Perfect in their insincere symmetry. 'The same little house where we spent countless hours hiding from your father—hiding from that robotic children's home manager—to *talk*.'

He didn't blink, those eyes holding fast to hers, and her stomach flipped. Painfully.

His smile faded. 'The same little house where I lost my virginity and you lost yours.'

Her breath caught tightly in her lungs. Memories claimed her. Just as he'd intended. Memories of the one and only time they'd made love. Of the night they'd surrendered their virginities to one another to seal their pact to marry. It had been the night before they'd agreed to tell her dad. The night before they would leave together and never return.

Instead he'd left her behind, with her father full of *'I told you so,'* because she'd strayed from the plan and told her dad everything before Akeem would arrive.

And he never had.

'I am not that boy any more,' he reminded her again, and reached for her. His fingers held lightly to the tops of her arms. 'I will not fumble or hesitate.' His eyes darkened. 'My touch will be...*controlled*.'

'You were never out of control.' Charlotte stared at him. 'Not with me.'

He released her. 'Wasn't I...?' He continued without a reflective pause. 'It matters not, because the pleasure you will experience in my arms now will be nothing like our night together. It will be...' He exhaled sharply, his nostrils flaring. 'It will be full of the pleasure only a king can give you. Only me. Only what I have become.'

'King?' she croaked.

'This is your last chance,' he warned, ignoring her question. 'Get in—' he stood aside, waving his hand towards the long red carpet leading up to a gigantic plane's entrance '—or stay exactly where you have always been.'

He dropped his hand to his side, turned and walked towards the plane.

'Wait!'

He snapped his head back round. 'Wait?'

Her heart slammed against her ribs, the breath in her lungs choking her. The funeral had been for her dad. The wake had become all about Akeem. But *this*...

This could be for her.

'I'm not the girl you remember, either.'

And she wasn't. She didn't want to be. She wasn't a secret royal, but she wanted to be someone else, if only for a minute. She wanted to be selfish. Bold.

Worthy of...*more*.

Her gut was gripped in a tight fist. She would never be

her father. She wouldn't allow herself to let life pass her by again. Her father had been nothing more than a shadow on the doorstep of death for far too long, and he'd been dead long before she'd found him.

A heart attack brought on by alcoholism and no one had been there. *She* hadn't been there. He'd died because she'd failed to do the one thing she'd been trying to do her whole life. Keep him alive.

Closing the memory down before it consumed her, Charlotte focused hard on the man before her. The living flesh of a man offering her *life*.

She was alive. She could live. The only person she had left to fail now was herself. And she was tired of failing.

Shaking her waist-length curls behind her back, she moved ahead of him, keeping her head high.

She was getting on board.

CHAPTER TWO

AKEEM HAD LIED.

The royal plane was a hotel. The double-decker private jet was the largest and fastest ever to take to the skies. He could have her right here, right now, in a multitude of rooms. Send her back to her insignificant life with only the marks he'd leave on her body with no one being the wiser. He'd bite and suck, and—

Beast.

His hand gripped the metal rail. Breaking his rhythm behind her.

The word was a murmur in his mind. An echo of the name his father had called his only son—his only child—and yet it scraped across his skin.

He was not feral any more. He did not cry when he was sad. He did not shout when he was angry. He was not the boy who, gifted with a small stuffed toy, had taken it to his room and torn the legs off. He was not the teenager who had answered with his fists when the boys in his class had mocked his trousers with their worn-out knees and his yellowing shirts.

He was not the boy who had been presented to his father, which had unleashed in him a rage knitted so tightly into his being that he'd scared himself. Even with guards holding his wrists above his head, his anger had swelled inside him. Bigger than him. Stronger. Untamed and ferocious.

No, he was not that boy any more, and he did not give in to his basic needs on a whim.

This was strategic, he reminded himself, shutting out the memory of those guards and his father's voice. He moved faster, urging her up the stairs. This one night was planned. *Necessary.* Seduce and destroy. Not only Charlotte, but the past, and any lingering remains of the boy he could never be again. The boy nobody had wanted. The boy his father had forbidden him to be.

Watching the gentle sway of her hips, he followed behind her as she climbed the stairs and entered the palatial aeroplane. There were no staff to greet them. Under his orders. No one would see her. No one would know. *Only him.*

She was his last tie to the past and he would sever that rope.

He stayed in sync with her every move as she tentatively padded onto the brilliant white carpet stretching the length of the first small lounge and acting as her personal runaway. Tight curls kissed the hollow at the base of her spine that he'd known so well. She was undoubtedly curvier. Even from behind, in that awful black blazer, he could see the swell of her hips and the prominent dip of her waist.

'Akeem?'

Her voice was gentle. Hesitant. She didn't turn. Simply stopped. Looking ahead and not behind. He'd spent nearly a decade trying not to look back. Not to feel. *Think.* But she'd always been there. Taunting him.

'Keep going,' he insisted, and after a brief hesitation she walked through the next open door in its gilded frame and entered the main salon.

With a press of a button the obscured glass came together as double doors behind them. His heartbeat raged to a deafening crescendo, so fast it almost hurt.

She was all his now.

Charlotte halted, and moved her head from side to side, taking in the shuttered windows lining the walls, the plush sofas draped in beige and gold running along each wall. A sound of awe escaped her, and he felt himself swell.

Open-mouthed, she drank in the surroundings he lived in every day. The slashes of light carefully designed to illuminate the highly polished wooden panels and hand-carved tables. Everything shimmered with a gold hue— including her.

She was looking straight ahead, and he watched her gaze stall. *The throne.* High-backed, and made from the finest yellow metal, encrusted with Taliedaa's very own rare jewels.

She gasped, and the sound was thrilling. He only wished his mouth was on hers so he could taste it. Taste the sweet taste of victory from her plush little mouth.

'Sit, *qalbi*,' he ordered.

Big green eyes turned to him. 'But *where*?'

Where did she think?

He strode towards her, backing her up into the only place she *could* sit. The throne with its clawed feet. It hadn't been designed for comfort. It had been created to bring everyone's attention in the room to the person who sat on it.

It was *his* throne now. And he wanted his eyes on nothing but her. Because only for today—only for one night— she would taste and feel everything that belonged to him. Recognise everything he had become. That he *would* become.

A king.

Her hands pinched together in front of her. *'Here...?'*

Akeem leant towards her and reached down beside her waist to grasp the seatbelt.

'I can do it,' she said, and her fingers brushed against his as she tried to take it from him. She stilled, craning her neck to look into his eyes.

He'd felt it too.

The surge.

'Allow me,' he said, pulling it around her and clipping it closed.

Licking her plump lips, she drew his gaze. He followed her tongue as it moistened the outline of those lips he'd dreamt of too often in the night's dark.

His eyes moved over her face. From the slight crevice below her nose to her high cheekbones. To her eyes. A deep emerald-green with slashes of gold highlighting her right iris. He had not forgotten those eyes. But he would.

Soon there would be no more dreams.

'Outside…' she started. 'You said King? Not Prince?'

He stiffened. 'My father passed away a few weeks ago and I will take his role as King, officially, in two weeks.' With one last tug, he fastened her tightly into the seat.

'I'm sorry for your loss,' she said.

But he wasn't sorry.

'As I am for yours,' he said instead.

'We're both alone now.'

She offered him a small smile, and it was a punch straight to his solar plexus. *Kindness.* He didn't want it. He didn't need it. Not any more. But he didn't move. Didn't speak. For fear she would somehow see the boy he'd spent nine years outgrowing. Pushing him into the shadows. Closing the lid…

'What was he like?' she asked.

His mouth gaped. 'Who?'

'Your dad.'

His jaw tensed. 'He was a king.'

'I know that.' She frowned. 'But was your dad everything you thought he would be?'

'No,' he answered honestly. 'He was a selfish man and a selfish king.'

'That's so sad—'

'No. It is anything but sad, Charlotte,' he corrected, keeping his voice low. Neutral. 'He taught me what not to be.'

Him, he added silently.

'How did he teach you?' she asked. 'Were there lessons in royal protocol?'

He nodded, pressing his teeth together.

'Were they hard?'

'I received my first lesson on arrival in Taliedaa. It was the toughest and the most successful,' he said, avoiding the impulse to grip his wrists, where he could still feel the pressure of his father's guards holding him.

He blamed her, he realised. Blamed her for the anger he'd travelled with to meet his father.

You let yourself get attached to her.

He *had* let himself, he corrected.

He was attached to nothing and no one now.

But the day he'd arrived in Taliedaa he'd been hurting from her rejection.

He'd asked his father why he hadn't rescued him from poverty the moment they'd presented him to the King. But it wasn't only that he'd been asking about. He hadn't been so naïve even as the boy he was. He hadn't only been asking why his father had forgotten him. He'd wanted to know why they'd all abandoned him. His mother... The foster families...

Charlotte.

His father had answered him. Told him in no uncertain

terms why he'd never come for him before. Why they'd all abandoned him. Because nobody wanted pathetic little boys or pitiful young men. He had been born into weakness, he had told him, and it was his nature to surrender to it. To be weak.

Like his mother.

Akeem had flown at him. In a heartbeat he'd unleashed a lifetime of hurt on the man—his father. Wounded. Crying. Screaming. The royal guards had caught him by the wrists and raised his arms above his head and the King had laughed.

There he had been, face to face with his father as he sat on his pretty throne, surrounded by men who would protect him with their lives, and every time Akeem had struggled, or sworn, he had instructed them to hit him—*harder*.

He had fought. He had cursed. And they had hit him with closed fists.

His father had had the clothes striped from his body to show him how primitive he was. He'd told him that he responded to his urges without thought or reason, acting on impulse like a basic dog, rather than thinking through his situation or how to respond to it to gain the best outcome for himself.

He was worse than a dog, the King had said, because dogs responded to stimulus. Akeem was a beast. Primitive. Untamed and useless.

His father had given him a choice. Forget the boy he was and the man he was becoming or go home. Back to his little English life. To his *basic* life.

Akeem's outburst had meant nothing. His father had used it as a teaching tool. The only reason his father had sought him out, wanted to place him on the throne, was for his own ego. To continue his bloodline, however diluted or illegitimate, because he'd sired no other children.

'What was it? The lesson?' Charlotte asked, dragging him back to the reason she was here.

To see the person he was now. Rich. Powerful. Different not only in name, but in body, in mind. He'd chosen to become Akeem Abd al-Uzza, Crown Prince of Taliedaa. There had been no other choice.

Be nothing—unwanted—or become someone else.

A prince.

He didn't shout any more.

'It was a lesson to leave Akeem Ali behind.'

Charlotte nodded. 'He wanted his son to have his name. Understandable…' She narrowed her eyes. 'But didn't you want to keep it?'

'That was not an option.'

'But surely your dad must have understood how important your mother was to you? If not to him?'

'All my father cared for was himself.'

'And his people? Surely he cared for them?' she asked, pushing for answers he didn't want to give.

He didn't want to tell her the disgusting parts of the King's life. The open sex. Women draped all over him in full view of his men. The greed. Wanting his toys faster—shinier—while his people suffered. The total disregard for his people's needs. His country.

His son.

'He cared for nothing but himself,' he repeated.

'What about you? Do *you* care?'

'I will not be the man or the King my father was,' he answered, each word measured and truthful, despite his need to rub his position in her pretty little face. 'I will claim his title and make it mine. I will not be *a* king,' he summarised for her. 'I will be *the* King, and my people will come first as they never did under my father's rule.'

And he would do it as he had been doing things for nine

years. Small steps. Small choices. Small changes. His people first. His needs… *Never.*

Until today? a voice mocked.

He pushed it aside. One day was all he wanted. Twenty-four hours to claim his revenge as a man, to take what he needed and close the door on the past for ever. Only then could he be the King his people needed.

'We are the mirror image of each other,' she said.

His brows pulled together. 'How?'

'You lost a mother you loved,' she continued, 'and I lost a father.'

'Do you compare what I felt for my mother with what *you* felt for your father?'

'Yes,' she answered simply. 'You loved your mother unconditionally. I know you were young when she died, but you spoke about her with pure idolisation. I know if you could've stopped her getting into that carcass of a car you would have. You would have kept her safe. I never idolised my dad, but I loved him. I tried to keep him safe, too.'

His eyes widened. 'And my father?'

'Absent—like my mum. She left me with my dad, as your father left you with your mother.'

'We are not the same.'

'I said mirror images—reverse. *Opposites.*'

She was right. They belonged to different worlds. But they had started out from a similar place. A point of reference they could both identify with.

He'd even dared to *love* her once.

His face contorted, his mouth twisting into a snarl, and he turned away from her. He knew better now—much better.

Love was an absurd ideology for the weak. It was a basic emotion and he would never let himself be primitive again. He wanted her. He acknowledged that. But it was physical closure he needed. No feelings. No emotion. Just sex and her recognition that he was no longer the boy she'd rejected.

Akeem sat on the sofa facing her, clipped himself in, and watched. He observed her as the man he'd taught himself to be. As a king would—with open appreciation.

'Are you just going to sit there and gawk at me?' she asked.

'Yes.'

Golden flecks burned in a sea of green as, back straight, knees together, she looked straight ahead and over his head, as if nothing could faze her. He smiled. He'd ruffle more than her inhibitions. He'd crush them to dust.

His legs spread, he lounged back. Here she was, within reach—not a photograph put on his desk with a breakdown of her yearly routines. She was tangible, with an energy he could taste.

'Charlotte?' he said, when she closed her eyes as the plane reached a furious speed.

She didn't respond as the plane climbed higher, nose-first, but held tighter to her knees and drew his attention to her ripped tights and exposed skin.

His world now was far removed from hers, with inexpensive stockings and shoes, with barely any soles on the shoes cradling her small feet. But he'd known that world with mended clothes, and he hated the reminder of who he'd been with her.

His jaw clenched, because it wasn't her clothes that were making him uncomfortable but the memories hurtling towards him, too fast to catch them. Because with her he'd been everything his father had told him he wasn't.

He'd been... *Calm.* She'd soothed him. Stroked the unnourished ego of a boy who hadn't known such arresting tranquillity before. Not since his mother. Not with the temporary families they'd placed him with, who'd all sent him back with a note to say he was too quiet, too tearful, too loud, too angry—*too broken.* The behavioural mentors who'd tried to draw him out of himself—out of his head— had given up when he'd made little progress and had still spoken louder with his fists than with his words.

The palace guards had held his wrists as his father had called out with every punch that the boy he was, was unwanted. With her, it hadn't taken vile words or clenched fists to stop his rage. It had only taken *her.* Her presence to soothe the anger in his gut. The anger he'd taught himself to hide, to replace with the determination to succeed.

But he wasn't calm now.

The temptation to rip the fabric from her legs rocketed through him, heating his blood.

But he would never be part of *that* world again.

A tightness he hadn't realised was clinging to his muscles was released.

They were airborne.

He clenched his jaw. The shoes. The tights. The clothes. She'd stayed in the world of *make do*, and yet she sat on his throne as regally as a queen.

He shifted, clamping his lips into a thin slit. Did he know *this* Charlotte? It didn't matter. For twenty-four hours she would forget her world of minding the pennies. And he would enjoy exposing her to every delight of the flesh and then send her back with only regret on her lips.

He sat forward, taking in her paleness, the concealed tension revealing itself in every line of her delectable body. He stood, closing the space between them, and unclipped her seatbelt.

She opened her eyes. Heat and want bloomed inside him instantly. He pushed a long lock of curls behind her ear. 'Are you airsick?'

A flush appeared on her high cheekbones. 'I've never flown before.'

She wasn't unwell—she was overwhelmed.

Thrusting an expletive from his mind, he pulled her into step beside him, and for his every large step Charlotte took two.

'Where are you taking me?'

He noted her breathlessness, the tightness laced through her fingers, as they moved through the next set of doors to a long corridor that splintered off into the master bedrooms.

'To show you to your room.'

'Don't you have staff to do that?'

He stopped and turned to her. 'You are only to be seen by me.'

He pushed open a door, and with a tug of his wrist pulled her into the room ahead of him. He lingered in the doorway as she took in her surroundings. Her gaze paused on the large bed. His eyes went to it too, and everything in him urged him to move into the room and push her down into the mattress, with his weight firmly between her thighs.

She turned to face him, her back towards the bed. 'Why can no one see me?' she asked, snapping him out of the heat pooling in his loins.

'You'll enter my kingdom in secret and leave before it's discovered that you arrived.'

'I'm to be sneaked in and out?'

'Of course,' he agreed.

Not a flicker of indecency haunted the velvet richness of his voice, but he felt it. The sticky fingers of doubt where triumph should be. Because to act so selfishly was close to being everything he did not want to be.

Like his father.

You are your father's son.

'Why the cloak and dagger?' Her brows knitted together. 'Surely even a king has needs?'

'My father blatantly took women to his bed, flaunted his affairs and mocked his people with his hedonistic pursuits, because he put his needs before his country—' He cut himself off. He'd told her too much.

'And you don't want to be a king who does that?'

'No,' he agreed, and let his lungs fully deflate before dragging in a deep, silent breath through his nostrils. This was nothing like his father's pleasurable pursuits. This was different. *She* was different.

'Why would you risk being seen with me if it would damage your reputation?' Her little button nose wrinkled. 'It's just sex.'

It wasn't *just* sex. For the price of one night he would be selfish. He would claim his revenge. She had made him get attached. She had made him forget that the only person he could rely on was himself. And he hated her for that.

She was his only connection to the emotional wreck of a boy he'd been, and after their night together—after he'd shown her all he'd become, all he was now—the memory of who he'd been would be obsolete.

That rope wouldn't pull any more.

She wouldn't haunt him any more.

Because the last remaining echoes of who he had been— Akeem Ali—would be gone. That boy would be dead. Lifeless. As his father had demanded the first time they'd encountered one another.

'No one will know, *qalbi*,' he assured her. Because his people couldn't know that his primitive need to have her one last time consumed him.

He would have one night to close the doors on the past, on who he had been, so he could fully embrace his future.

He would restore the monarch's reputation. He would make sure his mother's sacrifices had not been in vain.

He would have it all.

He would be King.

'You're to be a one-night stand—not my future Queen,' he finished, leaving her in no doubt of exactly where she stood in his future.

Nowhere.

It took every ounce of Charlotte's self-control not to react to the cruel sting of his confirmation. But it was as if a thousand bees had landed on her body with those words and jabbed at her exposed flesh.

One-night stand.

It didn't scream opulence. It screamed cheap and throwaway.

Her mouth ran dry. The words didn't appal her. She'd been made to feel worse. But they made her insides twist and pull.

'Get dressed, Charlotte,' Akeem ordered from the doorway when the silence sizzled, and she followed his gaze to some clothes laid on the table.

When he didn't exit the room, she jabbed a finger towards the clothes and said, 'Do you want to watch?'

Regret was instant, and it cut deep when he replied, 'Would you like me to?'

'No,' she said.

But the thought of him watching while she reached up beneath her skirt to pull down her tights…the thought of his eyes following as they skirted over her thighs, down to her knees, to land at her ankles…made her knickers damp.

Tension filled her. She didn't know what to do with her hands. They flexed and pinched together at her sides.

She turned to the bed and eyed the pattern on the bedspread. Gold. And there were gold sheets. She'd take any bet that they were actual gold—some blend, some mixture, that had softened the precious metal to his will.

She turned. 'You haven't said where it will happen. Only that it will be your bed.' Her voice pitched. 'How many beds do you have?' She arched a brow. 'Do you mean to show me all of them before we get to *the one*?'

'Many beds belong to me…in many countries. I mean to show you one bed. *My bed*. In Taliedaa.'

'I don't understand—' she started, because she didn't understand his hesitation, or her own. 'Why bring me in here, only to wait? Don't you want to do it in between gold sheets?'

Akeem screwed his face into a mask of displeasure. *'Do it?'*

'A bed is a bed. I don't understand this need of yours to wait and prolong this—especially if you don't want us to be seen.'

The click of him closing the door reverberated in the room.

'Sometimes the waiting is more pleasurable than the doing, Charlotte.' His eyes were trained on her, and he moved in, inch by inch, towards her. 'I have waited nine years for this moment and I will not rush. I will devour you with my mouth.' He stopped in front of her and her heart pounded. 'With my fingers,' he continued. 'My body will be on you. In you. I will savour you,' he promised, his voice silk. 'But only when you demand it, and not before.'

Her lungs refused to drag in air, because she knew the scent of him on her tongue, sweeping into her airways, would be fatal. She would be lost—not only to his words, but to him. Consumed by the delicious fact that he would wait.

Until *she* was ready.

The man who had abandoned her was willing to wait for her *now*. Just not when it had mattered…

She shut the thought down, because she wasn't here to confront the past, or the emotions pumping in her chest, because they scared her. They had a similarity to how he'd used to make her feel. Precious. Wanted. *Loved.* But she was here to claim her pleasure. To claim *life.* Not his love.

'Then I'm demanding it. I want it,' she said, and moved towards him, lacing her arms around his neck. 'You.'

He gently gripped the back of her neck, and the shock of his firm fingers sent little jolts of electricity through her to the depths of her stomach. 'Do you want my kisses, *qalbi*?'

She nodded, and taut, hard muscle answered her. He placed his mouth at the base of her throat, flicking his tongue in the hollow he found there.

She moaned. A tantalising pressure was building in her abdomen, and it made her press her thighs together. 'A little higher. Please…'

He moved his mouth up along the tight muscles, his teeth nibbling, his tongue caressing. His mouth closed around the flesh below her ear before he whispered, 'Always so polite, Charlotte.'

She pushed out of his embrace and he staggered, releasing her. Was she that predictable? A people-pleaser even in bed? Unexpected tears filled her eyes.

But she would not cry.

Why would she cry?

He reached for her, but she sidestepped him.

'I will not kick you out of bed for saying "please", *qalbi*.'

'What if I don't want to say it?' She bit at her lip to stem the sting in her eyes. 'What if I don't want to be polite?'

'You have a sudden aversion to manners?'

'I have a sudden aversion to being—' she inhaled deeply

and released her breath slowly, through parted lips '—predictable.'

All her life she'd done what was necessary to make others happy. To make her dad happy. Her dad had known the minute Akeem hadn't shown up nine years ago that she would stay with him. Look after him and forget everything else. Because she was *predictable.*

She closed her eyes, blocking out the gaze observing her with quiet intensity. Wasn't tonight all about her? But how could it be when she didn't know how to put herself first?

'I'm not ready,' she whispered.

Because it turned out she wasn't. Nine years he'd lived in her head. His mouth. His fingers. His touch. And now he was within reach—she was touching him. Her Akeem. Her friend. Her boyfriend. Her onetime lover.

She closed her eyes, swallowing down the sudden lump in her throat.

He wasn't *her* Akeem any more. He was the ex who'd broken her heart, and now he wanted to smooth over the cracks with something he called *closure.*

But closure didn't come from someone else, did it? Closure you had to find on your own. Or so some magazine article she'd read had said. It held true in her mind, because being in his arms—*his bed*—sounded nothing like closure. But his touch… To be touched… To find pleasure on a day when there shouldn't be pleasure…

'Then I shall wait until you are.'

His voice pulled her eyes open—pulled her back into the room and into his eyes.

He was giving her control.

'And when you are…' He moved the pad of his thumb along her cheek with a tenderness that defied the strength he radiated.

'And when I am…?' she said huskily, her insides trembling. Because she was being given the reins of something powerful—this hidden energy between them that was making her insides pull in every direction.

'It will be your choice, *qalbi*. You will lead the way and I will bring you so much pleasure.'

He rasped his promise from between open lips and she wanted to press her mouth to his. But she was afraid to lean in and capture his promise. To taste it. To take the lead.

'Rest, *qalbi*.' He released her. 'And then return to me.'

He turned his back on her, and she wilted as he closed the door behind him.

He'd pulled her from her life and thrust her into his—and she was out of her depth. But she'd got on the plane because she'd wanted to, she reminded herself. She wanted him. Wanted a moment in time she could call hers. But this wasn't her moment. It would not happen in between gold sheets because she wasn't ready and he knew it.

Keeping her clothes on, she stalked over to the bed, kicked off her shoes and ripped back the coverlet. She climbed inside, fully clothed, and pulled the golden sheets up to her chin. But something niggled at her. The way he looked at her. *Saw* her. Anticipated her needs.

No one ever did that for her. It was always her catering to everyone else. Her father... But Akeem? He'd known she needed rest before she'd admitted it to herself. He'd known she needed to control things even when she was baiting him to take her to bed.

A fatigue unlike any she'd known pulled her eyelids down despite her best efforts to keep them open.

Darkness claimed her.

CHAPTER THREE

AKEEM HAD BEEN RIGHT. She had needed to rest. But now…
Now energy consumed her.

Charlotte inhaled deeply and moved her feet to bring
her nose to nose with the door leading her back into the
lounge. She hit the rectangular touchpad and barged her
way into the room with as much confidence as she could
pretend to have.

She froze on the spot. Akeem was a vision of unques-
tionable authority. Her eyes skimmed down the length of
him. He'd changed. Gone were the western clothes and
there he was in swathes of black, and a headdress with a
band of gold securing it.

Her eyes moved back to his face and his clenched jaw.
His eyes were moving over the dragon-green fabric covering every inch of her skin and they didn't miss a thing—
from the opaque green headscarf with a gold trim that
loosely covered her damp curls, to the full-length sleeves
fluttering at her fingertips, the high rounded neck, and
down to the flared edge of her full-length trousers.

Head high, shoulders back, she said the words she'd been
practising. 'I'm ready.'

He stood, and in a single stride he was in front of her.
'Ready for what?'

She fixated on his lips. She could still feel them working along her neck. Each press of his mouth was imprinted upon her and even the shower hadn't been able to remove him…the feel of him.

She wanted those lips on her again. That was why she was here. She wanted—

'You,' she replied breathlessly.

She gasped, the throb of her heartbeat pulsing in her ears, as Akeem picked her up and brought the core of her to sit just above his. Instinctively, she wrapped her legs around his waist as firm fingers pressed into her hips. He walked with her wrapped around him like a second skin and set her down before the throne.

'What now?' she asked.

'Show me you are ready for me, *qalbi.*'

'How?'

'By removing your clothes,' he said. 'This time I want you to sit on my throne naked.'

Her chest tightened. *'Naked?'* Swallowing, she tried to ease the sudden dryness of her throat. 'I thought you wanted to wait until we were in your bed?'

The finger moving feather-light down her throat to follow the round neckline stilled. 'Are you not ready, then?'

'I am!'

He smiled. 'There is much I can do without claiming your body with mine,' he said, and his voice was a caress straight to the most intimate part of her.

'Here? Anyone could see us!'

'No one will enter without my permission.' His mouth curved in a fascinating movement, both sensual and terrifying. 'Right here, right now, you will remove your clothes.' He lifted his hands, removed his headdress, and dropped it to the floor. 'I'll go first.'

With an agile shrug he removed his robes, and pushed his boxers to his feet.

'You're naked...' she breathed, amazed at the ease with which he presented himself to her.

She couldn't help it.

She drank him in.

Every appealing curve of hard flesh.

'Does my nakedness offend you?' He stepped out of the puddle of clothes at his feet and her eyes moved down the length of him. Her mouth dried, her breath coming in sharp rasps. He was glorious. Bigger, taller—stronger than she remembered.

Her gaze stalled on the proudest part of him.

'No...' Her answer was barely audible.

She wanted to reach out and touch him the way she had nine years ago. To stroke upwards, along the hard muscles of his abdomen, to raise his T-shirt and close her mouth over a hard brown nipple.

They had been each other's first. She'd trusted him with her secrets and her body.

Did she still trust him?

Naively, she knew she did. With some false sense of security because of who they'd been. He'd offered himself to her then. Completely trusting. And he was doing it again. *Right now.* She wanted to do the same. To have the confidence of her younger self in her older body. To be as free as she had been before...*with him.*

She stood before him in front of his throne and toed off her shoes. She didn't dare to speak. She pulled her trousers down from her hips and stepped out of the clothes the way he had. She didn't dare to look away. This was life. This was *her* life. And she'd never felt as decadent or as revived as she slipped the green tunic over her head.

'Remove your bra.'

Her eyes shot back to his, and she saw his gaze was full of wild challenge.

He'd challenged her from the moment she'd walked into the pub. He'd prodded her to question why she hadn't become something *more*, understanding her doubts before she'd even given voice to them. In the car, he'd acknowledged her fears with pinpoint accuracy, and on the plane, he'd known she wasn't ready.

But he knew she was ready *now*.

He saw all the things no one had bothered to look for before. The things she'd thought were invisible. She'd thought that *she* was invisible. To her father. To the teachers she'd had in her teens, who had never recognised she was struggling. To the acquaintances in her never stable jobs. But he saw the things she'd thought no one cared to see.

Her needs.

The real her.

She slipped the bra straps from her shoulders and reached around with clumsy fingers to undo the hooks and let the fabric fall away from her breasts. Her nipples hardened into stiff peaks as he unashamedly caressed them with his eyes.

Thrilled and terrified, she hooked her fingers in the waistband of her panties.

He wanted to see her and she wanted to be seen.

By him.

He lifted his head. 'No, not those.'

Holding her breath, she stood as straight as she could wearing only her panties. 'Kiss me,' she whispered—because wasn't that what she wanted? The heat of him on her? A reminder that she was alive and really living on a day when death had been all around?

Akeem grunted and moved to capture her wrists. 'I will more than kiss you.' He drew her into his arms. 'I will devour you,' he promised, and pulled her mouth on to his.

His kiss was hungry, and she kissed him back just as

hungrily. He pushed her into the throne. The chair was cold and hard against her back, and without his heat against her she felt very naked as he kicked their clothes aside and bent to his knees before her.

'Now I taste you...' He groaned, deep in his chest. 'Kiss you where I long to most.'

Charlotte gasped as he pushed between her thighs. Her hands grabbed at him and moved onto his shoulders.

'Akeem—'

His fingers pressed deep into her hipbones, holding her in place for his viewing pleasure. He didn't speak—not with words. But he spoke with his hands. His fingers slid down the arch of her hips. Soft, feather-like touches whispered along the outside of her thighs to move inwards and between her legs. Spreading her thighs wider, he bent forward and flicked his tongue against her concealed opening.

It had never been like this during their youthful relationship. Never this wild or this totally consuming. But she wanted him there, between her legs. She wanted everything. More than his kisses and his soft, yet firm tongue stroking at her slick folds. Her body screamed to feel him inside her. His fingers, his—

His mouth moved up, capturing her nub of nerves, and sucked at her through the fabric of her panties.

'Akeem!'

The surge of pleasure centred around his mouth made her cry out and arch her body into his kiss. It was an explosion of sensation. Hot and blinding. Akeem's mouth moved over her with masterful precision, sucking her deeper and deeper into his mouth. The fabric between his mouth and her core was agony personified.

But Charlotte wanted his heaviness—the length of him—inside her.

Now.

Breathless, throwing her head back, she choked out, 'My panties!' not sure if her fingers at his nape were pulling him in closer or pushing him away so he could complete the task she'd given to him so brazenly.

He moved back, and she whimpered with his absence. His thumbs hooked into the elastic at her waist and he looked up at her from his position on the ground.

'These?' he asked. He tugged gently at the elastic and let it pop back against her skin.

She flushed, the heat searing up through the valley of her breasts to slash across her cheeks as his voice, pure husky tones of desire, penetrated her more than the sting of elastic.

'Take them off,' she begged, bold and brazen and not caring one bit.

'Tell me, Lottie—what is the magic word?'

'Please!' It was a roar—a plea.

Heat and excitement spread from her toes to her tingling lips as, millimetre by agonising millimetre, he pulled them down. The stretchy lace teased her in its slow descent to her ankles. Then with open palms, he worked his way up from her knotted ankle bone back to her thighs.

She wasn't sure if the rush in her ears was because of what Akeem was doing to her or because the plane was actually tilting.

He parted her legs, hooking her ankles on the jewel-encrusted armrests. He pushed his face into the dark curls and moved his tongue in confident strokes up and down her slick core.

'Ahh...' she grunted, clawing at his shoulders, moving her hands through his hair and thrashing her body onto his face.

His tongue pushed inside her and she tightened, every muscle stretched and aching for the ping of release. His hand moved over her stomach, pushing into the pressure there. She bit her lip, clamping down as his thumb moved rhythmically over her core and his tongue continued to penetrate her.

Her legs squirmed on the armrests but he kept her legs pinned open with his lips clamped to her core. Charlotte's control shattered, explosions taking off deep in her abdomen. The plane bounced hard, again and again, but the bounce seemed in sync with her body so she ignored it.

The earth was actually moving.

The orgasm ripping through her was unlike any other, and for a moment she was lost.

Akeem planted a kiss to her pulsing core and whispered, 'Now every time you say *please* you will see my face.'

She opened one eye and stared down at him. His face between her thighs was a surreal reality as she came back down to earth.

He smiled. 'We have arrived, *qalbi.*'

She winced as she tried to unhook her ankles, and Akeem reached for her. His palms, gentle but firm, closed around her ankles and lowered them for her, placing her feet carefully on the floor.

His eyes burned with glistening need and she felt…decadent.

Alive.

Anything but predictable.

'Please…' She smiled down at him, trying the word for size, and his face was all she could see. 'I want more.'

'More?' His mouth tilted into a crocked smile. 'There will be plenty of time for more.'

She stilled as he stood between her legs, proud and open in his desire for her. Her instinct was to reach for him and pull him down to her. Make him beg for the release he'd given her with his hands.

His mouth…

She wanted to use her mouth too. To taste him as she never had. To pull his ecstasy from him until he murmured *please* again and again as his hands wound into her hair.

'Does pleasure make you bold?' he asked.

Raising her eyes, she met his. Not only was he looking at her. *Seeing* her. He was acting on what he saw and she didn't know how to feel about that. No one had ever done it before. Put her needs first. Not even him. Their plan to elope—to run away—had been about them both. But now…? This moment…? It was all about her. Her pleasure.

Slowly, she took him in. Akeem… The power of his attraction to her gave her wings. Confidence. Allowed her to sit there on an actual throne—naked—without the urge to hide a single blemish.

Why *was* that?

Her heart thumped. Because she wasn't invisible. Here—now—in his eyes she was everything.

She felt empowered. Strong. *Bold.*

'Yes,' she replied.

The desire pulsing between her legs made her reach for him. For the erection she wanted to feel in her hands. It was his turn. She wanted to make him throb as she had. With her mouth.

He caught her wrist. 'I will enjoy you being bold.' He placed her hand, palm down, on his abdomen, and she splayed her fingers beneath his. 'But not yet.'

With his hand guiding hers, her fingers travelled up the firm lines of his stomach to his chest, and traced through the soft fuzz of dark hair. So soft. So hard. So surreal…

This wasn't real.

Alone—*here*—they were *this.*

She was this.

Different.

It would be all too easy to let herself keep falling. To fall into the heat of him again and again—to stay wrapped in the tingles of ecstasy. Forget who he was. Forget herself. Who *she* was. Only allow herself to remember the pleasure. This Charlotte felt visible. *Powerful.*

'Pleasure made me forget,' she said, reminding herself that just because she'd forgotten, it didn't mean the outside world didn't exist.

'Forget what?'

'Everything,' she whispered honestly, his gaze leaving her no room to mask her features from her thoughts. She dipped her chin to her chest. Breaking the agonising intensity of his eyes.

'Everything?' He pressed his hand down on hers and pushed her palm into him. Into the hotness of him. The hardness. 'Or,' he continued, eyes narrowed, 'have you only forgotten the parts that do not matter here?'

'But they do matter, don't they? Because when I go home it will all still be there.'

You won't, she finished silently.

But the grief? The regret? They'd still be there.

A bubble surrounded them, she realised. A mist of pleasure was wrapped around them, holding them suspended in time. *Together.* But after their one night they'd never be together again.

He shrugged, releasing her, and she watched as he walked to one of the sofas and tore free one of the golden throws.

Walking back towards her, he shook out the blanket and went on bended knee to cover her nakedness with smooth silk. The fabric imprisoned the ends of her hair and puffed it around her face. Akeem slipped his hands behind her back and pulled free the trapped hair until it fell about her shoulders and down to her chest in long, winding curls.

'If it will still be there, why not allow yourself pleasure

unreservedly? Permit me to make you forget, again and again. What waits for you no longer matters until it matters.'

For twenty-four hours surely she could let herself go? Why not let herself float as high as she could in his embrace, locked inside a bubble of make-believe?

But if she let herself float too far—too high—and he popped it before she could…left her again… Unprepared…

This time, would she recover?

She had to pop it. The bubble. She needed to shield herself from the influence of the pleasure Akeem could give to her. From the power of it.

'You made me forget before,' she said, the memory claiming her, 'but not with your body.'

Dark eyes snapped to hers. 'No,' he agreed. 'It was with my tongue.'

'At St John's,' she clarified.

It was a happy memory. She didn't have many. The bad often took over whatever good there had been. But she wanted to remember this.

She wanted *him* to remember.

'You let me draw you, again and again, until I got it right,' she reminded him, and sucked them both into the shared memory of sitting under a huge tree in the children's home garden.

He'd given her an escape from reality by simply offering his body—his presence—and she'd longed to stay there, under the oak tree, with her pencils and paper.

With Akeem…

Maybe for twenty-four hours she could stay with him again? But this time she would protect herself with the knowledge that the fairy tale would end, and then her reality could be whatever she wanted it to be. Hers.

Pulling her hand free from beneath his, she lifted it to his cheek. 'I'd like to draw you again,' she whispered, moving her thumb along his jaw, stroking it through the bristles of his short beard until she came to his mouth. A mouth she had drawn many times during their shared time in care.

It had been nearly ten years since she'd picked up a pencil. Since her father had destroyed all her portraits of Akeem.

The only memories she'd had of him—or of her dreams—were in her head, but drawing this newer, older Akeem would be a reminder of who she had been before. Of the dreams she'd tentatively told him about, of being a professional artist, until her father had reminded her it that she hadn't got time to dream.

Akeem had helped her to forget who she was once. Maybe this time he could help her remember who she wanted to be. Who she might become when this day was over.

She could still draw.

She could still dream.

There was nothing stopping her now.

Only herself.

Three sharp raps on the door and the sound of the double doors opening broke the moment between them.

Akeem spat out a word she didn't understand, but it set her nerves on edge and halted the footsteps of whoever was entering.

Charlotte tried to make a sound of protest—she was naked under the blanket—but with a small shake of his head he silenced her, his eyes wide, his jaw clenched…

She was in the presence of a king and not a lover now.

The bubble had popped, hadn't it?

And she wasn't ready—she wasn't prepared.

Her fingers poked through the blanket to grip onto her makeshift lapels, and she tugged the silk tighter around her shoulders.

'Do not enter,' Akeem commanded.

His voice was now controlled, and even. Focused and sure, his dark gaze stayed on hers. Her breathing sped up and she opened her mouth to speak, but before she could form the words his lips pressed against hers.

A feather-light touch of his mouth.

It was a promise.

His promise.

He stood, and it wasn't the fear of facing reality that she wasn't prepared for, and it wasn't whoever had started to come through the door that scared her, nor was it the embarrassment threatening to undo her that she'd been caught naked, wrapped around the son of a king.

It was him.

Covering her nakedness before his own. Not with the blanket but with his body. Big and wide, he shielded her, doing what no one else ever had. Protecting her.

He turned and walked towards the obscured glass double doors, towards whoever had been about to walk through the door, and continued to block her view with his physique.

His nakedness was its own flawless armour, she realised. It wasn't a handmade suit or the robes of a prince he required, but only his skin. Only the man had to be present. Because even without expensive fabrics, he still exuded the power only the son of a king could.

An unexpected thrill burned through her, catching her breath in her throat—because whoever was coming through those doors, a king protected her.

He'd made a mistake.

Scandal.

The word pulled at his insides, threatening to break the rigid control straightening his shoulders.

He could not hide her.

The skeleton crew he'd travelled with to England was all for nothing.

The moment those doors opened Charlotte would no longer be his secret, because there in front of him stood his royal guard and two of his most senior aides.

His men.

On arrival in Taliedaa, the moment the wheels touched the ground, his men would be ready to protect their new King. And here they were, ready—because it was their job to seek him out and assure themselves of his safety.

He'd forgotten.

In a single undeniable moment he'd become more than his father's son in his men's eyes. He had become his father. Because he'd taken his pleasure in the most abandoned way and forgotten himself.

A confident man often did things out of the ordinary without anxiety. But a king? He could do what he liked.

But not the kind of king he needed to become.

The embodiment of control.

His gut clenched. He would not follow his instinct and tell his men to get out again, because his men deserved the respect his father hadn't ever shown them. The respect his father demanded himself, although he hadn't deserved it.

He'd expected everyone else to be everything he wasn't.

His father had been a king of contradictions.

Nine years he'd spent, proving he was neither his father's son, nor the boy who'd arrived in Taliedaa. Because the Crown Prince made his choices based on the price of his actions.

Another lesson his father had taught him quickly.

He, the orphan heir, next in line to succeed to the throne, was stronger than his father. Better not because of him, but despite him. His father's reign of pleasure-seeking at the price of the crown's reputation—at the cost of his mother's reputation—was over.

Akeem's chest heaved as his men's narrowed eyes tried to see past him. To see *her*. He stepped forward, one step at a time, backing them up and away from the door. Blocking their view.

'Your Highness…' The head of his royal guard had the good grace to blush, and the three men behind him bowed their heads.

'Are my people well?' Akeem asked.

His bow deepened in response to the silent reprimand. 'Yes…' he answered, and then raised his gaze questioningly to Akeem's.

Akeem cocked a brow. 'Does the palace still stand?'

'Yes, it is as you left it.'

'Does the sun still set?'

'Within the hour, Your Royal Highness.'

'All is as it should be, then?'

Eyes as dark as his own widened as they glanced down at his nakedness. 'Yes,' he answered, the blush tingeing his cheeks turning from a slight pink to a deep red.

Akeem tutted his disapproval, but he felt his insides snake around his lungs and squeeze. He could not deny or explain what had taken place in the room behind him without making the situation worse.

Immediately, his path became clear. As it had when he'd been eighteen and thrown into his father's world.

He would not be *him*. His men deserved more, and so did his people. He would prove that the illegitimate Crown Prince was worthy to be their King. Worthy of the crown. And there was only one way to do it—to keep his reputation intact and make his people believe that he would never give in to his baser instincts like his father.

The scene behind him was not the beginning of the end

of his new reign. It was not a replay of his father taking his pleasure without decency or care—

Isn't it?

No!

Why not?

Because…

He couldn't answer.

In his men's eyes, it *was* a replay. A descent into his father's kind of chaos. In this moment he was just as bad as his father, ordering his men to stay and watch as women pleasured him.

He ground his teeth.

He would fix this.

He made himself stalk closer to his men, and with his voice low and sure he said, 'Imagine interrupting the King and your future Queen simply to tell him the sky is indeed blue…'

Tension radiated from every taut line of his royal guard's body. 'Your Royal Highness—'

Akeem shook his head and halted the stumbling apology with a lazy flick of his wrist.

'The helicopter,' he commanded. 'Fifteen minutes.'

Akeem hit the button, sealing the doors on his fate. He closed his eyes. A decade of ignoring his feelings—his urges—and for what? To risk it all? Jaw rigid, he looked at her then. *For her?*

She stood, her hair a crown of curls, trailing down her bare shoulders to fall over her breasts, and her skin shimmered as iridescently as the jewels surrounding her.

'Are you okay?' she asked.

His heart galloped into a frenzied beat. 'Am *I* okay?'

'Are you?'

Was he? He couldn't remember the last time anyone

had asked. His feelings didn't matter. Only his blood. Only his duty.

He nodded, but his heart refused to stop its treacherous double beat as she moved towards him.

'The one thing you didn't want to happen…'

She stopped in front of him, the scent of her dragging over his senses. What scent? What power did she possess to make a king become only a man before her? To make him revert to his most basic self?

'And now it's happened.'

She gasped as the blanket slipped from her shoulders. Akeem caught the falling fabric on instinct, and for a moment everything stilled as her nakedness beneath revealed itself.

He moved quickly, trying not to absorb the sight of her— her skin, her curves—trying not to remember what she'd felt like beneath his fingertips. He took her hand, ignoring the heat of her palm, and thrust the fabric into it. She wrapped the blanket under her arms and tucked it between her breasts.

Her cheeks high in colour, she asked, 'Does it matter that they caught us? That we—you—?' She stuttered and shook her head, her crown of curls bouncing on her shoulders.

'Yes,' he said, feeling low embers of the fire they'd shared threatening to burst into flame. He would ignore it—as he should have until he had her firmly in his bed, between his thighs. But still he couldn't resist, and continued, 'It matters that I made you come apart with my mouth.'

Her hand paused in tucking in her makeshift tunic. *'Exactly!'* she replied,

But he heard the quiver in her breath as she remembered. Remembered his mouth on her. Tasting her.

She crouched down with her back to him to pick up their

discarded clothes. 'I don't have a clue what's happening, or what you're feeling—'

'Feelings have no place here.'

Clothes in hand, she turned to face him. 'Who told you that?'

Every muscle in his naked body turned taut, from the tendons in his toes flattening his feet against the plush carpeted floor to the muscles elongating his throat. 'The crown must come before feelings or emotion,' he rasped deeply. 'One must obey one's duty first.'

The stab of those teachings still cut deep.

And now Charlotte Hegarty had unpicked the adhesive holding his life together and bared the truth. One misstep had been all it took to reveal that he was still reactive to his primitive urges. *Weak.*

The silken touch of her hand on his jolted him straight back into the room. Her small delicate fingers held out his robes to him.

'So they saw me?' she asked.

In the eyes of his men today he was like his father. But if he did what his father had not… If he married her. Made her his Queen. The *people's* Queen…

There was no other choice.

He snatched the robe from her and thrust his arms inside. 'They saw no one but me,' he said, because they hadn't. But they'd seen enough. The unmistakable truth…

'But you were naked—'

'Very.'

'So was I…underneath this.' The green of her eyes, bright with questions, searched his. 'Thank you for hiding me. Whether it was for you or for me…' She shrugged. 'I'm grateful you didn't let them see me fully.'

'Do not thank me yet.'

In a single stride he was on her. In her breathing space.

Close enough to be reminded of how sweet the musk was lingering on her skin and in the air. On his lips—his tongue. To be reminded of how desire had changed the game and now it was no longer a game of revenge—of getting even. But a game of duty.

'You may not like what comes next,' he said, capturing her waist in his palms and scooping her over his shoulder.

'Akeem!'

The weight of her over his shoulder and her perfectly pert bottom in his eyeline sent a rush of lava through his veins. The temptation to take her to bed returned.

He'd given himself a reprieve—a moment to think and save Charlotte from any embarrassment. But the truth was undeniable. He'd been caught behaving like his father, and he wouldn't allow himself—his reputation—to be so vulnerable again.

She swivelled on his shoulder. 'What are you doing?'

He moved towards the exit. 'I'm taking you back to your room.'

'To my room?' Her fingers pinched into his shoulders as he exited the lounge. 'You can't dismiss me and send me to my room because you don't like what I'm saying. I have a right to know what happens next—'

Thrusting open the suite door, he stalked towards the bed and lowered her onto the edge of the mattress. 'Get dressed and wait for me.'

He turned, pushing from his mind the image of a naked Charlotte waiting for him on this bed. It tugged at him…the idle notion of wishing he could be a man—nothing more than primitive need—and finishing what they'd started and finding ignorance in her body.

But he wasn't just a man. He was the son of a king. A crown prince. A crown prince who had surrendered to his baser instincts and proved his father right.

'I don't understand,' Charlotte called after him.

He couldn't say what made him stop. What made him turn around. But he did. And the sight of her—vulnerable and confused—almost broke him. *He'd* done that to her. Taken his pleasure and thrown her into a world so unlike her own.

He closed his eyes. 'Please, *qalbi*,' he said, because he was not averse to the word. He knew the power of it, and he saw it in her eyes and in her silence as she recognised his need for her to obey. As he had obeyed her. He had torn those panties straight from her body to give her the release she craved.

Yet his was a different plea.

He needed a moment to reconcile himself to what was to happen. What he *had* to do to be the King he'd spent almost a decade becoming.

He opened his eyes. 'You're not meant to understand,' he said, 'but you will.'

'When?'

'Soon,' he promised. 'Get dressed and wait for me.'

Closing the door behind him, he moved towards his own suite with an ease he didn't feel.

He'd demanded his night of revenge, and he'd been so close to victory.

But at what cost?

CHAPTER FOUR

HER WHOLE LIFE she'd been waiting for other people. For her dad to return home safely, before his nightly blackout occurred. And then for Akeem. She'd waited for him before…only to be given a firm reminder never to rely on anyone but herself.

Akeem hadn't bothered to turn up back then—because why would he? He'd got what he'd wanted. Her surrender. Her body. And then *whoosh*. He'd been gone. And that had been that until he'd wanted something…

She pulled the tunic top over her head and thrust her arms into the full sleeves, then bent to pull her underwear on. The dampness of Akeem's kisses still clung to her panties, making her pause and making her heart hammer. She picked up the trousers and pushed her toes in with force.

All the relationships she'd known had been *take, take, take*, and that was why she'd never give her heart again. Ever. Because she had nothing left to give. To anyone. Maybe not even to herself.

She'd wanted a night—one night—when her needs came first. *Hers*. And look where her stupid desire to be selfish had led her.

She wanted to go home.

She was done with waiting. Done with the promise of *soon*. Life was now, wasn't it?

Opening the bedroom door, she looked down the long corridor with doors on either side. Was that a staircase?

She moved towards it and grabbed the balustrade. Her bare feet connected to a smooth surface resembling reflective glass, and she descended to be met with another lounge of sorts. More beige sofas sat parallel to the staircase that spiralled into the room, reclining chairs, TVs, and—

Subtle vibrations teased her bare toes, and she flexed them against the smooth veneered floor. The vibrations got heavier, pulsing at her insides. There was a door in the middle of the floating staircase. And the white column descending through the middle was a…a *lift*.

It was!

The white lift's doors slid open slowly—the polar opposite to her pumping heart. Holding her breath, she stood rooted.

'Why are you hiding down here?'

Dressed and unruffled, Akeem appeared before her. Perfectly perfect in every way.

Something inside her snapped.

Caring for her dad had taught her to listen first and react later—*in private*—but not now. She wouldn't wait. She wouldn't hold back.

She couldn't.

She was going to cut herself loose from the control she'd so carefully maintained to keep her standing every time her dad lashed out or berated her for simply *being*.

She stirred her legs into motion, moving towards him with purpose. Her body was unstoppable as it realised its aim. It was thrilling—intoxicating. *Surreal*. Her stomach muscles hardened. She'd never felt so calm and yet enraged before.

Charlotte raised her arm, closing her fingers together

to create as much surface area as possible on her open palm, and—

Akeem caught her wrist in mid-air. 'You will not strike the King.'

'I'm not striking the King,' she hissed, the pressure of her raised arm keeping her face only millimetres from his mouth. 'I'm about to slap you—the man. Not the King with golden sheets and an aeroplane bigger than a high-rise flat. *You.*'

'The truth is always hard to hear, but they are one and the same.' He pinned her wrists and raised them to the sides of head, then moved in until they were nose to nose. 'Striking me is an arrestable offence.'

'Why break a habit of a decade?' she spat between tight lips. 'Why not take me to the police station right now and leave me to fend for myself, the way you've always done.'

He recoiled, breaking the contact of their over-sensitised bodies. 'I have never left you,' he corrected, his nostrils flaring as he half turned his body away from her.

She laughed, a hiccup of a sound, as she pushed herself free from the cold metal at her back. 'You just did!' She raised her hands and dropped them with a smack to her thighs when he didn't respond. 'Take me home, Akeem.' It was a hushed plea. 'Now.'

'You can't leave.'

'Why? Does the plane need fuel?'

He shook his head. 'No.'

'Then why not?' she asked, eyebrows high. 'You're the King. Make it happen.'

'I am not King yet, *qalbi.*'

'What does that mean?'

'How they found us…saw me…' He inhaled deeply, his shoulders widening as he seemed to grow bigger—taller.

'It was in a moment when I forgot my duty and became what I fear most.'

'Like your dad?'

He opened his mouth only a fraction, and she watched as his lips moved without sound. His lips thinned, and he nodded. 'Their catching us together will reinforce the doubt my people have. They think my rule will follow in his footsteps. That just like him my needs will come before my country.'

'Aren't they right?' she asked, before she could stop herself. 'You wanted to hide me—sneak me in and out of your bed—just to fulfil your needs.'

'I know what I did.'

'Why did you do it?' she asked.

His eyes held fast to hers. 'I couldn't help myself.'

'Neither could I,' she whispered. 'But that doesn't tell me why.'

'Can *you* explain what happened?' he asked. 'The intensity?'

Could she? Nine years had passed between them—it seemed like a lifetime but still…no, she couldn't.

'But if you didn't want to be seen with me…' Her stomach muscles tightened. He didn't want to be seen with the daughter of an alcoholic, did he? A nobody. She wasn't his future Queen—she was a mistake. But she needed to know why he'd taken such a risk. She hadn't asked before—she'd been too focused on her own reasons. Her own need to put the past behind her. 'Why did you put yourself in such a vulnerable position to be caught in the first place, when it was the last thing you wanted to happen?'

'My father had a lifetime of being reckless for his own amusement—'

'And you wanted a taste of it?'

'No,' he denied, his voice a harsh rasp.

'Then what *did* you want?' she pushed.

'A night—'

'You risked your reputation for a night?' She cut him off, her insides twisting. 'We haven't even made it to your bed.' She blew out a puff of agitated air. 'Not *your* bed. Not the only bed you deem fit for purpose.'

'Make no mistake,' he warned. 'Things have changed.'

'Changed?'

'My bed is off-limits.'

She laughed, a throaty gurgle. 'How dare you pull me from my life, fly me who knows how many miles into a kingdom I've never heard of and then turn the tables on me?' She fixed him with an exasperated glare.

'If the tables have turned on anyone,' he replied, 'it is me. Because you will be my wife.'

'Wife!' she scoffed. Old hurts bloomed fast, and his cruel joke hurt more than it should. 'I'm a one-night stand,' she reminded him. 'Not your future Queen.'

She exhaled heavily, forcing herself to blow out all the heaviness in her chest. In her heart.

'I'm done with this game,' she said, steeling herself to the truth. This was over before it had begun. He was a prince, and she was the daughter of Damien Hegarty. It was in her genes to fail. 'I don't belong here. Send me home, Akeem.'

'It's too late for that,' he said, and a deep flush stained his cheeks. 'There is only one solution and your leaving is not it.'

Her gut dropped to her toes. 'Solution?'

'When you leave this plane you will enter my kingdom as its future Queen.'

Her mouth open, she stared at him. He hadn't been playing with her.

He nodded—a small inclination of his head.

'They could have caught you with anyone…'

'But you aren't anyone.'

'No, I'm not,' she agreed, 'but I could have been. Would you have married someone else?'

'No.'

'Why not?'

'Because there has only ever been you, *qalbi.*'

'What?' she asked. 'What about no one ever complaining about your stamina? What about you being more skilled than the boy I remember? You're lying,' she accused, her cheeks tight with tension. 'Why would you lie?'

'No one has ever complained because no one has ever been in my bed besides me. The boy you remember had no control—he was a boy. I am a man. I have control in more ways than one,' he told her. 'And I do not lie.'

'If the only person you've ever been with is me, how could you possibly know that you could give me extreme pleasure?' she pushed, trying to catch him out in his unnecessary lie.

Why was he doing it? Telling her it had only ever been her. To persuade her to say yes? To get her to marry him? It wasn't her destiny to be a queen. If her dad had been right, she was only ever destined to fail. And he *had* been right, hadn't he? The one time he'd needed her she hadn't been there. The idea of her being a queen… *Ridiculous!*

'You couldn't,' she answered for him, because his lies would not convince her to say yes to being his wife when he didn't want her in his bed. Let alone his life! 'Then why…?' She searched for the right words, but she didn't have any. She knew why *she* hadn't been with anyone else. But him? The son of a king had denied himself. It made no sense.

'Because the only thing that matters here is my duty,' he answered. 'My people need stability. Not a king who puts his pleasure first—'

'But today—'

'I made a mistake.'

She furrowed her brow. 'Is that why you wanted me here? In your bed?' she asked, her gut twisting. 'Because I represent a life you can't have—?' She cut herself off as an acrid taste flooded her mouth.

'Yes. That is exactly why I wanted you in my bed, *qalbi*. Because I knew when you left it—when our night was over—the past and the boy you knew would be gone. For ever.'

'That makes no sense!' she screeched.

'It doesn't have to make sense to you.'

But it did!

She wanted to wail, but she folded her arms around her chest, felt the thud of her heart pounding against her palm. He was right. It didn't have to make sense. She was here. *They* were here.

'Our marriage,' he continued, dismissing her line of questioning, 'will show my people I am stable. Grounded. I will be secure in my role as King in the eyes of my men. My people.'

'And you think by making *me* your wife—their Queen— is the stability they need?' Raising her chin, she asked, 'But what about my life? I can't just up sticks and—'

'As we have already established, there is nothing at home for you.'

No, he'd established that she had no job, and soon she'd have no home. They hadn't talked about her non-existent friends, or how empty her life was now she didn't have to care for her dad. But what about her dreams? There was nothing holding her back any more.

She could have been anything... She still could be...

'I have plans. I'm going to college,' she told him, revealing her plans to them both before she'd thought them through. 'I'm going to enrol as soon as the college announces the new intake date and I'm going to get my Visual Arts diploma.'

'And your tuition fees?' Smooth as silk, he sliced through the rebirth of her old dream.

Money, time and her dad had always been the excuses for why she couldn't chase her dreams before. Why she couldn't go to college. Why she couldn't take her talent and do something with it. Now her dad was gone, and time was all she had. But money...?

'I'll find a way. A job. Something permanent.' She'd never had a permanent job before. Her dad had always made it difficult, and part-time work had been the only option.

At her last job—the call centre—she'd been on the phone to her boss once, about adding more shifts to her rota, and her dad had been screaming curse words in the background about something...a poor bet. And of course it had been her fault he'd lost. Her boss had told her not to come back.

But she didn't have to worry about her dad any more— not the poor bets, or the drinking binges he'd thought he deserved for losing, or putting him back together when he'd been full of regret.

It was just her now.

'I saw a vacancy at the local primary school before you kidnapped me from my life—for an assistant to work in early years education. Creative sessions...'

She frowned, trying to recall what the role had actually been and why it had lingered in her memory. She hadn't thought it was possible before. Her getting a job at a school. She'd barely made it through school herself. But that had changed.

'It was in art.' The words exploded from her mouth. The vacancy had stayed with her because it was about *art*.

Her dream. 'Messy play for children with additional educational needs. I like kids—'

'When have *you* come into contact with children?'

'Christmas work in retail,' she explained. 'Kids get bored when their parents are shopping. I talked to them.'

By accident, she'd learnt that children responded when spoken to like human beings. And it had always filled her with a sense of pride when one of the mums juggling more than one child had appreciated her intervention. She could work with children. *She could!* She'd combine her love of art and kids while working on her portfolio as a portrait artist.

She'd always wanted to be an artist. Her heart raced. She still could be.

Her face hardened as Akeem's lips parted to flash a gleam of perfectly white teeth.

'Are you laughing at me?' she asked. Because how many times had she been laughed at in school? Called stupid for drawing nudes? For recreating the pictures she'd coveted in art books well past their due date back in the library?

Wincing, she felt memories catch her between the eyes. How hard her father had laughed when he'd found her portraits. When she'd told him about becoming a professional portraitist. When Akeem had left her behind and she'd confessed she'd attended a taster session for a diploma in Visual Arts at the local college?

He'd hidden all her art supplies then. Destroyed her work. Her memories. But she'd still had her books. He hadn't taken those, and she'd devoured them. Repeatedly. Lost in fantasy, in fairy tale and romance.

'No, I am smiling at your ability to surprise me. I would never laugh at your dreams.'

She gritted her teeth and tried to dismiss the response her body was having to his obvious sincerity.

'You can do your diploma here,' he said.

'Here?'

'Why not here?' he countered. 'I can fly in a professor of the arts to give you one-to-one tutoring. You'd get your diploma, Charlotte.'

She could get her diploma...

What choice did she have, anyway? There was nothing at home for her, but here she wouldn't be standing still any more. She could start walking towards her dreams. Towards claiming back her identity with her art.

She could make a life to call her own.

But what kind of life would it be?

A restricted life.

A life where her husband locked his bedroom door in the name of duty.

She understood why he'd said it—that his bed was off-limits. But she could still feel it. The energy between them. The knowledge that in an instant they could both be naked and in the same situation they'd been in upstairs.

The attraction between them was powerful. She'd be a fool to deny it. But a sexless and loveless marriage sounded...*painful*. Emotionally. Mentally.

Was she strong enough to agree to be his Queen—to help him build a secure reputation as King—while forging forward and making her own life? If she left—went home— would she regret that she had never seized the opportunity? Squeezed every ounce of opportunity from it for herself?

Opportunity was to be had if she let herself. If she closed her heart to the people they'd been and accepted the people they were now.

And who were they?

He was a king, and she...

She was going to be selfish, wasn't she? *Bold*. Live her life.

But a night of sex and marriage were two different things. If she closed herself off to the emotions raging inside her chest—if she didn't let him in—she could be the Queen he needed *and* get her diploma.

Couldn't she?

Was he even giving her a choice?

She inhaled deeply and nodded. 'I'll do it,' she agreed with a firm, confident nod. 'I'll marry you.'

'For the price of a diploma you'd accept the consequences of our actions…?'

Akeem sucked in a lungful of air. He didn't get angry any more. He stayed in control of all things. At all times. But the thought that Charlotte would concede to his demand just so that she could get her diploma made him angry.

He alone wasn't enough. He, as a man, would never be enough. Not for his father. Not for *her*. He was an afterthought, a consequence, a burden she would have to carry—as he always had been. He'd only ever been wanted when he had something to give.

His blood.

A diploma…

The wildfire of her eyes met his. 'Of course not.'

Her denial sent the pent-up rage blooming inside him straight to the surface of his skin. His time in care came back to him. Foster home after foster home…surrounded by family and constantly being an outsider. Unwanted, but endured for the cheque at the end of the month.

Until Charlotte.

Until she'd wrapped him up in her lies and promises to do more than endure him, to love him. And in the end she'd rejected him too, because he hadn't offered her enough. Escape with him hadn't been enough when he'd been nothing more than an orphan, working his way up on a construction site.

He held his breath. His feeling on discovering he was a prince, needed but not wanted, and definitely not *loved*, returned with a tug and a twist to his innards.

He'd tested her back then by not telling her his secret, and she'd failed him like all the others. And she'd failed him again now. Because now she wanted what he could offer.

He focused hard on the woman before him. He needed to hear it. Needed her to confess. He moved towards her and she backed up against the wall.

'If I had told you nine years ago I was a prince,' he started, and placed his palms on either side of her head as he leant in, 'would my crown have brought your loyalty? Would you have made a different choice, *qalbi*?'

'What do you mean?' she asked.

The scent of her filled him, goading him to react to the betrayal that lingered in his soul rather than do what he should do and keep his distance from her, control himself. He could still taste the sweetness of her centre in his mouth, feel her orgasm ripping through her as he'd—

Dark brows rose above her narrowed eyes. 'I waited and you never showed up. That wasn't a choice.'

His fingers, gentle but firm, gripped her chin. 'Lies…'

She splayed her hands beneath his. 'Oh, how hard it must be for you to remember that day you promised to meet my dad now you are the *mighty* Prince Akeem.' She shook her head. 'My dad was actually really great about meeting you. He was really excited. He sent me out to get some nice bits in—'

'Nice bits?' he squawked, his dark eyes widening.

'Biscuits, cake…' She shrugged. 'I'd brought no one home before. Well, not through the front door.'

Her eyes flashed, and he remembered too. Sneaking in

through her bedroom window to hide from the drunken rants downstairs. Holding her until silence filled the darkness. How he'd sworn he would never leave her alone in the dark again.

'He was never sober enough,' she added, slicing through his memory. 'But I had no real friends. Friends who would understand that just because my dad was *him*, he wasn't *me*. It was special, my bringing you to meet him, and he saw that.' She sighed. 'When I came back from the shop we waited together, with my suitcase, but you forgot all about me—Crown Prince Akeem.'

'I have forgotten nothing.'

He released her, because the confident thrust of her chin bit at him. He'd been confident too. *Once*. He'd walked step by step through the garden gate hanging by one hinge, up the overgrown path to her front door, and he had knocked with the confidence of a man coming to claim his love. To save it. To cherish it. To protect it.

But love hadn't been there.

Love had not conquered all.

Love was a lie and she was a liar.

'How convenient that you have forgotten about the text message in your recap of events.'

'The text message?' Her eyes widened. 'What text?'

What text?

His hands fisted at his sides as he fought the urge to touch her and demand the truth. The truth she denied. The truth he'd denied too, until his phone had vibrated in his back pocket and the text message had proved every word her father had said had come from *her* mouth.

The mouth he had kissed.

The mouth he'd watched speak his name again and again as he'd thrust inside her.

The mouth that had claimed his as he'd driven them both

to a shared orgasm. Their first together. As one. They'd been born again, promising one another. To be together. To be married. To be a family.

All lies!

'The text message,' he growled, 'from your phone.'

'What did it say?'

'You know what it said—you sent it.'

She looked him dead in the eyes. 'I never sent you a message.'

Had she forgotten? Had he been so easy to forget? Only to be remembered when he had something to give her?

'How dare you stand there and lie?' he hissed between gritted teeth. He'd accused her dad of lying. Called him a drunken fool and told him that *his* Charlotte would say no such thing.

She was honest.

Kind.

But she'd toyed with him.

She'd made him believe he was wanted.

She'd made him get attached.

She'd made him weak.

The amber specks in her right iris blazed. 'What did the message say?'

My dad needs me. I'm not coming with you. I never was.

Verbatim, he said those three brief sentences out loud.

What a fool he'd been to believe she wanted him. No one had ever wanted him. Not his father. Not Charlotte. People only wanted what he could offer them. His blood. His time. His sacrifice.

At eighteen years of age he'd promised himself they'd rejected him for the last time. He would make himself better. Stronger. And not only would he be needed, *they* would want him. *Need him.*

What boy of eighteen would have taken the other option? Returned to his former life as a no one? A life that didn't need or want him?

Here, he had power. Here, he had choices. Here, he was the protector of his people. Duty-bound to his country. And now his duty bound him to the past, because he'd been reckless enough to flaunt it in his present.

His mistake had bound him to Charlotte.

His little liar.

'I didn't send that message,' she said.

Raising her arms, he laced them around his neck and pulled her to him, into his hardness.

'I will seduce you right here and now as an incentive to tell the truth,' he proclaimed.

He would kiss her until her bones melted. Until she didn't know where she started and he began.

'I am telling the truth!'

Her words shook him out of his angry haze and he exhaled fully, leaving his chest empty. He was drained. Mentally. Physically.

What was she doing to him? To his control?

'You left me alone to explain myself to your father,' he accused, all too aware of the memory of how he'd stood his ground for both of them. For Charlotte. Until she'd texted him with the truth. Her own words—typed by her own fingers. 'You couldn't be bothered to face me yourself and tell me you weren't coming with me. You left your drunken excuse of a father and a text to do your dirty work.'

'But I… You never came…'

He ignored her. 'Do you know what he called me?'

'What did he call you?' Her voice was so quiet…so timid.

'He called me a monster for wanting you by my side.' Damien Hegarty had called him much worse, but he would not repeat those words—he would not hear them again. He'd been called many things throughout his childhood: withdrawn, unwanted, a bastard. But a monster? And the other sickening words he'd called him? Only once.

What about your Father, Akeem? He called you much worse.

This wasn't about his father.

Isn't it?

He pushed the voice aside. No, it was firmly about *her*.

'I was newly eighteen,' he continued. 'You were sixteen. He said he'd told you about men like me who use young girls and then throw them away. Rotten men. Broken men. He was glad you had used me for your own enjoyment.'

He couldn't stop, even though everything in him told him to calm down. To breathe. To let it go. But he hadn't been able to let it go—let *her go*—for nine years, and it had brought him nothing but chaos.

'He said you were not as naïve as you'd made out. That you'd wanted a good time and used me to achieve it. You'd prearranged my meeting with your dad to make sure I got the message that you never wanted to see me again. And then my mobile phone pinged with a text to confirm everything he'd told me.'

'And you believed him?' she husked, her chest rising and falling as rapidly as his heart was pumping. 'After everything?' She paled. 'You believed everything my father told you?'

Her voice was quiet, but every word boomed through him like a bass drum.

Pinching the bridge of her nose, she pushed out a slow, deep breath. 'After everything we'd shared, you walked away because you believed I'd tricked you? Because my dad said so?' She released the bridge of her nose and turned her attention to him. 'Then you didn't really know me at all.'

'I believed the message that came from your phone and told me you weren't coming.'

And he had believed it. Why wouldn't he when it had been from her phone? Why wouldn't he believe she'd written it when throughout his life his caregivers had all written little notes in their brown manila files, explaining why yet again he couldn't remain with the family he'd been housed with?

'Told me you had no intention of coming with me.'

Her intense, stony stare held him captive. 'It wasn't me.'

'He betrayed you?' The question was out before he could digest it.

'My dad…' She gave a half-hearted shrug. 'He was a villain, wasn't he?' A weak smile tormented her lips. 'He used our own vulnerabilities against us. He trapped me into thinking he was all I had, and he convinced you I didn't want you any more.'

'It's not true,' he whispered—because it couldn't be. Damien had not cheated him.

'I didn't have my phone. My dad knew you were coming and he sent me out of the house,' she recapped, her breathing quickening into short little rasps. 'It is the truth. I see that now. Don't you?'

His heart forgot to beat. His lungs forgot to inhale. He'd held on to his bitterness—his need to get even—for nine years.

His veins pulsed and twitched in his cheek. 'It seems I do.'

He was so *angry*.

Angry with her, angry with her dad, angry with himself

and with the past he had no control over. Damien Hegarty had manipulated him into believing Charlotte didn't want him, and her dad had convinced her that he hadn't shown up. They'd both been tricked—catapulted away from their destinies.

And you have no control over your present either, do you? Your father made sure of that.

He pushed the voice down, because he *could* control *this.* He ached. Throbbed with the need to lose himself in anything but the past and how wrong he'd been. How naïve he'd allowed himself to be. How fragile he'd allowed her rejection to make him. He'd lumped her rejection in with all the others he'd experienced since he was a child.

Since the rejection of his father.

Yes, his father had claimed him eventually—but only because he was the only one available. *He'd wanted him for his blood.* Not for himself alone. He'd knocked that boy out of him. Moulded him into what he'd wanted.

But Charlotte...

He'd been wrong.

Her hand moved, her fingertips rising to his cheek. 'Akeem...'

His name sounded as if it had been torn from her lips. A breathless question. *A plea?*

They were both reeling from the revelation of her father's trickery. She was asking him to give her somewhere to hide—someone to hide in. Wasn't she? And just for a moment he would let her hide in him. In the intensity crackling between them as hot and wild as it had when he was between her thighs.

For one last time he would surrender to it. To the pull. *To her.*

Unable to contain the emotions building in his chest, he crushed her mouth against his. He let all his rage pour into her as he moved his lips against hers. And she kissed him back, her lips smacking against his, fanning the flames licking between them.

He couldn't stand it. The agony. He tore his mouth from hers, his breathing ragged. He couldn't do anything but focus on his next intake of air.

Pushing her away from him, he panted as hard as she did.

His need for revenge was unwarranted.

His insides clenched. All along he should have been giving his attention to his duty.

He should apologise. He closed his eyes. He couldn't. What would he be apologising for? For everything he was—*had been*—and for what everyone kept telling him wasn't enough? For believing she'd thought the same?

Akeem opened his eyes.

He grabbed her hand and pulled her inside his elevator in the sky.

'This elevator,' he said, releasing her hand and turning to face her. 'Is revolutionary in the aircraft industry. One of the first of its kind. My father was many things, but he always liked to be among the first. The first to win, the first to lose. But most of all he put himself first. Before his wife, his mistresses, his son and his kingdom.'

He turned away from her and pressed a button. Then he turned to face the doors, watching them close and seal him inside the elevator with the woman beside him, her reflection mirrored in the reflective doors.

His future Queen.

'I am not my father. I will marry because my duty to my country will demand it. But I will not succumb to the madness of passion again. My people will always come first,' he said.

Because he needed the reminder of who he was now, and so did she.

'You will always come second after we leave this plane.'

CHAPTER FIVE

'WHY WOULD YOU say something like that?' Her voice was small, and she hated it. Hated it that he'd made her feel that way.

Invisible.

'It's a simple truth you should understand,' he replied.

She snapped her gaze to the impenetrable figure beside her. *Understand what?* All her life she'd been under no illusion. She came second. Or last, if at all. And now, after everything that had been revealed—*her dad!*—he was asking her to put up, shut up, and do as she was told. Step aside for someone else. Forget her feelings—her needs because he said so. Like her dad.

She didn't think so.

Her dad had betrayed her. She bit hard at the inside of her cheek, stemming the tears, the anger burning in her chest. She had been his daughter. His *daughter*! And he'd lied. Tricked her. Manipulated her into staying in his shadow. Into helping him live his life while she forgot about hers.

She was tired of forgetting.

She wanted to live her way, and for herself first.

Her shoulders tight, her breathing rapid, she didn't allow herself to think the thought through. She stepped in front of Akeem, raised her hand, and smacked her palm against the big red button.

The lift shuddered to a standstill.

'What are you doing?' he asked.

'You don't get to talk to me like that,' she said, wishing her heart would beat normally, not with this frantic, chaotic drumroll it had had since he'd waltzed back into her life. She shrugged it off, made herself meet those eyes, fixed on her with disapproval. 'You don't get to speak to me like I don't matter—or *won't* matter,' she corrected, and pointed to the closed doors, 'after we step outside.'

'How would you like me to speak to you?'

The question was flat, with no hint of sarcasm or genuine curiosity. Only words.

She'd seen so many versions of Akeem today: the man with furious kisses whose hurt had been as visceral as her own when they'd confronted the past. *When they'd kissed.* And then there was the man who would be King. The man who'd faced their unannounced visitors without so much as a blush, and come back to demand she be his bride.

The Akeem she was looking at now was already King. No explosion of passion, just a cool regard. The King was looking at her now, and he didn't see her. Not the way he had when he'd stripped her to her skin and pushed her into demanding what she wanted.

No, this was a king who saw nothing but his people. *His duty.*

'You asked me to be your Queen and help you establish yourself as King in the eyes of your people—'

'And for me to do that they must come before you.'

'No.'

'It is not negotiable,' he dismissed.

'A lot has happened since London.' She blew out an exasperated breath. 'A lot neither of us expected. But you're not the only one who gets to set the rules.'

'It is my job to set the rules, and to have them obeyed without question.'

'Not with me. Not any more. Not after—'

'Your father?'

His interjection was low. Quiet. But just as he had in the limo and before he'd ordered her to rest, or when he'd stripped her bare in the lounge, he knew exactly what she meant—what she needed—before she'd voiced it.

He did still see her—even if the crown of duty was obscuring his sight.

She could feel it.

The *knowing* between them.

She nodded slowly. 'My dad manipulated me, and I sacrificed the last nine years of my life to care for him because he tricked me into it.'

Her head hurt. Her heart hurt. Her father and her grief were complicated, but she still missed him. *Loved him.* But…

'Don't pretend there are choices when there aren't any choices to be made,' she said. 'There is only what *you* want. Just like my dad.'

'I am nothing like your father.'

'Maybe you don't *want* to be like him—'

'I am *nothing* like him,' he repeated, his voice a sharp warning. 'Or my own father.'

'Did you love him?'

The pause was pregnant.

'Your dad?' she clarified. 'I loved mine, but I'm not sure he loved me, because he forgot about his duty to me—'

'Stop comparing our lives. They are not similar,' he bit, and the hard edge to his voice hurt.

'But they *are* similar,' she contradicted. 'You can't deny that.'

'Maybe once,' he conceded. 'Once we walked the same

streets in the same shoes. But not any more. That world is no longer mine, and it never will be again.'

'I was an accident—like you,' she continued, ignoring his resistance. 'Mum and Dad got married because of me, and continued their binge drinking regardless of the fact they'd made a life. My mum died because of her continued carelessness, and I paid the price by becoming a full-time carer for my dad.'

Their eyes met again in the mirror.

'Dad forgot that he should take care of me, and not the other way around. He forgot his duty so badly he tricked me into staying in that role for another nine years…'

She trailed off as flashes of the last nine years hit her. She'd lost so much time. How many people had she lost? How many friendships? Her career as an artist?

'You paid the price because your dad couldn't keep it in his pants and you ended up in care. I ended up in care too.' She watched as he hardened at the reminder of how they'd met. Both lost. Alone. Needing what the other had to give. *Sanctuary.*

'I know you were there much longer than I was. I got to go home when you didn't have a home to go to. But…' She shrugged. 'Forgetting about myself—putting myself last—isn't something I can agree to again.'

'I will not forget my people as my father did and allow *your* hurt feelings—'

'As King, your duty comes first.' She inhaled deeply, steeling herself to ask for what she wanted. *Needed.* 'But I need you to be a decent human being. No throwaway comments. Explain what you mean and why you want something. Don't hurt my feelings to get what you want.'

He grimaced. 'Feelings cannot win. We cannot put them first,' he continued. 'Because when you do, you end up in situations you never would otherwise.'

'Like losing nine years of your life because of your lying, treacherous father?' she asked. 'Like being promised a night of sex only to be trapped into getting married? Like agreeing to be your ex-lover's wife, only to be told you won't matter in the marriage, anyway?'

Her rant over, she glared at him. At the skin tightly pulled across his cheeks. At his flaring nostrils. At his eyes, dark and wide.

'Feelings don't always have to be so...*extreme*,' she started again when he didn't answer.

'We have been nothing *but* extreme, Charlotte,' he corrected. His voice was a low rumble. 'How can we be anything else?'

'So you've decided for both of us that it's all or nothing? No middle ground? No compromise?'

'Kings do not compromise.'

'What about friends?' She swallowed hard. 'What about husbands?'

'Friends?' He flinched, and she swallowed down the pain in her throat.

Akeem held her gaze as something unidentifiable flashed in his eyes, with the silence hanging between them.

'I cannot promise you friendship. I cannot promise you everything you have asked for.'

She opened her mouth to speak, but he shook his head.

'I'm not finished.'

She pressed her lips together, and he continued.

'But I can promise to treat you as a human being, and to respect that you are a woman who can make her own decisions. Going forward, I will ask,' he promised, moving in on her, 'not demand.'

His voice was silk against her frayed edges. His words. His promise. This might not be the life she wanted, but she could shape it into something good if he would *see* her.

Recognise that she would not remain in the background any more.

She would voice her opinions.

She would matter.

She pressed the red button again and the lift rattled, picked up a little speed, and stopped with an ungraceful thump.

He hit a button and the doors opened. A red carpet ran all the way from under the plane to a convoy of cars and a gathering of men.

And a helicopter.

'You are shoeless,' he said, and she looked at him, then looked at her feet. 'May I carry you?' he asked, his words articulated with effort.

She smiled at the tightness of his mouth. 'I can walk,' she assured him.

Because she could. She could walk forward with her head high and her feet bare because she wanted to. Because it was *her* choice.

Before he could comment again, she moved in front of him and onto the red carpet, through the parting throng of men and towards the helicopter doors, magically opened by invisible staff.

She climbed inside and Akeem was quickly beside her, pulling a harness over her shoulders, between her breasts, and clipping her in between her thighs with quick and steady hands, before climbing in beside her in the pilot's seat.

Her stomach lurched. '*You're* flying it?'

He turned to her. 'Scared?'

'No,' she denied. But the truth was she was exhausted with being afraid, and this moment, these changes of events, her agreeing to be Queen—

What if the people didn't accept her as their Queen? Her

dad had never loved her. If he couldn't love her, his own daughter, how could anyone else? How could a whole desert kingdom accept her when her family hadn't?

But how would she know if she didn't try?

She'd been afraid most of her life.

Afraid of never being accepted.

Afraid to fail…

The rotor blades turned. The sound was getting louder and louder, replicating the whooshing inside her ears.

She gasped as the helicopter turned in a three-sixty and took flight. All around her was desert. Miles of it. Before the city sprang up from the red sands themselves.

It was something both ancient and surreal. A wall spanned the city at the base of the mountain, and buildings with rounded peaks stood on tall columns and archways. And up it rose. The city ascended into the skies. And there, in the distance, above the walled city, was a palace set against the mountains.

'It's a fortress!' she exclaimed.

A calming realisation washed over her. The doubts and the fears were her dad's, because her sixteen-year-old self was still inside her. She could feel her, kicking inside her chest and demanding Charlotte take this second chance being offered to her.

On her terms she would claim back her art and her identity. Because this was her ticket to adventure.

To life…

She wouldn't fail this time.

Failure was *not* built into her DNA.

She flicked a glance at Akeem. Confident. At ease. Intuitively, she felt safe—protected. But wasn't that the most dangerous illusion of all? Because the scariest of all the things that were changing around her was *him*, and the part of herself that saw this as a second chance with Akeem.

Turning away from him, she refused to acknowledge *that* part, and focused on the views before her. On the golden globe of the sun descending behind the mountains and turning the sky a deep orange and the landscape beneath—a mystical brilliance of burning red, golden spires piercing the skies from doomed roofs, and splashes of green feathered throughout.

Taliedaa was breathtaking.

She watched, entranced, as with complete, confident control Akeem flew them towards the palace in the sky.

To her new home.

Where adventure waited.

He'd hungered for this. For nine years he'd dreamt of this moment—ached for it. Ached to rub all she'd thrown away to live a life of drudgery in her face. To shame her for doubting him. To hold the past by the hand and show it there was no place in his world for it now.

To show it—*her*—all he had become.

But her betrayal had never existed.

And now she would have a place in his world.

He unbuckled his harness and exited the chopper. Motioning to the staff at the gilded entrance to wait, he moved to Charlotte's door and wrenched it open.

He looked down at her feet. Her bare feet were slender and long, with a high instep. Elegant. *Unadorned.* Ready to be embellished. He would have her toes painted. His eyes moved over the green robes covering her body. He could wrap her in silk, but could she become the Queen he needed her to be? Could she leave the past on the plane?

He met her eyes.

Could he?

Palms forward, she said, 'Don't carry me.'

'Do you have a hidden pair of slippers?'

'No.'

'There is no carpet to cushion your feet here,' he said.

'Are you asking me if I can or telling me I can't walk?'

He bit the inside of his cheek. 'I am asking.'

'Then ask.'

He reached for her but she halted him.

'Questions require words,' she said, 'and I would like to hear yours. I'd like to hear your respect for the woman I am…a woman who can make her own decisions.'

His eyes flicked to the staff waiting for his command to come and greet them. He should cloak himself in his armour and become the Crown Prince—rightful heir to the Taliedaaen throne. He had been him for so long—the son of a king—it should feel like a second skin. *But it didn't.* He felt crumpled. Dishevelled. As if someone beneath his suit of armour was stretching the seams…

'May I?' he asked tightly, and she nodded.

He reached for her again. This time, she didn't resist. She came to him with open palms on his shoulders. He drew her in tight against him, feeling the quick inhale-exhale of her breath, and with one hand beneath her thigh, one around her waist, he carried her, step by step, to the front door of the royal palace.

Pride.

It burned in his belly.

'Your Royal Highness… Miss Hegarty…' the staff chorused.

Never had he thought to hear his title along with her name. He kept walking because his hands refused to release her, his feet refused to stop.

Formal introductions could wait.

What he needed couldn't.

Distance.

Akeem stepped into the tiled entrance hall with its high

domed roof and kept walking. He turned into a hallway lavishly decorated with ancient tiles depicting scenes of palace life, then walked through a courtyard lit with lanterns powered by unseen electricity and opened a door.

He hadn't held his past by the hand, he recognised. He'd carried it through the front door and welcomed it. Claimed it as his and given it a home. He'd turned his past into a spectacle of duty, and now he was bound.

Tethered.

He slid her to her feet, caught her wrist, and pulled her into the room with him, onto a floor littered with silk rugs. He closed the door. Her wrist was too small, too delicate. He dropped it.

She didn't move. She stayed too close…too near.

'Charlotte, you are not blinking.'

She blinked unnaturally several times. 'I'm not?'

'No.'

'I'm sorry. I'm a little overawed,' she admitted. 'The helicopter, the desert, the city… The *palace*,' she crooned. 'It's beautiful, Akeem. Your home is beautiful…'

His pulse was refusing to slow and his chest puffed. Her mouth was saying all the right words, but they didn't stroke his ego the way he'd thought they would. The *but* lingering on her tongue was too loud, too sharp—not what he had envisaged.

Nothing so far was what he'd envisaged his time with Charlotte would be.

And whose fault is that?

'But…?' he encouraged, keeping his voice even and ignoring the thud of his temples.

'But…' she started, and flicked her tongue against the dip in her bottom lip. 'But this is my adventure. I want to know what happens next before it happens—before you hoist me over your shoulder again.'

'*Adventure?*' he repeated, his brain refusing to understand her use of that word in correlation with his life. 'This is not—'

'An unusual, exciting or daring experience. That is the definition of adventure, and I'm pretty sure this fits the bill.'

'You have a dictionary with you?'

'I like words. I've read the dictionary quite a few times. Just for fun.' She slanted a slender shoulder. 'So adventurous was my life before you.'

'Then tell me what you make of this word.' He moved towards her. Closer. And whispered, 'Box…'

'Box?' she repeated, lips pursed.

'You want to know what happens next on this adventure of yours?' he asked. She nodded. 'Then tell me: what is the definition of box?'

'It depends—'

'No,' he said, redirecting her. 'A box—an everyday box. What is it?'

'A container with a lid.'

'Exactly. But sometimes boxes have locks. This box will need a lock.'

She pushed the scarf from her hair and let it hang on her shoulders. 'Is this a lesson?'

'Perhaps,' he said, resisting the urge to close the distance between them and push his hands into her hair, clench his fists around the curling softness. 'You will need a box.'

'A box?'

'A large box,' he agreed, and then he closed the distance between them and did what he'd told himself he wouldn't. He touched her. A finger to her cheek. So warm. So soft. 'Staff will enter this room when I leave, and they will help you pack it.'

'Pack it?' she asked.

He moved his finger. Slowly. Down her cheek. He

stopped at her chin and tilted it. Made her look at him as he moved his finger over the notch beneath her throat, down between her breasts and flattened his palm on her ribcage.

On her heart.

'How many years has your heart been beating?'

'That's a strange question.'

The words shuddered from her lips and he felt it. Her hiccup. The double beat of her heart beneath his palm. She was faltering.

'And that is not an answer.'

'Depends on who you ask.'

'How old are you?'

'You know how old I am.'

'Indulge me.'

'Twenty-five.'

'For twenty-five years you have felt every feeling, every doubt, every fear, and now you will let them go.' His palm pushed into her and massaged the flesh, caging her heart.

'Let them go…?' she breathed.

'You will not entertain them again,' he said, and then corrected himself with a speed that surprised him. 'Unless you want to. Keep the key if you must—if you *like*,' he said. 'But a queen must know control. Which emotion to display. Which fear to make use of to drive her. And you will be Queen, Charlotte. You will understand control.'

A sound escaped her lips and fired straight into his groin. Half-moan, half-sigh. He wanted to taste it. Inhale it—feed his lungs, his life's essence. But he resisted, and he would keep on resisting.

'Pack your feelings away,' he encouraged, and then he told her what he'd told himself on his first night here. 'Put them in a box, *qalbi*, and forget them.'

'Is that what you do, Akeem?'

She waved a hand towards the bed and he turned to it.

It was across the room. White organza drapes fell from wooden posts, and on it was a mattress so deep...

'Are all your feelings hiding under that bed?'

He snapped his attention back to her. 'I do not need a box,' he lied. 'All I need is here.' He touched his chest. 'An armour called duty.'

'Tell me.'

She pressed her hand to his chest.

Oh, but his heart hammered.

Thud, thud, thud.

'What was it like for you?' she asked.

And he did not like it. Her ability to call to the part of him he'd buried deep. So deep. He no longer had the key to his box. If it had ever had a key—a lock. But the lid was creaking back from its rusted hinges, and it hurt.

'What was it like?' he repeated, all too conscious of his hand on her body, of hers on his. 'I learnt how to represent my people. Not with wealth or pomp, but by using the privilege of being Crown Prince to guide a people. A country.'

'Who taught you how to do that? To understand?'

'Them. The people,' he said. 'They were talking, but my father wasn't listening. I listened.'

He had been right to become Akeem Abd al-Uzza and banish the boy Charlotte had known. The boy who had freely felt his feelings. Because now, moving forward, he wouldn't let himself feel anything for her.

It was the way he'd survived for nine years, and the only way he would survive now.

His father had abused his power to satisfy himself at the cost of so many people's lives. His people would not suffer the same under his rule. Not because of his negligence. His *feelings.*

'It can't have been easy for you—'

He stepped back, pulled his hand away as hers fell from

his chest. He did not want her to see—to know—how hard it had been for him. He wanted her to know only that he was *this*. A man of royalty. A would-be king. A crown prince. Anything but a basic boy with basic needs...

'I have never known anything easy.'

'Will it be hard for me?' she asked.

'The quicker you understand that everything you do from this moment will be to take care of something bigger than you or me, the easier the next steps will be for you,' he said.

'Like looking after my dad? That was bigger than me—than my dreams.'

He tilted his head to look at her. 'I know you understand sacrifice—'

'And this will be another?'

'No, not completely,' he denied. Because that part was true. He would pay for her time. Her sacrifices. 'This time you will keep your art. Whatever you need—ask. Selma will be with you shortly.'

'Selma?'

'Your personal assistant.'

'How long do I have to pack?' She laughed when he stared at her. 'My box?'

'Three days,' he answered.

Because he needed those three days away from her. Three days to compose himself. To stamp out whatever was between them. To put it back into his dreams, where only the darkness recognised its poignancy.

'What happens then?'

'We shall present our engagement to the people of Taliedaa. To dignitaries, the Royal Council...' He inhaled deeply. 'The world and its cameras will stand in the gardens of the palace as we stand above them on the royal balcony, and *nothing*,' he emphasised, 'nothing other than control and orchestrated smiles should be with us. Everything else—'

'Should be in the box?'

'Well done.'

She shook her head. 'I have less than three days to reinvent myself?'

'Not reinvent,' he clarified. 'Refine. My staff will help you,' he said, and then corrected himself. '*Your* staff will help you prepare for the announcement of our engagement and for our wedding.'

'Wedding?'

'One week from today.'

'A week?' she gasped. 'Why so fast?'

'We must be married before I take the crown,' he explained. 'That is why every decision—every item you pack away—is crucial.'

She nodded. Small continuous nods. 'Will I see you before?'

'No.' He turned away from her, ignoring the pull to stay with her—to stay *close*—and opened the door.

'That's it? That's all you're going to say?'

He didn't look back. 'There is nothing else to say, Charlotte,' he told her over his shoulder. 'Find a way to forget the woman you are and become a queen.'

Just like he had.

He closed the door without a second glance and walked back the way he'd came.

He had three days to bury his box deeper. Because he would not reveal what was inside.

Or who...

CHAPTER SIX

HE'D DISMISSED HER. Left her to prepare on her own for a situation she'd never dreamt she'd be in. Three days to turn herself into a queen. One week until she became a wife.

She wasn't ready. How could she be? She was Charlotte Hegarty, survivor of addict parents. The daughter of alcoholics. What right did she have to these things now being offered to her?

She closed her eyes.

She would not fail.

Her dad had been wrong.

'*Shukran.*'

'*Hasan jidana.*'

Selma, her personal assistant, smiled. 'Very good, Your Royal Highness.'

Charlotte wriggled in a little celebration dance and pressed her toes into the bedspread.

'Charlotte,' she corrected for the umpteenth time. She wasn't royal yet. She was a royal-in-waiting until tomorrow, and even then… *Your Royal Highness?*

'You cannot learn a language with many nuances in a few days,' said Selma.

Charlotte crossed her legs. 'I know.'

'In time, you will learn,' Selma soothed her impatient student. 'The palace will provide a tutor—'

'A tutor can't teach me what you can before the announcement.'

'Of course it is your choice, but the brain is much like a sandwich.' Selma pressed her palms together as she sat on the edge of the bed 'Too many ingredients and the filling spills out.' She clapped. *'Splodge.'*

Charlotte laughed. Hard. And then covered her mouth with her hand.

'It won't be funny when you can't remember anything because you've tried to digest too much and your stomach is still full and yet you must eat more sandwiches.'

'Are you hungry, Selma?' she asked, displacing her hand from her mouth. 'All your analogies are about food. You should have eaten with me. There was way too much food for just one person!'

'I'm always hungry—and you are always hungry for knowledge, yes?' Brown eyes twinkled beneath dark arched brows. 'Because you eat very little and ask many questions?'

'Nerves,' she confessed easily. 'It seems important to know as much as I can about my new home, and you've been an excellent teacher.'

'The best way to gain new knowledge is to let it sit with you.' She pointed to the mountain of plump pillows at Charlotte's back. 'Sleep, and let your subconscious do the hard work.'

'I don't think I'll sleep.'

She hadn't slept well since she'd arrived, and the thought of tomorrow's schedule wound her up too tightly to sleep now. Her eyes wandered longingly to the box of supplies she'd been gifted, which was sitting beside the low-slung sofa on the far side of the room. Her fingers itched to pull the paper free, to take the pencils from the packs and escape into herself.

Art. It was right there. Waiting for her to claim it. As it had been every night since her arrival. The one thing that made her *her*. She pushed down the longing because only later, when she was alone, would she continue to rediscover that part of herself.

'But you must rest.' She pulled her gaze back to Selma. 'Go.' She shooed her off the bed with the back of her hand. 'I'm so sorry... I didn't think...' She paused.

Selma had offered her something achingly close to friendship. She knew the dynamics were all wrong, but somehow it worked. *A friend.* Maybe soon a confidante? Her heart bloomed. She'd had no one to share her secrets with. No one since Akeem. But the moment Selma had introduced herself they'd hit it off.

'It's been so nice,' Charlotte continued. 'Thank you for making it nice, Selma.'

These last three days she hadn't been alone. Her days had been full, but her nights...

Akeem hadn't returned.

'You won't thank me tomorrow, after the stylist has plucked you within an inch of your life—'

'Like a chicken?'

Selma wrinkled her nose. 'And told a gazillion facts you'll never remember about Taliedaa by Kadar. He never knows where to begin or where to end. But he is passionate about his records, and continues to preserve the legacy of our young sovereign state. He's overjoyed that you are such an eager student, but tomorrow I will rein him in.'

'No, please don't.'

'There is too much to do for his lesson to go over its allotted time.'

LELA MAY WIGHT   107

'It's been fascinating, meeting with him every day over breakfast—he obviously loves this place.'

'He does.' Selma flushed. 'Very much.'

'And you?'

'I love him—but don't tell him.' She smiled, but the corners of her lips pointed down. 'He wouldn't know where to store *that* insignificant fact in his history books.'

'Maybe it doesn't have to be history?' Charlotte said—because hadn't her past very much become her present? If she could have a second chance, couldn't anyone?

Is that how you see this? As a second chance with Akeem?

Selma was shaking her head, and Charlotte ignored the punch of the question she'd asked herself.

She concentrated on the woman on her bed. 'Have you and Kadar known each other long?'

Selma coughed and rose, clearly not wanting to talk about Kadar further. 'Would you like me to help you settle down?'

'No, I'll manage.'

No one had ever offered to tuck her in before. Selma offered every night. Maybe she could ask her to check under the bed… Her stomach pulled. She didn't have to ask. She knew what would be under there. *Her fears.* But she wouldn't be afraid. She would let them go, as Akeem had told her.

'Sleep?' Selma suggested. 'Tomorrow will be—'

'Scary?'

'Busy,' she corrected. 'Your history lesson with breakfast, and now the designers have your preferences and sizes…' She smiled brightly, her warm brown eyes widening. 'You will have more than the off-the-rack collection they've left you to get by with.'

'All these clothes…' Charlotte smoothed her hand over

the layered silk organza dress she'd chosen to wear for tomorrow's lessons beside her on the bed. 'They aren't off the rack where I shop.'

'Where do you shop in England? London—so many shops!'

She picked up the dress and held it against her chest. 'Charity shops mainly,' Charlotte confessed, refusing to feel any shame. She loved charity shops. They'd kept her clothed throughout her teens and into adulthood, and her dad too. But she'd never have found clothes like *these* there.

She looked down at the brown dress. *No.* What had they called it? *Plum chestnut?* It was layered and striped. *It was beautiful.* It was a V-necked asymmetric style, with batwing sleeves, a fitted waist and a flared skirt, and a lop-sided hem overlaid by sheer panels…

She never had anything so exquisite next to her skin. And she loved it.

Was that materialistic? Probably. She didn't care. Wasn't it every girl's fantasy to have her Cinderella moment? Her whole life she'd known how she'd wanted to look, but she'd just never been able to afford it.

Akeem as a fairy godmother? She smothered the cackle in her throat.

The team who'd joined her very quickly after Akeem's departure from her room had supplied her with underwear, shoes, daywear, nightwear… In every colour she could think of and some she wouldn't have considered. *Umber?* She'd never worn umber…or burnt orange…or red…

Her core tightened. Tomorrow she would. Tomorrow she'd wear red.

'Well, no charity shop bags will enter the palace tomorrow morning.'

Selma winked, and held out her hand for the dress. Charlotte loved her familiarity. Her ease as she took the dress from her and hung it, ready for tomorrow.

'The designers will return with a wardrobe.' Selma whistled, long and low. 'A wardrobe with you in mind on so many rails.' Selma clapped. 'I can't wait to see their designs for your wedding dress.'

Charlotte's stomach dipped. She couldn't think about the wedding yet. She wasn't officially engaged, and her fiancé had gone missing...

She missed him, she acknowledged, but only to herself.

'And, of course, your finished engagement outfit...' Selma sighed wistfully, a hand on her chest. *'That dress.'*

Nerves made Charlotte's fingers bite into her palm. 'One dress at a time, Selma,' she chided playfully. Because that was exactly what she was doing. Taking one dress—one day at a time.

'Both will be perfect.'

She didn't doubt it.

But what about the woman *in* the dress?

For seventy-two hours she'd been in his home. Under his roof. And he'd resisted her. He'd controlled his impulse to seek her out, to replay their encounter in the flesh, to touch her—hold her...

Hold her?

Akeem toyed with the black leather strap in his hand, frayed and cracked from age. He'd always been impulsive as a child—and as a teenager. He'd said what he was thinking—*reacted.* He was no longer impulsive. Leaving her alone in his palace, depositing her in her rooms and stepping away—they were considered choices.

He'd given himself space—taken active steps towards addressing the intensity of his feelings for Charlotte. They were too intense. Everything he could not allow himself to feel.

No, you've just hidden from her like a scared little boy.

He was not little, and he was not afraid. He'd been working with his most senior aides from dawn till dusk to make this day move like a well-oiled machine. Everything was in place. Everything was ready.

All he had to do was wait twelve more hours…

He ran his fingers over the edges of the watch until he came to its small, round metal face. The silver-plated back was tarnished, with a copperish rim showing its worth.

Cheap.

You shouldn't have that, should you? Put it back under the bed like a good boy.

He wasn't *that* little boy any more.

If your father knew you had it—

He was dead. He couldn't do anything any more.

But Akeem knew exactly what his father would have done. He would have had one of his men take it. He would have laid it on the table in front of his throne and then he would have called him. Made him watch as he brought a heavy hammer down onto the glass face. Smashed it. The basic wristwatch of a basic woman. Just to smother the basic love of a boy for his basic mother.

So why do you still have it, Would-Be King? Do you need it? Will you cry without it?

His hand squeezed around the watch in his hand until it dug deeply into his palm.

Pain. He flexed his fingers. He welcomed it.

You didn't welcome it nine years ago, when you confronted your father on his pretty throne.

He shoved the watch into his pocket, but the intrusive thought persisted. He spat a curse to the rising sun, and the memory of the last time he'd seen the dawn with Charlotte emerged as vividly as if he were watching a replay.

The morning after they'd both lost their virginity.

The morning he'd said things would be different.

The morning he'd promised they'd make their own family—*be* a family.

Turning his back on the city, Akeem moved through the rooms he called his and, with the past biting at his heels, walked towards Charlotte's rooms.

Outside her room, he hesitated. Could he really not resist for twelve more hours? Had the last seventy-two hours been for nothing...?

He swept inside without knocking.

The balcony doors were open, and there she stood outside. Her body was covered in an organza dress and her hair hung between her shoulder blades in a loose ponytail.

Moving towards her, across the hardwood floor littered with silk rugs and past the vast bed, he detested the blood heating through him at the sight of her. Detested this tug inside him. It was the sensation of a rope being pulled so tightly that he couldn't withstand it for twelve more hours.

Before he could stop himself, he called out to her. 'Charlotte.'

She didn't turn.

He stopped statue-still, a foot before the balcony doors, and half turned, ready to leave as he'd entered. Unobserved. But she turned first.

'Akeem?'

He inched closer, calling for the control he needed. 'Are you drawing?' he asked.

'Only sketching...' She looked down at the pad resting on the stone balustrade and brushed a hand over it. 'It's not very good.'

Memories, fast and blinding, hurtled towards him and

plunged him into the past... Under the oak tree. *Laughing.* Handing her a sketchpad and newly acquired pencils, bought with his meagre wages. Her eyes moving over him as he'd sat and sat and she'd drawn him.

'How does it feel?' he asked. 'To draw again?'

A shy smile curved her lips. 'Like wearing my favourite pyjamas when they've just come out the tumble dryer. Comfortable,' she explained with a half-laugh, half-sigh. 'Worn in.'

'Bring it to me,' he demanded, wanting to see—*needing* to see.

'No, it isn't ready.' She turned her sketchpad over and turned all her attention to him.

'You would deny the Crown Prince?' he asked.

'No, I would deny *you*, Akeem. It's not ready.'

'Come to me,' he commanded.

Tentatively, she took a step towards him. Another step. The shawl fell from her shoulders to the stone floor. He'd approved her dress, as he'd approved the rest of her temporary wardrobe, but seeing it on her in the flesh, her tawny beige skin alight with golden undertones... His throat dried and his groin pulsed.

He reached into his pocket and pulled out the small watch. He enclosed his thumb and forefinger around her wrist and fastened it there with quick fingers. Not letting himself notice the delicate flesh of the inner side of her wrist, or how delicate and how soft the skin felt as his fingers brushed against it. Neither did he let himself analyse why he was doing this. Only accepted that he was.

'It's a watch...'

'It was my mother's.'

Charlotte placed her hand on his. He looked at their hands, hers so much smaller. She trusted him. Trusted him to cage the fire within him. The passion. Just as his mother had trusted his father to do the right thing when he'd seduced her away from her duties and made her take a leap of faith into his arms.

And then he'd crushed her.

Her reputation.

Her heart.

He snatched his hand away.

He did not want Charlotte's heart.

She rubbed her wrist. 'Why would you give me your mother's watch?'

He stepped back. He was eighteen again, confused, giving Charlotte his extra pillow.

No. He was twenty-seven and a crown prince. He was not confused.

'I don't need it any more,' he told her—because he didn't. He didn't want to feel attached to the past. To the boy that no one wanted, lost in the care system.

'You don't need it?' she croaked. 'It was your mum's?'

'I can't give you everything you asked for on the plane. So I am giving you this.'

'What can't you give me?'

'Decency.'

'You can't be *decent*?' She laughed. 'Why not?'

'Because I do not feel decent when I'm around you.'

Her smile vanished. 'Is that why you haven't come to me?' she asked. 'Why you've stayed away?'

He didn't answer. He couldn't. How could he admit he'd stayed away because every time he was with her it was a fight? A constant battle with his control?

'You've stayed away because you're angry, haven't you?'

Nine years and his smiles were practised...*perfect*. He did not show his feelings, let alone speak them out loud. But she could see.

He clamped his teeth together.

She stepped into his space and it hit him like a stray bullet. The presence of her. The calming balm she'd offered to him so many years ago, when he'd been about to leave the care system and embark on his own journey. A journey with her. And here they were again. *Embarking.*

She raised her hand and he made himself remain still. Quiet. All but for the thumping in his chest as she placed her palm to his cheek.

'You're angry with the past. With me. I get it. But I'm not angry. Not with you for staying away. Or with my dad.' She smiled. That small knowing smile. 'Because the past is the reason I'm here, in this beautiful dress, watching the sun rise over red hills and a city made of red stone. Am I still afraid of getting it wrong?'

Her eyes, emeralds embedded in gold, blazed and she caught him inside the flames.

'Of course I am. I've been getting things wrong my whole life. And my dad was in my head too long for him to disappear with an outrageous marriage proposal. But I'm here.'

Her hand moved down his cheek to his shoulder. A slide of her palm and every nerve-ending came alive under her touch.

He resisted. Stood still. Resolute.

She placed her palm over his heart. 'And so are you.'

'And so am I…' His reply was raw. Rough. He wasn't supposed to be here. He should be in his own rooms. He should be anywhere but here, letting her touch him. *Soothe him.*

'You told me feelings shouldn't matter here, but can you feel it?'

He could feel everything.

'Feel what?' he asked, denying that her touch did anything but pull at his groin.

'The past paving the way to the future.'

'Maybe for you. But for me…'

'You are to be the next King.'

He didn't answer. His every action since he'd stepped into this room had not been *kingly*.

She tilted her head. 'What makes you so afraid of your feelings? Of mine?'

'I am not afraid.'

'I am—but not of my feelings. Whatever has brought you here this morning, and whatever has kept you away since we got here, it isn't because you don't feel. It's because you *do*. I see you confronting the past—our shared past—' she watched him with compressed lips '—and it hurts.'

'I am not in pain,' he dismissed angrily. 'I do not feel pain.'

'Of course you do,' she contradicted him, her eyes zeroing in on his face, moving across every taut vein, the thrust of his hard jaw. 'If you weren't in pain, you wouldn't look at me like I'm an alien because I'm calm about a betrayal that affected us both.'

His eyes stayed on her plush little mouth, that was saying, oh, so sweetly, all the words he didn't want to hear. *Shared betrayal. Shared rejection. A shared past!* He did not want to hear them, let alone speak of them.

He could silence those lips—pin her tongue against his and stop it wagging.

She stepped back. *One step. Two steps. Three.* It would take him less than a millisecond to correct her error. It was a mistake to make him chase her. Hunt her.

She tilted her chin at him, elongating her throat. She was luring him away from duty, trapping him inside himself, and he wanted the heat of her on him. Not these feelings causing his chest to tighten and his temples to throb. He wanted *her* to throb. He wanted—

'Tell me why you're here,' she said.

Wisps of hair had escaped her ponytail and were curling haphazardly under her ears. He wanted to release the trapped mass, let it fall about her shoulders. Feel its thickness in his hands.

He stilled. 'I never should have come.'

'Akeem—'

'Shush.' He silenced her attempt to speak, but really he was turning up the volume on the song of duty that he could never mute. It was always playing, and whatever the volume he could hear it—because it came from within... because it lived inside him.

He would not allow this energy between them to leave these rooms. He had a duty to deny his needs—even the basic needs of a man—and show the people of Taliedaa he would not abandon them for pleasure. He would not abandon them as his father had. As his father had abandoned his mother.

Him.

Charlotte had known the boy. Akeem Ali. The son of Yamina Ali.

He took a breath, filled his lungs, and made himself stand straight. Tall. *Privileged.*

She did not know this man.

She did not know the King.

Charlotte felt it. The shift.

It wasn't a dramatic change. It was a change in the atmosphere. Akeem's head was bare, his hair ruffled, his bearded jaw squared, and his black tunic hung loosely from his broad shoulders. But inside his muscles were taut. Her eyes moved down his throat to the V-neck collar. He reflected nothing but steel, even though his clothing was relaxed.

'You never should have come at all,' she said. 'If you didn't—'

'Didn't what?'

'Didn't want me. I know you wanted the girl you thought I was. A one-night stand. But this woman in front of you now. She is an unwanted queen—'

'Wanting is not the problem. *This*—' he waved his hands between them '—is the problem.'

'Me?'

'This intensity.'

'You came to me,' she reminded him. 'Not the other way around.'

'I came because I understand—*intimately*—the disorientation of having nothing to ground you to a world that has been thrust upon you. I wanted you to have something—'

'Something to ground me?'

'Yes,' he lied. Because he'd come here because he hadn't been able to fight it. The need to be close. *The pull.* But he would fight it now. He would fight it with everything he was.

'And when you came in here the past caught up with you?'

'Not the past, Charlotte,' he said. *'You.'*

'At St John's I came to find you, didn't I?' she said.

She'd sneaked past the resident care workers and sought him out. She'd found him asleep and she hadn't had to say anything. Together they'd crept into the gardens, hand in hand, and hidden under that oak tree.

She'd told him everything. And when she had voiced all the secrets she'd been told to keep quiet—never to tell outsiders—he'd simply held her. He'd let her feel all the feelings she'd kept at bay her entire life.

'It is not the same,' he said.

'You let me grieve for the life I should have had and for the person I should have been.'

And together, over the following weeks, they'd made a plan. They'd chosen a different life.

'I am not grieving,' he said.

'Okay,' she conceded. 'But did you ever think that maybe the past has caught up with me, too? That my dad—his betrayal, my past, *our* past—is something we should talk about? Something I need to talk about?'

'Your father was a fool.'

'My father led us here.'

'I came back to England for you—because of you. Not your father,' he denied. 'But this—the past—cannot impede our engagement announcement tonight.'

'But I *am* your past,' she said. 'How can you separate the two without confronting what that means?'

'It means nothing.'

Exasperated, she asked, 'Why is today so important to you?'

'Imagine eyes, hundreds of them, watching *you*, knowing *your* name and everything about you when you know nothing of them. Then imagine standing before them, waiting for them to accept you.'

'It must have been hard…' she whispered, scared for the boy he'd once been. Alone. Craving acceptance. She knew the bitter taste of rejection from those who should have accepted her unconditionally. Turning their backs on her. Betraying her.

'Under the command of the King they had to respect his wishes and accept me. Did they want me? Absolutely not. To them, I was a bastard. Raised by a whore who had shared in hedonistic delights with my father.' She physically recoiled from his words, and he quickly added, 'The truth is the truth and I will not hide from it.'

'But your mum…?' she gasped, not knowing what she wanted to ask, exactly, but knowing she wanted to defend her. While they'd been in care together Akeem had spoken of her with nothing but pure idolisation. These words now did not reflect the woman he'd loved.

'I was my mother's son, but I am my father's heir.' he explained cryptically.

She called him out. 'Was?' she asked. 'Not am?'

'She is dead.'

'So is my dad—but I'm still his daughter.'

Bearded jaw twitching, he regarded her with intense eyes before answering. 'I was a stranger to the Taliedaaen people, to their way of life and their struggles. Did they respect me? They had no choice. I am of royal blood, and rightful heir to the throne. Did they respect my mother?' he asked, and waited for her reply.

But she didn't have one.

'No,' he answered for her. 'She fled her home in shame. She had no power. No privilege,' he snarled, his lips folding back to reveal perfectly white teeth. 'Here in Taliedaa I am my father's heir, and they will respect you, Charlotte, because I will command it.'

'You will command it the way your father should have done for your mother?'

'This is nothing like that. Their relationship—'

'Your father and mum had a *relationship*?'

'Whatever they had,' he dismissed heavily, 'the people did not want her. They did not want me, but I need them to want *you*.'

'How do we do that?'

'By convincing them we are real. Not fire and passion, but stability and strength. Not pomp and heirs and titles but something else—something *real*. Something my father never offered to his people or his country. He offered them false promises. Nothing but mistress after mistress. As his Queen stayed hidden in her quarters until she died, childless. You will not be *that* kind of queen.'

Eyes wide, she stared. 'You want me to have a baby?'

'No!' he denied, the word vehement.

His eyes flashed and her stomach tugged.

'I need them to want change. Appreciable change. You are that change.'

'I am?'

'If I had sent you home after what my men saw, doubt would have shadowed me as I took my rule. This is the first step to showing them I will *not* rule as my father did. That pleasurable pursuits are not my aim. That the changes I suggest are for the good of the people, the country. Stable. Honest. Good.'

'Like your mum?' She didn't know where the question had come from, but here she was, asking it. Defending his mother. A stranger who'd given up her life in Taliedaa to raise Akeem in England. *That* was strength. Giving up everything she'd known for her family. Her son. A bit like her. Charlotte had given up everything for her family. Her dad.

His eyes flashed. 'My mother was defenceless—powerless in my father's world and in yours. I am neither of those things here.'

No, he was a vision of animated strength. 'But you think you were defenceless before? In England?' she asked, as the question formed in her mind. 'Powerless?'

He flinched—only slightly, but she saw it. The shudder. 'The boy I was when I was with you was weak, Charlotte. Unwanted.' His nostrils flared. 'Untamed.'

She'd wanted him, but the look in his eyes told her to keep that to herself, so she asked, 'Do you have something to prove because of your dad's actions? Or because of who you were before you were a prince?'

'Both,' he confirmed, and her heart broke a little for him. They were so similar and so different.

'A bit like me…' She tried to smile but her lips twisted

uncomfortably. 'I have wasted so much time, and I have so much to prove, too.'

His face contorted. His full bottom lip flattening his jaw. 'I cannot let this—this need you have to compare our lives—get in the way. I need you to be—'

'To be the future Queen. And you'll be *him*?'

He frowned. 'Him?'

'The Crown Prince.'

'Who else?'

'Whoever came into this room.'

'*I* came in here,' he said.

No, he hadn't—but she kept her opinion to herself.

'You doubt it?' he asked, watching her face, her too-expressive eyes.

She couldn't lie. He'd know.

'I doubt nothing—I can feel it.'

'You're mistaken.'

'You're going to marry me,' she pushed. 'Won't you have to come to my room? Won't we share a bed? Or will I share a bed with *him*?'

'You'll share a bed with me, *qalbi*,' he promised, and moved towards her, towering over her with his scent, his heat. He stroked a finger across her cheek. 'The King.'

His scent was the same, but his presence…

'What if I don't want the King?' she asked boldly. 'What if I want the man on the plane…the man who came to my bedroom this morning?'

His wandering finger stopped its delicate tracing of her cheek to move to her chin. 'The King is all you will have, Lottie.' He tilted her face upwards, his eyes obsidian, boring into her. 'Because I *am* the King.'

He turned on his heel and didn't look back once as he closed the door behind him.

Lottie didn't want the King.

She wanted him.

Hadn't she always?

Collecting her shawl and sketchpad, she felt emotion hum through her. Because if all he could give her was a king, she'd be a queen-in-waiting he'd never expected.

And she knew just the woman to help her.

CHAPTER SEVEN

AKEEM'S SKIN TINGLED. The fine hairs on his arms rose to acknowledge her presence before he'd even seen her.

He turned, and saw that at the top of the stone steps someone had been delivered to him. But it was not *his* Charlotte. Not the girl with ripped tights and ill-fitting clothes.

His breath caught as one of her arms, covered in thin red lace down to her wrist, made contact with the stone balustrade.

She was a vision in cherry-red, with her hair curled around her face, and the candelabra positioned on top of the columns on either side of the staircase appeared to be for her own personal lighting. She glowed almost iridescently. The choker round her neck, its ruby feathering the dip below her throat, and the golden crown on her head, made her the perfect definition of what she presented herself to be.

A queen.

His eyes travelled down the length of her. From the boat neckline, to the bodice pulled in at her waist by a simple satin bow, to the flaring skirts meeting her ankles. A red-covered foot took a step, and then another, as a feather-light touch guided her down the stairs.

She glided towards him. 'Will I do?'

He swallowed thickly. 'Will you *do*?'

It was clear, from the crown in her hair to her carefully painted lips and her elegantly fitted shoes—which brought her almost to his height, lips to lips—that this Charlotte was...*different*. She'd been transformed...*for him.*

His hand moved to her waist. 'You will do,' he said, and no god, and certainly no man, would have believed he'd spent all day trying to forget going to her room...spent all day remembering who he was and who he'd become.

Because here it was—everything he didn't want.

Passion.

Plush lips hovered just in front of his. She didn't kiss him, simply kept her mouth just within reach, letting a hint of her sweetness and warmth seep into him.

He cleared his throat, breaking the invisible magic holding them in each other's aura, and pushed down those feelings of inadequacy that had haunted him his entire life. The reason he'd believed Charlotte's father so easily.

He held out his hand and offered it to her. 'Ready?'

A memory of the last time he'd asked her if she was ready pulled at his insides. He would not entertain it. Not now.

Straightening her spine, she exhaled a silent breath through pursed lips. 'Ready,' she said, and slid her hand into his.

He felt it then. The slight tremble. Was it him, or was it her? He didn't know, so he didn't acknowledge it.

He inclined his head, and the staff who'd been invisible before moved in front of them and swept open the double doors to the formal reception room which led to the royal balcony. They stepped inside, perfectly in sync. But he didn't see the surrounding room, or the staff standing beside the doors to the balcony, waiting for his signal that they were ready.

His heart hammered. There, on that same balcony, his

father had forced his people to accept him, the illegitimate son of the King. Now he was going to demand they accept his Queen.

His Charlotte.

'Akeem, you're hurting me.'

His heart remembered to beat, flushing blood through his veins in a tidal wave. He looked down at the hand beneath his and instantly loosened his hold. 'I'm sorry.'

His head swam with all the words they'd shared since London. All the angry words and unexpected confessions. His throat was tight, his mouth dry.

'Ready?' she whispered, a gentle smile tugging at her full lips.

Was he? Was he ready to put his past in front of his future? To give it a place? A home?

He nodded, feeling a tightness pulling at his cheekbones. He gave the signal. A long blink of his too-wide eyes.

Slowly, the black wooden doors opened onto the city below. His desert kingdom. He entwined his fingers in hers, resisting the urge to bring her hand to his mouth and place a kiss on the back of it. To reassure her that everything was going to be fine. It would be. He'd make sure of it. But he did not want to put doubt into her smile, nor into the confident presence holding his hand. He did not want to acknowledge the hand of doubt pressing down on his sternum.

Stepping forward onto the balcony, he kept her hand in his. Kept her near as he looked at his people, standing toe to toe with nobility and dignitaries, as cameras recorded this moment when the Crown Prince would reveal his bride.

Their future Queen.

His gaze worked over the crowd that filled the palace gardens. More trailed out of the enormous gates and down the mountainside. He did not smile. He pulled Charlotte towards him, into his side, and inclined his head.

The crowd erupted.

Cheers.

Akeem raised his hand and the excitement instantly stilled. He opened his mouth to speak, but it was not his own voice he heard.

It was hers.

'Shukran...' She spoke clearly, as if trained to make her voice move over each face in the crowd. 'Thank you,' she repeated in English. And then, slow and choppy, she continued in his mother tongue.

In his mother tongue.

'In time, I hope to be as crucial as the rubies mined at the northern border, in the valley of Dalah, where the Dead Sea gifts life. As valuable as the emeralds from the south and the gold mined right here in Taliedaa. Because I intend to mirror those jewels.'

She licked at her lower lip.

'I will serve you, the people of Taliedaa, by spending my time amongst you, offering support and comfort to your future King.' She turned to him then, and the green of her eyes was as vibrant as those minerals mined by his people. 'The Crown Prince,' she said. 'The future. The rightful heir to Taliedaa's throne.'

She bowed to him, dipping her chin to her chest.

Applause.

A sense of restlessness itched at his skin and locked his jaw. *Regret.* It ate at him. He'd tricked her by seducing her with the word 'closure', and now here she was...the perfect Queen for an imperfect king.

He raised her up and pulled her to him, leant down and brushed his mouth against hers. A touch of softness. Of warmth. Of her *presence.* There it was—duty's kiss. Mouth to mouth, lip to lip. Perfunctory.

But it didn't feel perfunctory.

It felt powerful.

He wasn't alone.

There was someone on his side. Standing with him—*for* him.

No one had ever been on his side. Yes, he'd stood with his father on this balcony, but they'd been separate entities. Standing only for themselves. In the group pictures at the children's home he had been one of many, but they had been alone. Apart. On different journeys. And in the foster families... He'd never been with them long enough to stand with them—to be a part of what they were. *Family.* But here, with her—in front of his people...

He moved back, his hands still in hers, and stared at her. He'd ripped her from her life, thrust her into his, and she had sold the lie that this marriage was something real because he'd asked her to.

She'd made the people want her.

Want change.

And she'd done it for him.

For so long he'd pushed for change—to bring the best and be the best for his people—and now Charlotte had gone above and beyond to help him succeed.

He couldn't have done it without her. Not so swiftly. The roars of applause had never been so genuine. His country needed a queen.

He needed a Charlotte.

He turned to his people once more and raised their hands.

And so the cheers rang again.

Acceptance.

But her words from this morning clawed at him.

'Did you ever think that maybe the past has caught up with me, too? That my dad, his betrayal, my past—our past—is something we should talk about? Something I need to talk about?'

She was right. He should have considered it. Her need to talk. He owed her for his. To listen. To treat her like a human being and be decent.

He gripped her elbow, and after a deep inclination of his head and chest he turned them away from the crowds still cheering.

He would listen now.

The enormous doors closed behind them on their iron hinges. Akeem gently removed his fingers from her elbow and walked further into the room, leaving her staring at the broad expanse of his back covered by a black outer cloak.

Adrenaline pumped through her. 'What's wrong?' she asked. 'Did I do something wrong?'

He turned. His dark eyes were luminous beneath the white scarf feathering his cheeks. He held a finger to his lips and the gold-tipped sleeve fell back to reveal a thick wrist. Her eyes followed the golden seam to his black inner robes. She bit her lip, waiting for the staff to leave as he dismissed them.

'There *is* a problem,' he confirmed when they were alone.

Tension gripped her. 'Problem?'

He pointed a long, steady finger at her chest. 'You made the crown fit,' he continued, 'and became a queen. You did everything right.'

'Then what is it?'

He dropped his hand. 'If this is going to work…'

His eyes travelled from the crown pinned in her hair,

over her carefully made-up face, to the choker at her throat. She burned wherever his eyes lingered.

'We need to be alone. Completely.'

She raised a brow. 'What for?'

'To talk.'

'Who will talk?' she asked, wrinkling her nose.

'You.'

'What do you want me to talk about?'

'You said you wanted to talk this morning.'

'I did?'

'You said I should have considered that you need to,' he reminded her. 'I have considered.'

'And what did you decide?'

'That if you need to talk, I will listen.'

'Because you want to?'

'Because we need to get to know each other again.'

'What do you mean, *"get to know each other"*?' she asked, wrinkling her nose. 'I'm in a better dress...' She fisted the fabric at her waist and pulled it out. 'But underneath it's me.'

'And who *is* that?' he asked, his face unreadable. 'The girl I knew couldn't have been like *that* out there.'

'Been like what?'

'Perfect.'

She wrung her hands together in front of her. 'Selma helped me,' she explained, her throat clogged. 'She helped me craft what I wanted to say. What I wanted to project to your people.'

His eyes narrowed. 'And what did you want to project?'

'Myself,' she husked. Because that was all she'd ever wanted to project. 'Here, in your country, I can be all the things my dad said I couldn't be. And all the bad things—' she grimaced '—I believed about myself, I can lock in a box and throw away the key, can't I? Push it under the bed and only keep the good things. The parts of myself that make me *me*.'

He didn't move. Didn't contradict her. He stared at her. 'If this is going to work,' he said again, 'I want to understand the person you have become. I want to know the why and the how. Who you were and who you are now.' He extended his hand. 'Let us know each other again, *qalbi*.'

She didn't know who moved forward, but her awareness of his fingers sliding between hers was explosive. *Intensity.* It was always there—even out there on the balcony. His lips had pressed against hers in the most chaste of kisses. But the first kiss after the plane had not been a kiss from a king. It had been a kiss from Akeem.

And she would find him again.

'Where will we go?'

'Every palace has its secrets,' he said, running a hand through his hair. 'I will show you mine.'

But would he show her as the man or the King?

CHAPTER EIGHT

'WHAT IS THIS?' Charlotte smoothed her fingers over a carv-ing that resembled a flower. She turned to him, the gravel crunching beneath her feet. 'Is it a tomb?'

'No.'

'A dungeon?'

'It is neither of those things.'

She squinted at the primitive entrance. It had to be a tunnel. 'A cave?'

Something clicked above her right ear and she turned to him.

'We both need a little magic,' he said, holding out a long wooden stick for her inspection.

'The magic of fire?' Her nose wrinkled. 'Mankind dis-covered fire long before our times.'

He raised it above their heads and ignited a flame. 'There is more,' he promised, and caught her hand.

She gasped as, with a powerful arm around her waist, he pulled her inside with him.

She couldn't see a thing.

'The first and only time my father brought me down here,' he told her as he moved in front of her to lead the way, 'he left me here in the dark.'

'Why would he do that?'

Akeem sneered. 'To see if I could find my way back.'

'Did you?'

'I did,' he said. 'But not before I found something else first.'

'It's so dark… I'm surprised you found anything,' she whispered. 'I can barely see my own hands. There's nothing here but rock.'

'Look with better eyes, *qalbi*.'

'I can see…' She squinted. 'Rock.'

'Look further than the end of your nose.'

'But that's the safest place to look when you can only plan your next step.'

'Is that what life has been like for you?' he asked. 'Only planning the next step?'

'I thought what my life has been like was easy for you to figure out?'

'It was,' he said. 'But I want to know the why—the how.'

'That's not a simple thing to answer…' she said, and suddenly the past became too visceral, the hunger she could never sate pulling at her abdomen. 'I just did it.'

'Did what?'

'Survived, of course.'

He stopped in front of her. His eyes still on the path ahead, he said, 'Then let there be more light, *qalbi*, so you can plan your next step better.'

He placed his torch on the cave wall, and as the flame caught and blazed its heat was transferred to the lamp next to it, and the next, until all around them lights raged like fireflies.

Akeem threw the torch into a corner. Pre-prepared kindling lit up like a furnace in aceramic bowl, and just as the flames had kissed each other to rage into light, so did the ceramic pots buried in the ground. All around them was light, where before there had been none, coming to life around them, from deep within the red earth, one flame after another.

The red stone walls burst into life around them, bringing the cavern and a natural pool to life. The waters, so still and so blue, became almost translucent before them. Unexpected lush green and foliage climbed the walls.

Shadows and flame had turned the darkness into something living. Something oozing life. Left by the generations before them who had passed through here.

It was an oasis underground.

She moved to stand beside him. 'It's beautiful.'

And it was. It was almost alien in its beauty. And its unexpectedness overwhelmed her with its utter abundance of life—so much alive and living where it shouldn't. She felt so small before it. So insignificant.

'This reminds me to be better,' he said, his eyes forward. 'Bigger.'

'I feel it,' she replied. 'Something bigger…something more…' Filling her lungs with a fortifying breath full of heat, burning wood, and the scent of death and life, she said, 'I was always scared I'd never become something bigger. Something *more*.'

'More?' He turned to her. 'More what?'

'I used to think there was only one type of "more". More money to pay the bills so I would never see a red bill again. That would bring me peace. More food so I could have a full fridge and feel full…content. More clothes so I'd feel warm, and—' The word *loved* was on the tip of her tongue. She stopped herself. 'I believed that more…' she searched for the words '… more physical things would bring me to a place of happiness. But after these last few nights in the palace…'

His face twisted into a mangling of harsh lines. 'The palace wasn't enough?'

'The palace was plenty,' she soothed. 'But I haven't slept well there,' she confessed.

'Why not?'

'The sheets are so soft.'

'And…?' he asked.

'The sheets are so soft I can't sleep,' she clarified. 'Not because they're uncomfortable, but because comfort itself is very new to me. I haven't been comfortable. *Ever.* I'm afraid of it.' Her eyes turned large. 'A few days ago I buried my father. I was facing eviction, and the prospect of throwing myself on the mercy of the benefits system.'

'What does this have to dowith anything?' he asked.

'It has *everything* to do with everything. Because after talking with you this morning…' She trailed off. This morning felt like another life, not a few hours ago. She started again. 'After talking with you I realised the "more" I wanted was inside. I needed to believe I was worthy enough to accept the quality of fine cotton sheets.'

'And do you believe it now?'

She held his gaze. 'I've never believed it. That I am worthy of more. Worthy of the things others took for granted. I was always on the outside, waiting to be let in. Nobody wanted to be friends with a girl whose dad roamed the streets with a can of lager and stumbled and fell into people's gardens.' She wanted to close her eyes, but the intensity of his held her fast. 'I'm still afraid. *Inside.* That the world will only ever recognise me as his daughter.'

Akeem remained silent. Still. So very still. 'Why?'

'My dad…' Her eyes grew hot. 'He never loved me. He told me. Told me he could never love something he'd made because it was in my genes—in my DNA—to fail. Like he had at everything. And if he couldn't love me, his own daughter, how could anyone else?'

'Charlotte…'

'I was determined to make him live. Determined not to

fail my father.' She closed her eyes tightly. 'I was determined to make him live and I failed him.'

There—she'd said it. The whole truth. Why she was so adamant that here she would be more. Would be all the things she'd promised herself she would be until her dad had told her she wasn't capable. He had convinced her that she was his daughter and therefore destined to fail. And in the end she had failed. He'd died because the one time he'd needed her, she hadn't been there.

'You failed no one,' Akeem said quietly.

She opened her eyes and met his. He was watching her intensely. 'I did,' she corrected.

'Charlotte—'

'So, yes….' She cut him off. 'I'm still afraid, but I'm no longer scared to try. I'm not scared of being here. I'm not scared of this, or of cotton sheets. I'm not afraid to live any more. I will not live my life in the shadows, in fear of failing—like my dad.'

Closing the space between them with a purposeful stride, he kissed her. Her eyelids first. Then her cheeks.

'Our brief whirlwind affair,' she said, 'was the best time and the worst time of my life. The worst was when social services came and found my dad drunk on the sofa, the house empty of food. They took me into care at the children's home because I had nowhere else to go. Then I met you.'

'And?'

'And you were everything.' A trembling smile tugged at her lips. 'Strong. Resilient. But most of all you didn't care where I'd come from—*who* I'd come from,' she corrected. 'You were kind. You showed me the ropes in an environment I never thought I'd be in. No one had ever helped me before. No one had ever helped me to survive.'

'I remember giving you a sketchpad and pencils.'

'And I spent all my time drawing you.' She smiled. 'When I got to go home, and we made all those plans to leave when you turned eighteen, I believed that there was more—that I could be more. That I was worthy of a different life. A better life. That I was enough. But after you disappeared it was easier to believe my dad's version of my life. Because you'd left me behind. Because in the end I hadn't been worth the trouble. I hadn't been enough for the one person who'd made me question how I was living my life.'

'It was not the truth.'

His words scraped at her skin. It would be all too easy to fall back into the heavy ache of worthlessness that had been an unwavering constant throughout her life. But his eyes held fast to hers. Locking her into him. Into the moment.

'I didn't know that,' she said. 'I was sixteen—you were the only person to make me question my life. To convince me there was more out there.'

He laughed—a gentle sound. 'I only showed you where to find the best cereal in the communal kitchen.'

'You showed me there was more,' she corrected him. 'That I could *be* more. If I took a chance the way you were taking a chance. You were leaving the children's home behind and you were determined to learn your trade as a labourer, so one day you could build skyscrapers in the sky.'

'And instead I became this.'

'Is this life better?' she asked. 'Being the son of a king?'

Deep lines appeared in the smooth skin between his eyes. 'Yes.'

'Why?'

He smiled. 'Why is it better?'

'Yes... You said your dad was selfish?' She grimaced when his eyes shot flames, as if trying to incinerate her line of questioning. But she wanted to know. 'I want to know what it was like for you,' she said. 'Were you afraid of coming here?' she asked. 'Afraid that they—the people—would only see a boy in care?'

'I was angry,' he confessed. 'Angry with you, with your father, and most of all with my father.' He shook his head. 'There was too much rage for me to be frightened.'

'What did he say?'

'Who?'

'Your dad,' she replied. 'Did you confront him about your mum?'

'You do not confront a king.'

'But you're a prince—his son.'

'All he saw when he looked at me was his legacy being continued. If I had questions—needs—there were other people for that.'

'But you were so much more than that.'

'Was I?'

'Yes! You were a little boy who'd got left behind. A boy who turned himself into a capable young man.'

'My father needed an heir,' he interjected. 'Not the boy I was or the man I was becoming.'

'What about family?' Her heart broke for him. 'You were his *son*.'

'I was an illegitimate bastard,' he corrected her, and she recoiled from the hatred in his voice. 'I was nothing. I came from nothing. And he did not let me forget it.'

Her mouth flew open. 'You came from him and your mum. You came from love.'

'I came from the swapping of bodily fluids. I was a child who'd grown up in a foreign land, in a system that did not grow men—it broke them.'

'You were not broken,' she whispered. 'How?' she asked, rage heating her cheeks. 'How did he not let you forget?'

'There was a contract...'

'A *contract*?'

'I had to forget the man and become the Prince. Become Crown Prince Akeem Abd al-Uzza and leave Akeem Ali where he belonged. He made me change my name. He made me—'

'Put him away in a box? He made you put who you were in a box? Like you told me to do with my feelings. Hide them. Shove them out of sight. Forget them.'

His nostrils flared. 'Something like that.'

'No,' she corrected. 'Not "something like that". That was it, wasn't it? Like my dad... Oh, my God. He made you feel exactly like my dad did when you came to the house. Like a monster.' She covered her mouth, holding in the scream gurgling in her throat. 'He made you feel like everything you were was ugly. Bad. Destined to fail. Like my dad.'

'He did not make me feel like that,' he denied. 'He made me a king.'

'No, you did that on your own,' she corrected. 'You never would have failed—with or without him.'

'I do not believe you're scared any more,' he said. Deflecting her.

She let him.

'Why not?' she husked.

'You were fearless on the balcony,' he replied. 'And you are fearless now.'

Fearless? A lightness fluttered through her.

She stilled. 'I may not have chosen to be here, Akeem, but I can choose who I am. Who I want to be.'

'And you want to be the woman on the balcony?' he asked.

'I want to be myself.'

'Yourself?' he repeated. 'And who is that?'

'I'm not sure,' she said, a hesitant smile on her lips. 'But I'm excited to find out.'

'On the balcony you were a queen, and in here you are—'

'A woman?'

'Yes…'

'I can be both and still me.'

'It is not possible to be two people in one body.'

'Not two people,' she corrected. 'Only one. I'm not hiding one part of myself in favour of another.' She stilled. 'Is that what you do? Split yourself? Show your people the King you were out there and conceal this man, hiding in the dark with me?'

He didn't answer. Instead, he stared at her with an intensity she'd never seen before. He lowered his head and crushed his mouth against hers. Kissed her so hard he drowned out the voices in her head. The doubting voices. The voice of her dad. Just the way he had almost a decade ago. He'd listened to her, to every word she'd had to say. He'd seen her. And now he knew what she needed, just as he'd known when he'd taken her to his hiding place at St John's. Behind the tree.

Except this time she didn't need to be soothed. She needed to be touched. Touched by him. Set on fire as she burned the parts of her past she no longer needed in his arms and kept only the parts she wanted.

His mouth pushed hard against hers, his tongue pushing through the barriers of her lips to stroke at the insides of her mouth. It would be easy to let herself fall into the pleasure he was offering her, to resist the knowledge of what he was doing. But she couldn't.

She didn't want him to hide from the past. From hers or his. Because it had made them and this moment possible. It deserved acknowledgement.

She twisted free, her hands on his chest. She pushed away. 'Are you trying to hide, Akeem?'

'I am standing firmly between your legs, *qalbi*,' he said, and backed her up against the wall.

He was lying. She could feel it. The distance.

His mouth moved down, kiss by kiss, until he met her hardening nipple. He closed his mouth around the bud, sucking her and the fabric into his mouth.

Charlotte closed her eyes and let him run. He hadn't run away from the intensity like he had this morning. He was falling into it. Into her. But still she felt that distance. His refusal to acknowledge the boy she'd known.

As as he ran, so did she. She ran from the past, from the present, to be right there in his arms. *In the moment.* Alive and living. She let herself enjoy the pressure of his mouth on her.

The cave wall was hard against her back, but she didn't care.

This was life.

She had chosen life.

Her fingers slipped into the hair at the base of his head and she moaned. Low and deep.

'Oh…' Her hands reached for his shoulders, holding on as need ravaged through her. 'Oh, my…'

He stroked his fingers firmly down the valley between her breasts, to the bodice of her dress where the skirts flared out. Her insides throbbed as he put his hand beneath her skirt and trailed his fingers up the length of her leg, to graze gently against the fleshy inside of her thigh.

He put his fingers to her core, moving over her centre in a tantalising swipe. 'Do you want me to touch you here, Charlotte?'

'Yes,' she said. 'God, yes, I do.'

He didn't hesitate. He swiped her panties aside, pressing his fingers down along the wet folds of her to part her sex and open her up to him. He thrust a finger inside her.

Her core clenched around it. *'Akeem!'*

'I know my name,' he told her, and eased another finger inside her. Everything tensed—pulled tight like a stretched elastic band.

She looked up into his face, everything in her body urging her to bear down on his hand. 'Do you?' she husked. Did he even know that the man between her legs was not the Crown Prince?

He didn't answer. Deft fingers undid the choker at her throat and it fell to their feet. Charlotte didn't hear the tear of fabric, only felt the heat of his mouth on her. He moved down her throat, sucking and nipping as he came to her breast. His free hand tugged down the red lace covering her breasts and bared them to him. The hard nubs were waiting for him to claim them. He sucked, bringing a nipple deep into his mouth, and feathered his tongue over the tight bud.

Her hands dived from his shoulders to his hair, pushing and digging their nails into his scalp. He worked her body, her flesh. An explosive need made her push down on to his hand, seeking more, seeking friction.

'Please…' she begged.

Please, please, please, she wanted to say, because it was his word now. It belonged to him. It was only his face she saw. He was the only one she would ever beg for release.

And he didn't deny her.

He pushed another finger inside her, imitating what she wanted him to do with the bigger and harder length of him pushing against her stomach.

'Oh, my!'

He answered by pressing more deeply inside her, his fingers sliding smoothly in and out and his thumb moving against her in a hypnotic circling motion. She moaned into his mouth, giving herself up to the pleasure, to the feel of him against her and his fingers between her thighs.

'I…' She closed her eyes. She was too many sensations. Too much everything. She reached for him. 'I want to touch you.'

She moved her hands over his shoulders, over the taut muscles of his back. His chest. Lower.

He caught her wrist. 'No.'

The pad of his thumb moved over her clitoris and he leaned into her, keeping her trapped between the wall and the hardness of him.

'I want to touch you,' she pleaded. She ached to touch him. To bring him the pleasure he was bringing her.

The tempo of his fingers increased. 'I've dreamt of this moment for too long to find release at your touch like an inexperienced teen,' he answered, his voice dry and hoarse. His words weren't a compliment, but a statement—a breathless sentiment acknowledging his need.

Her body grew tight with the thrum of his fingers. She couldn't help it. She said, 'Then don't. I want you inside me.'

The noise that left his mouth was half roar, half battle cry. He pulled his fingers out of her with a quickness that caught at her breath. He grabbed her by the hips and picked her up, pushing her against the wall until the hardest part of him, still concealed by his trousers, pushed at her centre.

'When I take you,' he told her. 'When I push myself inside you because you beg for me—and you *will* beg,' he promised. 'It will not be against a stone wall. It will be in a bed. My bed.'

His tongue plundered her mouth and he rocked against her. Harder. Faster.

She screamed. 'Akeem!' His name was a plea. A gasp, a moan—a guttural cry of need. It was animalistic to her own ears. A primal call for her mate. Her secret confessions hadn't made her feel uncomfortable, she recognised.

They had set a primitive part of herself free... And Akeem needed to confront his past too, not hide it, or he'd never be able to let it go as he'd instructed her to do.

He was hiding his true self in plain sight. He was hiding behind the version of him that was the future King. But this Akeem, bringing her pleasure and ignoring his own... This Akeem listening to her tales of woe because he wanted to, because he wanted to know her... *This* was the Akeem she wanted to know.

The man of fire and passion between her legs.

Her Akeem.

The Akeem she'd known...the Akeem she knew still.

He pushed harder, grinding against her throbbing core and taking her to an edge she'd never leant over. A pulsing, electrifying edge.

'Come for me, Charlotte.'

Her body tightened, her nails clawing into Akeem's shoulders as convulsion after trembling convulsion burst through her and tore her apart.

She sagged against him and splintered into a million pieces. He stilled, and she couldn't stop trembling.

He was so warm against her. Hard. But there was a softness in the hands holding her to him. Shielding her... protecting her as she came back down from the heights of ecstasy. And it was all too easy to let him hold her up.

Maybe, when they found this bed of his, she could set Akeem free, too.

What was she doing to him? He'd dry-humped his future Queen against a wall. The thought of pushing inside her—filling her with himself—had almost undone him.

She smiled up at him and it crushed him. He couldn't smile back.

He'd lost control, and she'd given him permission to do

it. To give in to the carnal urges driving him. He was everything his father had told him he was.

Primitive.

He'd destroyed her dress. Ripped the seams to expose her red lace-covered breasts.

He lowered her gently to her feet and shrugged the outer cloak from his body and wrapped it around her shoulders. He moulded his hands over her. Over the reality of her shoulders.

He needed her to understand.

He caught her chin. 'Who are you?' he asked.

He had to make her understand what he'd failed to make her believe nine years ago, because he'd been weak and believed her father. Someone needed to believe in her, and first it had to be herself, but he would guide her on her way as no one had guided him.

He owed her this small gift. A gift she'd given to the boy he could never be again.

'Charlotte,' she said. She moistened her lips with the tip of her tongue. 'Who else could I be?'

'Tell me who you are.'

'Charlotte...' It was a murmur this time, confusion narrowing her eyes.

'Charlotte who?' he demanded.

'Charlotte Hegarty.'

'Say it again.'

'I am—' She inhaled deeply.

The smell of burning wood and the heat of their mingled arousal infiltrated his senses as he watched a veil lift from her eyes.

'I'm Charlotte Hegarty.'

'And Charlotte Hegarty is enough.' He pulled her to him and lifted her against him, pressed her firmly to his heaving chest. 'Charlotte Hegarty is worthy of more than high-quality cotton sheets.'

A hiccup of a sound left her lips. Not a laugh…not a moan or a gasp. 'And are *you* worthy of top-of-the-range sheets?'

'I have never denied myself comfort.'

'You've denied me at every opportunity,' she husked, and his heart raged, along with the harder, pulsing length of him.

No, he'd denied himself.

'Did I not give you release? Pleasure?'

'What about *your* pleasure?'

'If I'd torn the panties from your body and thrust myself inside you…possessed you… I would have been everything my father told me I was. A basic boy, with basic needs and basic desires.'

'There was nothing basic about what we just did, Akeem,' she said gently. Too gently.

But she was wrong.

He would have been nothing but flesh and hard muscle finding release. That was *basic* at its core definition. The impulse of the man who had driven to London to exact his revenge would have taken over. An impulse he could not give life to in this world.

He would have been a pleasure-seeker at the cost of others. At the cost of Charlotte. He had no protection with him, and if his seed had taken root inside her—made a life because he hadn't been able to control himself…

'Can you tell me your name?' she asked, and his face contorted.

He was nothing but a name now. Nothing but his blood. Nothing but his kingdom. He had one name, and she knew it.

'I am Akeem Abd al-Uzza, Crown Prince of Taliedaa. The only heir by blood to the Taliedaaen throne,' he answered. Because that was the only person he could be. Even down here, with the world nowhere to be seen, no one to see them. Because it didn't matter if they couldn't see them. *He* would know.

'Is he worthy?' she asked, and he sucked in a sharp inhalation of air. He'd been trying to prove his worth as the chosen Crown Prince for nine years.

'We claim our own worth, *qalbi*,' he answered truthfully. Because that was what he was trying to do now—claim it by proving it. By not being his father or the boy he'd once been.

'I'm so glad you've claimed yours, Akeem,' she said. 'I'm so glad the boy I knew found his place, despite his father and mine. Despite St John's… I'm so glad that, despite it all, he found his *home.*'

She breathed the word 'home', and the word felt distant. Alien. He lived within the palace walls. He ruled a kingdom. The desert was in his genes. But was it *home*?

Home was belonging. Acceptance.

He had neither.

He steeled himself against her words about belonging. *That* boy had never found his place—his home…

'The world told him there was no home for a boy like him,' she continued. 'His father told him that everything he was, he didn't care for. And you proved them all wrong. You did it, Akeem, and your mother would be proud of you. Of that boy.'

Her words were a knife in his heart. All he'd done was for her. His mother. To make her sacrifices worth it.

He choked back words and tugged Charlotte into him. Lifting her effortlessly against him, he moved towards the exit.

Her hands around his neck, she leant into the crook of his neck and said sleepily. 'I can walk.'

'Shush,' he soothed, because he needed her against him, needed her presence…because he was raw, electrified and stripped to the bone. He had not felt this disjointed since his arrival in Taliedaa.

It had been a mistake to bring her here. He hurried back the way he'd come, carrying Charlotte tightly against him. He'd brought no one here. He'd exposed himself. Revealed the secrets to his survival. And now every time he came here to remind himself to be better…stronger…he would see her face…

He did not want to feel. *Not this.* This pure, undiluted desire and a need, as she had said, for more…

There was going to come a time when he wouldn't be able to distract her with sex. She'd want him to share himself, and she'd keep asking questions because it was her nature…

What would she do when he couldn't answer? When she found out that the boy she kept pushing him to show her was dead?

CHAPTER NINE

ROUGHLY, CHARLOTTE SMUDGED the pad of her thumb against the sketch, to blend the thicker lines of charcoal into lighter tones. She was attempting to draw his hands. The hands that had held her against that wall. The hands that he had used to turn her on and melt her bones so mercilessly. The hands that belonged to Akeem. The man who wouldn't show himself to her. The man she wanted desperately to remember that he was more than a dutiful king.

The servants had brought an easel last night, and a trolley to keep her art supplies on, and it had been...*wonderful*. Making lines and smudges, expressing herself—

'Lottie.'

Hurriedly, she flipped her drawing over and turned to face the doorway. Akeem stood there, wearing white loose-fitting trousers and a long tunic.

'Still not ready?' he asked, and a guilty flush heated her cheeks.

'No, it's not ready.'

'You weren't so shy before.'

'It's been a long time.' She brushed off her hands. Trying to free her fingertips of soot. 'I'm feeling my way back in.'

'I have something that will help.'

'What is it?'

He stepped closer to her. 'Come with me and I'll show you.'

'Where?' she asked, her body all too aware of his approach. His closeness.

'It's a surprise.'

She arched a brow. 'More caves?'

He laughed and pointed. 'You have charcoal on your nose.'

She didn't laugh back. She placed her charcoal on to her new art trolley and stood. This was her chance.

'I'll come with you,' she said, reaching for the watch at her wrist and unbuckling it with trembling fingers, 'if you tell me about this?'

She held it out to him. He stopped moving and she felt it. The distance he immediately put between them.

'What is there to tell?' He frowned. 'My mother tied that watch around my wrist on my first day at school and reclaimed it when she collected me. She gave it to me and retrieved it every day until she couldn't. That is it. That's the story.'

'No.' Her bare feet soundless, she moved closer. 'They're the facts.'

'There is no story. You asked me to tell you and I have.' He reached for her. 'Now we leave.'

She evaded him. 'What about the boy she left with it around his wrist every day? What about the boy who kept it? I want to know the *why…*' she repeated his words back at him '…the *how.*'

His expression controlled and unreadable, he replied, 'It is what it is.'

'Instinct?' she said, recalling her words to him last night. 'He survived, didn't he?' Her heart squeezed for the little boy he had been. Alone in his grief. Her eyes filled with unexpected tears.

'I guess he did,' he replied, his eyes sharp, watching her face, her expression.

'It must have been hard, surviving on your own for so long. With only this…' She looked down at the watch and swallowed down the lump in her throat.

His expression turned from passive to enraged. 'We both know you were as alone as I was.' His bearded cheek pulsed. 'We both survived.' His black eyes flashed. 'On our own.'

The past came hurtling back to her. 'Are you still surviving?' she asked.

'What do you mean?'

'Since I arrived you've used mechanisms…places where you hide.'

'I am right in front of you.'

'Yes, you are,' she said, 'but you pull away every time I get close. Last night you pulled away…' she shifted uneasily '…in your head.'

She made herself stand still. She wanted him to know, so she told him.

'You ran away.'

'I ran straight to you.'

She shook her head. 'You distracted me and I let you, because I understand running…'

She stalled, thinking about the right words—the right way to tell him that she got it. That she understood it— *him*—better now.

She swallowed. 'I understand how hard it is to let anyone close, because it's scary. Scary to think someone might *see* you. I let you see me last night, because I think we could be a family, Akeem.'

Eyes narrowed, he scoffed, 'A *family*?'

'If not a family…at least we could be friends.'

'Friends do not feel what we feel. They do not feel this intensity—'

'We're going to get married. We can choose what we are, can't we?'

His face gave nothing away, but his hands moved, his thumbs and forefingers grinding against one another at his hips.

'I was alone growing up with Dad,' she admitted. 'Glossing over that—what growing up with him was truly like—is a habit that isn't easily broken. But I want to stop glossing over it. Because telling you set a part of me free.'

She stopped talking for a moment, because she wasn't sure she was making sense.

'It will take time to get my dad's voice out of my head… telling me to keep quiet,' she continued. 'But I don't have to be quiet any more.' She inhaled deeply. 'And neither do you.'

'Our marriage benefits the crown. The people.'

'It will still be a marriage,' she insisted. 'Two people who should be honest with each other. When one wants to run—the other runs with them. Catches them up and tells them they're worthy. When I ran in the cave, you caught me and told me I was enough…'

And, oh, how those words had moved her. It was the first time she'd ever heard them. But she shook it off. Right now, it wasn't about her. It was about him. The man who kept coming back to her. In London, to her bedroom … He had something to say, and she wanted to hear it.

'We made a deal,' she said. 'And now we need to make the deal work. So next time you want to run, Akeem, I'm going to run with you—because whether or not you like it, you might have bargained on getting yourself a temporary queen, but you got me too. A temporary family. So run all you like, but I'll catch you. Because that's what friends do. What *family* does.'

'Why is it so important to catch me, *qalbi*?' he asked, taking back the control he needed, when his urge was to run.

She'd tied her long hair back, and he wanted to release it. Set her curls free until they feathered her waist and the dip in her spine. He longed to explore with more than his hands…

'You have told me how—why—you have become *this* Charlotte,' he continued, 'but you did not tell me why you're helping me?'

'You didn't give me a choice, remember?'

She smiled. That small, knowing smile. He wasn't running. He was walking slowly towards her. Slackening the tension on that rope.

'There are always choices,' he said—because there were. He could have decided to be a no one. Instead, he'd become this. And he'd made the right choice.

Had she?

He raised his brow, his heart giving a painful double beat. 'A diploma?'

'I can do that on my own,' she dismissed, too easily. 'Why are you changing the subject? Stop deflecting.'

'I'm not deflecting.' *He was.* 'Tell me why?'

Another step. And there it was again. The stray bullet. Her presence. Her scent. He couldn't help it. He reached out, grasped her by the back of her neck, felt his knuckles cushioned by her curls, and reached up to remove the tie in her hair. It tumbled, heavy and long, around her face. He pulled her towards him.

'Why are you helping me?' he asked, and his eyes flicked to the pulse pumping hard at her throat. His lips thinned, and he answered for her. *'Kindness?'* It was a sneer, because it disgusted him.

The King did not need kindness. The King did not need the emotions tied to family or friends. Because emotions had no place in royal life. His father had administered that lesson, but *he* had put the teachings into practice.

He had decided long ago that to be a true ruler he would set aside the part of himself that needed answers to the question *why*, because his destiny was to repair a broken legacy—not to weep over his mother or the love his father had denied him.

He didn't need to know why they'd abandoned him any more because he wasn't that boy. He was a king. *The* King.

But here she was, offering help anyway.

'No, not kindness,' she rejected. 'I knew a boy once who became a prince,' she said. 'I didn't see him for a really long time. I owe that boy a great debt, because he showed me once that there was another way to live. He gave me sanctuary, and when I lost him I forgot there could be another way.'

'And now?'

'The debt stands. I understand that now. I understand it wasn't his fault,' she continued. 'I stood still because of *me*. It was *my* fault. And now I hope I can move forward.'

'With the boy?' His voice was deep, the words low, conflicted.

'With the boy and the Prince,' she answered. 'One and the same, he told me. But the Prince also told me he could never really be the boy again, because he'd had to become someone else. Some*thing* else. But I think he can be that boy again. I think he can be both. And I would like to meet them in the same skin, breathing the same air and in the same room.'

'I'm not the person you seek. This is not a fairy tale. There are no transformations at midnight—no toads to be kissed, no princes to rescue.'

'You can be the boy with *me*,' she said, ignoring him.

He could never be that boy again.

'The boy is weak.'

'And the King is strong?'

'The King has power, respect. The boy knew neither.'

'You're going to kiss me now, aren't you?'

'Yes.'

And he did.

He ran straight into the warmth of her body. Her kindness. And he closed off the voice in his ears telling him he wasn't worthy of friends—family. That he was weak for wanting them. Because he was starting to wonder if it was wrong.

He was distracting her again. Asking her lips to accept the thrust of his tongue and moving his hands under her tunic to grasp her hips and pull her core into the hard heat of his.

But Charlotte put her hands on his chest and pushed. 'No.'

'No?'

'No more running,' she said. 'You let me whisper all my secrets in your ear in the cave. It's time to whisper in *my* ear, Akeem.'

His nostrils flared, but he nodded, knowing that next time she wouldn't accept his attempts to divert her.

'I do not whisper, *qalbi*,' he said, and stalked back to the entrance of her room and opened the door wide. 'I roar.'

Charlotte remained silent. Breathless as she followed him up a staircase and down a long corridor.

Akeem came to a halt. 'Here it is.'

She frowned. 'A door?'

'A room.'

Her heart cinched. 'Your room?'

He shook his head.

She inhaled deeply, feeling regret or relief washing over her. She didn't know which. 'But I already have a room. Several.'

He reached for the handle. 'And now you have this.'

He pushed the door open and stepped aside.

Charlotte didn't move to touch him. She didn't dare. Because touching him would spiral her into a thousand splinters of emotions that would stream from her eyes in an unstoppable stream of— She inhaled deeply, trying to quiet her mind, to think. Of *delight*?

She whirled to face him. 'Why would you do this?'

'We will make this marriage work despite the circumstances that have brought us here, *qalbi*.' His eyes darkened. 'Your lessons begin tomorrow.'

Breathless excitement quickened her breathing. 'Lessons?'

'Your diploma,' he answered.

'But how…? Who…?'

'An artist in her own right, with substantial success in the European art world, and a retired teacher, is currently settling into her rooms. This—'

He waved his hands and her eyes moved across walls lined with different casings. A wide cupboard with thin slots holding different paper. Another with paints in bottles and tubes. Another with pencils, charcoal, and an array of other mediums.

'This will be your classroom.'

Her very own studio.

Hers.

'Why?'

'Proof,' he said. 'Your dreams will not be forgotten here.'

'What about your dreams?'

His eyes trained on her; Akeem stepped inside the room and closed it behind him with a flick of his wrist 'I dream to be the King my father wasn't.'

'Why? Why is it so important to be him? His heir, but not your mother's son? Why are you not both?'

* * *

He swallowed, pushing down the angst that had travelled with him throughout his life.

'The boy you speak of knew only one type of life. The care system embedded uncertainty into the little boy with scraped knees, too troubled to keep. Into the teenager too angry to place in a family home. He grew into a loner in the children's home. He was too quiet—too withdrawn—to engage in meaningful conversation. Too angry to soothe. The boy was unwanted. The teenager hated. The man...' He shrugged. 'He became a king.'

'I wanted the boy.'

'You wanted escape, *qalbi*. Not me. You wanted a new life away from your father. We are both grown enough now to recognise the truth.'

'You can't presume to know that.'

'I presume nothing. It is a truth I recognise. A truth that, if you wanted to, you would also recognise.'

'Tell me more about the boy who became a king,' she asked, moving on.

Or moving back.

He'd said enough in the cave. He did not want to go back.

'Tell me,' she urged, her voice soft. Tempting.

And there it was. The flare of kindness in her eyes, softening the green to a moss-like effect. Kindness. The reason he'd become besotted with her in their shared time in care.

His hands sought her out before he could tell them not to. They went to her hips, feeling the hard bones there as he tugged her into the length of him.

'All my life I wanted this "more" you talk of. And now I have it. I have it here—*power*,' he breathed between clenched teeth. 'The past is irrelevant.'

'You want power?' she asked, and leaned into the pressure of his palms. 'Control?'

'I have it already,' he said, and loosened his grip. Because that was not the power he wanted. He did not want power over her.

She already has it over you.

He dismissed the voice and hammered his kingliness home. 'Power I imagined impossible is now mine. I have respect. Control.' He moved back, away from her. 'My mother's name was as unwanted as mine before I was King. They called her a whore. And me a bastard. Only when I'd worked hard to be the perfect image of a crown prince did they call her by her name, and me by mine.'

'Your new name?'

He didn't answer.

'Whatever title you have, you'll always be him. You know that, don't you? Not the illegitimate legacy of your dad, or the result of whatever relationship your mum had with your father—'

'Don't.'

'I just don't understand how you think hiding away from who you once were makes you a better king.'

'Charlotte…'

'No!' She dismissed his warning. 'Your past isn't the enemy. Your dad lied to you. Like mine lied to me. Your feelings are valid. They make you strong.'

'Enough.'

'You said your dad was a terrible king. That he did not cater to the troubles of your people and followed his pleasure-seeking lifestyle and destroyed others in the process. You know the troubles of *real* people. Powerless people. First-hand. Why not tell them—*show them*—that because of your past you will be the King they need, if not the King they think they want.'

'They do not know what they want.'

'Then tell them—because they need you. Not this shell

of a king, fighting against anything that might bring him joy—fighting against me.'

She lies. Feelings are not strength. Your past makes you vulnerable.

'My mother's name will always be in the gutter if I do not prove I am neither my father's son nor hers, but something else. Something stronger. *Better.*'

'You are strong,' she corrected him. 'You always were.'

He swallowed and closed his eyes.

'You can roar now, Akeem.'

He opened his eyes, his breathing coming faster and faster. 'Yes, I'll roar.' He jerked her forward with a snap of his wrists. Moved his hand up to caress the sensitive flesh at the base of her throat, swiping his thumbs against the erratic drum of her heart. 'And so will you.'

He pulled her with him, through one of the doors in the studio and then another adjoining door. He kicked it shut behind him. Everything in the room was a shadowed blur. All he could see was the bed. A huge, imposing four-poster of extraordinary wooden proportions.

Silently they walked towards the bed and he wasn't sure who was leading who. Only that they were here.

His bed.

A moan escaped her as he laid her down in the middle of the bed. Her hands moved on him, seeking an edge. She found it—the hem of his tunic—and lifted it up.

'I want to see you,' she said.

'I'm right in front of you.'

'I know…'

Her eyes held his, her hands against the flat of his stomach.

'I want to feel you against me. The man beneath those barriers of an adopted legacy.' She lifted the hem higher, exposing his hard, peaked nipples. She touched one. 'I want to see *you*.'

Groaning, he tugged off his tunic, throwing it to the floor. 'Touch me,' he commanded, and she did.

She touched him, placing her hot palm against his chest and stroking her fingers over him.

'You're perfect,' she said, running her fingers through the fine fuzz of hair to follow the ripples of his washboard chest.

She ventured lower. Tentatively moving her hands to his firm, full backside. Her hands stroked around the tense globes. She hooked her fingers into the band of his trousers and pulled, testing the elasticity.

His hands clasped hers and dragged them back up over his flat abdomen, raised them above her head.

'I've dreamt of this moment,' he confessed, leaving her hands to raise himself above her.

'Akeem!'

Eyes wide, Charlotte squealed as he gripped the seams of her tunic and tore it in two, ripping the fabric apart to expose her black lace-covered breasts.

He tugged the ripped top from her body and bent to expose her golden flesh. He trailed his fingers down her upper arms. 'I've dreamt of being a king between your thighs,' he confessed. 'Extreme pleasure, surrounded by opulence.'

'And now?' she whispered.

Akeem set to work on her exposed throat. He kissed the arched tension from her neck slowly, tasting the sweetness of woman and the earthy, fresh sweat of passion. The slight tingle of salt on his tongue tempted him to suck deeper and bring her skin between his lips in a kiss that would mark her.

His mark.

She's already marked. And so are you.

Forcing himself to go slow, to stem the urgency demanding that he find her slick core and push inside her, he unhooked her bra.

'So beautiful,' he murmured, exposing her breasts and moving his mouth, licking and kissing the length of her collarbone, moving down to a dark nipple. He sealed his mouth over the puckered tip. Her moans grew faster, her nails digging in anywhere they could as he sucked her nipple deeply into his mouth while teasing the other beneath the pad of his thumb.

He flicked his tongue again and she quivered against him, panting hard. 'You are so responsive, *qalbi*.' He kissed and licked his way through the valley of her breasts.

'I want you....'

He raised his head. 'Say it again,' he commanded throatily.

'I want you, Akeem Ali, son of Yamina Ali.' Her eyes, green fire, thrust into him, inside him. 'And I want you too, Crown Prince, future King of Taliedaa.'

He lunged. She would have all of him. Take him deep. Until she didn't care who was inside her. The boy or the King. Only knew it was *him*.

He buried his mouth against her skin and kissed her harder, silencing the voice inside him and moving his mouth down her stomach. He kissed the waistband spanning her hips and tucked his fingers inside, then pulled the trousers off in one swift movement and threw them to the floor.

He returned to her. Positioning himself between her thighs, as the length of him found her core, he pressed against the entrance.

'Say yes,' he demanded, tilting his hips to apply more pressure.

One more nudge and he'd be inside her, and he needed

her to tell him to push, to cement this moment with his body inside hers.

'Tell me this is what you want.'

'I need you, Akeem.' She wrapped her legs around his hips. 'Both of you.' The heels of her feet pressed into the dip of his lower back. 'Inside me.'

He swelled—his chest, his shoulders, his every muscle expanding to accommodate the realisation that she was giving herself to him. *Completely.*

The room whirled around him, disappearing.

He thrust deep inside her.

'Akeem… Oh, Akeem!' Charlotte lifted herself and tilted her hips.

'Charlotte!' he cried as she brought him deeper inside her.

Her hands grabbed at him, pinching his flesh between her fingers as wave after wave of pressure ignited inside him, taking him to the edge.

She gripped his chin, making him look at her, and kissed him. It felt like a promise. A wordless pact. The way it had nine years ago. The night they'd shared then had been a promise.

He sank deeper inside her and he was lost. They both were. The boy and the would-be King were lost to Charlotte Hegarty.

And from the song of duty there was not a peep. Not a sound.

'Akeem!'

Charlotte sobbed into his shoulder, holding on to him as he pumped into her body, keeping his promise to bring her extreme pleasure.

But she couldn't see the opulence surrounding them. She could only feel him.

The man she'd always wanted.

The man she'd never stopped wanting.

It was all-consuming and overwhelming. Because in nothing but their skin they were everything they had once been and everything they had become. They were nothing but a man and woman, seeking sanctuary in one another.

Escape.

He was her oasis and she was his.

That had always been the case.

But it's only sex, the broken voice in her head admonished. *Sex fixes nothing.*

The voice was right. Sex fixed nothing. Not even amazing sex. And this *was* amazing.

But love…love could.

She loved him.

She gasped at the realisation. Her limbs tightened, her legs curled around his hips, and her core clenched around his mass. Clenching and unclenching, she screamed, noisily urging him to love her faster—harder, because she loved the love of his body. And she loved him.

She made sense with him.

She always had.

Under the oak tree. In front of the TV. In rundown pubs. In helicopters across the desert. In nothing but her underwear on a throne. In a red ball gown. Against the cave wall. In his bed…

She loved the boy he had once been and the uncertain Prince he'd become under the veil of perfection—the persona of the perfect King.

Sex fixed nothing.

But love could.

And this was love, wasn't it?

And it wasn't neat or tidy.

'I'm— I'm—' She stuttered, because he'd exposed every

nerve and she was burning with him in this ascent to the unknown as they travelled deeper into the oasis of their bodies, into their sanctuary—into each other.

He kissed her breasts, her neck, her mouth. 'Come for me, *qalbi*. Come now.'

And she did. A sheer blinding light burst behind her tightly closed lids and she let it claim her. The light. The brilliance. The release of love…of knowing she loved him. The shuddering climax was one only he could give her. Sanctuary in his body, and in his touch. The ultimate escape.

He roared, his neck straining backwards as he thrust one last time, filling her with himself. And she roared too. Loud and free.

He collapsed onto his elbows and she held him to her, his heart echoing the rapid pulse of hers.

For a long, breathless moment they stayed locked in each other's embrace, until their raging hearts slowed. Then he eased out of her and pulled her hips into his from behind, held her to him. He pulled the sheet over them.

'Sleep, *qalbi*.'

Safe in his arms—protected by the security of her love—she did.

CHAPTER TEN

THE BOY WAS still alive.

In him.

The illegitimate child of Yamina Ali was still breathing. Charlotte had pressed her lips to the lifeless body of a boy who belonged in the history books. She'd pressed her hand to his heart and pumped. Again and again. Until she'd seen a glimmer of life. And in his bed he'd been born again.

And now the boy was beating his fists against his chest. Demanding he recognise the fact that the woman who would walk through those doors towards him was more than a woman prepared to meet her King.

She was his.

He swallowed and fixed his gaze on nothing in particular. Not on the walls billowing with white drapes, drawn back to showcase the carved and intricate high arched windows, and not on the treacherous thump of his heart as the scent of foliage and flowers from every corner teased his nostrils.

He'd indulged her little game of playing in the past when he'd gifted her the studio. That night he'd let her draw him, with and without his clothes. He'd let her touch him without restraint, as he'd touched her. She'd whispered in his ear again and again about who they'd been, about family. She'd slept deeply. Contentedly. And for the first time in a long time so had Akeem—because he'd been home. The only home he'd ever really known.

Her.

The studio, making love and giving in to passion, confessing how his past had shaped him—*still shaped him*—had all been too much. It had made him weak. Put him in a position he'd vowed never to put himself in again.

So he'd returned her to her own bed. Because there were always choices. And he had made his. He'd left her alone after that afternoon which had turned into night and then to dawn. He'd buried his head in the duties of the King, and caged whatever man it was she'd released that afternoon.

Until today.

His wedding day.

The boy inside him howled like the feral beast he was—calling for her. Her presence. Her touch. Her soothing calm. But the boy could beat against his ribcage as much as he liked, because it was not his time.

It was time for the King to claim his bride.

He turned, ignoring the fact that his body—the howl inside his chest—knew she was behind him before his eyes did.

And there she was.

In her wedding dress.

His bride.

His Charlotte.

Gold feathered the cream veil covering her hair and shadowing her eyes. It ran over her shoulders and met in a high collar at her throat, tied at the neck by a string of gold between the notch of her clavicles. It trailed down her back in a short train. He could not see her face. Only the tip of her button nose and the shine of her full lips.

Her throat was bare, but panels of cream fabric embellished with sequins sewn in lines and swirls of silver hid every other inch of flesh. The embroidery at her midriff was a triangle, directing his gaze downwards. It ran the length of her torso and pulled in at her waist to mould over her hips, where more fabric flared out.

The dress sat against her body like a second skin, and every time she took a step towards him it moved tightly against the sway of her shoulders, flattened across the breadth of her thighs.

His eyes moved over the obvious lines of her thighs, her hip bones. He had gripped those—thrust inside her again and again until he'd forgotten his name. But he remembered it now: Crown Prince Akeem Abd al-Uzza, son of the late King Saleem Abd al-Uzza and soon to be King of Taliedaa.

Her promise pulled at his groin, but there was no escaping the cameras live-streaming their nuptials, or the princes, princesses and other dignitaries who surrounded them, who had travelled from the four corners of the earth to see the Crown Prince of an up-and-coming small desert kingdom take a bride.

After the ceremony there would be introductions, politics, food…

But after that…

One more night, the boy inside him urged. *Our wedding night.*

Yes. This would be his night. The night he'd promised himself in London. He would sleep with her one more time as a king with his queen. Seal their new pact. And then finally he would be rid of him. The boy she'd brought back to the surface—the boy who, after today, he couldn't risk remembering. He would put him back in his box and bury him deep. And then he would become the man he was destined to be.

The King that Taliedaa deserved.

What about her?

He'd give her the space to grow into the woman she was destined to be, too—a queen by day and an artist by night.

But his bed? He could not have her in it. He could not let himself feel the way he did when she was there.

He dragged his eyes away from her—tore himself free from the lust threatening to undo him. The world and its eyes were on him—on *them*. He would do his people and his country proud.

And your mother?

An image of his mother's dark hair falling forward, obscuring her eyes, flashed in his mind. He could remember her scent. Her warmth. *Her love.* But he could not see her face. With every day that had passed since her death, she'd faded a little more.

Guilt. It passed through him in waves. As it always did. He could not remember her now.

He moved his eyes over the crowds assembled in neat rows on either side of the aisle as Charlotte descended. Their eyes were not on their King, because they could not yank their eyes away from the display he'd gifted to them.

Her.

Their future Queen.

She stood before him and his heart jack-knifed as she pushed back her veil to reveal her eyes.

Her voice broke the bubble in the most delicate of whispers. 'I've missed you,' she said.

His mouth flattened as he took her elbow and turned them both to the man who would bind them together.

Eyes forward, he said, 'I've missed you too.'

God, help him. He had. So much.

She was born again as Crown Princess Charlotte Abd al-Uzza. Future Queen of Taliedaa.

She was married.

Excitement feathered over her skin, raising every fine hair under her wedding dress.

Tonight was the night.

He would be hers again, as he had been in the studio. In his bed. The man beneath the crown. Her Akeem. The Akeem he kept hidden from everybody but her. The man no one had noticed reaching for her when no one was looking.

He squeezed her hand as they chatted with some bigwig. He'd been by her side with every step, every introduction—every forkful of the delightful meal served at a table as long as her row of houses back home, covered in the crispest white tablecloth, the shiniest of tableware, seating an A-list of guests. He'd shown her with small gestures that, whatever disguise he was wearing, beneath he was the man in the studio. The man in his bed.

The man she loved.

A bell chimed and unseen hands flung the doors along the furthest wall open, bowing their heads.

The grand finale. Fireworks.

The crowds inside, who had already moved from the banqueting hall into another room of equal lavishness, now moved outside.

Akeem's hand, with a firm hold on her elbow, guided her across the highly polished floor and out through the exit, down into the courtyard to the views of Taliedaa and the rolling hills of the desert under a night sky.

But he didn't stop. He walked past the crowds and past the views of his kingdom, through an arch in a high red stone wall, and unlocked a gate. He pulled her through, into another courtyard, and locked the gate behind them.

High walls surrounded them on either side. But at the heart of the courtyard was a low pool, scattered with underwater lights resembling candles. At its sides, pink-tinged columns of differing heights lined the cream-and-red-tiles. Everything glowed in warm tones of red and pink.

She craned her neck and saw that above them was a clear night sky. A single light flew into the sky with a whistle, and exploded above them in sprays of gold.

'Charlotte…' He moved in front of her.

The air shifted and she shivered. 'Akeem?' She took a step forward. 'You're here—it's *you*.'

'Here and in the flesh, Charlotte,' he confirmed.

Her eyes locked on to his lips, to those full brown lips making each syllable of her name sound…*right*.

And it *was* right—her name belonged in his mouth. Because she belonged to him. She always had. To this man—the man beneath the crown. The man who had disappeared until their wedding day.

Her husband.

They appeared to be opposites, pulled together by an unseen power to stand face to face in the same disguise… But underneath…? Underneath, they were the same. They were each other's secret haven from the world outside. They always had been.

He dipped his head at the same time as she leant up. Their mouths met. The kiss was not perfunctory. Not the seal of commitment he'd offered to her in front of their guests. It was the kiss of a man kissing a woman. The same kiss that had met her in the studio—in his bed—when he'd surrendered to the past. To the intensity between them. *To her.*

And now he was surrendering again.

Hands grabbed and pulled at cloaks and veils until they lay discarded at their feet. They were primitive. Primal. They were *them* again. Everything they'd been that night in his bed.

She wanted him to roar again.

Now.

She cupped his face and kissed him deeper. Pushing her tongue into his mouth. Tasting him. Savouring him.

A trickling heat of a desire neither of them could deny burst between them.

Hard and unrelenting, his tongue probed, tasting her, skilfully dipping in and out the way his fingers had moved inside her in the cave. Releasing her wrists, Akeem slowed his kisses and moved to her neck. It was a slow assault of her senses as his hands moved over the sharp points of her hipbones and then flipped her around to face the wall.

'I can't wait,' he murmured, his voice tight and husked. He pressed a kiss to the underside of her ear. 'I need—'

'I need you too.' She placed her hands on top of his and guided them up her body to cover her breasts. 'I don't want to wait.'

He squeezed her breasts, pushing his hips into hers. The hard heat of him pressed into her and she moaned deeply as his mouth sucked at the sensitive part of her neck.

'Akeem…'

His hands moved from her breasts, down her ribcage and lower. He smoothed his fingers over her stomach, pressing into the pressure building there.

'Say it for me.' His fingers moved over the seams of her core, through her dress. 'Say please.'

'Please, Akeem,' she said.

Because it was his word, his face she saw when she said it, even with her face pressed against the wall. She pulled her hand away from his and reached behind her, finding the hard ridges of his thigh and then moving over to the hard heat of him. Stroking him. Up and down.

'Please,' she said again.

She stroked him faster, feeling him pulse beneath the black fabric of his trousers.

'Please…' She found his zip and caught the end of it, dragged it down. She eased her hand inside the opening and gently pulled him free.

'Lottie…' he moaned, and it fed her confidence. Fed her hunger to feel him hard inside her.

She smoothed her hand over the wet tip and closed her palm around his thickness. Smooth and hard. She pumped him.

'Please, Akeem, make love to your wife,' she said, and the words *your wife* made her heart race harder in her chest. They were a family now. By law. 'Make love to me,' she urged.

And he gripped the wrist of her hand that was working him, and the other one that lay on top of his hand working her, and dragged them both up her body, above her head, positioning them palm down on the wall on either side of her head.

'Wife…' he drawled against her cheek, and his hips pushed into her from behind, making her stomach press into the wall.

He flipped her hair over her shoulder and planted kisses to her nape as his hands trailed down her wrists to her elbows and back to her body, her waist. He grabbed her hips as his mouth moved with hard kisses down her spine.

On his knees, he reached for the hem of her dress and folded it upwards as he stood again, exposing her bare calves, her knees, her thighs. He rolled it all the way up until the dress sat on her hips, exposing her white lace-covered bottom.

His hands stopped, and she didn't move as she felt his eyes burning over her. This was her offering to him. Her surrender to the intensity between them.

'Wife…' he murmured again, and then he was on her. His hands moved between the apex of her thighs as she turned her mouth up to him and he claimed it. Kissing her hard as his fingers moved aside her panties until he found the pulsing heart of her.

'Mine!' he roared into her mouth. 'Wife!'

With his hand on her pulsing nub, he spread her legs open with his knee, grabbed her hips, and thrust into her.

'Akeem!'

'Husband,' he corrected.

He pumped into her and she couldn't catch her breath. She moaned too loudly, too fiercely. She was his. All his.

'Husband!' she roared, and she tightened her core, clenching around him. He was so deep. So completely a part of her...

They were here—despite everything and because of it. They were married.

But did he want her? His wife? Could he love her? Not only her body, but *her*?

Could the King love his Queen?

Could she love them both, the man and the King? Love him enough to keep them together—their new family—if he didn't? If he couldn't love her back?

Her love hadn't been enough for her dad. Not enough to keep *that* family together. But this was her new family. *Theirs.*

She shut down the voice in her head. Let herself fall into the panting of their breath, the sealing of their mouths and bodies.

She broke free of his lips. 'Love me harder!' she begged. *'Love me!'* she cried. Because that was all she wanted.

His love.

He did not deny her. He loved her. *Hard.* And she met every thrust of his hips, backed herself into every entry of his hardness into her heat.

She shattered, falling against the wall, as wave after wave pulsed over her.

'Charlotte!' he roared. 'Wife…' he said. And with one last thrust he filled her with himself. Hot streams of love. And she came again. Shuddering against him as he leaned into her. She screamed loud as her orgasm, harder than the last, made her legs shake and her knees give way beneath her.

Breathless, he held her against the powerful wall of his chest, holding her up so she didn't fall. Just as he'd held her up in London, when she would have fallen into a wall of grief and despair. Just as he'd held her up on the plane. And now he was holding her up as his wife.

A firework of rainbow colours burst above them. Simultaneously, they craned their necks to watch the grand finale of their wedding day. An explosion of colour littering the night sky.

She couldn't help herself. She spoke.

'I love you.'

What had he done?

He eased out of her, steadying her on her feet, and with quick precision pulled her knickers back into place and rolled her dress down her thighs.

'Love?' he repeated and tugged up his fly.

For four days he'd resisted her. Resisted the need to bury himself inside her after that day in the studio—in his bed.

He was everything his father had accused him of being. A simple man with basic needs—and basic emotions. A man never in control, who lashed out with his tongue and didn't think of the consequences.

Your father showed you the consequences, didn't he?

'Love,' she agreed, turning to face him. Her beautiful

face was flushed. Her lips swollen. 'You asked why I was helping you and I told you a half-truth.'

He wanted to ask about the other half, but he could not speak. His throat was too tight. His jaw was locked and his tongue was a dead weight in his mouth. She made him everything he didn't want to be—a man who followed his needs before his head. A man who consummated his marriage against a wall.

And she loved him? This weakness in him?

She was lying.

'The other half of the truth is love,' she continued. 'Not debts of gratitude or kindness. *Love*,' she emphasised. 'That will never change. I will always love you, Akeem. And I think a part of you will always love me. Because this marriage—'

'Is in the name of duty,' he reminded her.

'Is it?' she questioned gently. 'I think you already had everything in your possession to establish yourself as King.'

You didn't have her.

He clamped his lips together as she continued. 'The crowds cheered for you—not me. This marriage…you asked for it—demanded it—because somewhere inside you, you recognise the girl in me—inside this woman—who sees the boy in you.'

Her words made his skin itch. He wanted to claw at it. And at her version of what had happened. He wanted to rip it off his skin, pull it out of his ears, because it sat too neatly. Wrapped around him like something old and worn-in.

Something he already knew.

But he did not love her. He couldn't.

His black gaze intense beneath arched brows, he said, 'That boy does not deserve love.' And he didn't. He hadn't deserved it back when they were teenagers. And he did not deserve it now.

'Why not?'

She shivered, and his every instinct told him to pull her against him, pull her into his arms and crush her to him. Warm her up. He didn't.

'Everybody deserves love,' she said.

'No, not him. Not Akeem Ali. And not the King. They will never be allies. They are too different. Too—'

'Similar?' she interrupted. 'Because underneath all the noise they both want the same thing.'

'What do they want?'

'What we all want. To belong. To be a family.'

He reached down and collected her veil, held it out to her. 'You will freeze,' he told her, when she hesitated to accept it.

'I'd rather freeze than never hear your truth.'

'There is no truth, *qalbi*. There are only facts.'

'Then tell me the facts.'

'Love is never enough on its own—as my mother found out to her cost. Because love did not put food on the table. Love did not buy shoes for growing feet. Love did not pay for the car's MOT. Her love did not save her. My love couldn't save her.'

'She died in a car crash, Akeem. It was an accident. It had nothing to do with love.'

'I killed my mother,' he said, his voice level. 'The boy you are so determined to breathe life into killed her.'

'You were five—'

'I am the reason she is dead. That's how he made me remember. My father...' he breathed. 'Every time I questioned his choices he reminded me of mine. The basic nature of my conception. He said no family wanted me. Not even my own. Because I was primitive. I ate when I was hungry, cried when I was sad, shouted when I was angry. I had no control over my impulses because I was a boy with basic instincts—'

'Your father called you an *animal*?'

'Exactly. No better than a feral household pet that should have been euthanised at conception. Because my breed was primitive. And he was right.'

'He was wrong, Akeem. So very wrong.'

'Was he?' he asked. 'My mother worked until her knuckles bled—until she was so tired from feeding a boy who ate and ate. She died behind the wheel because she shouldn't have been driving.'

'He hurt you, didn't he? Your dad? I can feel it…' She placed her hand on her chest. 'In here.'

'My father wanted his heir on the throne, but he did not want his son. He did not want angry Akeem. He beat his flesh to drive out everything he was.'

Appalled, she gasped. 'He hurt you *physically*?'

'No, not him. Not the King. But his men…'

Shame threatened to silence him, but he'd already said too much. And he was not ashamed that men twice the size of him with his eighteen-year-old body had hurt him. There had been too many to fend off.

It didn't matter. He was bigger now. Stronger. They wouldn't hurt him again.

He looked at her, at her too-big kind eyes. Pitying him. She couldn't hurt him again, either.

No, you're hurting yourself.

It wouldn't hurt. He wouldn't let it.

'I showed my father exactly who I was when I arrived. *Angry.* I demanded to know why he'd let my mother die… In answer, he had my clothes stripped from my body the minute I raised my voice. Bigger men, stronger men, held me and beat the angry teenager from me in front of him.'

And he'd controlled his anger every day since…controlled his impulses. Until her. Until he'd forgotten himself.

Her hand flew to her mouth, her eyes brimming with unwanted tears. But he would not touch her. He swallowed down his instinct to soothe her.

'I'm grateful my father had me beaten,' he continued, 'because he turned me into this. A prince. He taught me control. To bury my impulses. To smother my feelings and—'

Are you a Daddy's boy now?

He was no one's boy.

Mummy's boy…

They'd called him that with every thump against his body the day he'd dared to question the King—dared to show him the angry teenager he was.

Mummy's boy.

'Your father taught you lies. Because all he taught you was to hate yourself,' she said, her voice heavy. Broken. 'Why didn't you leave?'

'Why didn't *you*?'

'Duty,' she answered. 'Duty to my dad.' She shook her head. 'Akeem…' she sobbed. 'Your dad was a villain too. But you didn't hurt your mum by living. You didn't kill her—that's ridiculous.'

'Yes,' he corrected. 'I did. If she hadn't chosen me—if she hadn't left Taliedaa—she would still be alive. She died so Akeem Ali could live. If I had left I would have been running away from my duty. I would have dishonoured my mother. Her people. They deserved more than my father was giving them.'

'*You* deserved more, Akeem,' she corrected. 'Your father…' She gasped—a sound he would not let deter him. She'd wanted this. But now she was stepping forward, arms outstretched.

'Do not touch me,' he said, because he could not have her hands on him. Her softness against his rough. Her kindness…

Her mouth grappled soundlessly with unspoken words. Then she closed her eyes, inhaled a deep breath.

Softly, she spoke. 'He lied to you. He was selfish. He wanted what he wanted and made no allowances for anything else—any*one* else. He wanted an heir. He didn't deserve one. He didn't deserve *you*, Akeem Ali.'

'It is not that man—not Akeem Ali. I am the King my father taught me to be. With the new name he gave me. A new identity. I will carry my mother's memory on the shoulders of a king—not a beast who ruts in the dark and follows a basic urge to survive. Not this primitive man you make me.'

'There is nothing primitive or basic about you,' she denied with venom, pursing her lips and wrinkling her brow. 'You're more than instinct, Akeem. But instinct got you here. Got you through the life that was handed to you. If you were only built to react, you never would have survived the children's homes, the foster families, the social workers who talked about you in the third person. You should have broken, but you didn't even bend.'

He had broken. Had bent to his father's will. In order to forget everything that mattered.

The past matters, does it?

'My mother should have died at home, in her own country, in the desert where her heart belonged. And I am the reason she didn't.'

'Well, if that's true…' She blew out a heavy breath. 'Then we both killed our parents.'

'Nonsense. Your father killed himself.'

'We could go all the way back to my conception—'

'Stop it.'

'Or to my birth that drove my mother to drink more—'

'Stop.'

'Or we could go back to a few weeks ago, when I took an extra shift, didn't come home… I left him all alone and he died.'

'His death was not your responsibility—'

'And neither was your mother's yours. It wasn't your responsibility to protect your mother from herself. From her choices. You were a child. You are their child. But you are also your own man, and you're afraid to embrace that.'

'I fear nothing,' he lied—because he feared this. *Her love.* Her ability to look beneath his armour and make him question his mode of survival. 'I know the facts. The story does not matter. My story does not matter here.'

'Of course your story matters. It matters to me. So tell me and I will listen—like you listened to mine. Accepted mine. You are the son of a king, but you're also a man. A kind man. Just as you were a kind boy.'

'He was weak—'

'No,' she said firmly. 'That boy was kind.' She pointed at his chest. 'You are kind. You took me to your secret haven. You gifted me my dream. *My art.* Knowing I was all alone, you travelled to London to get me. You forgot your duty and dropped everything for me. You are everything that came before in *your* story. Not theirs—not your parents' story.'

She moved into his space and grabbed his hand. He let her take it.

'*That* is the man I love,' she said, 'and I don't care what his name is any more. Because you are him and I lo—'

'Do not say it again.'

She ignored him. 'I love you.'

She must be all out of bullets because they did not penetrate his skin. Her presence. Her words. He wouldn't allow them in. He would not be that man in the studio, roaring his secrets into her body. He would not be the man thrusting into his wife against the wall.

He could only be one man, and she wouldn't let him be him.

There was only one choice to be made.

He would let her go.

'You might care,' he said. 'And you might choose a completely different name when I tell you why I came to London.'

'For me,' she answered. 'For closure.'

'I came for you,' he agreed, 'but not for closure.'

'Then for what?'

'I came to crush you.'

Instinct told him to draw her nearer, but he pushed her away. She could take her love with her.

'Crush me how?'

Her voice was small, but it needled him. The strength in her eyes was telling him she could take what he gave her. That she knew what he was doing and wouldn't allow it. But he wouldn't give her a choice. This hunger, this desperation between them, was…weakness.

'Revenge.'

He let the word sit with her. Watched it penetrate. Felt the tremble of her fingers in his palm.

'My dad—'

'You pushed for this, Charlotte. Ever since you arrived here you have pushed me to confront the past—what it means to me, how it shaped me. So you will take it. You will understand how the past—our shared past—drove me dizzy with the need to pluck you from your life and thrust everything I am in your face. To tease you—tempt you— and then snatch it all back when what you craved was me. Throw you back into your pitiful life. I wanted to crush you under the weight of my power. The power of the Crown Prince. Of the King. Of *me*.'

'That's not who you are.'

'That is exactly who I am.'

He knew it now, and he knew what he must do to become the King his people needed. No temptations from the past. No whispers in the night about a person he could never be again. Because she was right. He was a man in his own right, and today he would embrace it.

Today he would let them all go.

'Are you sufficiently crushed, *qalbi*?'

'No.'

Her response was barely audible. Everything he had become over the last nine years stared at her. Not at the girl she was. Not at the Queen he had made her. But at the woman in a wedding dress. The woman determined to change him. To make him *feel*…

He felt nothing.

'You won't be free until you confront what hurts you,' she said. 'And I want to be here when you do. But if you can't…if you can't reach out and take what's in front of you…*me*—all of me.' She swallowed, the delicate tendons in her throat tightening. 'Then I'll walk away.'

He would not reach out.

He couldn't.

He couldn't be with her. Not when she questioned the very fabric of who he was—who he'd turned himself into. A king. She regarded his crown with disdain. His riches— his power—she treated them as if they were nothing. As if *he* was nothing—an empty shell surrounded by opulence. Everything he'd wanted to prove to her that he was…*meant nothing to her*.

She wanted the past—a boy long forgotten. She did not want him. She did not want the man he'd become. She wanted to stay in her basic world of having to *make do* even after everything he'd shown her—rubbed in her face.

He would never make do again.

He wouldn't be basic.

'Then walk—I won't stop you,' he said, and his voice was not his own. 'I cannot be this man you seek because I am not him. I will never be him again.'

She didn't say a word. She turned her back on him and opened the gate. With her veil obscuring her face and her dress clenched around her midriff. She walked away.

She was a liar.

She hadn't run with him. She'd run away. Like they all did. Because no one wanted angry Akeem. Hurt Akeem. Broken Akeem.

The rope snapped.

Untethered and alone, he sank to his knees.

Charlotte crashed into her room and leant against the door, drawing deep, long breaths into her tight lungs.

The truth was out. He didn't want their past. He didn't want her. Not the woman she was now. Not the woman he'd given her the choice to become. She couldn't stay here. She couldn't give herself to a man who only shared the physical side of himself.

She couldn't. She couldn't be part of a one-sided relationship ever again. Her relationship with her dad had taken everything from her and given nothing in return. He'd convinced her she had nothing to give to anyone else. Not even herself. She would not do it again. She would not open herself up to be shot down—to be shown she wasn't worthy of respect.

Of love.

Selma hurried towards her, her hands splayed, her eyes wide. 'Charlotte!' She came closer, gathering her against her. 'What has happened? Why are you here? You are trembling.'

She was trembling—but not because she was cold. Because he'd broken her. Her heart.

She'd pushed too hard—too quickly.

'Let's clean you up,' Selma said, and pulled her into step beside her.

She leant on her shoulder and walked to the bathroom with Selma holding her up. She was grateful for the support because she was ready to fall, to pull herself into a ball and weep. But that was the old Charlotte. This Charlotte would walk away with her head high. However much it hurt.

And it wasn't a pitiful existence that she'd return to. For all his cruel words, he had fixed her. Wrapped her in the light of hope. And she would cling to it. She would continue to chase her dreams. Her diploma. She would be all the things she wanted to be—with or without him.

She stopped walking and took Selma's hands in hers, grasped them tightly. 'I need your help,' she said, her stomach flipping upside down and inside out.

'Of course.' Selma squeezed her hands back, just as tightly. 'Anything.'

She'd never had a friend other than Akeem, but now she had Selma, and she could cry for the girl who had never known this.

Friendship.

She'd thank her later.

Charlotte steeled herself to ask for what she needed to do next and then asked it, pulling the words out of her throat and spreading them into the air.

And it hurt.

'I need you to help me leave the palace.'

CHAPTER ELEVEN

SHE WAS QUEEN—of course he knew where she was. Did she think he didn't? The moment she'd left the grounds a guard had spoken in his ear. They'd followed her—for her own safety, of course—told him she was safe with Selma.

He hadn't chased her because he'd been right to push her away. To let her go. He'd been right because the moment she'd seen it—*him*—she'd run. He'd been right to tell her he couldn't love her. Because how could he love her when he didn't love himself?

You're nothing without her.

'Leave me,' he said, in answer to the soft rap at the door. A rap that had come three times a day for six days. Today was the seventh. Today was the day he would officially succeed to the throne without his Queen.

'Highness…' The voice was hesitant, but still his senior aide ventured across the threshold.

'Leave me.'

'You must ready yourself—'

'I *am* ready,' he replied, without looking at or acknowledging the tray of refreshments that was being placed on the low table by the door even as another, untouched one, was removed.

He'd been readying himself for this for nine years. What did he have to prepare that he did not already know by heart? By rote? A few practised words, a bow, a crown, a new title.

King.

But wasn't he already King in every way that mattered? Did he not already rule them? Lead them? Had he not led them when his father had been busy, distracted by his latest obsession?

Hadn't he shown them he was worthy to be their King? Hadn't he, to become the King they needed, shown that the past had no place in this world? Hadn't he shown her there was no place for either of them? Because he, the forgotten orphan heir—soon to be the ruler up on high—couldn't be King with any ties to the past, to the emotional boy now in front of him, staring at him with big brown eyes.

His eyes.

His legs cramped beneath him and he shifted, splaying them out flat. He looked again. Stared at the easels lined up against the windows overlooking the city. *His* city. Pictures by Charlotte—of him. Her drawings of a life he'd tried to forget and a life he was barely living.

So many of them…

Him at the children's home, under the oak tree. Him asleep in a small single bed. Her at her bedroom window in London as he looked up at her from below. Both of them together, locked in an embrace surrounded by fire in the cave—his secret oasis. Both of them on the balcony… And a double portrait. A boy and a would-be king, side by side, staring straight back at him with the same brown eyes.

He'd swapped one life for another, hadn't he? Without claiming either? Neither of those lives—the boy's or the King's—belonged to him. He'd been a puppet of the system until his eighteenth birthday and then he'd been his father's puppet, claiming a heritage he'd never known belonged to him and changing himself to repair a legacy he hadn't broken. His father had. And yet *he* had claimed the responsibility.

But at what cost?

'The ceremony starts in two hours.'

'Please, leave.'

'As you wish.' Resigned, his aide complied.

The door closed silently behind him—Daniyal, his right-hand man, and he couldn't bring himself to care about his unkindness. Kindness had brought them all down. It had brought *her* down. His Charlotte. His Queen. His wife…

No, you brought her down.

He had.

He looked down at the aged paper in his hands. He'd found the picture Charlotte had drawn of him in care. He'd found it in a suitcase battered from his time in the children's home.

The suitcase was scuffed from trailing it behind him to every temporary home he'd spent time in. He hadn't even unpacked it when he'd arrived in Taliedaa.

Because you expected to leave again, like every time before.

Exactly! He hadn't unpacked it in those foster homes, because he had known those big smiles and open arms were fake. Those hands hadn't been reaching for him. They'd been reaching for the cheque they'd be given at the end of his stay. A brief stay before they sent him back with the same suitcase.

His father had been reaching for a legacy. His name. His lineage. His continued bloodline. Not his son. So he hadn't unpacked again.

He clenched his fists too tightly. Then he prised his fingers open and felt his insides twist.

It was the first portrait she'd ever drawn of him, and she'd gifted it to him as a thank-you. *Thank you?* He'd destroyed them both with his weakness. He'd left her behind and now he'd thrown her back into her old world because he was an indecent bastard. His father had been cruel and selfish. Her father had been a mean drunk. But he was something worse. Maybe her father had been right—maybe he was a monster.

What have you done?

He laid the paper out flat on the floor, trying to smooth the creases his destructive hands had crunched into it. But he only blurred the lines. Smudged the face of the boy she'd drawn.

He destroyed everything.

Everything good.

Blew out the light of hope.

Hadn't he been to blame for never finding a home? He'd never given anyone a chance to want him. He'd never given Charlotte a chance to love him.

It was your fault nine years ago too, wasn't it?

The voice was right.

It had been his fault. The blame was solely at his feet.

Because he'd let her go. He'd believed the lies that seemed so brittle when he thought of them now. Her father's words. The trickery. But he hadn't been tricked. He'd allowed himself to believe those lies because he'd been afraid. Afraid of her. Her presence. Her stray bullets. Her kindness.

Her love.

He looked at her pictures again. She was everywhere in the studio. In the portraits lining the walls. On the sofa, where her shawl spread out haphazardly. In the lids left open. The drying paintbrush by the sink.

You're still afraid, aren't you? To show them who you are?

Instantly, he saw everything.

Everything she'd been trying to show him.

She'd drawn his story. The story he'd pushed down into that place where he'd hidden everything that mattered.

He'd forgotten to keep the parts that made him *him*.

He was both.

A boy in the body of a king.

That rope…it hurt. It always had. For nine years. But now… It had snapped. Irreparably. She'd gone because he'd pushed her away…because he'd refused her encouragement to be himself.

He loved her.

He'd sat here for a week. Sat here on the floor, in her studio, in sky-blue jeans ripped at the knees, and a T-shirt so thin and tight it defined every muscle beneath. Clumsy fingers had repaired the socks on his feet. *His* fingers. And the shoes he hadn't been able to bring himself to slide his feet into had lasted him three winters in the coldest temperatures the British weather could offer. They were almost soleless now.

He jumped to his feet.

He could not drag her back to the palace and demand she listen to him. *Forgive him.* He needed to show her. He needed to show them all. But would she come? Would she come to see him named King before his people?

He didn't know, but he needed to do it. Not just for her, but for himself. His father had never listened to his people, never given them the privilege of choice. But he would let them choose now.

He would let them choose *him*.

But first he would change. He was no longer this boy with ripped jeans—he was both a boy with a challenging past and the son of a king. And they both deserved finery. Top-of-the-range quality fabric…

They were both worthy of *more*.

It never lessened. The lurch in his gut as he looked down over the city below… But it was one face he looked for amongst the crowds gathering outside. *Hers.* And she was everywhere and nowhere.

Striding towards the door, he pulled it open, ignoring the bowing men and the curtsying women. He moved through the winding halls laden with pictures of ancestors he would never meet and stepped out into the day.

In the flower-adorned courtyard with its sound of cascading fountains Akeem didn't stop. His face stony, he entered the royal gardens.

He shrugged off the staff, directing him back inside to the royal balcony. He wouldn't be there. He would not stand up there and look down at them.

He would stand amongst them. *His people.*

He would tell them a story. *His story.*

He would give them the choice his father never had.

'I came to you nine years ago with nothing...'

They'd taught him how to project his voice, to make it boom in the loudest arena. It boomed now. The people surrounding him moved away, creating a circle around him and giving him space.

'I was a stranger to your ways...' he continued, keeping his voice neutral.

He was not neutral. He was alive. Breathing. His royal guard infiltrated the crowd and discreetly made the space between him and his people wider. He continued and spoke to them too—to the royal guard, his inherited men—because they needed to hear his words too.

'I was a stranger to the personal struggles of this Kingdom of Taliedaa. But I am not a stranger to struggle or to hunger. Not only for food, but for the warmth of stability. I was a man when I came to you—when I stood above you in fine silks and asked you to accept me. And you did. Because my father asked you to—he demanded it. I thought on that day I had left the boy I was behind. But my wife...

your Queen-in-waiting…has reminded me that that boy's struggles—his losses—are universal. I have lost much, and so have many of you.'

Pain sliced through him, but he would raise his mother's memory up—the memory of who she had been, not who he had turned her into. The woman—the mother—he had forgotten.

'My mother… She was a young mother. A single mother in a foreign land, who worked her fingers to the bone to raise me. Her son. In my early life she wrapped me in hope, in love, in warmth, and I did not hunger because of her. She was one of you. Born here, raised here. *Loved* here. Until she made a mistake and fell in love with a king. And I am that mistake. It shamed her. *I* shamed her. Forced her to leave all she'd known because of her love. Her warmth. Her desire to see her son flourish. Now I ask all of you—would you not do the same? For love? Would you not abandon everything you'd known to raise your child? She did. She did not allow me to live in shame. My mother, Yamina Ali, raised a king.'

Oh, how his heart thundered. Beat painfully against his ribs. No, it was not his heart. It was the boy. Charlotte had removed his gag.

'My wife, Charlotte Hegarty, left behind her life to make a home here—for her love of your Crown Prince.'

Oh, he felt it now. *Love.* All around him. In every caress…every word. She had not let him forget just because he had not taken the good parts with him. She had shown him he needed the good parts of his past.

He needed her most of all.

'The Queen understands struggle,' he continued. 'She also understands what it means to overcome it. She has kept her promise to you. She has offered comfort and support to your Crown Prince. She has reminded me why I can be the King you need, if not the King you want, because your struggles are my struggles. And unlike my father, who stood above you in fine silks and then shut you out, closed the doors and forgot about you, I will not forget. Akeem Ali, the son of Yamina Ali and the late King Saleem Abd al-Uzza stands here today along with your Crown Prince. Because I am both in one body—in one flesh—and I will not choose one over the other.'

There it was, all out in the open, and he did not feel shame. He felt lighter. Better. Stronger than he ever had. But he needed to know. He needed his people to tell him… And even if the answer was not what he hoped for, at least he would have given them the choice. The choice of who was their King, their leader, regardless of blood or legitimacy. It was their right to choose and he would give them the choice his father hadn't when he'd thrust him upon them.

He would ask them now.

'Do you want me—this half-man, half-son-of-a-king— to be named your leader today? Your King? Because it is your choice and yours alone, people of Taliedaa. I will not demand to be King as my father did. So, tell me now, is this Prince of both worlds enough? Is he who you want to lead you into the future? Because I can be no one else? I am Akeem Ali Abd al-Uzza.'

The crowds roared.

He was their King.

He saw her then. Not her face, but her eyes. A simple black headscarf covered her hair and her face, and a black dress fell to her ankles.

But it was her.

She was here.

Running with him…

Charlotte slid back the scarf.

He moved, and the crowd parted, and then he stood

before her. Before his wife. His Queen. He had no words left. None. So he dropped to his knees and swore his allegiance to her. To the only woman who had cared enough to see him.

The true him.

The man and the King.

Akeem Ali Abd al-Uzza.

For nine years she'd wanted him on his knees. And now he was, Charlotte did the only thing she could. She got down on her knees too.

'The new King,' she said, in her newly found authoritative voice, even though her insides were trembling. She bowed, her chin to her chest, her knees turned to stone. 'Akeem Ali Abd al-Uzza—rightful heir to the throne.'

His hand sought hers. His fingers pushed through hers. And she let them.

Together, they raised each other up.

The surrounding crowds roared.

She hadn't intended to stay in Taliedaa, but she hadn't been able to leave. Leaving the palace with Selma, travelling into the city…every step had been agony. Every step taking her away from him. She hadn't been able to bear it—the thought that another decade might pass before she saw him again. *If* she saw him again. So she'd stayed close to Selma. Hidden in plain sight.

She hadn't intended him to see her today—hadn't wanted him to think she was there because of duty, to hold the hand of the Crown Prince. Because the King didn't need her to hold his hand. He would be the King with or without her. She was here for Akeem the man. To offer her support even if he didn't know it was there.

But she was holding his hand anyway—and he was holding hers.

His expensively tailored black suit was moulded to every inch of his body, a golden tie was at his throat, and he was every inch a king, surrounded by opulence, with the power of the people in his hand. But not because of his lineage, because of *him*.

The man they had never seen coming.

The only man she had ever loved. Still loved.

The boy and the man. Both in the same skin. Her husband the King.

She leant into him and whispered, 'I'm proud of you.' And she *was* proud of him. Proud of him for embracing who he was and what he could become.

Black eyes held hers, and she saw herself in their reflective depths.

Did he want her there—inside him? Because he'd always been inside her. He'd never left.

Wordlessly, he took her elbow and led her inside. And she let him walk her in with fear in her stomach.

This might be the last time he guided her anywhere.

This could be their last goodbye.

She would not cry.

The doors closed behind them and she inhaled a stunted breath.

'I'm sorry,' he said.

She closed her eyes. Her heart was pumping too loudly. *He was sorry?* She waited for the excuses, for him to turn his wrongs into hers... Because where there was pain, wasn't it always her fault? Hadn't life taught her that not everyone could own their mistakes without hurting others with their reluctant apologies?

She waited until she couldn't wait any more. She opened her eyes.

'Say it again.'

He didn't hesitate. He dropped to his knees. 'I'm sorry,

Charlotte. I'm sorry I hurt you. I'm sorry I was too stupid to see that those moments in the cave, in the palace and in my bed—' he swallowed, jutting out his lower lip '—were the only moments where I revealed the true me to anyone. You saw me even when I didn't want you to.'

He knelt motionless, still but for the heavy rise and fall of his chest.

'I couldn't tell you my name because underneath it all—the opulence and the power I'd longed to rub in your face—I was no one. An empty vessel of nothing. A mass of broken flesh and bone. I'd swapped one life for another without claiming either for myself. Neither of those lives— the boy's or the King's—belonged to me. I was a puppet of the system until my eighteenth birthday, and then I was my father's puppet. Thank you, Charlotte,' he finished, and every line on his face was taut. Pained. 'Thank you for setting me free.'

She so badly wanted to jump into his arms, to tell him she was right here, with him, and she was going nowhere. But words were cheap. His words outside had been for himself, for his people. But now she wanted words for her. Proof that he could embrace the past—because it was the only way they could move on together.

So she didn't raise him up. And she didn't feel victorious, and neither did her sixteen-year-old self. She felt... *abandoned.*

He might not have abandoned her on purpose nine years ago, but he'd abandoned her on their wedding night.

Would he abandon her again?

'What will you do with your newfound freedom, Akeem?' she asked. 'What will you do with *me*?'

Her heart was beating so hard because he didn't need her any more. Not to be his Queen. His wife. But did he want her? Did he need her as she needed him? As a lover? A friend? Family?

'I want to love you hard…'

His eyes flashed and her stomach pulled. That night he'd loved her fiercely with his body but abandoned her with his mind.

'So hard,' he continued, 'that you are breathless with my love.'

'I'm not talking about sex.'

'And neither am I.' He swallowed, searching her face as she searched his. 'I thought my riches, my power, would make you want me.' He held up his huge hand, the slender digits halting her rebuke. 'I was wrong. You cared for none of it. Not even for a diploma.' He smiled, oh, so weakly. So tentatively. 'In the cave you asked if I was worthy.'

'Are you?'

'The man before you is worthy. I am worthy of love. I am worthy of the happiness I find in your arms, in bed, against the wall or on the floor, or simply by being in your presence while you sleep…watching you draw.' He hushed her again when she tried to speak. 'But more than that we are worthy of happiness, Charlotte. Of love.'

'Love?' she repeated. She wanted—no, she needed to touch him. But she didn't.

'Love,' he agreed. 'All week I have wanted to drag you out of Selma's house in the city. Drag you into my bed and love you so hard you wouldn't be able to leave my bed for days. Because sex is what we do—how we talk.'

His Adam's apple moved up and down his taut throat.

'I wanted to keep you in bed for weeks,' he went on. 'For however long it took you to forgive me. Instead…' he said, and then he exhaled heavily, a shudder escaping his lips. 'Instead I sat in your studio. I sat there on the floor and stared at your drawings—your portraits. Of me. In the cave. On the balcony. In the children's home… And the double portrait.' He exhaled heavily. 'You were the only one to ever see me when I was standing in plain sight. I want to be the man you see. I can't make you forgive me, but I can promise I will talk with my mouth, as well as with my body. I will use my words and my actions to show you how much I love you. How sorry I am for not listening. For making you pack a box with your feelings.'

'I never really packed it,' she confessed wryly, and her heart was so light—so full—she could burst.

'I want to unpack mine, and then I want us to fill a fresh box—without a lid. I want us to fill it with the intensity between us. I've tried to deny that I feel it, but it has never diminished. It has only grown. Grown into an all-consuming need to be in your presence. To touch you. Be with you. Love you. And I don't want to deny it any more. I want to keep it in a place where we can both see it, feel it, embrace it. Use it to drive each other to be better. *Stronger.* Because it was never a weakness. You are my strength, Charlotte. You make me a better and stronger man.'

She rushed to him. Fell to the floor with him and landed in his arms. She scrambled with the too-long light cotton sleeve and unbuckled the watch. Her heart pumping. Her eyes too wide. She grabbed his wrist, pushed up his sleeve and attempted to wrap the delicate watch around his wrist. It was too tight. It looked ridiculous. She pushed the fine silver pin through the last hole.

Perfect.

'She's been here today with you…your mum.'

'I know,' he whispered.

'Your dad too, watching his people. And my dad—' She choked. 'He was here as well.' She grabbed his hand and placed it on her chest. 'In here.

'There were two sides to your father,' she told him, because she got it now. Understood it for what it was, right or wrong. 'There was the man who abandoned you, and there was the King. Your father the King moulded every sentence you spoke today.'

'How do you know that?'

'My dad had two sides as well. The side social services saw, so he could get me back home, and the side he showed to me. Maybe getting me back was in his eyes doing the right thing. Standing by his duty. The way your father stood by his in the end. He was cruel, but he came for you. Turned you into a king. I hate him for how he treated you, but he was still your dad.'

'Determined as ever to compare our lives, Charlotte?' said Akeem.

'We walked the same streets in the same shoes once, didn't we? I can see your path as clearly as I can see my own. Your father made you a king, and your mother made you emphatic and compassionate.'

'And your father made you strong. Invincible against all odds.'

'For all his faults, I am his daughter. And I loved him.'

'I cannot say I loved my father, but I loved my mother. I loved her so much—' His voice broke, and she finished for him.

'It was easier to blame yourself, to be angry, than to let yourself grieve.'

'Yes,' he said, his eyes heavy with unshed tears. 'I see that now.'

'Love is not the enemy. Life can be hard sometimes, and then at other times it can be...*magical*.' She smiled. 'As magical as fire when your eyes aren't accustomed to the dark.'

'I want to be your light in the darkness, *qalbi*. I want to be your oasis when all around you is sand.'

Together, they said, *'Sanctuary,'* and laughed.

Her hands moved to the back of his neck and she toyed with the hair at his nape. 'Are you scared?' she asked.

'Yes,' he said.

'It's okay to be afraid when everything is changing.'

'Is it, *qalbi*?'

'Yes—because what you're feeling is growing pains.'

'Do you feel them too?' he asked.

'Yes,' she smiled weakly. 'And it hurts. But I want to hurt with you. Change with you. Grow with you. Love you.'

'I'm not afraid of my feelings any more,' he told her. 'I'm not afraid of this. Of us. Of what we are.'

'And what are we?'

'Husband and wife.'

'King and Queen?'

'We are both and we are more.' He tugged her into his arms. 'We are family.'

'Family,' she agreed, and let the tears fall.

'Qalbi...' Big, solid hands came about her waist and pulled her into him. 'My heart,' he said.

Akeem tilted her face to search her eyes. And he saw himself in them. The man and the King, on the floor in her arms.

'Call me by my name, my heart,' he demanded, with everything he had been, with everything he was, and with everything he would become. 'Tell me I am yours.'

'Akeem. The boy of my dreams, the man of my heart,' she whispered. 'Husband. King. Mine.'

He kissed her, and she kissed him.

It was a promise.

A promise of today, tomorrow and for ever.

* * * * *

INNOCENT IN
HER ENEMY'S BED

DANI COLLINS

MILLS & BOON

In loving memory of my mother, Sharon,
who taught me to love reading
and left romance novels on the coffee table
and showed me what a loving relationship looks like
with her fifty-five-year marriage to my dad.

We all miss you, Mom.

CHAPTER ONE

THIS MUST BE what it would feel like walking to the gallows, Ilona Callas's imagination whispered as she passed through the security gauntlet in the lobby of the Vasilou Tower.

Her skin was clammy and her stomach was filled with lead. Her heart raced and her breathing was so shallow and rapid, she grew light-headed. Her nostrils burned with the scent of danger. *Flee!*

Perhaps it was the glass elevator. The guard showed her into it and pushed the button, but left her to rise alone. She averted her gaze from the way the plants and people abruptly shrank beneath her and grasped the rail for balance.

She didn't care for heights, not since her older half brother Midas had dragged her to the edge of a cliff and terrorized her with threats of throwing her off. *A joke*, her stepmother had insisted. *Boys will be boys.*

Deep down, Ilona suspected the reason she was here was because Midas was at it again. He was so funny with his destructive pranks, he ought to have his own comedy special on the streaming networks.

The Parthenon came into view then even that behemoth shrank as she continued to rise. Buildings this tall were a rarity in Athens. Most kept to twelve floors or less, ensuring the Parthenon was always in view. The fact the owner of this tower had been allowed to double that height told her he did not confine himself to the rules that governed others.

Much like Midas.

The knives in her stomach turned.

The door pinged and opened. Ilona entered a top floor reception area of stunning design. The marble tiles were arranged so the veins created a river effect, guiding her through a gallery of modern art to a desk stationed before a glass wall etched with a map of the globe.

A woman sat behind the desk, but a scrupulously groomed young man stood by to greet Ilona.

"Kyría Callas. *Kaliméra.* I'm Androu. Kýrie Vasilou will be with you shortly. May I ask you to wait here?" Androu led her to a door adjacent to the reception area, one that opened into a small, stuffy glass-fronted room. It held a round table and four chairs that were a chic, modern design made from polished wood. He didn't offer coffee or water before he left her.

The lack of respect was obvious. This room was a prison where she had no privacy. The lighting was artificial, the music not piped in. The only sound was the loud tick of the clock. Ilona didn't bother trying her phone. The service would be poor; she was sure. This room was deliberately uncomfortable so meetings here would be kept short.

It was not the place to leave a peer.

If Leander Vasilou thought she would depart in a huff of indignation, however, he was deeply mistaken. Ilona had been insulted, attacked and disregarded her whole life. Rather than taking offense, she was grateful for the time to sit quietly and escape the coming confrontation with more pleasant thoughts.

She admired that marble floor and wondered how she might obtain the name of the mason so she could plagiarize the effect in her flat. Or, as she often fantasized, perhaps she would sell her flat and move to the island of her mother's birth. She loved her work, but today was a perfect example of why it was also draining. It would be far less stressful to work in a café the way her mother had. On Paxos, she would have a view of actual water. She could feed the stray cats and try her hand at pottery. That had always fascinated her. So tactile and magical to create shapes from silt. She would have to look up whether there were appropriate clay deposits—

"Kyría Callas?" Androu was back. "Kýrie Vasilou will see you now."

A glance at the clock revealed she had been waiting thirty-three minutes.

Since the young man held the door with an air of expectation, she rose.

"Thank you," she said, but the blanket of dread returned to her shoulders, heavy and cold.

She followed him down a blessedly air-conditioned corridor, through a far more comfortable waiting area, one that provided a small banquet of refreshments and a view of the city.

He waved her into a massive office.

Here, the marble veins in the floor created a mountain effect. On one side, there were a sofa and chairs with a television mounted above a wine cooler set in a cabinet of glasses and bottles of spirits. The other side held a meeting table with six ergonomic chairs, a projector and a blank whiteboard.

In front of her, at the pinnacle of the mountain, natural light poured through a wall of glass, backlighting the occupant of the office, Leander Vasilou.

He sat at a desk made from a curved slab of polished mahogany set atop drawers arranged in a slant. The whole thing looked offset, but dynamic and ultramodern. He wore an earpiece and was speaking in French, booking a tennis match with someone.

The doors closed behind her, but his conversation only lapsed into whether a certain piste at a Swiss ski resort had been attempted, then the merits of protein shakes over whole foods after working out.

He didn't look at her once.

Ilona hadn't been invited to sit so she didn't. She waited with the patience she had gathered around her through a lifetime of being least and last and deeply unwanted. It usually served her well, cushioning her against most of life's spears and arrows.

Not today.

She knew he was aware of her, knew he was deliberately trying to get under her skin. To her chagrin, it was working. She wanted to put it down to the attack this stranger was waging on her. Many would label it "just business," but it was deeply personal to her. It was *her* business he was attacking.

That wasn't what was piercing her bubble of detachment, though. It was him.

She had seen photos of Leander Vasilou, but she hadn't expected his suit-model looks to be so mesmerizing in real life. His eyelids sat heavy and bored over gray irises. A scruff of beard accentuated the height of his cheekbones and the hollows of his cheeks. That same scruff might be hiding a cleft in his squared off chin. It certainly framed a mouth that gave her a small thrill when his teeth briefly caught at the inner flesh of his bottom lip.

"Oh, yes, I remember her very well," he said, voice dipping into smoky amusement rife with sensual memory.

That tone had the strangest effect on her, turning the greasiness of dread in her belly to warm butter laced with honey.

A flush of heat rose from that same place, radiating into her breasts and turning to an embarrassed heat as she realized she was reacting in a very sexual way to that timbre in his voice.

She *never* reacted to men. Or women. Not to anyone. Not like this. She dated when an escort was expected—like a gala or holiday party—but she rarely allowed more than a kiss at the end because that was when her interest always dried up.

Oddly, this man, whom she was predisposed to fear and dislike, was making her wonder how his lips would feel against her own. How would they feel in the crook of her neck? His wide hands became a source of fascination as he briefly squeezed the back of his neck and laughed, causing the fabric of his shirt to strain across his well-built shoulders and thick biceps.

She had never once in her life felt her breath leave her because the beauty of a man appealed so strongly. Or experienced a compulsion to unbutton a man's shirt and nuzzle the hair on his chest because a few fine hairs at his collar caught her attention, but she was envisioning doing that to him and was appalled with herself.

She swallowed, discovering her throat was hot and tight. Her cheeks were beginning to sting as her blush arrived from her chest and swept upward.

She averted her gaze to a sculpture that could have been steel flames. She thought about the time Midas had thrown her doll into the fire at the Pagonis chalet in Switzerland. It had been the last thing her mother had given her.

That painful memory helped her remember why she was here. At nine, she hadn't had the courage to pluck her doll out of the fire and save it. She wouldn't be so cowardly today.

She firmed her feet to the floor and drew a long subtle breath of patience.

Leander Vasilou finally ended his call. He dropped his earpiece onto his desk and looked at her with a distinct lack of interest.

"Kyría Pagonis. You wanted to see me." He didn't rise, didn't offer his hand to shake.

She didn't even glance at either of the chairs she stood between.

"Callas," she corrected with a polite smile. "My mother wasn't married to my father so I use her name." Ilona always corrected that. It was a whole thing with Odessa, her stepmother. "But given you're attempting to take over my company, I expect you already know my name."

"I *am* taking over your company," he assured her. "Ilona."

His facetious tone was dangerously close to that other, intimate timbre he had used a moment ago. It had the same effect of unfurling frond-like sensations deep in her belly.

She tried to ignore it, but her throat was constricting again.

"You have acquired forty percent of the shares in Callas Cosmetics. I own forty-five. Pagonis International owns the remaining fifteen, so I don't know how you—"

"Does it?" he cut in.

The sweet sensations in her stomach curdled. The text from her younger half brother Hercules appeared in her mind's eye.

You should be here. They're making decisions without you.

"I understand you've made an offer to buy those shares

from Pagonis. May I assume you're prompted by product loyalty? Your skin is certainly flawless," she said.

There was a flash behind his sharp gaze, like the glint off a knife blade.

"You may assume that my intention is to take over Pagonis International. Acquiring their cash cow is the first step."

Ilona had been called many things, but never that. And Midas must know he was the real target. That's why he was throwing her company forward as a sacrifice. Big surprise.

She tightened her grip on her clutch, fighting to keep an impervious expression on her face.

"I've bettered your offer," she said with false calm. "If they sell, it will be to me. I'm here to offer for the forty percent you've already obtained. I'm prepared to pay above market value."

"I've upped the ante myself, promising ten percent over any offer you make. The sky is the limit. That was one of the Pagonis board members on that call." He flicked a finger toward his earpiece. "We're old friends and he owes me a favor. He's also greedy as hell. Pagonis will not be selling their shares to you."

The churn in her stomach grew into a tangle of thorny brambles.

"Why is it that you're targeting Pagonis?" she asked, lifting her brows in absent interest. "Cosmetics and biotechnology fall outside the Vasilou bailiwick, doesn't it?" His conglomerate took on large infrastructure projects like bridges and airports.

"I want to take back what's mine and destroy the rest," he said very casually, as though mentioning his errands for the day.

Her blood went cold as she began to see where Midas was dragging her. Here was the cliff, and its churning sea was in Leander's eyes, mercilessly crashing against sharp rocks.

"What, um, what exactly is yours?" she inquired, fighting to keep a level tone.

"The speech recognition technology that your brother 'developed' sixteen years ago." He only curled the fingers on one hand to indicate the air quotes, not even lifting the heel of his palm off the blotter on his desk. Contempt dripped off his tongue. "Most of the credit goes to my father, but I worked with him on it. Then Midas talked us into allowing him to assist us with taking it to market. That was the last we saw of him or any profit we should have earned."

Of course, Midas had stolen that technology. She kicked herself for not seeing it long before now, but she had still been at boarding school when he had been impressing their father with his business acumen. Then she had focused on building her own enterprise, distancing herself as much as possible from Midas and the corporate headquarters, not wanting to work at Pagonis International because she would have to work directly under Midas.

"That doesn't explain why you're coming after my company, rather than some of the subsidiaries that Midas controls," she said.

"I entered the door that was open. Your shares aren't as expensive or well-protected against speculative trading. Which doesn't make sense to me when your company has been infusing the mother ship with much-needed cash for over a year."

It made sense if he knew her family, but she didn't let their greed and scorn of her value distract her in this moment.

"Your intention is to persuade the board to sell you its share in Callas Cosmetics and take it over from me? Then what do you plan to do with it?"

"Let it wither and die."

That pushed her onto her back foot. "Why?" she asked with anxious bafflement. "You just called it a cash cow."

"Because I want your family to know that I don't need it the way you do. I want it to *hurt*. I want you all to feel sickened at the mistake you made, living off the fruits of my father's labor, stealing the credit and driving him to ruin."

The gravel rolling in her middle stopped. It became heavy and nauseatingly hard, but at least it was a feeling she was used to. This was very familiar ground.

"Your takeover is motivated by vindictiveness," she acknowledged.

"Yes." No hesitation or apology.

Perhaps he was entitled to his antipathy, but *she* hadn't stolen from his father. There was no defusing hate, though. Ilona had learned that with Odessa. It didn't matter that Ilona was her father's mistake. Ilona had always borne the brunt of Odessa's resentment.

That seemed to be what Leander had in store for her. He would take the majority share in Callas Cosmetics, then force her to watch as he ran it into the ground. That would crush her, given she had built it from a patch of dry skin on her cheek to a global enterprise.

A familiar despair at injustice floated around the edges of her periphery, but she mentally batted it away. Crying or fighting against the bullies of the world had never served her. The best she could do was soften the punch and get away as quickly as possible.

"I don't want innocent employees to lose their jobs." She made her decision with the swiftness of self-preservation and acted on it before second thoughts could creep in. "Our customers depend on the efficacy of our products, especially those with facial scars and burn injuries. It would be a shame to deny them something they need. I propose you buy my shares."

He snorted and his chair squeaked as he threw himself back in it. "I know what it looks like when a rat jumps ship, Ilona."

No fernlike tickle when he said her name this time. She was nothing but granite inside, hardened with resolve.

"I propose that you buy my shares for the amount my father gave me when he approved my business plan. That was one hundred thousand euros of start-up capital and a fifteen percent share. I don't know what I'll do next, but I'm happy to maintain those terms on any venture I pursue." A café, for instance. With dolmades served on hand-thrown crockery.

He was taken aback, not that he showed it, but he went very still and his eyes narrowed as he tried to discern what the catch might be.

She enlightened him. "In return I would insist you hire a qualified CEO and do everything in your power to keep Callas Cosmetics thriving."

"Your forty-five percent is worth ten million euros."

"Yes, I know." She offered a flat smile. "And I assure you that if you pursue the Pagonis shares just so you can destroy Callas, I will drive up the price until you pay thirty million for *fifteen* percent. Or you may have forty-five for one hundred thousand. My research tells me you're a shrewd negotiator. Well done."

"Your negotiation skills are terrible. What would you get out of that?"

Freedom.

"A clean conscience," she said. "I accept that I benefited from your father's work. It was unknowing, but I did. Losing ten million is a blow. Losing something I built with great pride and care would also cause me great distress.

But having served me my just deserts, I assume you'll leave me alone in future." She hoped.

He steepled his fingers and swiveled his chair, head cocked as he reassessed her. "Are you trying to protect Midas by handing me the keys to your company? Did he send you here to make this little gesture to distract me from going after Pagonis International? It won't work. I won't give up."

She bit back a hysterical laugh. "I can see you're very determined." His ruthlessness was glowing like a neon sign. "The only people I'm trying to protect are the innocent ones."

Her employees from top level to floor-sweeper were a tight, dedicated team. There was already an ache behind her breastbone at knowing she wouldn't see them every day, but she was good at compartmentalizing. Showing this man how distraught she was wouldn't help her case. In fact, he would probably use it against her.

She stood tall and aloof as she waited for his next move.

His head fell back as he regarded her through the screen of his spiky lashes. "Are you angling to stay on as CEO?"

"No." She suppressed another choke of laughter. "My company is being used as a pawn between you and Midas. I refuse to become one myself. Take the spoils and fight your fight, but leave me out of it. Shall I have the paperwork drawn up?"

"Your eagerness to run is suspicious." His gaze flickered all over her, leaving little burn marks everywhere it touched.

She had made a mistake. She preferred to stay in the background, but she had caught his full attention and it was deeply disconcerting, both because his antagonism was plain and because she was reacting to him in such an inappropriate way. Some girlish part of her was squirming, worried her hair was out of place or there was a drip of coffee on her blouse.

"What if I asked you to stay on as CEO?" he questioned. "What if I made that my condition for accepting your offer?"

Her heart skipped then stretched with longing. She had built her company with more than pride and care. She had put her soul into it. She didn't care that her father had eventually decided Midas was the better businessman based on his stolen technology and named him president of Pagonis International. Ilona knew in her heart she outpaced Midas when it came to financial intelligence, marketing insight and management skills.

Much as it would kill her to walk away from what she had created, however, the idea of finally escaping the Pagonis tentacles was even more appealing. That 15 percent in Callas Cosmetics had kept her beholden to Midas after their father passed. If she gave up her company, however, she had no reason to continue associating with any of them.

She would finally be free.

Thanks to this man with the broad shoulders and glinting silver eyes and a sensual mouth that put shocking thoughts in her head.

"Tempted?" he chided in that infuriatingly seductive tone.

"No," she lied. Her skin was still prickling, wondering if he found her appealing which was so stupid. "The idea of partnering with a man who hates me and wants to use me to exact revenge against my family sounds like a marriage best not undertaken. I suggest—"

"Marriage," Leander cut in, sitting straight up with another screech of his chair. "Now *there's* an idea."

CHAPTER TWO

"What?"

Ilona Callas's eyes widened as Leander shot to his feet and came around his desk toward her. In fact, there was a split second where he glimpsed genuine fear flare behind her startled gaze.

Then she blanked her expression and seemed to subtly rebalance her weight, but her knuckles turned white where she held her shiny black handbag. The tendons in her neck stood out with distress.

With a disconcerting swerve in his chest, Leander veered across the room to throw ice into glasses. He opened a bottle of sparkling water, glugging it over the cubes, using the action to steal a moment of reassessment.

Marriage to the illegitimate Pagonis daughter had already occurred to him as the ultimate means to his revenge, of course it had. For a decade and a half, he had mulled every possible path into their empire.

He had set aside approaching Ilona for several reasons, the primary one being that it would tip his hand. Making a stealth move on her company had put him in this first, fail-safe position of having a foot in the door. Morally, he had balked at romancing a woman under false pretenses, even one whose family he categorically despised.

Now that he had met her and she had brought it up, however, marriage returned as a possibility. That stark fear he had just witnessed was concerning, though. It had even briefly eclipsed his blinding desire to destroy the Pagonis family. Much as he wanted to make them pay, terrorizing a woman with sexual threats was not something he would ever do, under any circumstance.

Most especially if he was trying to talk her into marriage.

Is that what he wanted, though? Marriage? To *her*?

"I realize you didn't steal the tech yourself, but you've lived off those profits, Ilona. That's how your father was able to invest in your company. That's why I'm coming after you along with the rest. You don't get to be a Pagonis only when it works to your advantage."

There was such a loaded silence behind him, he glanced over his shoulder.

Her glower at his back quickly reconfigured into calm dignity. "I just offered to make good on that."

She had and he was still puzzling through that offer.

He set the fizzing glasses on the coffee table, nodding at her to join him as he took his customary armchair.

After the briefest of hesitations, she came to perch on the corner of the sofa farthest from him, ankles crossed, hands folded, demeanor one of polite interest.

Damn, but she was beautiful. He had noted that, too, in his many online research trips, but he was far more interested in whether a woman had an engaging personality or a unique perspective on life that challenged his own.

Still, he was red-blooded enough to react to Ilona's unadulterated sex appeal. She had a supermodel figure—tall and slender, but rounded in all the most alluring places. Her bone structure was delicate, but her depthless brown eyes were steady and unflinching. Her shiny black hair was clasped behind her neck. Her manicure and makeup were natural shades. Even her lipstick was a nude shade with only the barest hint of berry pink.

Somehow that was more tantalizing than garish red, drawing his gaze back to her wide, lush mouth again and again.

She wore simple gold jewelry—hoops in her ears, a chain with an ornate knot that sat in the hollow of her throat and a ring designed like ivy that twined toward the knuckle on her middle finger. Her clothing was a classic navy skirt suit with a pinstripe and a white shirt with its collar popped. Her shoes were a matching blue-black with red soles.

She wasn't flirting or throwing out lures, though. So he wasn't sure why he felt such a tremendous *pull*. It had accosted him the moment she had entered his office, quiet and graceful as a ballerina. Slithered, he had told himself of her near-silent entry. He wanted to view her as a viper, like Midas.

She was too sensual looking to be a cold-blooded reptile, though. He couldn't tell what she was beneath her understated, faultless demeanor.

Inexplicably, a hummingbird came to mind, one that appeared pretty and small when she was still, but with a heart that was beating a mile a minute. He didn't know that, but he sensed the way she remained alert, ready to dart away at the least startling movement.

She didn't touch her water, didn't fidget or press him to speak. She sat very quietly, exactly as his receptionist had reported she had behaved in the pressure cooker, the room in the reception area where he sequestered those he didn't really wish to see.

Rather than grow overheated and angry at his rudeness, or trying to maximize her time by making calls, Ilona had sat and waited.

Waiting was hard. Leander knew that because he had had to wait for his opportunity to take Midas down. The wheels were in motion but had yet to pick up momentum. Marriage to Ilona could provide the rocket fuel, but thinking about something like that and doing it were very different.

She was a Pagonis and not to be trusted.

On the other hand, she held a stake in the company. Pagonis International was publicly traded, but the family owned a substantial interest. Their father had bequeathed his shares equally between his three children. His widow owned a similar amount and the family always voted together, maintaining control.

But what if Leander could disrupt that? At the very least, marrying into that family would allow him to reap some of the financial benefit that should have been his all along.

He nodded, warming even more to the idea of capturing this reluctant little pawn.

"You're not married," he noted. "Are you engaged? In a relationship?"

"I don't think it would be wise to offer you any more leverage than you currently possess," she said with a faint smile.

"Interesting that you think a relationship would be a weakness, not a strength."

"Goodness," she said with a glance at her naked wrist. "Did my therapy appointment overlap with my business meeting? I'll speak to my assistant. There's no reason you should feel compelled to do double duty."

He refused to like her, but he was a sucker for sarcasm delivered on such a frosty platter. *May I assume you're prompted by product loyalty?*

He was still privately smirking over that cheeky remark.

"I find committed relationships to be a liability myself,"

he volunteered, presuming he would have unearthed any serious liaisons while he'd been researching her and her family. "I have no problem with monogamy, but demands on my time are very high. I don't like people in my space, expecting me to answer to them. I don't like being emotionally accessible. It's...*tedious*."

"Hmm." The noncommittal noise neither agreed nor disagreed.

Such a mysterious creature. He was reluctantly curious, wondering what it would take to get a real reaction out of her. Not a reflex like pain or fear. Laughter. *Passion.*

She must possess some of the latter. Callas Cosmetics was enormously successful in a crowded market. Her father's initial investment was well-documented, and the family name had definitely helped her along, but she hadn't relied on gimmicks or risky gambles or dirty plays that he could find. She had scaled strategically, always raising money through outside sources with sound proposals.

As someone who had grown his own business from next to nothing, Leander knew there had to be a deep emotional driver to propel a person into doing the hard work every day. His motivator was revenge. The way Ilona was prepared to sacrifice herself for her employees and customers suggested something less dark. It had to be passion.

He could definitely work with that.

"If we were to marry—" he began, then surprised himself with a fantasy of her long, slender legs squeezing his waist while he plumbed the depths of her sensuality, his mouth catching her cries of culmination.

A hot bolt of desire grounded itself behind his fly, causing the flesh there to twitch and thicken. He bit back a curse, nearly missing what she was saying.

"You have completely misconstrued my remark." She brushed at her knee. "I meant that taking a position under you in my own company sounds like an arrangement that is doomed to fail. It would be similar to a marriage where everyone says, 'It was obvious from the beginning that it wouldn't work out.' I don't like making obvious mistakes."

"Thank you for connecting those dots for me. I've moved to a new page where I am proposing—" Was he really going here? *Taking a position under you...*

Her words rang in his ears, but this wasn't about sex. It was about using her as a Trojan horse to get inside the family so he could deal Midas the lethal blow he deserved.

"I propose you allow me to buy the fifteen percent from Pagonis," Leander stated, growing more resolved as he located pieces from one of his many plans and modified them to fit this moment. "I will then give you *all* of my shares in Callas as a wedding gift. You will own Callas Cosmetics outright and may run it however you see fit."

Her eyes widened with exhilaration before she dropped her lashes, screening her reaction while she looked to the hands she had arranged in her lap.

"That's an attractive offer, but I don't wish to marry." Her gaze came up again, thoughts shuttered. "At all. It's not personal."

"No?" He thought again of that flash of fear she had revealed. Was she afraid of all men, not just him? That thought caused an uncomfortable prickle across the back of his shoulders.

Maybe she wasn't into men at all. He didn't see that as an impediment to a marriage for business purposes, though.

"I wouldn't think marriage was something that interests you, either," she said in a remote tone. "You said you don't like people in your space. Ironically, we're a perfect match in that regard. I'm also very private. That's why it's best if we stick to our own corners."

"We could have our own corners," he decided abruptly. "Separate bedrooms."

"A marriage without sex? That *is* a compelling offer." She was being facetious again, the minx.

"I'm serious. I happen to be straight and was under the impression you are, too, but sharing a bed with my wife is not a deal breaker for me." He couldn't believe those words were emerging from his mouth. He loved sex.

He wasn't an opportunist, though. He didn't take whatever was available for the sake of it. Besides, he'd be a fool to trust her. Yes, there was often a power imbalance when a man brought a woman into his bed, one that typically favored a man, but there were plenty of men who became ruled by lust. He wouldn't become one of them.

She tucked her chin, brows coming together with skepticism. "A marriage in name only? Really?"

"Disappointed?" he mocked. "Do you want to have sex with me?"

"Of course not," she said a little too quickly. "I only met you five minutes ago." Her snippiness was the first hint of true emotion she'd displayed since walking in here. A stain of pink touched her cheekbones and her gaze slid away from his. Her spine inched a notch taller.

So defensive and wasn't *that* interesting.

He rubbed the backs of his fingers against the nap of whiskers under his chin, biting back a smug grin.

"You don't want children?" he prodded.

Her averted gaze widened as though he'd sucker punched her. She recovered in a blink and swiveled her head to look him dead in the eye.

"No."

Such a lie. One she baldly made straight to his face. That ought to be ringing all sorts of alarms inside him, but he was far more interested in why she refused to admit she wanted children. He had always assumed he would have a few one day, after he'd achieved the justice he sought.

His desire to marry her took on a new angle, one where he would have the time to pry out all these little secrets and evasions she was hoarding behind her standoffish exterior.

Don't, he warned himself. She was a means to an end. That's all.

"So, it's agreed," he stated, having discovered years ago that those words made his wishes come true. "We'll marry and live in the same home, but within our separate spaces. We'll confine our marital duties to public appearances and hosting events like family dinners…" He grinned in anticipation of that bloodbath.

"It is not agreed," she said, quiet, but firm. "I cannot marry a man who hates me. How can you even consider tying yourself to someone you loathe? Unless the point would be to make my life as uncomfortable as possible?"

"On the contrary," he assured her. "In exchange for switching your allegiance to me, I would provide you with a more comfortable life than ever. You would take full control of your company and all of my wrath would be directed toward the other members of your family."

"Mmm. And I'm sure being extorted into a marriage of revenge would soon provoke my affection toward you." Her pained smile fell away. "But I've thought of a new avenue I can pursue." She rose so abruptly he practically heard the burr of wings in his ears. "Keep your shares. I'll sell mine to my employees. If you then wish to harm the company, you'll be destroying the livelihoods of invested co-owners who have nothing to do with your thirst for vengeance. If you need a referral for a good PR firm to help weather that scandal, I'm happy to provide some names. Thank you for your time today."

"You're really going to walk away from all of this?" The

bold black line of her hair down her spine was as enticing as a ribbon to a cat. He wanted to snare it with a claw and drag what was attached into his mouth. "You don't care that I intend to level Pagonis? You'll be impacted, too."

She turned, appearing collected, but he scented the adrenaline running through her. Her throat flexed as she swallowed and her lips were thin with tension.

"I've already expressed my concern for innocent people. It's a global economy and small disruptions in supply chains can have far-reaching consequences. I would hope you're not so overcome by antipathy you want to cause harm all around the world, but I can't stop you if that's your goal. I certainly don't believe marrying you will give me the power to change your mind."

"What are you going to tell your brother about this meeting, then?"

"Nothing. As I said, my company is the pawn, not me. If you wish to convey a message to him, I'll have my assistant forward his contact details. *Antio sas.*"

Ilona walked straight from his office to the powder room across the lounge. It was as well-appointed and sumptuous as the rest of this top floor with subdued lighting, a selection of her competitor's luxury soaps and lotions, even a change table and a rocking chair suitable for nursing an infant.

She sat down and did her slow breathing exercises, clearing her mind and bringing her heart rate back to normal before she allowed herself to react.

Marriage?

Her heart took a skip and she clenched her eyes shut, counting to ten as she inhaled, then backward as she exhaled.

Marriage wasn't remotely possible, she assured herself.

She didn't have to consider it at all. No. She only had to focus on the other piece, where she divested her company to save it. Heartbreaking as that would be, she was proud of arriving at that solution. From a financial and personal standpoint it would be a horrific loss, but she had built it with her own sweat and tears. She could start over with something new. Perhaps she would start a cat café. She could paint cats on the dishes she used to serve spanakopita and souvlaki.

That was such a lovely thought, she actually smiled at her reflection when she rose and dabbed a cool towel at her temples.

She smoothed her hair and examined her makeup. When she was satisfied there was nothing to criticize, she left the powder room, still mentally planning her new life.

"Ah. Good. You're still up here. That saves security detaining you." Leander halted midcharge from his office. "Tell them to stand down, Androu," he said to the young man who caught himself a hair's breadth before slamming into his boss's back. Leander held Ilona frozen with his sleet-colored gaze. "Let's continue our conversation over lunch."

Ilona fought to speak around the pin that seemed to have punctured her chest. "I have other appointments."

"Advise Kyría Callas's assistant to clear her schedule," Leander told Androu over his shoulder.

"Very good, sir."

Very *not* good, but at least Leander was waving her toward the elevator. Ilona gladly made for the exit, needing out of this building and away from this man.

You don't want children?

Of course, she did. She couldn't take that step right now, though. Not without bringing the hell of Odessa's wrath down upon herself.

"It's not my nature to be obstructive," she told Leander as the doors closed them into the elevator. "A lifetime of being around domineering men has taught me to pick my battles so I'll go to lunch if you insist, but I won't marry someone who is already demonstrating he wants to control my life."

"It's lunch," he said pithily. "Where we will negotiate the fine points of your taking complete control your company. If yours is anything like mine, it *is* the bulk of your life. Surely that's worth skipping a marketing presentation or whatever you had on."

She wished he would quit dangling the prospect of sole proprietorship. It was a very tasty carrot. The shareholders Leander had recently bought out had been mostly reasonable, but Midas occasionally flexed his influence, backing her into a corner for his own enjoyment. She would love to be free of that.

She would love to be free of Midas. *Love it.*

"You moved your ring," Leander noted.

"Pardon?" She followed his gaze to her right hand where she had reflexively clasped the rail as the elevator plummeted. "Oh." Should she tell him? What would he do with the information? Steal her ring? It wasn't particularly expensive and there was no real way he could weaponize this quirk of hers. "I move it when I want to remember something."

"Such as?" Suspicion narrowed his gaze.

"Picking up my dry cleaning." She lifted a shoulder in an absent shrug. "In this case, I want to remember to look up something when I get home." Clay deposits on Paxos. "I use this ring because it's a coil. I can shrink or expand it for different fingers. If I have more than one thing to remember, I wear it on this finger." She pointed to her index finger. "If it's on this thumb, it's an event I can't miss. If I put it on that one, it's travel."

"Foolish me, paying for an assistant," he said dryly. "So anytime I want to clear your schedule, I can just take that ring?"

"You can try," she shot back, and saw immediately what a mistake it was to challenge him, even mockingly.

Excitement for a wrestle flared in his eyes.

At that exact moment, the elevator dipped below the lobby into an underground parking garage. The glass walls became solid concrete. The lighting changed from bright sunshine to subdued gold, closeting them in intimacy.

The elevator stopped and Leander swayed onto his toes.

He was going to kiss her.

All of her…softened. Her clasp on the rail tightened and her gaze dropped to his mouth. She stood very still, waiting. Wondering. *Wanting*…

CHAPTER THREE

THE DOORS OPENED, releasing all the charged air from this little capsule.

Leander shot his hand out to hold the door and amusement indented the corners of his mouth.

No. She ducked past him, mortified. He knew. He knew she had expected his kiss and now he would use that against her. A meteor shower of fiery ulcers returned to her stomach.

And now she was staring into the open back door of Leander's chauffeured car while her own was at the curb of the lobby above.

"Where shall I have my driver meet me?" she asked stiffly as she slid inside and removed her phone from her bag.

"Dino will take you wherever you wish to go when you're ready."

"The Callas building on Ermou, please," she said promptly. She was *so* done.

"Cute. I'm growing smitten with that sense of humor of yours," Leander said as he came in beside her and the door slammed. "It's charming."

And there it was. He was taunting her for betraying her attraction. Her chest filled with the hot pressure of helpless persecution and a desire to lash out. She firmly quashed it.

"Take us to that place with the tables, Dino," Leander instructed the driver as he took his seat behind the wheel. "And check the score, would you?"

"Very good, sir." Dino plugged his ears with wireless buds.

Ilona texted her driver to enjoy some personal time and ensured her location was on for her assistant. Then she glanced at her messages and saw Midas wanted her to call. Ugh. She dropped her phone into her clutch.

"You don't seize these moments to be productive?" Leander asked with idle curiosity. His own phone was in his hand, but he seemed to be watching her the way a boxer might study his opponent before climbing into the ring.

"You requested my schedule be cleared. What could possibly be more important than giving you my undivided attention?" she asked to the window as they came up to the street.

"Again with the flirting," he chided.

She turned her head to regard him, trying for a look of infinite patience, but she caught him with his head angled so he could see her ankles.

"What?" She tucked her feet in the other direction and glanced to see if she had scuffed a shoe. Dear heaven, she hadn't paraded through his building with toilet paper stuck to her heel, had she? That really would take the cake. No. She was fine, thank goodness.

"I'm thinking," he murmured as she met his gaze again. There was speculation there, *masculine* speculation.

Ilona knew she was attractive. Her mother had been classically beautiful and Ilona took after her. If anything, she downplayed her looks, but it didn't stop men from coming on to her.

She often wished she had stayed in that awkward stage when she'd had uneven teeth, a flat chest and oversize features on her elfin face. Odessa had reveled in humiliating her over her flaws then, but at least Ilona hadn't been slut-shamed or treated like a sex object.

The older girls at boarding school were responsible for her transformation. They had taken her on as a makeover project, proud of themselves until Ilona finished blossoming with pinup curves and starlet features. At that point she became a rival, whispered about behind jealous hands. Nascent friendships had been cast off in favor of knocking her down.

When she returned home, Odessa had despised and punished Ilona *especially* because she was younger and more beautiful than Odessa would ever be.

Beauty was a form of armor, though. Ilona wore hers at all times and kept it polished to blinding perfection. Which was another reason she had no interest in marriage. Men didn't want her. They only wanted to possess her beauty like a shiny car.

"I honestly can't think of one thing you could offer me that would persuade me to marry you," she informed him.

"Can't you?" His gaze drifted across her features like a caress, settling on her mouth with such intense interest, her lips tingled.

Her heart rate picked up and she rolled her lips inward to press the buzzing out of them.

"No," she choked and snapped her attention forward. Her whole life had been on the wrong side of a seesaw's power imbalance. She wouldn't fill her future with more of it. Her heart constricted at the very thought. "I've explained that I don't wish to be used as a weapon. That goes doubly for being one that's used against myself."

Her stilted words caused a sting of humiliation to crawl up her neck into her cheeks. She couldn't look at him and only hoped he wouldn't play dumb and demand she spell it out further.

After a beat, he said, "You're refreshingly frank."

"Better to call it out than pretend it's not there. That really would allow you to use it as a weapon." Her face was on fire, her chest a cavern of ice, but defensiveness and denial only emphasized a weakness. She'd learned that the hard way.

"You don't see sexual attraction as a weapon *you* can use?"

"On you? Pfft. No." He was far too sophisticated and experienced with seduction. His sexually charged, *I remember her very well* on that phone call when she'd arrived had told her that.

Her sexual experience was confined to rebuffing it. Before him, that had always been relatively easy. Today, she was battling herself. It was distressing to feel so helpless against such a strong attraction. Her gaze kept wanting to swivel back to him and slide all over him. Sitting close to him was agony, making her skin feel tight and prickly. Aware.

She knew he hated her and some puerile part of her wanted him to *like* her, which was self-destructive. She had been taught long ago not to wish for positive regard from people who despised her. That way lay madness.

She smoothed a wrinkle from her skirt, ensuring the hem covered her knee an extra centimeter.

"You've already explained that you'll use any door to debase my family," she said stiffly. "The one to my bedroom is firmly dead bolted. Don't bother knocking."

She expected a tasteless comment about picking her lock. She got profound silence.

She glanced at him.

His features had turned to granite, causing a small lurch in her chest as she realized she had made a mistake.

"Don't judge me by the standards you're familiar with, Ilona. Unlike your brother, there are certain legal and ethical lines I will never cross."

Had she *insulted* him? That would suggest he cared what she thought of him.

He left her pondering that as they arrived at the restaurant. They were shown through a busy dining room with a full outdoor patio.

It certainly was a place with tables, one so full it would afford them very little privacy.

The host led them to stone stairs and Leander briefly touched her lower back to indicate she should precede him.

With her spine tingling from that innocuous touch, she followed the host upward to a wide breezeway with a half wall that hid them from the dining area below. Here, a half dozen tables were spaced well apart. Between each, tall planters overflowed with fragrant geraniums and colorful petunias. The shade ensured the temperature was several degrees cooler and the din from below was muffled. Plus, they were high enough to see the blue line of the Aegean as well as catch the soft, salt-flavored breeze that floated in from the water.

"This is lovely. I didn't know it existed."

"It's one of my best-kept secrets. Kindly keep it that way. Wine?"

"Light and white, please."

He ordered, requesting the special which was a seafood platter for two.

"Now. Tell me all the reasons you are hesitant to marry me. We've established that bedroom activities will be negotiated separately. What else?"

She opened her mouth, but was briefly too bemused by his assumption to find words.

"Because I don't wish to tie myself to a stranger for the rest of my life," she finally blurted. "Is that something that genuinely appeals to you?"

"It doesn't have to be a lifetime. Ten years would do."

"I'm not throwing away ten years of fertility," she assured him.

"You said you don't want children."

"I don't want children with you," she clarified, grateful the wine arrived. She washed away her fib with a gulp of icy tang flavored with fruit and smoke and a hint of nougat.

Because, as potential mates went, Leander was ridiculously fit for the job. He was healthy and strong, powerful and prosperous, not to mention easy on the eye. At twenty-four, she wasn't in a hurry to start a family, but he was the first man who had made her think seriously about starting one.

He was the first man to make her think about *making* babies.

His eyes narrowed on her and she had the sense he was affronted. She took another gulp, cooling the heat rising in her throat.

"Five years," he suggested.

"That still puts me at thirty before I'm divorced and looking for a suitable father. No."

"Five years, separation after three."

"Are you really willing to go three years without sex? Or are you proposing an open arrangement?" She didn't know why she asked. Yes, she did. Because it would humiliate her to sit at home while he was out getting his jollies with someone else. For the first time in her life, she felt a pinch of empathy for Odessa, forced to raise the consequence of her husband's habitual wandering eye.

"We'll keep it simple." Leander made every statement sound as though it was an agreed decision that would go into a contract they were negotiating. "No affairs. Yes, I'm confident I can survive three years without sex. Why? What's your record?"

Twenty-four years and four months, not that it was any of his business.

"I honestly don't understand how you see this marriage benefiting you," she said with fraying patience. "What would you gain beyond the ability to make my life difficult? I am not Midas, Leander. If you want to punish him, please highjack him into lunch and invite him to partake in your honeymoon of celibacy."

"What I will get, *glykiá mou*, is your shares in Pagonis," he explained with exaggerated patience and a self-satisfied smile. "They will be *your* wedding gift to *me*."

"So you can dismantle and destroy the company my father's grandfather started? I already told you I think that's awful. I won't facilitate it."

"I'm not asking you to." He sobered. "You made your point. Harming the workforce is poor justice and it won't cause Midas to lose any sleep. No. I'll use my influence to oust him instead."

"As president? I admire your optimism, but if my portion in Pagonis afforded that sort of influence, I would have done it myself by now."

"No, you wouldn't. You said you pick your battles and you clearly don't want one with him. I have more of a taste for blood. If someone picks a battle with me, I stay in it until I win."

She didn't doubt that for a second. If she wasn't very careful, she would wind up married to him despite her best effort to avoid it.

"Be honest," he cajoled. "Who would you rather see running Pagonis? Midas or me?"

"That's not a fair question. I don't know you." She rolled the stem of her wineglass between her fingers, considering what she had read about him, once she had realized he was buying up shares in her company. Leander had seemed to innovate his way to the top of his field. He had taken big risks and leapt on opportunities—like shares in her company—but there weren't any whiffs of bribery or other heinous tactics.

Unlike Midas, who was capable of anything.

"Is your recipe for low-carbon cement really yours?" she asked.

"There you go lumping me in with your brother again." Leander curled his lip. "I don't steal my innovations. I develop them myself. Answer my question."

"I'm thinking." She was thinking about having complete control over Callas without Midas interfering. She was thinking about Midas facing a comeuppance that was long overdue. Dear heaven, that was such a tempting vision.

However.

"You're right. I don't want a fight with Midas. He makes a ferocious enemy, as you must know. I'm not actually an object, Leander. Do you realize that? You want me to be your blade or bullet or *pawn*. That's not how Midas will see it. He will see it as a betrayal. All this anger you have toward him will be gathered up by Midas and turned onto me. There is no win for me in what you're proposing. At least while Callas is under the Pagonis umbrella, I have some protection."

"I'm not going to let anyone, least of all that bastard, come after my wi—" Leander sat back, mouth setting into a grim line as his laser-sharp gaze fixed on something over her shoulder. "Speak of the devil. Did you tell him where we were?"

"Who? Midas?" Her heart came into her mouth and a wash of ice water went through her, stilling all the what-ifs and maybes that she had allowed to swirl inside her. She didn't turn to look, saying woodenly, "My assistant likely did."

"Why?" Leander's infuriated gaze stayed on his enemy, but she felt his anger flaring out to encompass her, eroding the small degree of respect she'd earned from him.

It was startlingly painful to feel his regard yanked away so abruptly.

"Hey," an American man called from one of the other tables. "My wife is using that. She's coming right back."

Ilona turned her head to see Midas was ignoring the American and coming at them with a stolen chair. He set it backward at their table and straddled it as he sat, arms folded across the back. His glare of bitter accusation fell over Ilona like a jar over a spider.

He looked so much like their father from his square face to his barrel chest, it was always disconcerting to see stark hatred thrown at her from features that had usually worn an expression of patronizing fondness.

She forced herself to meet Midas's filthy look with an impassive one, but her pulse was galloping and a fizz of alarm shot through her when Leander abruptly stood. Was he *leaving*? Well, that was just great, wasn't it?

Leander handed his chair to the man who'd chased Midas. Then Leander folded his arms and looked down his nose at both of them.

Ilona had to admire how neatly he had turned the tables on Midas's attempt at a power grab. Perhaps he *was* strong enough to take on the bane of her existence.

If he was, that was a caution in itself, one she should heed.

"I told Feodor that you should call me," Midas said without preamble.

"I got that message, but I'm having lunch with my new partner in Callas." She waved at Leander.

Midas didn't look at him. His cheek ticked with barely suppressed rage.

"Why? Rideaux is rallying the board members, insisting we sell our Callas shares to him." He jerked his head at Leander. "I told Rideaux to hang tight because you had promised to counter. That is what you're doing, isn't it?" The threat in his voice poured terror into her blood.

But she saw immediately—*immediately*—that Midas had lied when he had said he would accept her counteroffer for the Pagonis shares. His goal was to instigate a bidding war between her and Leander. He didn't care who got the shares in the end so long as the price went up, filling his coffers before he cut her loose completely.

No wonder he was incensed to find her conspiring with Leander.

How could she still be so naive that she had missed the depth of his avarice?

"Tell me you are not cutting a deal with him, Ilona," Midas said grimly. He would never let her forget this. Never. She wanted to cry at Leander. *See what you've done?* But Leander wouldn't care that he had called this punishment down upon her. In his mind, she was a Pagonis and deserved nothing but pain.

She wanted to run. Literally run away, but she was cornered both physically and figuratively. Midas sat on the chair and Leander stood in the space to the left of the table, both blocking her into the end of the breezeway.

"Ilona and I have been discussing options," Leander

said. "She has made clear that she doesn't wish to be used as a pawn or a weapon against you."

A contemptuous curl arrived at the corner of Midas's mouth, one that said, *I knew it*. Pathetic little Ilona, too afraid of him to betray him.

"I've assured her that I wouldn't dream of putting my wife in such a position," Leander continued.

"What?" Midas finally snapped his attention up to Leander.

What? Ilona's heart nearly fell out of her mouth.

"Ilona and I are getting married," Leander stated, holding Midas's gaze while thrusting out a hand to her.

"That is not true." Midas's hand curled into a fist on the back of the chair. "Is it, Ilona?"

A choice had to be made. Stick with the devil she knew or align with a new one.

The waves were crashing and frothing angrily below, but it suddenly struck her that *she* was the doll. *She* was on fire, slowly being scorched and damaged and turned to ash.

There was only one way to douse those flames. *Leap.*

She rose and accepted Leander's hand. Her heart exploded with trepidation as the ground fell away from beneath her.

Leander was right there, pulling her into the solid wall of his body as though he could shelter her from the impact.

"Between us, we have a majority in Callas," Leander was saying to Midas. "My offer for the fifteen percent stands, but tell the board to sell it to whomever they wish. We don't need it."

Menace darkened Midas's complexion. "You're making a mistake, Ilona."

She couldn't speak. She was in that disorienting, breathless place where sound was muffled and everything had become a blur. She couldn't tell which way was up.

Leander's arm was crushing her. Maybe that's why she couldn't breathe, but his firm grip told her she wasn't in this cold, airless place alone. She let her arm slide behind his back, clasping on to him while she searched for something to say.

"Excuse us," Leander said dismissively. "We're celebrating."

"I bet you are." Midas jerked to his feet, toppling his chair and leaving it where it fell against the stones.

As he walked away, he met the waiter with the platter of seafood they had ordered. Midas knocked it out of the man's hand, raining shrimp and calamari onto the patrons below.

He ignored the shouts of anger and kept walking.

A surge of triumph had Leander barking out a laugh and throwing both his arms around his *fiancée*, squeezing her lithe form while he started to plant an exuberant kiss—

She went stiff with rejection. Her face had drained so her complexion was more olive than honey-gold. Her arm was bent against his chest, not pushing him away, but tense enough to hold him off. Her thick black lashes were lowered to hide her eyes, but her mouth was tight with anxiety.

She was trembling so hard, a different compulsion rocked through him, the kind that wanted to cradle her close. He smoothed his hand over her narrow back, disconcerted to realize she was much slighter than she seemed. The way beauty radiated off her created a halo of presence that was bigger than she physically was.

"Are you going to faint?" he asked with concern.

"Of course not. But I've lost my appetite. I'd like to leave." She extricated herself from his hold and reached for her handbag on the edge of the table.

Somehow, her hand took a wild lurch and knocked over her glass of wine.

Her inhale was a sharp tear of sound. He braced for a scream to come out of her, but she only stared at the spreading stain, body so taut he thought one touch would cause her to shatter.

She carefully released her breath and looked at his shirt button. Her mouth was quivering, her eyes unblinking. "I'll find my own way back."

"I'll take you."

She didn't argue, only started for the stairs.

The server met them there and assured them their meal would be remade immediately.

"We're leaving. Bill me for our meal and for all the guests who were affected. Allow them to order anything else they wish." Leander left Androu's number for the invoice.

As they slid into his vehicle, he was still hungry for food, still thirsty for blood. Still grimly gratified, but wondering if he had overplayed his hand. It had been very satisfying to watch his enemy take that kick to the stomach, but he would have preferred to spring the marriage on Midas when it was a fait accompli.

The way Ilona was reacting had him wondering if she would try to back out.

"What made you side with me?" he asked curiously.

She was bringing her phone to her ear and held up a trembling finger. Her voice was unsteady as she said, "It's me— Yes, I know, Feodor. I just saw him. No, that's fine."

"Is that your assistant? *Fire him*," Leander said in a spark of temper. Everything he'd been trying to do today had been jeopardized by Midas showing up in the middle of it. If Androu had ever revealed his whereabouts without his consent, he would know he was terminated before Leander had to think the words.

Ilona ignored him. "Tell Eugene to make a code yellow

adjustment and meet me at the curb in fifteen minutes. Do that now, then come back to me." She angled the phone away from her mouth. "Please take me to my office, Dino. I mean it this time."

"Yes, *kyría*." Dino pulled out and headed east.

"I don't expect my employees to stand between me and my family," Ilona told Leander. "Feodor knows to be as circumspect as possible, but Midas would only install spies in my company if he didn't get the information he wants when he wants it. Feodor weighs the cost benefit and— Yes, I'm here." She went back to her call. "I need to meet with accounting and legal as soon as I'm in the building. See if you can get my own accountant and lawyer into a room in the next day or two. I also want to speak with the property agent who found my flat."

"I have a property agent," Leander interjected. "We'll meet with her together to find a house that suits us both."

He should be on his own phone, telling Androu to set up his own meetings, but he was morbidly fascinated by Ilona's swiftness to action. Disturbingly, it reminded him of those initial hours after he'd found his father, when his mind had been crystal clear and he'd done all the things so fast he couldn't even remember how the emergency personnel had been notified or his father's body removed. He'd come back to awareness two weeks later, rocked out of his stupor to realize he was in a utility vehicle rambling across the tundra without any recollection of how his father had been laid to rest or who had tried to console him.

"Hold a moment, Feodor." She lowered the phone. "We can meet with your agent, but I need mine for something else. What is our timeline? Do you want a proper wedding? I don't. They take ages to organize and I'd prefer something quiet since this isn't—"

"Short timeline, big splash," he stated. "Weeks not months. I'll arrange the wedding if you don't want to."

She made a face and went back to her assistant. "I need you to hire a wedding planner—" Something Feodor said broke through her shield and she gave a bemused shake of her head. "You're such a cliché sometimes. Yes, take the lead, but you can't do it all yourself. I have a lot to accomplish in the next short while so hire a professional planner and— Pardon? Oh, it's, um…" Her stark expression slid to Leander. The pinpoints of her pupils exploded to swallow the dark brown of her irises. "I'm marrying Leander Vasilou."

Her words struck in his ears like a hammer, reverberating through his whole being. He was doing this. Marrying her. A Pagonis.

He didn't even know if he could trust her. A phrase he'd heard his English mother once use emerged from his suppressed childhood. *Marry in haste, repent at leisure.*

"Almost there," Ilona said, peering forward. "Send my private number to Leander's assistant. I'll see you in a moment." She ended the call and dropped her phone into her clutch.

Callas Cosmetics had manufacturing facilities around the world, but its head office and research laboratory were still located in its original building, one that Ilona had taken over from a long-defunct textile plant, revitalizing a depressed area into upscale industry.

Dino drew to a halt outside the glass-fronted entrance and left the car, coming around to Leander's door where he waited for Leander's signal before opening it.

At the same time, a nondescript man in a dark suit emerged from the lobby. He had a hand to his ear as he spoke through an earpiece to some unseen party.

"You ordered an escort into the building?" Code yellow

explained. Leander scanned an alert gaze up and down the block. "Are you concerned Midas will confront you here?"

"He'll send Hercules first. Maybe Odessa." She clamped both hands over the top of her clutch. "I don't know if you realize what you have unleashed, Leander. Don't let his name fool you. Midas turns everything he touches to poison, not gold."

"I know." His chest tightened as his mind conjured his last glimpse of his father. "Is that why you sided with me? You consider me the lesser of two evils?"

She ran restless hands over the smooth patent leather of her bag, seeming to choose her words carefully.

"With respect, I sided with myself. As long as my father was alive, and Pagonis International owned a piece of my company, I was forced to maintain positive relations with Midas. Today, you offered me a way to sever ties. I took it. I *will* take it." Her eyes were hollow caves, her cheekbones like tent poles beneath gaunt drapes. "I'm under no illusion that you won't cut me loose if it serves your purpose. I'm prepared to do the same if it comes down to a choice between you or me."

"We continue to prove how well suited we are," he drawled.

"Will you let me out, please? People are waiting for me."

Leander knocked on the window and Dino opened the door. Leander rose and helped Ilona from the car. Her hand was pure ice in his.

He held on to it for an extra second, preventing her from walking away, forcing her to glance questioningly at him.

"I'll collect you for dinner at seven."

"If you'd like," she said in the tone that said she picked her battles and had no desire to engage in this one. "I'll see you then."

CHAPTER FOUR

ILONA WAS EXHAUSTED from a day of sustained stress made worse by pretending she was overjoyed about a marriage she had deep reservations about agreeing to.

By the time she was dressing for dinner, all she wanted to do was crawl into a bath and go to bed early. She wanted to lock the door of her flat and stay here forever, rather than march forward on the path she'd charted.

She still couldn't tell if she had exercised agency or pushed the self-destruct button on her life. It had been enormously satisfying to get the better of Midas—for about three seconds. Which was about how long her actions would impact him. He *would* retaliate and the dread of waiting to learn what form it would take was agonizing.

She might have withstood his attack, might have been able to take every precaution and feel protected against him, but she had this other unprotected flank—the one she'd exposed to Leander.

If she had wanted to finally take on Midas, she really ought to have chosen a partner she could trust. Instead, she'd made a bargain with a complete stranger—one who was equally powerful and dangerous and had a grudge against her.

In fact, he was *more* dangerous to her. Rather than intimidate her into doing things she didn't want to do, he had *enticed* her. He had inspired her with his complete lack of fear where Midas was concerned, making her believe in his strength. In her own.

But her mind kept wanting to go back to that moment at the restaurant when she had stood and grasped his hand. If only she could push Undo. Nothing about this felt safe. It felt like the longest long shot and she had never been a gambler.

There was no going back, though. The scene at the restaurant had turned the paparazzi's interest on to them. Her PR department was already fielding calls asking if their association was business or romantic.

Whatever happened from now on would play out under a relentless spotlight of media attention so she took extra care with her appearance, expecting to be photographed with Leander tonight. Her midlength dress was a figure-hugging satin slip with an emerald-green lace overlay. An onyx clip over her left ear held her hair off her face, but she left the rest loose. She added drama to her eyes and lips and slipped on shoes that were an inch taller than her typical day wear.

The doorman called up as she was moving her things into her evening clutch, informing her that Hercules had arrived to see her.

Right on time, she thought dourly.

"I'll meet him in the lobby." In the past, she had let Hercules up, but not today. Not for the foreseeable future.

Hercules was two years younger than she was and had once been a wellspring of affection toward her, back when they'd been small enough to snuggle while watching cartoons. Eventually, he had been forced to choose, though. His mother didn't care for rivals, especially when it came to the men in her life. Ilona didn't blame Hercules for taking the less painful route of allowing Ilona to be the target of censure so he didn't have to be, but it still hurt.

She felt for him, though. He hadn't had the chance to prove himself to their father before Apollo Pagonis had died. It had been an uphill battle anyway. Apollo had fostered an atmosphere of competition among his children, promising the most successful would run the corporation he'd inherited from his own father. Midas had been several years ahead of them and had stolen Leander's technology to win that race. Ilona had come a close second with her honestly earned cosmetic enterprise—even if that had always been seen as a folly of little consequence.

Hercules had the soul of an artist. He had struggled with economics and spreadsheets, compromising by turning his talents to marketing, but his heart wasn't in it. He suffered in lonely silence on the inside of the wall that separated her from being a "real" Pagonis.

Tonight, he was more melancholy than usual. His shoulders were a sloped line, his mop of Technicolor hair mussed by his own hand. His eyes flashed wide with persecution as he spotted her coming off the elevator and he rushed forward.

"Ilona. *What* are you doing?"

"I have a date," she said, deliberately misunderstanding him.

Hercules dipped his head to speak in a low voice. "He'll make your life a living hell. You know that, don't you?" He was speaking about Midas and shot a look to the doorman behind his desk, as if that man would report him for speaking ill of his brother. "I can't protect you this time."

"How is that different from the status quo?" she asked with a blink.

His features tightened. "That's not fair. You don't know what I do."

No, she didn't. She experienced another pang that he might have tried in the past to help her and yet his efforts remained invisible. Ineffectual. How demoralizing for both of them.

"Now you don't have to put yourself out," she said gently. "My car is here," she noted as Dino halted outside and Leander stepped out.

"Ilona." Hercules grabbed her arm as she started to brush by. "*Not him.* Not like this. Midas was *incensed*. So was Mother," he added abstractly.

Because marriage meant children. Ilona *should* get pregnant with Leander's baby. There would be a macabre delight in tormenting Odessa with that nightmare scenario.

"Ask Midas why *not* Leander," she advised. "Excuse me. I don't want to keep my fiancé waiting."

Hercules tightened his grip while Leander yanked open the door into the lobby and asked in a lethal voice, "Do you need help, Ilona?"

"No," she said mildly while his tone caused her heart to crash around in her chest like a loose cannonball.

"You don't even know him," Hercules accused as he released her. "What makes you think you'll be better off with him? Ask *him* why *you*."

She already knew why her. And no, his motives weren't lily white, but at least he'd been up-front with her about them. She ignored Hercules and walked outside where she manufactured a smile for Dino as he opened the car door for her. She stole a calming breath as she slipped inside.

"Are you all right?" Leander asked as he came in behind her.

"Perfectly," she lied because what was the use in admitting she was petrified? Hercules might not be very good at protecting her, but he was never wrong when he forewarned her.

"Did you read the press release?" Leander asked her as they got underway.

"I did. That date will work." Even though it meant she had only three short weeks of freedom before she walked into a new cage. *What* was she doing with her life?

"I'll tell Androu." Leander placed the call as they drove. That didn't surprise her. He was locking her into her decision. She understood that. It compressed the air in her lungs, but there was no going back. She knew that, too.

"Excellent news," Leander said as he finished his call and tucked his phone away. "After he left us, Midas tried to stop my purchase of your shares. Rideaux squeezed another two percent out of me, but I only gave it on condition he rally the board by midnight. He rammed it through and those shares will be yours on our wedding day."

"That is good news." She forced the corners of her mouth upward. "My lawyer is working on the language to give you control of my shares in Pagonis. I can't give them to you outright, but I can designate you to manage them and vote in my stead. She'll forward my terms for the prenuptial agreement to your lawyer by the end of the week. For the most part, I suggest we retain the property we bring to the marriage so we'll only have to split what we acquire jointly, like the house we purchase to share."

"Agreed."

So civilized.

Ilona supposed she should be grateful, but she had always imagined that if she did marry, it would be driven by a burning desire to be with that other person. Trust would be so deeply ingrained in the relationship, cold details like contracts and conditions for their divorce would be completely absent from the process.

Next time, she assured herself ironically while also feeling a pang that this marriage was temporary. He didn't really want her and that was so much like the rest of her family, it scored deep lines behind her heart.

They arrived at the restaurant on Lycabettus Hill and caused a small stir as they were shown onto the terrace. Their table overlooked the twinkle of the city, the glowing Parthenon and the three-quarter moon casting its light on the smooth Aegean.

"Our reputation precedes us," she murmured as he helped her with her light wrap. "I don't suppose anyone will notice the view tonight."

"I certainly won't. You look lovely. Are you cold? Would you like to keep this?"

His casual compliment and the brush of his touch against her shoulders had caused goose bumps to rise on her skin.

Discomfited, she murmured, "I'm fine."

He handed off her wrap to the hovering maître d' before he held her chair for her.

Between his solicitous gesture and the melody of stringed instruments and the soft breeze, this was the most romantic date she'd ever been on. Yet it wasn't that at all, she acknowledged with a pinch of melancholy.

Leander studied her as he took his seat, gaze delving into hers while his expression remained inscrutable.

"Second thoughts?" he asked as though he could read past the serene mask she had learned to wear in self-protection.

Her pulse tripped, but she pressed a light smile onto her lips. "And third, fourth and fifth. You?"

"None."

His resolve made her nerves jangle.

"Shall we make this official?" he asked.

"I thought our lawyers were doing that?"

"I mean this." He reached into his jacket pocket and set a velvet box beside the small lantern between them.

"Oh." Her breath rushed out of her and, inexplicably, the backs of her eyes stung.

Gasps rose from nearby tables. Her throat went dry and she clenched her hands in her lap, but there was nothing to grasp on to. Her grip on her previous life was gone.

"You know how to keep an audience in suspense, don't you?" he murmured when she only stared at the tiny box. "I was going to ask you to pick it yourself, but when I saw that it reminded me of the ring you were wearing this morning. See what you think."

Had it only been this morning that they'd met and agreed to this caper?

To her mortification, her hands were visibly shaking as she reached for it. She heard another ripple of amused emotion travel through their audience.

How excruciating. She was a private person at the best of times and now everyone saw how she was reacting. *He* saw it.

She pried the box open and a dazzling marquise-cut diamond flashed like an arc weld into her eye. It was bridged over a spiral band of pavé-set diamonds, echoing the style of her day ring.

"It's beautiful." She was nearly struck speechless, unable to think of the last time she had received a gift of any kind, let alone something so lovely and personal. Something she instantly adored with her whole heart.

"It should fit. Your assistant really does give up too much of your personal information." He pinched the ring to remove it from the box, then held out his other hand in request for hers.

His warm fingers cradled the fine bones of her hand and the cool weight slid up her finger, nestling into place as though it belonged there. A signal seemed to pulse from the flashing stone all the way up her arm to spark in her chest.

"No moving this one," he said with a light tap against her knuckle. "It stays here to remind you that I'm in your life."

As if she could forget! It was such a patently silly thing to suggest, a day's worth of tension sputtered out of her in befuddled laughter.

His remote expression altered, softening into something that made her heart skip and the rest of her say, *Oh*.

Then applause rose around them, reminding her they were under intense scrutiny.

She started to withdraw her hand from his, but some joker started clinking a knife against a glass in that annoying demand for a groom to kiss his bride.

"Shall we?" Leander kept her hand and stood to draw her to her feet.

Did they have to? Sex was off the table, but they hadn't said anything about kissing. She could have demurred. She could have done anything, but she let him draw her to him.

Goodness, he was tall! She was five-eight and wore three-inch heels, but he still towered over her. His broad shoulders blocked her from most of the prying eyes, which was a small relief, but his arms were sliding around her, gathering her close. His gaze held hers as his head dipped.

Her lips softened and parted as his mouth arrived...at the corner of hers.

That might have been all it was, but she accidentally turned the two millimeters needed so her mouth was under his. She lifted her chin to invite more. More pressure. More heat. More of the swirling fog that closed over her as he waited a single beat before his mouth sealed firmly over hers, commanding and suddenly hungry.

She hadn't realized she was calling up a storm. His arms firmed around her as his tongue dabbed, then he devoured her. It wasn't the taking of a ferocious wind that stripped her naked, though. It felt a little like that. She was bowed and defenseless against an unseen force, but in the same way he had coaxed her to detonate her own life, he brought forth a burst of sensuality from within her. She was suddenly soaked in need. In *yearning*. In a compulsion to lean into the wildness and become part of it.

As sensations rocked and ripped through her, she lost track of where she was. She swayed and clung to his strength, reveling in the movement of his hands across her back, giving herself up to this plundering kiss. His strength was all that held her up and, for a few moments, she felt safe here, even as every ounce of her self-possession was incinerated.

Joyful laughter and applause penetrated, reminding her they were in public.

She wanted to cringe away, then. Hopefully, he would believe she was only playing her part the same way he must be. *He* hadn't completely abandoned his pride, though. Only her. How debasing.

"Will you let me go, please?" she asked into his throat.

"I can't," he growled. "My cuff link is caught in the lace of your dress. Also, your lipstick is smudged. Is it all over my mouth?"

She dared a glance upward. What a depressing comedy of errors.

She stole his pocket square and, staying close against the shelter of his chest, surreptitiously swept the linen around the border of her lips. She lifted her lashes in question.

"Better," he assured her and took it with his free hand. He scrubbed it across his own mouth before he thrust it into the side pocket of his jacket.

Then he peered over her shoulder, arms encircling her as he carefully untangled himself.

She belatedly realized what was pressed against her stomach. His erection.

A bolt of shocked delight—and shock that she was de-lighted—went through her. Perhaps he hadn't been faking the passion in his kiss?

He released her and cool air swirled across her over-heated skin. He helped her with her chair and used the drape of his jacket to hide his fly as he retook his seat.

She might have sat there in a state of complete shock, but a server arrived with champagne. The cork popped and please, *please* let that be the last time the rest of the diners clapped and cheered.

"To us," Leander said as they touched the rims of their tall flutes.

She drank hers way too fast.

CHAPTER FIVE

LEANDER HADN'T SEEN ILONA since their engagement dinner two nights ago. After their passionate kiss, she had steered their conversation to pedestrian topics like a tentative guest list and their preferences for a house. They had said their good-nights outside her building without another kiss or an invitation to join her upstairs—not that he had expected one, previous, mind-blowing kiss notwithstanding.

That kiss had kept him hard nearly every minute since, however. It had been meant as a brief stamp of finality on their deal, but she had turned her head ever so slightly and her mouth had melted like spun sugar beneath his own. Who knew a kiss could catch fire? Not him, but in seconds a conflagration had surrounded them.

He had stood within it, reveled in it, while her lithe body pressed against his in surrender. If he hadn't felt his cuff become snared in her dress, he might be kissing her still.

But he had and that had been a necessary moment of sanity.

Even so, he wondered through the next hours and days if they really would eschew sex when they had such incredible chemistry. He wasn't a masochist so why torture himself if she was amenable?

Thirty minutes ago, he had received his answer. His head of PR had tipped him off to a rumor circulating about his intended. He didn't want to believe it, but it would explain why Ilona had leapt on his proposal so unexpectedly and kissed him with such fervor.

Did she think he was born yesterday? What he had briefly forgotten was that she was a Pagonis. They were born without a conscience.

The question was, would he go through with marrying her to achieve what he wanted despite the way she was trying to pull the wool over his eyes?

"There she is." Ursula, his property agent, noted Ilona's car was approaching up the drive of the villa they were here to view.

When the car halted, Leander opened the back door himself. Ilona's calf and half her thigh briefly flashed from the slit in her skirt, sending an irritating jolt of heat into his groin.

He didn't *want* to respond to her, but now that he'd had that brief taste, he couldn't help it. Everything about her appealed to his basest instincts, making him want to touch and taste and explore and own.

As she straightened, she started to slip on her sunglasses, but he stopped her.

"We'll be inside. You don't need those." He stole them and dropped them into the backseat, wanting to see every thought and machination that crossed her deceptive heart.

A hundred emotions glinted and sparked in the melted chocolate of her irises, from surprise to nervous searching of his gaze to wary vulnerability. Her lashes flickered as she dropped her attention to his mouth, seeming to expect a greeting.

He was tempted to kiss the hell out of her. Would she give herself up in the same way every time? He was dying to know, but he confined himself to a brief brush of his lips against her cheek.

Erotic memory wafted into his brain with the subtle fragrance of anise and roses that clung to her skin, enticing him, but he didn't give in.

"Meet Ursula," he said abruptly.

Ilona's mouth might have briefly trembled in rejection, but he was learning that she had a talent for overcoming moments of transparency. It was as maddening as it was admirable, but it was also a reason to be cautious, reminding him she kept a lot hidden.

"It's nice to meet you." She shook the agent's hand.

Leander walked behind them as Ursula escorted Ilona inside and extolled the virtues of the property. The neighborhood of Ekali was a prime location and this terraced estate was very private, surrounded by trees while still affording mountain views from its tiers of verandas and balconies.

They paused in the foyer where black-and-white tiles were arranged in concentric circles beneath a dome that poured sunlight onto the wide spiral staircase. Grand archways ensured the entire ground level flowed from one room into another. An airy lounge became a music room and then a dining area. At the back, a wall of glass opened onto the garden and further along, the pool.

Ursula knew Leander well. She mentioned the indoor pool and the servants' quarters in the lower floor, then wrapped up her pitch, suggesting they explore the rest on their own.

That suited him. He wanted a private word with his fiancée.

Ilona was quiet as they returned to the main staircase and walked up, but he sensed her glancing surreptitiously at him from beneath her lashes.

A second, equally splendid spiral took them to the top floor which was completely reserved as a master suite with separate bedrooms, each with its own bath. A small lounge connected the two rooms. The house was built into a hill-side, so there was a walk-out to an upper garden along with a balcony that overlooked the pool.

As they squinted against the sunshine, assessing the view, Leander considered whether to ask her outright if she was using him to hide an unplanned pregnancy or whether it was better to feed her enough rope to hang herself.

"I think it's perfect," Ilona said in the exceedingly polite tone he found so unsatisfying.

"Really? I hate it." He really did. There were too many stairs, too much deliberate opulence. It was both claustro-phobic with the surrounding trees, and yet had a view that was uninspiring. Also, he was in a very bad mood, unin-clined to like anything.

Ilona jerked at his antagonistic tone, but quickly recov-ered. "We're being honest?"

"I expect honesty at all times," he shot back.

Her chin briefly wobbled before she firmed it, but she held his gaze without flinching.

"Very well. I see value in the fact it's available immedi-ately. It meets our basic requirement for separate bedrooms and a convenient location to our work. If we close today, we won't have to waste time on further searching. I don't love the decor, but it will impress guests and has enough room for entertaining large crowds. It's not meant to be our home, only something we'll occupy for three years, so perhaps I should have said, 'It will do.'"

Three years. She wasn't looking for a father to actually raise her child, only support it and give it a name?

"'Large crowds?'" he repeated. "What happened to not wanting people in your space?"

"I thought entertaining was a legal requirement once you marry. While my father was alive, my stepmother threw dinner parties two or three times a week. She had several larger holiday bashes and charity galas throughout the year."

"Good God. Is that something you want to do?"

"Not in the least. After a busy day at work, I might entertain the neighbor's cat, but that's about all the interaction I'm up for."

Not the neighbor. The neighbor's *cat*. He didn't let himself be diverted by that whimsical little revelation, but he did enjoy it.

"I typically buy out a restaurant when I'm required to host anything. Or use my yacht."

"We could continue to do that. Or…" She went back inside where she looked around thoughtfully. "We could buy this as an investment. It could serve as a venue for our own events, but villas like this are in demand for destination weddings. It could provide an income when we don't need it."

That was actually a solid proposal.

"*We* could marry here," she continued, brightening. "Feodor would love that. He's having trouble finding a suitable location."

"Seriously, why do you keep him?" Leander asked with exasperation. "He seems completely incompetent."

She paused at the top of the stairs, jaw slack. Then her chin came up.

"It's not his fault. My stepmother keeps undermining him. She threatened two designers with ruin if they worked with me and fired one of her favorite caterers from a standing lunch contract simply because they submitted a quote for our reception."

"Which sounds like they're available. Where's the problem?" he drawled.

"That's not the point I'm making." She started down the

stairs. "Odessa is going out of her way to be obstructive. As I just explained, she made a career of entertaining. She knows everyone and put the word out that she will punish those who work on—or attend—our wedding. The invitations haven't even gone out, but Feodor has already received a dozen regrets."

"Why would she do that?" He moved to catch up with her, expecting Midas was behind it.

"Because she can. My relationship with her has always been difficult." Her lashes shielded her eyes as she continued downward.

"Why?" He kept his tone conversational, taking all of this with a grain of salt. She was clearly trying to discredit her stepmother in order to undermine any rumors that had reached his ears from that quarter.

"Why do you think? My father had an affair with my mother and, when she died, had the bright idea of insisting Odessa raise his bastard alongside her legitimate sons." Her profile was the deep carving of a cameo, still and sharp.

She stopped again and released a hiss of consternation.

He paused two steps lower so he was eye level when she pensively bit her bottom lip, reminding him how plump and lush it had tasted when he had roamed his tongue across it.

Why the hell did she have to be *so* enticing and *so* impossible to trust?

"I should tell you…" Her throat flexed. "Odessa is spreading some very ugly rumors about me. The most tasteless is that I'm pregnant. She's telling people that's why we're rushing this marriage, but that it's not even yours."

And there it was. She was attempting to get ahead of it by telling him herself, but he steeled himself against giving her any sort of credit for that.

"Are you?" he asked, forcing a tone of vague interest.

"Pregnant? No!" She was taken aback. Then, as she read

his skepticism, her mouth pressed into a line of grim resignation. "I see. This isn't new information. You already heard it and you believe it."

"She knows you better than I do." He canted his head. "I'd be a fool to discount it, especially given how quickly you agreed to marry me. If something seems too good to be true, it usually is."

"You think this marriage looks too good to be true? Pah!" She moved across the step, intending to brush past him.

He shifted to block her path.

Ilona pulled up short and straightened her spine, trying to look down her nose at him, but she wasn't quite tall enough for it to have an effect. Plus, her heart was racing at this confrontation and her head was about to explode. It was taking all her effort to maintain control of herself and not start to cry. True disdain was beyond her.

"If I were pregnant, I wouldn't have agreed to a celibate marriage," she pointed out. "Even a sucker who snaps up Odessa's lies like they're shares in Callas Cosmetics could figure out he wasn't the father if I never had sex with him."

"But you kissed me like you wanted to have sex on the table of the restaurant," he reminded her in a mockingly helpful tone.

Humiliation stabbed into the spot beneath her throat. She knew she was going red with guilt and shame, but she'd been attacked by sarcasm and false accusations enough that she kept her temper. Barely. Her voice shook when she spoke.

"It sounds as though you also bought the one where I'm a whore who gets her kicks by breaking up marriages. I genuinely don't care what you think of me, Leander, but let me assure you, there is *nothing* that could induce me to raise a child in a household where one parent resents them. Would you excuse me, please?"

She returned to the inside of the step and this time he let her pass. She reached the bottom and hurried her way across the foyer to the lounge where Ursula stood outside the windows, pacing in the shade of a tree as she spoke on her phone.

Leander came up behind her, but she refused to look back to see what was on his face. She held her arms crossed, but ensured her tense shoulders remained down and back, not hunched and defensive the way she wanted to pull them.

"Dumping me now will do nothing to hurt Midas," she pointed out, barely turning her head. "He'll dance a jig over my public disgrace, but that is the only effect it will have. Do whatever appeases that sickness inside you, though. I knew I couldn't count on you." She had contingency plans in place. Her agent hadn't found her a property yet, but she was looking.

"I didn't say I was dumping you." He arrived beside her at the window, hands shoved into his pockets. "I said I expect honesty."

She choked on a laugh of disbelief. "You don't believe a word I say! What does it matter if I tell you the truth or not?"

"You switched sides without remorse. It follows that you have ulterior motives."

"I told you what they were—to sever ties with them. I hate them more than you do."

"I doubt that."

"Of course, you do. Again, what's the point in telling you the truth if you presume I'm lying?" The backs of her eyes were hot and a scalded line sat behind her breastbone. It was the familiar ache of her feelings being dismissed and ignored. Disbelieved.

She sensed him looking at her, sensed his frustration that she would throw his words back in his face like that. Did he expect her to grovel and beg him to believe her? Been there, done that, had the emotional scars to prove it.

After a long minute, he grimly acknowledged, "This *is* war. They were bound to try to divide us."

Another choke of disparaging laughter escaped her. "I hate to dent your ego, Leander, but this isn't about you. I mean, Midas is always thrilled when Odessa makes my life difficult, but she's not doing it for him."

"Why then?"

There was an agonizing wrench in her chest. "It doesn't matter," she decided wearily.

"It sounds like it does matter. If you want me to trust you and believe what you say, tell me the truth, Ilona."

Persecution had her glaring her astonishment at him, wondering why he insisted on turning the knife within her.

"I *am* telling you the truth," she said on a burst of bitter outrage. "I was a child who was given no choice in where I went after my mother died. My father took me into his home, but I never had a place there. I wanted to be with him because he was all I had, but he was a tremendous sexist. He expected great things from his sons and very little from me because I was a girl. My education wasn't as important as my looking pretty and he thought he was indulging me when he invested in my company. He doted on me when it suited him and Odessa hated me for it. From the time I was five, she told me I was stupid and ugly, an abomination, a mistake, a burden and an embarrassment. Later, when I grew curves, I was a harlot and a source of shame. *Like my mother.*" She flicked out a hand, batting away the countless other insults that had been hurled over the years.

"Now that my father is gone, and she has this excuse, Odessa isn't holding back," she continued. "She will do everything in her power to make me regret my own existence. She's more than capable of it. I have often wished I had never been born, but that doesn't matter because *I* don't matter, as she has made clear a thousand times."

"Ilona." Leander's breath hissed in and his hand came out.

She tucked her elbow into her side, going stiff with rejection.

"Think what you want of me, Leander. I don't care." That was mostly true. She didn't want to care what he thought of her. "Just tell me whether I should cancel our engagement party this weekend. I could use the time more productively elsewhere."

He was staring hard enough to scorch the side of her face, but she only watched Ursula happily chattering away out there, oblivious to the war going on in here.

In a sudden move, Leander knocked on the window to catch Ursula's attention.

"The party is on," he said darkly. "We'll marry here and find something else that suits us better as a home."

CHAPTER SIX

DO WHATEVER APPEASES that sickness inside you.

That serrated knife of a remark from Ilona stuck itself deep in Leander's gut and slowly turned.

You don't know what they put me through, he had wanted to rail at her, but maybe she did. Maybe she did.

It was a disturbing thought that kept closing his hands into fists, as though he was trying to catch hold of something he hadn't glimpsed long enough to identify before it was gone. His mind kept conjuring her stillness, her sadness beneath that cloak of dignity that had struck him as tattered and torn while she explained why she wouldn't risk asking him to raise a child who wasn't his.

It had sickened him to hear it. He hadn't wanted to believe her.

But he had. Midas, it seemed, had not fallen far from the proverbial tree. His mother sounded equally sadistic and conscienceless.

So Leander was going ahead with this twisted alliance of theirs.

The rest of his week was nonstop meetings, allowing no time to see his fiancée. They mostly communicated through their assistants, much of it benign queries. Did he have opinions on wedding themes, menus or the font for the invitations? Leander did not. Did Ilona have a special request for their honeymoon? She did not.

The day of their engagement party arrived and it was one more appointment in today's packed calendar. Leander was on his way to his barber when Androu handed him an envelope marked Private and Confidential. The return address was Ilona Callas.

It jolted him to a halt in the middle of his office, but he didn't shy from whatever the envelope contained. He didn't know what he expected. A scathing suggestion he go forth and multiply? Perhaps the ring he'd given her?

It was a report from Ilona's physician certifying her pregnancy test was negative. She was also free of sexually transmitted infections and was deemed generally healthy, if slightly anemic. Her blood type was O positive.

Not pregnant. This was meant to satisfy any lingering doubts he might have, but it made him feel small. He swore tiredly.

"Kýrie?" Androu was hovering in anticipation of instructions.

"Book me an appointment with my doctor."

"Blood tests are only mandatory if you're marrying in a church. I looked it up."

"Book me an appointment, Androu."

"Immediately," Androu mumbled into his shirt front and exited the room.

A few hours later, Leander stopped by the clinic for the necessary procedures before making his way to his yacht.

Ilona was already aboard. On his instruction, she'd been given his stateroom for whatever entourage was helping her dress. He was already in his suit and found her in the shade of the lido deck, eating finger foods off a plate while listening intently to a young man who was gesturing as he spoke.

Leander's breath was punched out of him at the sheer beauty of her.

Her lightweight dress of ivory and seafoam green was pressed to her curves by the breeze. Most of her gleaming black hair had been gathered into a professionally messy pile of curls, but wisps drifted around her face. The style would allow the wind to muss it without damaging the look, he imagined, but that hint of dishevelment was sensual and touchable. Playful and enticing.

The young man splashed something invisible onto his own face and Ilona burst into laughter, covering her mouth. Her profile was so bright and naturally joyous, her body language so relaxed and graceful, Leander had to catch his breath again.

"May I bring you a drink?" someone asked at his elbow, forcing him to drag his gaze from her.

"Scotch over ice," he said abstractly. When he looked back, Ilona had ironed her expression into an aloof mask. She offered him a cool smile.

"Leander. I don't think you've had a chance to meet Feodor in person." Ilona introduced the twentysomething who wore glasses and a goatee.

"It's a pleasure to meet you, Kýrie Vasilou," Feodor said with a respectful nod. He glanced at Ilona. "Shall I help with guest arrivals?"

"Thank you."

Feodor melted away and Leander watched him go with a hostile gladness he'd never experienced before. Was he really threatened by his fiancée's nerdy employee? How adolescent of him.

But the PA obviously knew Ilona very well. Well enough to make her laugh.

"Did he tell you a joke?" He hated himself for wanting to know.

"Hmm? Oh. No." Her expression softened. "His niece and nephew are characters. I enjoy hearing about them. This yacht is beautiful." She quickly changed the subject and set aside the plate she was holding. "I can see why you like to host parties here."

"I like it because it forces people to show up on time or miss departure. The sunset waits for no one. You look lovely."

"Thank you," she said automatically, as though she thought he was only saying what was expected and she was returning in kind. He meant it, though. He could hardly take his eyes off her.

"I got your report," he said, wondering if that would make her look at him.

"Good." She smiled at the server who brought his scotch and requested a glass of wine.

"I took all the same tests today," Leander informed her as the server moved out of earshot. "Most of the results will take a few days, but they were able to tell me right away that I'm not pregnant."

"Reassuring," she said without inflection, but her lips twitched. She glanced away to hide it.

The most ridiculous tickle of triumph spread through his chest.

They didn't have time for any more banter. Guests were arriving.

They had kept the party semiformal and small enough that it felt exclusive. "Small" was still a hundred guests. Once underway, Leander circulated with Ilona through the various saloons and outer decks, accepting congratulations and making small talk.

It would have been boring as hell, but he was fascinated, watching her navigate the different social connections. Her manners were impeccable and she was charming in a way that kept all the focus on their guests. She was incredibly good at deflecting while revealing very little about herself. It made him feel privileged to know that tiny bit more about her than she allowed anyone else to see, even though it was only a microscopic amount.

He reacted to her presence beside him, too. The crush of people had her standing close enough that her body heat radiated into his while the cobweb weight of her skirt fluttered against his pant leg. His ring glittered on her finger when she dragged a wisp of hair behind her ear and a caterer passed close enough behind them that Leander protectively set his hand on her lower back to ensure she didn't bump into the tray of drinks.

A soft pink flush touched her cheeks and her lashes lifted in question.

The noise fell away and the crackling awareness between them intensified. His hand was still on her back and his thumb moved in a restless caress. He had the nearly irresistible urge to draw her into an embrace.

"Ilona. I thought your family would be here." A middle-aged woman with zero sense of timing broke into their moment with an abrasive, "I was looking for Odessa."

There was a brief, hunted flash behind Ilona's eyes before she adopted her serene, welcoming expression.

"Leander, do you know Mira and Theodore? Mira lunches with my stepmother."

"Theodore and I are well acquainted," Leander said, shaking the husband's hand. It was clammy with sweat. "My mother couldn't make it, either," Leander added as an explanation for neglecting to invite anyone with the name Pagonis.

"I thought we had a scheduling conflict ourselves," Mira said through a pinched mouth. "But Theodore made it happen." That curled lip wasn't a smile.

"Wouldn't have missed it," Theodore assured Leander as he swept his handkerchief across his beaded forehead. "Congratulations to both of you. I'm sure you'll be very happy."

"I'm sure we will. And I'm glad we were able to clear up our own scheduling conflict with your project," Leander said magnanimously.

"Yes, yes. Excellent news." Theodore shot a warning glare at his wife as she made a sour noise.

"We're in demand tonight. Excuse us," Leander said.

"Enjoy your party," Theodore said behind them.

"She looks like she'd rather jump overboard," Ilona murmured as they moved away.

"She's welcome to," Leander retorted.

Ilona stifled a snort and shot a laughter-filled look up at him.

He bit back his own grin and set his hand on her waist again, liking the supple feel of her and the way all those feminine fragrances rose off her hair and skin to tantalize him.

"Let's see if we can find someone we can stand." He brought her to a business partner who had since become a friend, Mikolas, and his wife, Viveka. Viveka was an artist and very eager to tell Ilona how much she loved her products.

"Between painting and children, I'm washing up nonstop. I'd have hands like a scullery maid if not for your lotion. Have you thought of developing a children's line?"

They spoke with the couple until the champagne was served. The toasts were mostly bland platitudes, but Leander thanked everyone for coming and set his arm around Ilona as he lifted his glass to her.

"Finally, to my beautiful fiancée. By agreeing to marry me, you're giving me something I've wanted for a long time." The words were exactly as he'd rehearsed them, but they didn't come out with near as much irony as he had used to compose them.

The yacht must have hit some wash from a passing freighter at that moment. The deck seemed to shift beneath him as he watched her drop her lashes. Shy at being the focus of attention? Or aware that he had intended to be facetious and was stung by it?

"I mean it, *glykiá mou*." His voice sank into his chest and he grew hot and prickly. "Thank you."

Ilona didn't know what to make of Leander's toast. Of any of this.

She had sent him that medical report in a passive-aggressive huff, hurt and affronted. The last thing she had expected—the very last thing—was that he would make a joke about taking a pregnancy test himself.

It had been such an absurd remark, she'd been privately laughing about it all evening while resenting him for making it hard for her to hate him. He was the loveliest date which was annoying, always nearby without smothering or hovering. He checked on her drink and neither monopolized a conversation nor left it all to her. He knew how to get away from the boorish guests, too.

And he'd gotten the upper hand with Odessa! Ilona couldn't help enjoying what a ruthless flex it was for him to neutralize Odessa's influence by pressuring Mira's husband into showing up, even if it meant the odious Mira was here.

Ilona couldn't help admiring the strength of his muscled frame, either, when the yacht rocked beneath them and his arm firmed to steady her. She honestly felt light-headed for a moment and feared he was about to kiss her. She would dissolve again; she really would and couldn't bear to do it in front of all these people.

Thankfully, Feodor was keeping to his efficient schedule and the loud bang of fireworks drew everyone outside.

The gasps and sighs of the crowd, the music and the bursts of sparkling color, barely made an impression on Ilona. She stood with her back pressed to Leander's chest, her head resting in the hollow of his shoulder, her bottom brushing his hips and thighs. Her blood shot and fizzed with each shooting star then her heart exploded and her mind scattered.

It finally ended to great applause and the yacht pointed itself back to shore.

Leander's warm hands rubbed her cool arms. "Are you cold?"

"I brought warm clothes for nightfall. I'll go change."

She excused herself, skin still sensitized by a touch that surely wasn't meant to turn her on the way it did.

It was starting to hit her that this would be her life for the next three years. She would share a house with him and they would go to events and he would touch her shoulder to get her attention and her knees would go weak. How would she survive it?

The distress of her thoughts made her fingers clumsy. She couldn't seem to get these crisscross laces to close her linen trousers and threw off her pullover, growing hot and agitated.

"Oh." Leander walked in and firmly pressed the door shut behind him.

"What—?" She snatched up the pullover and hugged it across her naked breasts, keeping her other hand on her unlaced pants so they wouldn't slide to the floor. "What are you doing here?"

"I thought you'd be finished changing. I need a clean shirt." He removed his jacket to reveal the stain of red wine on his chest.

"Did you lose a duel?"

"One of our guests had too much to drink." He began unbuttoning his shirt, gaze on the cuffs he was releasing. "If I were in a duel, I wouldn't lose."

"Says the man defeated by a glass of wine."

"Touché."

"Oof. I see what you did there. You should be ashamed of yourself."

"Yet I rarely am," he said in a blithe tone while stepping into the closet.

She seized the opportunity to shrug on her pullover again. It had a wide neckline that didn't allow for a bra. Its loose sleeves and drawstring cuffs got in the way as she hurried to work on the cords of her trouser fly. Why was looking chic always so inconvenient?

She finally managed it and set her bare foot on the bed so she could turn her pants cuff. She used her comb to measure the width, ensuring they were exactly the same.

"You don't have to try so hard, you know." He spoke from the door of the closet and his voice had shifted to a lower gear. He was closing the cuffs on a clean shirt that hung open, revealing his bare torso. He belonged on a romance novel cover, he was so muscled and well proportioned. She swallowed, gaze fixated on that intriguing pattern of chest hair that bisected his six-pack then disappeared into his boxers as he opened his fly and tucked his shirt.

That knocked her out of her staring. Nervously, she stepped in front of the full-length mirror and smoothed the hint of a wrinkle near her pocket, then adjusted the fall of the pullover on her bare shoulders.

"This necklace doesn't work with this collar, does it?" Its square links had contrasted appealingly with the sweetheart neckline of her sundress, but they were too heavy a statement for the soft, bohemian knit.

She searched with her fingertips for the catch behind her neck.

"Did you hear me?" Leander appeared behind her in the mirror, a loose tie slung beneath his popped collar. His warm fingers brushed hers aside and worked the catch on her necklace. His breath stirred the fine hairs at the base of her skull, sending a shiver down her spine.

As he brought his hand in front of her, offering the necklace, his smoky gaze met hers in the mirror. "You're beautiful. That's not false flattery. I'm being completely honest."

"That's nice of you to say, but Odessa's friends will make a full report." She accepted the necklace. "They'll buy themselves back into her good graces by disparaging me for any little infraction they can find."

He made a dismissive noise, but his dark brows came together as his attention went to the spot where her shoulder met her neck.

"You have something here— A birthmark?" His thumb rubbed where she'd had laser treatments until it was only a slight discoloration. "Is it a scar?"

"Is it unsightly?" The question was a deflection. She didn't want to admit Midas had once pushed Hercules on the swing hard enough to hit her and knock her down, leaving a cut that would have concussed her if it had been on her scalp. "I should have brought something else to wear. I can take my hair down to hide it."

"No, I only noticed because I'm standing right here…" His thumb was still brushing over the scar, sending little tingles into her breasts. "Is it the result of a hot curler mishap? I'm serious. Don't hurt yourself trying to improve on perfection." His gaze flickered to hers in the mirror, gently admonishing, but filled with the warmth of masculine admiration.

"You really are laying it on thick," she chided, trying not to melt under that look.

To her eternal shock, he dipped his head and pressed a warm kiss against the old injury.

Her nipples blossomed with a sting beneath the sensual knit and she drew in a shaken breath.

His gaze came up. "No?"

"I—" She didn't know. Except she did. Because his hand flexed at her waist and her eyes were growing hot and damp. She had become one live wire of pulsing sensation. Her whole body, which had been tracking him at a subconscious level all evening, was now fully awake and aching for his touch.

All from one innocent kiss.

Was it innocent, though? He knew what he was doing. His gaze was hazed with lust as he watched her.

"Tell me what you're thinking," he coaxed.

It was embarrassing and far too revealing, but try as she might, she couldn't look away or dissemble. Not right now. Not with him.

She bit her lips together, helpless against the reaction that was taking her over.

His breath dragged in and his eyelids grew heavier.

"I'm dying to know if this scent on you is the result of all your lotions or if it's just the way you smell." His nose and lips brushed her nape, barely grazing her skin, but the caress made her scalp tighten and a soft moan climbed in her throat. "It's intoxicating." His hot breath pooled against the side of her throat. "You have to tell me, Ilona. Do you want me to kiss you? Touch you?"

"Yes," she whispered. Whimpered. Her assent slid from her lips before she could think better of it.

"Good." The low word seemed to emanate from the depths of his chest. He opened his mouth more deliberately against her skin. Her whole body went weak.

His arms came around her, one hand sliding under the edge of her pullover, splaying across her bare abdomen as he dragged her into the strength of his frame.

"This is what I wanted to do to you when we were outside. Could you feel how much I want you?"

She opened her mouth, but no sound came out. She was too inundated by wild sensations. He wasn't even doing anything except setting those soft kisses under her ear and lightly kneading her belly, but she grew shakier by the second. She could feel his heart hitting her shoulder blade, heavy and strong, and there was a pressure against her bottom that should have intimidated her, but it thrilled her. She was affecting him, too.

She didn't know what to do with her hands except to cup his jaw and turn her face, seeking his mouth with her own.

With a groan, he dragged her even closer. His hot mouth stole over hers and instantly she was drowning. She didn't care. This was the primitive jungle of that night at dinner. A place where she didn't even feel self-conscious when his hand found its way up beneath her shirt to cup her braless breast. She could only tremble in reaction and let her mouth part wider so he could kiss her more deeply.

He turned her and sandwiched her against the cold, smooth wall of the mirror with the warm press of his body. Both his hands came up beneath her pullover to possess her breasts while his mouth plundered hers.

She hadn't known any kiss could feel like this. Like a drug. Like a craving. She swept her hands up and down his sides and around to his back, tracing the indent of his spine and urging him to crush her because his weight felt so good against her.

"This is all I think about," he growled against her cheek, thumbs circling and circling her distended nipples, sending runnels of heat and need deep into her loins.

His knee barely suggested inserting itself between hers and she flowered open, accepting his hard thigh against her mound with a shaken gasp of gratitude.

While the edge of his teeth stole down her neck and he sucked on her earlobe and swept his tickling caress across her breasts, all her focus drilled down to the bright, hot place where his hard thigh pinned itself to her pulsing flesh.

She was moving against him, she realized. Seeking those sharp, piercing bolts of pleasure. She was as shameless as she was mindless. Her hands were clenched in his hair and she was arching and shifting, needing that hard pressure, needing everything he could give her. She returned his kiss with flagrant passion, sucking on his bottom lip, asking him for something. *More.*

He muttered something about never lasting three years and loosened her laced fly. The wide strength of his palm went into her pants and covered the lace underwear she wore, hot and sure.

"Yes? Tell me yes." It was both a command and a plea. His eyes sparked stardust from behind the filter of his spiky lashes. His knowing touch stole beneath the silk and—

"Oh." Lightning struck as he caressed that spot, that sweet, taut, needy spot. Again and again.

"Say it," he urged, rubbing and circling.

"Yes," she panted helplessly. "Yes. Don't stop. Oh, Leander. Oh, oh—" She was on her tiptoes, seeking. *Needing* the invasion of his finger. Needing the rocking of his palm that utterly owned her.

"Now, *glykiá mou.*" His mouth covered hers and the

oblivion swept up in a shivering wave, taking her out of herself for long moments where she was only dimly aware of how uninhibited she was as her body pulsated in ecstasy.

CHAPTER SEVEN

"WE'LL STAY ABOARD TONIGHT." Leander's thick voice dragged her back to herself. His gaze was smoldering as he eased his hand from between them.

Ilona was still trembling and so embarrassed, she wished she would die of it. Please. Right now. An iceberg. *Anything.*

He was holding her up because she was still clinging to him. Had she really let him touch her like that? And make her orgasm while he was fully dressed and in complete control of his own body? He was aroused, yes. The press of his erection against her was unmistakable, but he wasn't panting and melted and falling apart the way she just had.

"Unless you want to forget about saying good-night to our guests? I could definitely be talked into not leaving this room for the rest of the week." His teeth were at her earlobe again, letting her feel the scrape of them.

Even as her hair seemed to stand on end with renewed stimulation, she knew she couldn't sleep with him. For a multitude of reasons, not least of which was the fact he had the power to make her forget every one of those reasons.

With an inner cringe, she realized people would be noting their absence and their change of attire when they reappeared. Rumors would get back to Odessa that something had happened in here and that could turn ugly very fast.

"I'll go out first," she decided, opening the hands that were clenched in his shirt and pressing him back.

"Good idea. I need a minute," he said wryly before catching her lips in a final, pulse-fluttering kiss that had her mouth clinging so helplessly to his.

He closed himself into the bathroom, but she stayed exactly where she was, still too shaken to move. Too mortified. *Scared.*

For all those rumors Odessa had circulated about how promiscuous Ilona was, she was actually a virgin. Sex meant babies and, much as she yearned for a family, she knew how vulnerable children made a woman. She didn't remember much about her mother, but she remembered her counting out money and crying. She remembered her watching Ilona eat without placing a plate in front of herself.

And that was without someone actively trying to destroy her because she had dared to have a child.

She couldn't stay the night with Leander! She wasn't on the pill or anything.

Pushing off the mirror, she turned to confront herself and, even though he had just rewritten everything she had believed about her sexual self, she looked remarkably untouched. Her trousers needed retying, but they were barely wrinkled. Her nipples were still tender, but they were relaxed beneath the soft knit. Her makeup was unsmudged and she only had to reapply the lipstick that had faded through the evening.

Her hand wasn't quite steady, but she managed it. Then she sat to fasten her wedge heels with their ribbon ties.

She wasn't fast enough. Leander emerged as she was rising. She turned to give herself a final inspection, mostly to avoid his gaze.

"People are going to think what they think, Ilona. Screw them." He held out a hand. "Let's finish this so I can have you to myself."

She didn't tell him she would leave as planned, thinking it was better to wait until they'd both cooled off.

Despite her intense self-consciousness and latent tension, the rest of the evening was pleasant, if disconcerting. Each time her arm brushed Leander's or he glanced toward her, a spike of renewed desire shot through her, shutting down her brain and amping her nerve endings back to life.

Finally, the guests were filing off the yacht, all professing the party a wonderful night.

Then Mira proved herself to be the drunk who had ruined Leander's shirt. She lurched out of her husband's arm and jabbed her sharp fingernail into Ilona's breastbone.

"She knows what you're doing," she slurred. "You think you can cash in with a baby? She won't allow it. She told me she won't."

Theodore muttered an imprecation and firmly steered Mira off the yacht while the handful of remaining guests pretended nothing had happened.

Ilona could feel the demand for answers radiating off Leander's stiff presence, though.

As the last guest departed, Feodor approached. "I think that went well. I'll see you Monday?"

"I'm coming back with you," Ilona said, swallowing the nervous quaver that arrived in her voice. "Would you mind fetching my things?" She didn't look at Leander.

"Of cour—"

"I'll take you in my car," Leander told her. "Feodor can drop Androu."

Feodor bounced his surprised gaze to Leander then back to Ilona. As the silence drew out, he said, "I'll fetch your bag," adeptly solving half the problem and leaving them to work out the rest.

"I'll have the cars brought around." Androu hurried away in the opposite direction.

Moments later, Ilona was settling into the shadowed interior of Leander's car. He told Dino to "check the score" and waited for the man to put in his earbuds before saying in a dangerous tone, "Care to explain what *cash in with a baby* means?"

Not especially. She rolled her lips inward as she considered how much to say, but he was likely to find out once he was voting her shares at Pagonis anyway.

"There's a provision in my father's will to reapportion the family shares when babies are born."

There was a stunned silence, then, "Spell it out for me. Are you saying that if I get you pregnant, our child will eat up shares that belong to the rest of the family?"

"Yes."

"Why haven't you told me that?"

"Because I don't wish to be used as a brood mare or have my child used as a property stake."

"That's not what I'm suggesting."

"Tell me that's not the first thought that popped into your mind," she scoffed.

His cheek ticked and he looked away. "I've trained myself to look at every option with an objective lens, especially when it comes to taking your brother down. That doesn't mean I would follow through on something so coldblooded. Midas would, though. Why hasn't he?"

Ilona bit back a sigh, finding this whole topic distasteful. "He tried as soon as he married. That was seven years ago, but they didn't have any luck. Apparently, he had gonorrhea when he was at uni and left it untreated for years. Four years ago, after his divorce, he supposedly got another woman pregnant, but our father was still alive. He insisted on a paternity test. The baby wasn't Midas's. Our father wrote in a condition that the family shares can only be held by Pagonis blood."

"That all tracks," Leander said with a disgusted snort. "What about the other one?"

"Hercules? He isn't interested in women or children."

"So that leaves you. If *you* carry a baby, it's definitely a Pagonis. No wonder they're so threatened by you."

"Yes, and everything they put me through would be visited upon my child tenfold so I *can't*."

"I would protect both of you. You have to know that."

"I would love to believe it," she assured him. "But why do *you* suddenly want a baby? I was raised on spite, Leander. I refuse to conceive a baby simply to get the better of them. Kindly don't ask me to."

"I'm not." He didn't flinch. "But you do want children. Don't you?" It wasn't really a question. He was prodding for confirmation.

She did. Deep down, she had a flicker of a dream where her life was filled with love. Where high small voices said the words to her and a deep one said it across a pillow and she even said it herself. And meant it. She wanted it to spill out of her in the most sincere and healing way, making her feel worthy and needed. Whole.

She didn't tell him any of that, only left a thick silence that had him turning his face to the window.

They didn't speak again until they were at her building. As he got out to hold the door and assist her, he said, "We'll talk more about this tomorrow."

"No we won't," she muttered and went inside.

Why do you *want a baby?*

Children hadn't been at the top of his immediate list of goals; Leander would admit that. Conceiving an heir was something he had firmly placed on the back burner while he spent all his concentration and effort on righting the wrong Midas had done to him.

He had always assumed he would have children at some point, though. His relationship with his mother was strained, but he had been close with his father. Maybe there was even a sense of something left undone. He had lost his father when he was sixteen. It was a time of life when many an adolescent walked out on their parents, determined to mature on their own terms.

Leander hadn't had the luxury of choice and often wondered what his father would think of the person he had become. Would he be this jaded, driven man if his father hadn't died? Would his father appreciate what Leander was trying to do in his memory? Was there any sense in doing it if he wasn't going to pass his name and legacy on to another generation of Vasilous?

So yes, he wanted children for deeply personal reasons that had nothing to do with any advantage they might afford him with his mission against Midas Pagonis.

Obviously, he wouldn't force any woman to carry his child if she didn't want to, but given the security he could offer, he had been a little insulted that first day when Ilona had said, *I don't want children with* you, summarily rejecting him as if he failed to measure up.

There were extenuating circumstances; he saw that now, and he understood her suspicion of his motives, but he was the product of an accidental pregnancy. He wouldn't be cavalier about bringing children into anything but a committed, healthy relationship.

Which was *not* what they had.

They *did* have incredible chemistry, though. If they hadn't had guests to get back to, they very well might have risked a pregnancy while they'd been aboard the yacht. That encounter had been erotic and exciting and Leander had suddenly seen their three-year stretch of marriage as something that would be the furthest thing from celibate.

He wasn't taking anything for granted, but if they had

sex, a baby became possible. For that reason, they had to discuss how they would handle pregnancy and children.

Over the next two days, he tried to reach Ilona to hash it out, but she put him off, canceling a dinner date and claiming she had too many things going on at work.

Annoyed, he instructed his lawyer to add baby bonuses and other settlements to their agreement.

Ilona's response came through her own lawyer. She accepted his terms as a contingency, but she expected him to abide by their "gentleman's agreement" regarding separate bedrooms. Also, she had a dress fitting and couldn't make lunch.

So childish.

Her silent treatment continued as he was called to Rome. Midas was being a nuisance, interfering with a project there, but Leander quickly got it back on track.

He returned two days later to a text that Ilona didn't need to view the property his agent had found. If he liked it, he could proceed with the purchase.

Was this what their marriage would be like? Hot and cold? He could have accepted that more easily if he wasn't still tantalized by the knowledge that when it was hot, it was *very* hot.

He would have to be the adult and reach out yet again, he supposed, but he had just arrived home and wanted to work off his tension. He changed into his gym clothes and started on the treadmill, watching financial headlines while he ran.

He was so deep in thought, he nearly missed a call that jammed his otherwise healthy heart.

Ilona knew Leander was back in Athens, but he didn't call or text.

That shouldn't bother her. They weren't teenagers where every text or lack thereof held a dozen hidden meanings.

She hadn't meant for their discussion on children to turn into such a bone of contention, but the way Mira had brought it up on the heels of their intimacy had made Ilona very defensive.

For the first time in her life, the idea of having sex was very enticing, but she wanted Leander to want *her*, not an incubator for another figurine on his chessboard. When the email had come through from the lawyers, listing all the benefits—bribes?—he'd offered if she became pregnant, she'd felt pressured and struck back with firm boundaries.

Even though she wanted sex with him. She couldn't lie to herself about that.

As for having a baby, well, it was a huge step, but she and Leander were both very wealthy, not counting pennies the way her mother had been. Pregnancy and child-rearing wouldn't be a hardship, not the way it was for some who had much less.

As for the danger of Midas and Odessa coming after her child, Leander *would* do everything in his power to protect what was his. She believed that.

No, now that she'd had time to think calmly about it, she wasn't as adamant against the idea of children, but she still saw issues in having a baby with a man who, at best, felt ambivalent about her. Eventually that lack of a bond between them would either force them to stay in a loveless arrangement for the sake of their child, or part and bring stepparents into the equation.

Neither of those outcomes appealed to her.

Amid her ruminations, her door buzzed.

Probably her neighbor Rasmus. His cat was forever leaping from his fire escape onto the outside ledge, then walking around to cry at the windows of the other units on this floor. Rasmus left his door unlocked so residents could return Snuggles, but Ilona often kept him if she was having a night in.

She'd been about to step into the bath, but she tightened the belt on her robe and hurried to tell him Snuggles wasn't here. She glanced through the peephole and saw flowers.

Leander? Her heart softened like butter in the sun.

She swung the door open, a smile dawning on her face because there was no reason to suspect it would be *Midas*.

CHAPTER EIGHT

LEANDER IDENTIFIED HIMSELF as Ilona's fiancé and the flustered building manager took him up to her floor.

"We're still investigating how the intruder was allowed up," the manager said in the elevator. "We have protocols around announcing visitors, but a new employee was in today."

Convenient.

"He was only here a minute or two. Security came up immediately, but he was already gone down the fire stairs."

"Have you reported it to the police?"

"Kyría Callas asked that they not be involved."

"Involve them." The doors opened and Leander stepped into a hallway where someone with a security badge snapped to attention. A resident shrank into their flat and closed the door.

One door stood open. Roses were spilled like bloodstains across the hardwood. Leander could see a lamp was overturned and a floor rug askew.

A grotesque premonition came over him. An echo of the day he'd found his father. He swallowed, stomach sour and skin turning clammy as he approached.

"Ilona," he called out, voice thick and unsteady.

"She's in there," the security guard said, pointing to a closed door.

Leander knocked. "Ilona, it's me. Let me in."

There was a pause, then firm footsteps approached. A man of his own age let him in.

A whirling tornado of emotions pushed him inside. A dozen questions were on his tongue. *Why did you call Feodor, not me? Why did you let Midas in? Why don't you want the police involved?*

He wanted answers and—

He froze, unable to breathe.

Midas had only been here a minute or two, but she looked…broken. She wasn't crying, but her eyes were swollen and her face ravaged by tear tracks. There was a bin of crumpled tissues beside the sofa and a box of fresh ones on the coffee table. The light that usually radiated off her was nearly winked out. Her shoulders were hunched, her legs covered with a soft yellow blanket. Her hands were protectively folded over a tortoiseshell cat.

As he approached, her eyes swallowed her face and her mouth trembled. What kicked him in the stomach hardest was the glint of embarrassment in her eyes. She hated that he was seeing her like this.

"You said Feodor was coming." She darted a look to the man who had let him in.

"I…" The man shrugged. "When he called back, he said to tell you he was coming. I didn't know he meant someone else."

"He shouldn't have called you," she said to Leander. "I'm fine. I just need a minute." She dabbled a tissue into the corner of her eye and took a big breath, trying to rally herself.

The air in his lungs turned hot. *Don't*, he wanted to say. He wanted to squeeze her hand and gather her up and whisper that everything would be okay now, but she looked so brittle, he was afraid she would disintegrate if he touched her.

He wanted to know what Midas had said to scare the hell out of her like this.

"Androu was with Feodor," Leander said absently. "He called me when he realized what was going on." Leander suspected the pair had been in bed. What his employee did in his off time was none of his business unless there was a possibility of professional compromise. In this case, it had definitely worked to his advantage. "I told Feodor I would take care of everything."

"Can I get you coffee? Tea?" a woman asked.

"No. I'm taking Ilona home."

"I don't want to go in there." Ilona's voice was a whisper-thin husk of its usually sensual self, thick with a plea not to make her face it.

"I'll take you to *my* home. You'll be safe there." He crouched beside her. "Do you want me to go pack your bag for you?"

"Would you?" She seemed anxious, as though it was the biggest ask in the world to walk across the hall. "There's one in the closet that I keep packed for travel. And my phone. It's on the charger. And my purse? I know I'm being a coward, but..." She bit her quivering lips and looked to the ceiling, trying to catch back the fresh tears that were welling.

That's when he saw the red marks on her throat. They nearly knocked him on his ass.

Blackout rage might have taken him then, but the woman said, "You need clothes to wear in the car. Do you want me to find something? Then I can help you dress?"

Ilona nodded.

Leander stood and took advantage of the moment to step away from Ilona and get hold of himself. He could hardly breathe, he was so explosive with fury. He went across to her flat and into her bathroom where he emptied the tepid tub. Then he splashed cold water on his face and the back of his neck, trying to cool his temper enough to behave like a civilized human being.

Trying to quiet the voice that said, *Kill him.*

The neighbor woman was gone when he came out. He looked around Ilona's apartment. It was small, only one bedroom, but it was nicely laid out and welcoming. He liked the warm tones and lack of clutter and comfortable textures. It smelled like her.

It was clearly her safe space, but she no longer felt safe here. That infuriated him all over again. He cleaned up the flowers and glass, then found her bag. He had security take it down with some fresh dry cleaning and her laptop. He threw all the medications he could find into her handbag along with her phone and the keys from a bowl by the door.

When he came to collect her, Ilona was dressed in matching track pants and jacket, bare feet tucked into a pair of sandals. Her face was washed, her hair combed and gathered in a ponytail. She was still sallow, but the shaken vulnerability of twenty minutes ago was firmly packed away behind a mask of polite gratitude.

"You've been very kind," she said to the couple. "I'm sorry I interrupted your evening."

They reassured her it was no trouble and Leander nodded his own thanks before he escorted Ilona into the elevator. There was a robotic quality to her body language. Her gaze was unblinking, her expression blank, her movements seeming to be on autopilot.

He wasn't much better, but his jerky sightlessness was the result of the tight control he was using to suppress his bloodthirsty wrath. She needed reassurance, not an exhibition of further male aggression, but that aggression was there and it would emerge when the time was right. Midas would definitely pay for this.

"You drove yourself?" Ilona was briefly confounded when Leander opened the passenger door of a green-and-silver convertible.

"Dino was already home for the evening." Leander placed a call as he started the car.

"Androu," his assistant answered.

"Order curbside. Chicken for two."

That confused her, too. She wasn't hungry and time had ceased to move while she had sat on her neighbor's sofa.

Thank goodness her neighbor, Rasmus, had left his door unlocked. Midas had attacked her, but her self-defense training had kicked in just as quickly. She had dropped him with a knee to the groin, then barged into the apartment next door, before locking Midas in the hall to shout profanities. His voice had faded even as Rasmus was calling security. Ilona suspected Rasmus had been making love with that woman, but Ilona had stayed there anyway, ruining their evening, too afraid to go into her own home.

That's why she was in Leander's car, valiantly trying to work out what she ought to do next, but her brain simply refused to work. She could hardly make sense of simple things like why there was so much traffic when it felt like the middle of the night. When had she opened her door to Midas? An hour ago?

"Is Kyría Callas with you?" Androu's disembodied voice was asking. "Feodor has dispatched bodyguards to escort her—"

"She's with me. I'm taking her home."

"Ilona?" Feodor's voice came through the speaker. "I've initiated red-level security at the Callas building and amber levels at all the international facilities. I have a secure location for you to stay in. Where should Eugene collect you? What else do you need? Clothes? Personal products? Are you hurt?"

"I'm fine," she said, more baffled than ever. "Why are you with Androu?"

"She's not fine," Leander cut in. "Have her doctor come to my apartment." Leander poked to end the call. "They're seeing one another."

"Feodor and Androu?" Her brain was still stumbling over his doctor edict. "Since when?"

"Since they went home together off the yacht, I imagine."

"Oh. That's nice for them. Is Androu nice? Feodor deserves someone nice." He was more than her PA. He was her best friend. Her only friend and she paid him very well to be as trustworthy and accessible as he was. She had had to use Rasmus's phone to call him so he hadn't picked up the unknown number, but he had listened to her voice mail straightaway. He had dealt with everything while she had sat on Rasmus's sofa, numb, incapable of helping herself.

"Androu is smart, efficient and loyal enough to call *me* when you were in trouble. Why didn't you?"

"It didn't occur to me." She slouched deeper into her seat. "Feodor knows what to do. Don't be angry."

"I'm not angry at you. I'm angry at Midas and myself for not seeing how truly dangerous he is. Has he assaulted you before? Is that why you have all these security protocols that can be activated with a word?"

"Not recently." There had been that incident at the funeral, the one that had left her arm in a sling. Odessa had witnessed it and pretended she hadn't, but Feodor had talked Ilona into making a report to the police—which Leander would probably insist on as well. She headed that off by saying, "Look, I know I should make statements

and everything, but it's *hard*. And nothing will happen.
I can tell you right now Odessa will provide him with an
alibi. She always does."

"Even when your father was alive?" He didn't raise his
voice, but the simmering fury that imbued his tone thick-
ened the air in the car. "Did *he* know Midas was violent?"

She turned her face to the window. "He put a stop to
the worst of it."

A profound silence, then a grim, "But not all of it."

No. There had still been the pinches and shoves and
her father hadn't had the patience for tattling so she had
learned to keep her distance and her guard up.

"I know you think you can use this against him." Her
voice cracked and she wanted to bury her face in her hands
at the thought. "But I don't want to be your hammer, Leander. I just want to get away from him."

"You are away. I'm taking you away," he said firmly.
"But this isn't about my desire for revenge, Ilona. He *hurt*
you. That can't happen again. Together we'll make sure
it doesn't."

She looked across at him, mouth trembling at how badly
she wanted to believe him, but why would he help her?
He didn't care about her, not really. Only as much as he
cared about gaining access to an easy door to get to Midas.

"Can we not talk about it right now?" She was trying
not to cry. "I don't want to think of it."

Leander couldn't stop thinking of it. He was incensed and
gripped by the urgency to annihilate Midas, but he needed
to know Ilona was safe, that she *felt* safe.

"You have the whole floor?" she asked when they
stepped off his private elevator into his penthouse.

"One of the perks of building the building. I set this
aside for myself." It had three bedrooms, but one was his

office. The other was his personal gym. He hadn't thought of that when he'd brought her here, only that it was a suitable fortress. He had wanted to bring her into the place where he could protect her best.

He showed her the alarm panel and gave her a code to come and go, then explained the emergency system and how an alarm would sound and security would descend if anyone tried to override it. She seemed to relax a fraction as she took it all in.

While he plated their food, Ilona drifted through the living area like a ghost, pale and lifeless, pausing to admire his view of the Acropolis, his pool and the dining area that opened to a terrace that offered sunset views. His decor was an ultramodern style of clean lines and practicality. He wasn't one for pillows with froufrou tassels or colorful throw rugs like he'd seen at her place and he regretted that choice now. He would have liked to offer her those softer touches so she would feel more at ease.

Neither of them ate much and her physician arrived while they were still picking at their meals. She took Ilona into his bedroom to examine her. The doctor didn't say much as she left, only that Ilona had gone into the shower and would take a sedative and go to bed when she came out.

Leander made some calls, learning the cameras in Ilona's building had been disabled, the doorman who had let Midas up couldn't be located and Midas had been with his stepmother all evening—exactly as Ilona had predicted.

Leander swore under his breath, but he wasn't the least bit surprised. These sorts of dirty tactics were familiar to him from his own attempts to seek justice against the man. That's why he'd had to attack Midas through the unprotected flank of Ilona's company.

His desire to obliterate the man had increased a thousandfold, but he could no longer use Ilona to do it. His gut churned with guilt at having set her up for this attack. She might not have come right out and told him she was afraid Midas would assault her, but all the signs had been there. Leander had been too blinded by his thirst for vengeance to see it.

He had seen Ilona as Midas's weakness, but now she was his own Achilles' heel. Any further strikes Midas aimed at her would impact Leander. His conscience couldn't abide it and there was also something deeper. He'd tasted her fear and felt her shaken anguish inside his own chest. He hurt because she hurt.

It had been a long time since Leander had felt this vulnerable. He cared about people, but only collectively and superficially. He ensured appropriate policies were put in place for workplace conduct and safety. He paid livable wages and "gave back" and his company was founded on green principles.

But after the devastation of losing his father, he'd been careful not to become too emotionally attached to anyone. The worst he'd felt since then was when his PA had abruptly left with pregnancy complications. He'd hired Androu to replace her in a very sexist attempt not to experience such acute concern for an employee again.

In fact, one of the attractions of proposing to Ilona had been his initial antipathy toward her. He had been convinced he wouldn't come to care for her. Not in a way that would leave him open to being hurt. Yet here he was, knocking softly then slipping into his bedroom to stand over her sleeping form, ensuring she hadn't fallen in the shower and was resting comfortably.

She had aligned herself on the edge of the mattress, blankets pulled over her ear, hair woven into a shiny black tail he wanted to touch.

How arrogant of him to assume he could bring a woman

into his life and not bear any responsibility for what happened to her. The scope of that responsibility, one that encompassed the bruises on her throat, was deep enough to make his torso ache.

He didn't want this responsibility, this weight, but he definitely wanted Midas to pay. It was a dilemma that had him circling the bed and sitting down on the far side to consider his next moves.

There was no going backward on his plan to marry her. If anything, he had to double down and make it clear they were a team that Midas couldn't break. That meant they would have to begin to really trust one another.

It was still eating at him that she hadn't thought to call him and had been so shocked that he had turned up. His ego was more than dented over that. He felt genuine shame because why would she think of him as an ally when he was the reason Midas had come after her?

They needed to build a bridge between them, one that spanned a deep, jagged distance of familial betrayal and painful history. Bridges were his specialty in real life, but earning her trust and proffering his own was a much trickier project. It wouldn't be accomplished through a few exercises in eye contact and backward falls. They would have to genuinely open up and be honest with each other. It would take time and commitment.

It would mean completely letting his guard down with a Pagonis.

All his instincts knotted into a tangled shield at the very idea, but it was the only way to best Midas. He knew that.

He dropped onto his back beside her, considering how to go about it.

Ilona woke thirsty and disoriented. Weak morning light was coming through the crack in the curtains. Where—?

Memory rushed back. She was in Leander's home. His bed!

With a small gasp, she sat up, head swimming.

"You're safe, Ilona." Leander's voice was a quiet rumble beside her. "Go back to sleep."

He was still dressed in last night's clothes. Part of the bedspread was pulled across his waist. He had one arm thrown above his head, his eyes were closed and stubble shadowed his jaw.

Had he said the same thing in the night? She had a vague memory of waking with a whimper and hearing his reassuring voice beside her. He might have held her hand…

"I need to go to work," she said, reflexively looking for escape.

"Why?" Leander cracked one eye. "We can work from here."

"I want to go in." It was what she did. Carry on. Pretend it hadn't happened. Do the things she could control so she wouldn't dwell on things she couldn't.

She pulled up her knees and hugged them, considering whether that was the healthiest way to keep responding to Midas, especially if he was escalating from insulting and antagonizing to physical assaults.

As she closed her hot eyes and pressed them to her kneecaps, she started to relive that horrible moment when she had opened her door and—

Her hair shifted, sending a tingle across her scalp. A shiver went down her spine that made her lift her head and sit up straighter. That caused a light tug on her plait.

"I couldn't help myself," Leander said wryly as he released her thick tail so its weight landed against her back again. "It looks like it's carved from obsidian, it's so glossy and smooth."

She self-consciously brought the plait to the front of

her shoulder and petted it, liking the silky, ropey feel of it herself.

"Feodor has made arrangements for me. I don't want to intrude on you longer tha—"

"Ilona." He came up on an elbow. "We're going to live together in ten days anyway. Stay here until then."

"Here?" She was striving for a cynical reference to the bed they were currently occupying, but she wasn't as averse to sharing it with him as she should be. Her stomach was tilting all over the place at the daunting yet alluring thought.

He inhaled sharply and caught the hand she was sweeping down the rippled line of her plait. Her pajama sleeve had fallen back, revealing the black bruise on her forearm.

"That—I hit it on something when I was…" She tugged free and drew her sleeve to cover her wrist.

"When you were running away." His voice had turned bludgeon-hard again. "I want you to stay here, Ilona. Go into work each day if you must. I'll take you there myself, but he's not getting near you again. Not without going through me."

She didn't know how to react to that. It had been a long time since someone had been on her side. Feodor was, but he wasn't in a position to offer real protection. On the contrary, she protected him and the rest of her employees, taking whatever Midas dished out so they were shielded from it.

The pattern in the bedspread blurred. She couldn't look at Leander, she was so touched. He had come to her when she'd been too shocked to look after herself. He had said he was taking her away from them, that he wanted to *help* her. To guard her when she was so tired of guarding herself.

She had to bite her lips to still their trembling.

"Ilona?"

"Shall I make the coffee?" She threw back the covers and escaped before she broke down and threw herself at him.

CHAPTER NINE

ONCE LEANDER WAS SATISFIED that the security precautions in her work building were top-notch, he left her there for the day which helped settle her nerves. Work was Ilona's safe place. Her happy place. Here she made things that helped people and was liked and successful and valued.

Before she knew it, the day was gone and Leander had returned for her, which surprised her.

"You didn't have to come. I have bodyguards." They'd been relegated to following in her car behind them since Leander had escorted her into his own. "I was planning to work late and get ahead on a few things before the wedding." Mostly she had wanted to put off facing him again along with all the changes that were happening so fast. Before last night, she had been counting on these final days of singlehood to come to terms with everything.

"I want to start dating," he said.

"Other people?" She was floored.

"Each other," he clarified dryly, mouth twitching.

"Oh." Her cheeks abruptly stung with a blush, as though she was an adolescent and he was the first boy to ask her to dance. "Why? We're already engaged. Living together." Kind of. Her things were being boxed from her apartment in preparation for their moving into the home they would share after their honeymoon. "I have a ton of things to do." She was restructuring at work and had fittings and decor decisions, not to mention signing her statement with the police and finishing up negotiations on their prenuptial contract.

"We need to get to know one another better."

In what way? Spend the night on his yacht sort of way? The heat in her cheeks intensified.

Things had changed so much since that interlude at their engagement party. She'd been embarrassed by her response that night, then conflicted over Leander wanting to discuss children.

She still had huge reservations about making a baby with someone she didn't love, but she wanted a family. And she was so *tired* of being afraid to go after what she wanted. She was tired of trying to live up to impossible expectations set by people who didn't care about her.

Agreeing to marry Leander had been an act of defiance, one where she had finally seized control of her own life. Deciding her future, choosing what happened to her body and whether she had a family, should be her choice, too, not something dictated by whether Midas and Odessa would approve.

Since last night's attack, she had been considering more about that. She kept thinking that having a baby would be more than a rejection of Midas's control over her. It would be a defiance against her own mortality. Life was fragile and temporary. She had to get on with living the one she'd been given.

And there was that other, secretive defiance within her, the one where she *felt* things. Where she had discovered a sensuality she hadn't known she was capable of experiencing. Did she want to spend the next three years ignoring that? Then explore it with someone else?

Or did she want Leander to show her everything her body could feel?

"That wasn't a euphemism." Leander briefly squeezed her fingers where her hand rested on the seat between them, sending a zing up her arm and into her chest.

"Pardon?"

"I realize Midas has made it hard for you to trust any man. I'm not referring to sex. We need to know we can count on each other. That means spending time together. We need to be honest and work through any fears or disagreements we might have."

"You're afraid of me?" she asked skeptically.

"I'm afraid *for* you," he said gravely. "I'm bothered that you're afraid of me."

Was she? Not in the way he meant. She'd been sedated last night and even though he had shared the bed, the most intrusive thing he'd done was tell her to go back to sleep. She had awakened surprised, but not frightened.

Which was strange. The idea of sleeping next to someone had never appealed. Sleep was a very vulnerable state. She'd been taught that every weakness could be exploited, but waking next to Leander had been almost reassuring.

It was something she could easily get used to. Which was disturbing.

"I'm not afraid of you. I'm afraid to trust you," she clarified haltingly. "Finding my way to being as self-reliant as I am was hard. I try not to count on anyone. That way they can't disappoint you."

"I'm not like him. I don't lie or go back on promises. I say what I mean and mean what I say. I will draw the line at murder in cold blood—reluctantly," he pronounced with disdain. "But Midas will pay for all he's done, Ilona. To you and to me. He'll pay until he has absolutely nothing left. I swear that to you."

A bitter wind passed over her heart, making her shiver inside.

He meant it. She felt it. For the first time she believed *in* him. Unequivocally. He wouldn't stop until Midas was on his knees.

That ought to be satisfying, but she was disturbed by his vow. She was, paradoxically, afraid for him. She was afraid of what he would lose along the way. Midas would make sure Leander didn't come away unscathed. More concerning, Midas had a way of causing a person to twist themselves in ugly ways. Look at Hercules, deeply unhappy, never standing up for his own principles and often dispatched to do Midas's dirty work. Perpetually miserable.

Even she had become a crumpled form of herself, too fearful of further dents to let herself be all that she could be.

She didn't know how to articulate that worry in a way he might accept, though. And they had arrived at his building. His warm hand closed over hers as they walked up and that innocuous contact had the ability to empty her brain of all those worries.

In fact, a girlish lightness entered her heart. They were going on a *date*.

It became their habit to go out for dinner every night. It was both a low stress event and high. They went to quiet, intimate places and talked about the wedding and travel and foods they liked. In that way it was companionable and easy.

But Leander did courtly things, holding her chair and asking her to dance.

Every time Ilona was in his arms, she struggled to hide

that his spicy scent and the brush of his body made her bones weak, but she never refused. It was the most delicious torture to put herself through. She liked feeling his strength and his confidence as he led her around the floor. She liked how cherished she felt when his thumb brushed the heel of her palm or his splayed fingers shifted on her waist, strong and possessive.

It always made her long for him to kiss her or make a move when they got home, but he always stayed well on his side of the wide bed they continued to share.

Tonight, as he seated her and took her wrap, his thumb brushed into the hollow beneath her ear. His caress sent a tingling rush into her breasts.

"No makeup tonight. That's good."

The bruises, she realized with a sick lurch in her stomach. They had finally faded and she was glad they were gone, but there were plenty of other reminders of that dark night—the police report that had gone nowhere because Midas had an alibi, the fresh rumors Odessa had started about Ilona being in financial straits, the RSVPs to the wedding that were weighted far more heavily to Leander's guests than to hers.

Leander's warm hand gave her shoulder a squeeze. Affection? Reassurance?

It was gone too quickly for her to interpret. He circled the table, leaving her in a confusion of shy pleasure. He'd become difficult to read, offering those small, unexpected caresses before withdrawing. They left her bereft and swimming in yearning. She kept waiting for the fiery desire he'd shown her on the yacht to reemerge, but each time it sparked, he always seemed to douse it and move away.

While she quietly drowned in unrequited lust.

He paused with his hand on his chair and she looked up

at him with her heart in her throat, wondering if he had any clue of her feelings. His handsomeness nearly undid her, with his alert profile, his tall bearing and wide shoulders, his nail beds going white as he tightened his grip on the back of his chair—

With a gasp, she swung her head around, expecting Midas to be swooping down at them, but it was only a woman of fiftyish years.

Oh! She had completely forgotten.

Ilona rose and smiled in flustered greeting. Now she felt extra foolish for the way she was mooning over Leander, but she was excited to have arranged this little surprise for him.

Her flashing glance revealed he was staring coldly at the woman, his mouth held in a grim line.

Ilona's stomach plummeted and her blood went ice-cold in her veins. She'd made a mistake. A terrible one.

But Susan Vasilou was upon them, the moment unavoidable. Her hair was dark brunette with shots of silver, her build slight and graceful, her mouth wide like her son's as she smiled in a way that struck Ilona as being forcibly bright.

"Darling." She touched Leander's arm and offered her cheek.

"Mother." He bussed her cheek and shot a glower at Ilona. "You invited her?"

"I—" Culpability had to be painted all over her face.

"Oh, don't scold her. I asked her to let me surprise you." Susan tapped his wrist. "Yes, I'm joining them," she told the server who appeared beside her.

While a chair and place setting were procured, Leander said, "I thought we would see you at the rehearsal dinner tomorrow."

"I wanted a chance to have you all to myself." Susan

held out her hand to Ilona. "And to meet your beautiful bride. Please call me Susan." Her Greek lilted with her British accent, but it was smooth and unhesitating.

Leander politely helped both of them with their chairs. This time, he didn't touch Ilona as he did. He radiated so much irritation, her toes curled in her shoes with anxiety.

"Tell me about the wedding." Susan turned her eager interest on Ilona. "How did you two meet? Tell me *everything*."

Ilona practically choked on her tongue. Where to start? Not with the truth.

"Using Ilona is beneath you, Mother," Leander said in a chilly undertone as they were left alone. "If you want to see me or know something about my life, call *me*."

"But you so rarely pick up," Susan said mildly. "And I'm genuinely interested in the woman who has captured your heart."

I haven't, Ilona silently moaned. If anything, she had alienated Leander by making an assumption. She had blindsided him when she was supposed to be earning his trust. *I'm sorry*, she tried to telegraph, but he had averted his grim expression to glare at the view of the Parthenon.

"I'm sorry I didn't make the engagement party. Your family must have thought it odd." Susan slid a wounded glance toward Leander that Ilona interpreted to mean she hadn't been invited.

Why was he so hostile toward her? In their brief telephone conversation, Susan had struck Ilona as charming and likable, not cruel or objectionable. Did she overspend or speak out of turn after a few drinks? What?

"My family wasn't there, either," Ilona volunteered, wading carefully through the thick undercurrents. "My mother passed when I was young and my father died last year. My relationship with the rest is extremely difficult.

I don't expect you'll meet them at all." Not if she could help it.

"I'm so sorry." Susan sounded sincere. Compassionate. "Every bride should have a family member who is as excited as she is. Allow me." She propped her chin on her hand. "I adore talking about gowns and floral arrangements. Do you have a theme?"

Ilona couldn't help it. She *liked* her. Conversation flowed easily between them and the meal would have been very pleasant if Leander had warmed up a degree or two, but he remained withdrawn, barely speaking.

While they were waiting for dessert, Ilona excused herself to the powder room, thinking to give them a moment to clear the air.

"I'll come with you." Susan rose at the same time.

"Really, Mother?" Leander gave Susan a frosted look.

"Are you afraid we'll talk about you?" she chided.

"I know you will. Whatever you have to say can be said here, to my face." He nodded at her chair.

They held some sort of contest of wills, one that made Ilona feel she had caused this discord between them. She nearly wilted back into her chair in miserable defeat.

"It's all things you've heard before, darling. What difference would it make where I say it?" Susan sounded almost anguished, but she quickly covered that impression with a warm smile for Ilona. She tucked her arm through Ilona's and steered her toward the ladies' lounge.

Ilona's heart was heavy when they returned to the penthouse. She was in the oddest position of wanting to know Leander's side of things while wanting to defend his mother. She wanted to ask questions, but given his shuttered expression, she also wanted to respect his privacy. She settled on a sincere apology.

"I should have mentioned that she would be joining us. She called to welcome me to the family and I invited her on impulse. She said she wanted to surprise you so I…" Put him into a situation he didn't want. "I'm very sorry. It didn't occur to me you wouldn't want to see her."

The whole point in "dating" had been to get to know each other, but as she looked back on their half-dozen dinners, she realized they hadn't revealed anything deeply personal. She knew his taste in music was eclectic and he preferred snow skiing over water skiing, but she didn't know what his childhood had been like.

So much for honest and open communication.

"She manipulated you. Be on guard for it in future," he warned crisply. "Take everything she told you with a bucket of salt. And don't pretend she didn't try to pull you to her side when she got you alone."

She had, but Ilona didn't feel manipulated. She felt sorry for her. Sad for both of them.

"Do you want one?" Leander was pouring himself a drink.

"Thank you." She didn't really want it. Most nights she changed and they spent the rest of the evening working on their laptops or watching television. Tonight, she curled up on the sofa and accepted the glass he handed her, gently asking, "Will you tell me your side of it?"

"What's to tell? She didn't want to be a mother, didn't want a relationship with me when I was a child and needed her, but now she expects my attention and affection. I send her money to ensure she lives comfortably. I don't know why that isn't enough."

Because Susan was lonely and regretful and had been in a no-win situation from the start, if even a smidge of what she had told Ilona was true.

"You were eight when she moved back to London?" she pried carefully.

"To star in a musical. Not even a particularly good one. Her career has always been more down than up, but she insisted on pursuing it." His tone was dismissive.

"That's entertainment, I think. Eternally hoping for the big break." And wasn't everyone entitled to dream? "Perhaps she was homesick. I used to suffer it quite badly."

"When you were at boarding school?" He looked over his shoulder from the window.

"When I came to live with my father."

He made a noncommittal noise and returned to glowering at the city lights.

"It sounds like she was very young when she had you."

"They both were. My father managed to stick around so I don't see why she couldn't."

I got pregnant on holiday, Susan had told her, adding with a papery laugh, *I don't know how. Leander's father was so shy he could barely speak to me, but we had a little fling. I felt so grown-up until I was forced to grow up. My mother told me I'd better hope he married me because she wouldn't have an unwed mother in her house.*

"I have to ask..." Ilona bit her lip. Her own mother hadn't left her by choice so it wasn't particularly fair to say this, but, "Would you be as judgmental if your father had gone away to pursue his career?"

"He involved me in it," he said flatly, adding with scathing sarcasm, "But I take your point. My desire to star in musicals is nonexistent. It's my fault I didn't see her most of my life."

Ah. Well, then. She looked into her drink. "She never asked you to join her?"

"What was the point? I would have been at school during the day. She worked nights and weekends. We wouldn't have seen one another."

He and Niko were so close, Susan had lamented. *Leander wanted to stay here with his father so I didn't fight for him. I don't think he's ever forgiven me for that.*

Leander swore and squeezed the back of his neck. "I know it's childish to resent her. You're right. A father can absent himself without such harsh judgment, but she made a lot of promises to me that never panned out. She took the support my father sent her, but never took *me*. When I told her that Midas was offering to take our software to market, she encouraged us to trust him. She wanted the financial benefit of what Midas promised without having done any of the work to earn it."

Not unlike Midas, Ilona inferred. And the promised benefits hadn't arrived. Leander must have felt so foolish when he realized that Midas had tricked them. It was natural to look for someone to blame. He probably thought that if his mother had cautioned him, instead of encouraging him, he might not have lost everything.

"When I found— When my father died, she didn't turn up until the funeral service."

Found. Oh, no. She hadn't known that part. "I'm so sorry, Leander."

He shook off her murmur of sympathy.

"But—" Ilona frowned. "I was under the impression she arrived right away."

"Is that what she told you?"

"Not explicitly. It was just an impression," she mused, recollecting Susan's anguish.

He didn't cry, not even at the service, he was so traumatized. He didn't say a word to me until it was all over.

"*Then* she wanted me to come live with her," he said bitterly. "But she didn't have anything to offer me, just a flat-share and a poorly executed dream. My father had had to stop sending her support after Midas's trickery so we were both completely broke. The house had been mortgaged to finance the development of our technology. It was already in foreclosure. My father had legal bills from trying to sue Midas for what was ours. The stress and failure were so heavy on him..." He slugged back most of his drink.

He'll never forgive me for not being here, but I didn't love Niko. Not the way a wife should. Marrying so young, I felt cheated of the life I should have had. I kept thinking I would prove my dreams were worth the time I had invested in them, but I never have. Not in Leander's eyes. Somehow, I turned into my mother. I caused my own child to resent me. By the time Niko was gone, Leander wanted nothing to do with me.

"Did your father love her?" Ilona asked curiously.

"Yes." No hesitation. It was a fact delivered with a side of scorn.

Her heart felt stretched completely out of shape then, for all of them.

"He never looked at another woman and always said he wanted her to be happy. He let her disappear and keep his name and his money... But he was miserable without her. He didn't say it, but I could see it. How could she expect that I would side with her when she had treated him that way?"

"She let him raise her son, though. It's fine that you're angry with her, Leander, but surely it counts for something that she didn't make you live away from him? She said you wanted to be here with your father so she didn't fight for you. That you never wanted to come see her so she quit asking."

She could only see his profile, but his expression twisted with distaste.

"Is it such a crime that she wanted to live where *she* chose? On her own terms?" Ilona could relate to that; she really could.

His body seemed to bunch up with tension.

She braced herself to have her head bitten off, but he shrugged away whatever impact her remark had made.

"Maybe I would have had more sympathy for her if she hadn't lived off my father all that time. Off of me." He turned and jabbed his chest. "I sent her home with what I got from selling the little I had left. Then I hired on with a remote labor camp and sent her half my paycheck. I still support her. So tell me again how that makes her someone I should respect?"

"Don't then," she said, setting aside her drink and rising to her feet. "Your relationship with your mother is your business. But from my perspective, she didn't mean to hurt you. She was young and idealistic and misguided. Maybe she didn't show her love the way you wanted her to, but she does love you. I would have given anything to have had that much, rather than the mother figure I had in Odessa who destroyed my self-esteem. Enjoy nursing your grudge. I'm going to bed."

CHAPTER TEN

ILONA WASN'T ENTIRELY WRONG, which was irksome.

Leander much preferred to sit atop his high horse, but at thirty-two, he had to feel some pity for his parents, both a very young twenty when he had been born. They couldn't have been prepared for the responsibility. His father, nerdy and chronically anxious, had still been at university. His mother had struggled to make friends in her new country because her husband had been reluctant to leave the house. When she had suggested they all move to England, his father had outright refused. He hadn't liked change of any kind.

Ilona's remark about suffering homesickness as a child had briefly diverted him from wondering if his mother had experienced it, too. He hated to think of how powerless and lost Ilona must have felt at five, when she'd gone to live with a stranger who failed to fully care for her.

At least he'd had his mother for eight years. She had stayed until Leander's father earned his doctorate, then she had given her own aspirations eight years. Perhaps she would have come back on her own if his father hadn't passed, but they would never know. Leander hadn't given her a chance to make overtures in the subsequent sixteen years.

That remark Ilona had made about his mother coming

to Greece before the funeral was niggling at him. Had she arrived sooner? He genuinely couldn't remember those blurry days. They all bled into one another.

Very quickly, as a means of dealing with his grief and guilt, he had focused on revenge. The first step had been to make money. Fast. He had lied about his age and gotten on with a company that wanted a strong back willing to fly to remote locations and push a wheelbarrow full of wet cement. The mindless work had allowed him to plot meticulously how he would rise to Midas's level, then take him down.

Thanks to working next to his father's broad education in science, Leander had known a little about everything. He had quickly become an on-site resource for any sort of technical question. If he hadn't known the answer, he knew how to find it. Soon he'd worked his way up to being flown out to solve oddball problems on difficult projects.

The bean counters had always wanted the fastest, cheapest solution, however. They had never looked at the greater costs. The need for a company that would use greener technologies became glaringly obvious, but cultural mindsets were hard to change from within. He had started his own company and, by then, had known enough people in the industry he had been able to cherry-pick the ones who didn't need convincing. They had embraced his mindset and he'd been on a growth trajectory ever since.

Through those years, he hadn't let anyone—including his mother—distract him from his goal. Maybe he had held on to his resentment toward her so he wouldn't feel guilty about holding her at a distance. That's also why he'd sent her money, to soothe his conscience.

When he had finally started his own business ten years ago, she had tried to give him all his money back, revealing that she had saved every penny he'd sent her.

He'd been *furious*. She hadn't made herself more comfortable all this time and she hadn't invested it properly either, leaving it to gather anemic interest in a daily savings account. Most excruciating, however, was that it had been hard for him to send that money to her. It had been hard to earn and hard to part with it when his desire to wreak his vengeance against Midas consumed him.

But she hadn't seemed to value what he'd sent or even to want it. That had *hurt*.

He used a swallow of alcohol to burn away the ache in his chest.

It was childish to still feel a sting over that. He'd made her buy a flat with it and now, at least, she didn't have to suffer eccentric roommates and other inconveniences.

He almost heard Ilona ask, "Why would you care if she suffers?"

Because he was his father's son. He understood that he had a responsibility toward his mother and lived up to it, regardless of his feelings toward her. That's all this was. He did his duty and he didn't need her buying him cardigans or asking whether he'd seen a dentist in some pretense that she cared. He wanted her to stay out of his way and out of his life.

She'd caused Ilona to light up, though, making all the right noises over mention of Venetian lace and calla lilies. Leander had left all the wedding decisions to his bride and, as he had listened, had realized there were a disgusting number of them. It had meant a lot to Ilona that his mother had applauded all the choices she had made. He'd seen shy pleasure glowing within her under the simple praise.

Meanwhile, *her* stepmother had been the subject of a security meeting. How would Odessa be escorted from the house if she tried to crash the ceremony? Would the police be called for her? Or only if Midas turned up?

Leander's mother might be clumsy with her affection and was maybe a little too self-involved, but Ilona had made a fair point. His mother didn't intentionally hurt anyone. If she wanted someone to fuss over, and Ilona wanted to receive that fuss, Leander shouldn't stand in the way of it. He would have to make clear that Ilona wasn't to be toyed with, of course. If his mother extended a friendship, she couldn't disappear in eight days or eight years, leaving Ilona as abandoned as he'd felt.

He glanced at the clock, deciding he had waited long enough. Ilona ought to be asleep.

Sleeping beside her was pure torture. Sharing his home with her was, but in the best possible way. Her aromatic products lingered in the bathroom after her shower, imprinting on his brain for the day. Her phone and laptop looked very feminine and cute next to his meatier electronics when she left them in the office to charge. She *snored*, but softly, like a kitten purring. Her weight barely made a dent on the far side of the bed, she never stole the covers, but he struggled to fall asleep or stay asleep because he couldn't stop thinking about the way she'd shattered against his touch on the yacht.

It was rare to have that sort of connection. He was dying to explore it more deeply. Pun intended.

Stop, he ordered himself, and ran his hand down his face.

Every night, as he lay awake beside her, he resolved to buy a bed for one of the other rooms. Then he woke beside her and *liked* it.

It didn't make sense. He wasn't a cuddler. He had always found having another body in the bed too hot. He didn't like the sense that someone was so close to him while he was unguarded, but with Ilona, he was the one on guard. He had developed a subconscious alertness to any danger that might approach her and he only relaxed when she was in his sight or sleeping beside him. When he knew she was safe.

She seemed to sleep soundly there, too, which also pleased him. She'd been jumpy and anxious that first night, as anyone would be, and continued to have tense moments. When he stepped close, she often went very still, seeming to hold her breath as though uncertain what he would do to her. That always disturbed him enough to have him moving away. He didn't want to intimidate her. He wanted her to be comfortable with him, to know he would never hurt her.

If Midas hadn't terrified her out of her mind, he might have reopened the sex question, but that would have to wait until… Hell. Hopefully not three years from now.

He drained his glass and set it aside, then quietly entered the bedroom.

Ilona was still mulling over everything she had learned about Leander when he entered the bedroom. He paused as he saw her sitting in the pool of lamplight, chin on the mountain of her updrawn knees.

She lifted her head, pulse tripping. She was usually fast asleep by the time he came to bed.

"I didn't think you'd still be up," he said, closing the door and tugging at his tie. "Is something wrong?"

"Just thinking."

"About my mother? I'm over it."

She'd been contemplating more than that, but as he threw his tie toward a chair her brain blanked entirely. Was he going to strip in front of her like one of those exotic dancers? *Okay.*

"I'll call her tomorrow and lay out some ground rules. I don't want her asking you about my private life, but if you two want to go for brunch or text each other cat videos, do so with my blessing."

"Where does picking out wallpaper fall? Too personal? Or…?" She waved her hands in the air, blinking with innocence.

He only gave her a flat stare, not seeming to enjoy the joke.

She bit her lips in compunction. "Thank you. I like her. And I feel for her, chasing something that never panned out the way she wanted it to. That's hard for anyone. She's really proud of you, you know. That you were able to make your own dream come true."

He paused in dragging his shirt free of his trousers. "My company isn't a *dream*. It's a means to an end."

Midas. He really was a four-letter word.

"Don't you think he takes up too much real estate in our heads?" She'd been thinking that a lot lately. "I think the best revenge would be to forget about him altogether and live our lives without his shadow hanging over us."

"Give up now? When I'm so close to squashing him like a bug?" Leander pulled his belt free and threw it after his tie. "Is that what you want to do? Let him get away with everything he's done?"

He sounded so aggressive, she pressed back into the pillows.

"No. But chasing revenge allows him to win in other ways. We can't be happy if we're angry and we deserve to be happy." She saw that so clearly now, how she had refused to allow herself real happiness because there had always been this dark fret that Midas would punish her for so much as a smile. He probably would continue to try to spoil her fun, but that didn't mean she should do his harmful work for him. "He shouldn't be allowed to steal our moments of pleasure from us."

Leander hung his hands on his hips and stared at her a moment, then he toed off his shoes, muttering, "I'm a little too drunk for this conversation."

"Am I making you angry? I'm not defending him." He didn't even *seem* drunk.

"No," he said dryly. "But my mind leapt to our little moment of pleasure on the yacht. The fact he stole your ability to enjoy that sort of thing only fans my flames of hatred."

"Oh." A blast of fiery heat burst alive within her, part alarm, part acute self-consciousness, part remembered ecstasy. "You, um…" She swallowed. "You think about that?"

He stopped halfway to the bathroom, shirt loose and open, feet bare. "Did you think I could forget it?"

"I don't know." She rubbed her chin on her knee. "We had that argument after and you've been so reserved ever since, not even hinting that you were interested in me that way."

"Because you were assaulted." He shoved his hands into his pockets. "You need to know I can control myself."

She did know that. Or rather, she had never thought he couldn't. She had moments when she felt vulnerable around him, but emotionally, not the kind of vulnerable where she didn't want to be trapped in an elevator with him.

His voice plummeted to a dark rasp that sounded as though it originated in his chest. "Do *you* think about it?"

"I don't know what you're talking about," she blurted, then dropped her guilty face onto her knees, hiding her culpable blush.

He gave a snort of amusement.

"I do think about it," she conceded, blushing harder as she lifted her head. Her voice thinned with plaintive emotion as she forced herself into that open honest place they were trying so reluctantly to find. "I think about it and about what I just said, that I don't want to live my life in reaction to what Midas might do. I don't want to think about him *at all*. I want to think about what *I* want." She hugged her knees even tighter into her chest.

Leander's cheeks went hollow. He stood rooted and still, as though carved from oak. "And what do you want?" he inquired.

Here she was leaping off a cliff again, this time of her own volition. Air rushed around her and her breath was gone. Her body braced for the icy plunge into the unknown.

But this yearning in her was too soul-deep to keep it contained. "I want a baby."

He swayed like a tree sustaining a hard gust. "You said—"

"I know what I said and that stands," she rushed to say. "I don't want a baby out of spite. I want a child. A family. And before you offer to make one with me, I need you to think about what that would really mean, Leander. Not what it would do to Midas, but what it would do to *you*. Especially..." She bit the corner of her mouth again. "Especially coming from parents who separated because they couldn't make it work."

He sucked air through his teeth and looked away. "That is completely different."

"No, it's not. We're *planning* to split up. Plenty of couples divorce with little impact on their children, but we would have to figure out how to do that before we start down that road."

He was still an inscrutable monolith, profile craggy and shadowed, jaw clamped tight.

"Or not," she mumbled, shrinking into her hunched shoulders. "I don't want you to have a baby with me for any reason than that you want one. Please don't agree otherwise, but…" Now she was floundering in the foam, getting knocked about by the choppy waves, unable to fully orient herself, but casting out for that final other thing she wanted. "I thought you should know that I'm open to it. And that…" She searched his profile, wishing she could see inside his head. "That even if you don't want children, I want…" She couldn't seem to swallow. Her throat had constricted too much. "I would like a real marriage. If you do," she ended in another rush.

"Sex." He grunted out the word like a caveman, swiveling his head to pin her to the bed. "You want sex. Unprotected sex."

Her heart was thudding so loud, she thought he must hear it across the room, calling to him like a drumbeat.

"Only if you do." She wanted to die. To smother herself in the pillows around her, but she was unable to move, unable to tear her eyes from his edgy, wolfish expression.

"I do." He sauntered toward her, holding her gaze. When he was close enough, he cupped her cheek.

She didn't pull back. In fact, his touch felt so good, her eyes fluttered closed for a moment. When she opened them, her whole body was trembling with nerves. A bigger jolt went through her as she read the hunger in his eyes, completely undisguised.

She might have been alarmed by that glimpse of unfettered lust, but he wasn't making any other move beyond caressing her cheek with his thumb, letting her see the intensity of his desire and that he could control it.

"I, um—" She could hardly form words. Her lips were nerveless, her voice a wavering sound in her throat. "I thought we could wait until our wedding night, though?"

"Quaint." His mouth twisted ruefully and he dropped his hand to his side.

"Only because…" She had to tell him. Had to. But she was worried about his reaction. Would he laugh? Dismiss her? There was only one way to find out. "I'm kind of a virgin."

Leander's soul briefly left his body before he slammed back to his earthly form in a discordant rush.

"Kind of?" he repeated.

"I am," Ilona confirmed, chin tucking defensively. "The yacht was the farthest I've ever gone with anyone."

"You've never had sex. With anyone." Leander couldn't match up the sensually abandoned woman who had exploded in his arms, the woman who had recalibrated his gauge for pleasure, the one who haunted his dreams every night, with the words that had just come out of her mouth.

"Correct."

"Then why the hell did you have that screen for STIs?" He wasn't modest, but the questions and exam were pretty damned personal. She shouldn't have put herself through all that when he hadn't even asked for it.

"I was mad at you," she said to her manicure. "And it wasn't your business until I decided it was your business."

Such an exasperating woman. He frowned, compelled to ask, "How old are you?"

"Twenty-four. And it's not that I'm against sex before marriage. It's Midas. I've spent my whole life denying myself, worried that every little thing I want to do will only bring negative attention from my family. It's *my* body. If I want to have sex, I can have sex." Her back shot straight and her chin thrust out with defiance.

"Agreed," he said, more at a loss than he'd ever been in his life.

"And if I'm going to have sex, it should be with someone who…" She cleared her throat. "Makes me want to have sex. Right?" The dignity and logic she was using to hide her discomfiture was adorable.

"You're talking about me, right?" He pointed at himself. "I'm the one who makes you want to knock boots?"

"If you're laughing at me, then definitely not you."

"I'm not." He was laughing at the situation and only because he was so astonished. Very little got by him, yet she continued to shake up his presumptions about her.

"Can I ask you one more thing?" Her dark eyes went wide with vulnerability.

"Anything," he assured her, unable to think of one thing she could ask him that would ruin his elation.

"I won't be mad," she insisted, "but I have to know so please be honest. Do you want *me*? Or is this just about Midas?"

An arctic wind seemed to gust through him, chasing out the tenderness that had crept into his heart. All the cracks and fractures inside him began to ache.

"Everything is about Midas," he said with brutal honesty.

She flinched, but nodded acceptance of that.

He didn't like hurting her, but, "I wouldn't be marrying you if you weren't who you are. You're tempting as hell, Ilona. I would have *wanted* to date you if we had met some other way, but I can't waver from the course I've set. If you weren't part of my attack on him, you would have been a distraction. An obstacle. I would have pushed my attraction aside and stayed focused on him."

She was biting the inside of her lip, lashes hiding her eyes, nodding convulsively.

"You wouldn't trust me if I lied and said something different," he ground out.

"I don't think I would have believed you if you had said

anything different." Her tone had gone hollow. Her face had lost its rosy color.

Her words were a hard kick, one that cooled his blood.

"After, though. After I've dealt with him, this marriage will only be about us."

"You just told me why it will *never* be about us. Midas will be baked into our vows." Her eyes were glistening as she looked up at him. "And you don't know how long it will take to be satisfied that he's paid enough," she noted sadly. "It could take years. Decades."

"True." He didn't hesitate to deliver that harsh reality, either. "But you told me once that you pick your battles. This one I'm in with him is worth having."

She shrugged, not seeming convinced.

He would prove it to her, though. And they would both live happier lives once he did.

CHAPTER ELEVEN

THE MORNING OF the rehearsal dinner, they convened with their lawyers in Leander's office tower where they signed the appropriate contracts including the one for their new home.

Ursula had found them something in Glyfada, a seven-bedroom contemporary villa with all the amenities, an established staff and gardens that created a shroud of privacy without walling them in. It was almost boxy in design and seemed made strictly from glass and polished marble, but it was bright and welcoming and the view of the infinity pool blended into the horizon so the property appeared to extend into the sea. The decorating would be finished while they were on their honeymoon and they would move in on their return.

Ilona was of two minds about that. She was excited for it, because it was such a lovely property, but she liked sharing her husband's bed. Would they make love then part ways every night? The question was plaguing her, but she hadn't found the courage to ask.

As they stood and shook hands all around, Leander asked Androu and Feodor to wait while he pulled Ilona into a small studio apartment adjacent to his office. Ilona was so distracted by the utilitarian space, she didn't immediately take in what he said.

"I want to make this official right now."

Ilona dragged her eyes off the wide bed. "Make what official?"

"Our marriage. All the paperwork is done, the license is good. There's an officiant waiting to join us."

"You want to get married *right now*?"

"You object?" His gaze narrowed keenly.

Her stomach somersaulted. He still didn't trust her, even after all she'd told him about herself and invited him to make a baby with her.

"I wasn't expecting this." Obviously. She had a feeling that was his purpose in springing it on her, to test her. That hurt, but even more than that, "I'm not…wearing my gown," she mumbled in a small voice, feeling silly for being so excited about wearing it. She rarely let herself truly shine, though. She had pulled out all the stops for tomorrow.

"You look lovely," he stated, dismissing that detail.

She looked down at her bone-colored skirt suit and pale pink blouse, mostly so he wouldn't read the depth of her hurt and disappointment. She looked as though she was attending a business meeting, which she was. That's all their marriage was. A merger. She really was a silly fool for thinking it could be anything else.

"Tomorrow will go ahead as planned," Leander assured her. "But in case it doesn't…"

Midas. Always Midas.

Ilona forced a smile past the ache that had arrived in her throat. "Of course. Let's close this deal."

If he found her remark as cold as his own behavior, she didn't see it. She led him back into his office.

Androu invited the officiant in and the ceremony commenced without ceremony, with only their two assistants in attendance.

For a moment, Ilona consoled herself that it was better

this way. She had been worried all the pageantry of speaking her vows in front of a crowd would play on her nerves, but it was actually worse in this little office where the silence of their surprised witnesses was intensely meaningful. They watched her grow emotional as the weight of her words caused her voice to shake and her eyes to fill.

The words weren't even particularly sentimental, just legal statements about the contract of marriage imbuing obligations and responsibilities that she must promise to uphold. Still, when Leander cupped her face and repeated them in his deep rumble, she had to bite her lips to keep them from quivering.

This was big. Profound. If she had had any lingering worries or fears about going through with this marriage, they no longer mattered because it was done. She was tied to this man who claimed he would never hurt her. She believed that, to a point. She was confident he wouldn't attack her physically or deride her, but as she looked into his eyes and the skin on her heart grew paper thin, she knew he could destroy her emotionally.

Because she was more than susceptible to him. She was growing to care for him. Deeply. She wanted him to care for her in the same way, but she didn't believe he was capable of it. Even if he was, he would refuse to let himself care too deeply because of who she was. Because he was too obsessed with Midas.

If you weren't part of my attack on him, you would have been a distraction.

It was heartbreaking to realize all of that, but then he lowered his head and kissed her. His lips brushed across hers, tender and sweet enough to cause a colorful explosion behind her closed eyelids. For a few precious seconds, she was convinced they were soul mates.

Then he drew back and the moment was gone. There

were more handshakes. Feodor gave her a misty hug and said something about how it was a relief to know that if anything went wrong tomorrow, at least the most important part had already happened.

It hadn't, though, Ilona realized with a lurch of her heart. She caught Leander—her *husband*—looking at her with banked hunger and it struck her like a wrecking ball that her wedding night had arrived a day early.

Leander watched Ilona kick off her shoes as they stepped off the elevator into the penthouse. He tried to catch her eye to read her mood, but she wasn't allowing it.

"I suppose I can use this time between now and dinner to pack for the honeymoon," she said in a tone that was not nearly as casual as she was likely striving for. She had mentioned going into her office this afternoon, but Feodor had looked at her like she was out of her tree and assured her there was nothing so pressing it couldn't wait.

Leander had sworn the pair to secrecy and brought her home, high on the triumph of being able to call her his wife. Strangely, his satisfaction went beyond vengeance. He was thrilled in deeply primitive, remarkably possessive ways. She was *his*.

He could tell she was still taken aback by his change in plan, though.

"You're angry with me," Leander surmised.

"No. Why would I be?"

"Because I didn't tell you what I wanted to do."

"Because you didn't trust me to go through with the wedding tomorrow," she extrapolated. "You don't trust me."

"I can't," he said bluntly, steeling himself against the bloom of hurt in her eyes. "The dominoes I've set in place are so delicate, it would only take one false breath to wreck it all."

"Don't tell me what else you're planning, then. Let it be a surprise for me as well as him." She moved into the bedroom, peeling off her jacket as she went.

Leander sighed, but he had no regret. The cascade toward Midas's downfall would start now and there was nothing the other man could do about it.

Midas would try, of course. Leander had no doubt about that. There would be some attempt to disrupt tomorrow's wedding, but it would not only fail, Midas would expose himself as the villain he was.

That was the first prong of Leander's attack. The second was to put the screws on Midas financially. Midas lived beyond his means—which was saying something considering the depth of the family fortune. Most of his assets were either leveraged to the hilt or bought on credit he couldn't pay down. Leander had been quietly positioning himself to buy up the other man's debts and loans so he could call them. That, too, began tomorrow.

The third and fourth tine on his barbed fork were aimed at Hercules and Odessa. By taking them out, Midas would lose his most loyal supporters and have little to fall back on.

Hercules had made himself an easy target by spending the last two years painting for a gallery showing. The gallery in question had recently been purchased by a shell company owned by Leander. It would close its doors indefinitely, locking all of Hercules's work inside, tying up any funds or acclaim he might have earned from those sales. Hercules could sue to have them released, but it would cost him a pretty penny to do so.

As for Odessa, did she think she was the only one who could grind gossip through the rumor mill? Misuse of charity funds wasn't even an unfounded lie. Leander literally had the receipts showing a profound difference in the actual costs of catering and the amount claimed against the raised donations. All of Odessa's pet caterers and planners would think twice about allowing her stink to attach itself to their reputations in future.

Within a few weeks, the entire family would be in such a shambles it would be an easy sell to the board that Leander should take Midas's place at the helm of Pagonis—especially if his wife was carrying the heir to the company by then.

I don't want you to have a baby with me for any reason than that you want one.

He did want one. Ilona might not believe it, but he wasn't thinking of their child as an instrument of vengeance. Only as a signpost of where the future was headed. Ilona's children would inherit the company and thus the board's allegiance should fall to her.

More than that, he wanted a baby for *her*. She wasn't the spoiled heiress he had originally judged her. She was privileged, but deprived. Strong as hell, yet vulnerable. Isolated. He wanted to give her the family she craved.

He wanted to give her things no one else had. Freedom from fear. Security. *Orgasms.*

He closed his eyes, still astounded she hadn't had any lovers. It was a crime that she had denied herself all this time and, if he delved around in his bucket of motivation, he knew his rush to marry her wasn't purely about revenge, either. He *wanted* her.

Why? He didn't harbor any secret fetishes for an untouched innocent.

But something about being with her while she discovered her sexuality pleased him. It turned him on and made him feel protective and indulgent and proud. It made him *hungry*. He wanted to show her everything they could do, make her tremble and moan and cry out in joy.

Maybe he did have a secret fetish.

Maybe he just wanted to have sex with a woman who had been on his mind constantly from the moment he'd met her.

He followed her to the bedroom.

Ilona was in a state of confused anticipation. She *was* angry with Leander. She was hurt that he didn't trust her. She was also nervous.

They were married. That meant they could have sex. Which wasn't to say she had been waiting for some sort of permission. She had only set that deadline because she was so darned *daunted* by the prospect and now that excuse was gone.

Which didn't put her off. She wanted to sleep with him. They had hours before the rehearsal dinner. A prickly heat coated her skin with something akin to urgency, but what if she wasn't good at it? What if they were both disappointed? The first time was always said to be a letdown. Anticlimactic.

Who had come up with *that* stupid pun?

How did she even make overtures to get things started? What would he think of her if she did?

She was standing in her robe, trying to work out what to put on so she might look enticing without looking desperate, when the bedroom door opened and he came to prop his shoulder against the open door of the closet.

"There's this thing I've heard married couples do," he drawled.

She sucked in a breath so loud his mouth twitched.

"It's called kissing and making up."

Make-up sex? Was that what she wanted her first time to be?

She hugged herself and stared into a hollow space between where her clothes hung beside his.

He sobered. "We don't have to do anything you don't want to do, Ilona. But we need to talk this out."

"I'm not angry," she insisted. "Not really. I'm..." Pressure built in her chest, then the words came out in a rush. "I'm scared. I'm afraid that if you don't trust me, it means I can't trust you. And now look what I've done." She was married to him. She was going to start sleeping with him. She was going to be more physically defenseless than it was possible to be.

She was also afraid of what he could do to her, what he was starting to make her feel. She feared becoming dependent on him for confidence and pleasure and self-worth. For a reason to wake in the morning.

"Believe it or not, I'm trying to protect you," he said gravely. "All of the actions I'm taking from now on are mine. He can't accuse you or blame you if you have no part in it, not even knowledge of what I plan to do."

She jerked a shoulder to dismiss that, but she was slightly mollified.

"Let's agree to do one thing for the next few hours," he began.

Her eyes widened and he barked out a laugh.

"Not every word out of my mouth is about sex, Ilona. Relax." He ran his hand over his face, rearranging his amusement into something more kind. "Let's quit talking about him. Or thinking about him. When we're in this room, in our bed, it's only about us."

"That's frightening, too," she realized as she felt the full weight of his attention. It was as though his words had removed an invisible wall that she had been using to hold him off. Now she felt exposed. Defenseless.

"Why?"

Because there was no "us." They didn't have enough between them that wasn't tainted by their history.

Maybe that's what sex was for, though. To build the connection they needed.

With an awkward memory? She rubbed her brow, not relishing making a fool of herself.

"Does it bother you that I don't really know how it all works? I mean, I *know*." She rolled her eyes upward. "I know what happens. I lack *practical* knowledge." Her cheeks were so hot they hurt.

"You seem to be a quick study. I'm not worried."

"Don't laugh at me." She covered her face.

"I'm not. I swear I'm not." He was definitely chuckling as his warm hands came around her wrists and drew them down. "I won't rush you. You can stop me anytime. You know that, don't you?" His quicksilver gaze delved into her own, so deep her insides quavered.

She was barefoot, much shorter than when she wore shoes. She was inundated by emotions, too. Unsure but excited, inadequate but wanting to learn. Safe, but aware this would change things in her. She would feel different about him and herself after this. The intimacy of the act, the way she would have to strip away all her defenses and reveal herself, was terrifying.

But she gave the barest hint of a nod, too overwhelmed to speak.

A smile ghosted across his lips, then he drew her arms up to encourage them to twine around his neck while he pressed his mouth to hers, brushing softly.

It was a chaste kiss. A greeting and a quest. A promise to go slow and wait for her.

It was lovely and for a moment she simply enjoyed it, allowing her fingertips to play against the stubble that faded into a line on the back of his neck.

But her shy desire had been simmering for weeks, ever since that first wild kiss at the restaurant. Their interlude on the yacht had teased her with what could be and now her yearnings were gathering into a tangle with her anxious determination, forming a knot of frustration. He was being too careful. Too slow. She wanted the storm. The hurricane she knew he could deliver. She wanted to be swept away.

She instinctually opened her mouth and pressed more firmly into his kiss, allowing her breasts to squash against the wall of his chest, willing him to plunder.

A small jolt went through him and then his arm firmed around her. He abruptly angled his head to seal their mouths more thoroughly. His other hand cupped the back of her head. He held her where he wanted her as he took. Ravished.

But he gave, too. Oh, he knew how to inject delicious joy into her with the thrust of his tongue and the way he palmed her backside. An electric current formed between all those points of contact, making her nerve endings hum. When he scraped his teeth at her lip, she tightened her arms and rose on tiptoes. He tilted her hips into the thick presence between them, letting her feel his arousal against her mound and she nearly fainted with excitement.

An involuntary moan left her and a grunt of satisfaction left him. He abruptly broke away, leaving her dazed, but he gathered her up and brought her to the bed, setting her there with a dark look of intention in his eyes.

What had she done?

The door was open, the sun pouring through the slats of the blinds, illuminating the bed and her. And him, as he undressed, unhurried and watchful.

She eyed the fine pattern of hair across his chest as it appeared, noted how tight his dark brown nipples were, admired the sheen on his powerful shoulders and the way his taut abdomen held such a well-defined six-pack. She wanted to touch him there. Kiss his navel. Why? What a strange compulsion, but it was real and nearly impossible to resist.

"Take off your robe," he commanded as he dropped his shirt to the floor.

She barely heard him through the rushing in her ears, but she timidly rose onto her knees and slowly unbelted, watching him watching her. It's like a bathing suit, she tried to tell herself, but it wasn't.

"Tease," he chided with smoky pleasure as shyness slowed her movements and she unwound her hair before she loosened her robe and only let it fall to the point it cut across her shoulders.

He shed his pants and socks without hesitation then made an adjustment to himself inside his briefs. The thick shape of him was obvious, though. Butterflies battered in her middle as she stared at that hidden, mysterious part of him.

Leander joined her, knees splaying wide outside her own demurely closed ones. He finished brushing the silk off her arms so it pooled onto the mattress behind her.

A considering noise rumbled in his chest as he took in her pale yellow bra and matching underwear. His finger dropped one bra strap off her shoulder, then his mouth set itself there, branding the spot with heat and dampness and an electrifying sensation that shot straight into her nipples.

His mouth nuzzled and climbed up her nape, lifting goose bumps on her arms and scalp. Then he was kissing her again, gathering her in his arms as they both rose to kneel in the middle of the bed.

She could hardly breathe, could hardly hold her balance and clung to his shoulders, startlingly weak. It was the on-slaught of sensations. Not just the kiss, but the hardness of his flexed muscles beneath her hands and the brush of his skin against hers. The intriguing shape of him and the way his flat hand thrust into the back of her panties and cupped her cheek.

Her stomach turned to jelly and she broke from their kiss to gasp, "This feels really good."

"It does." His deep, rasping voice was as much a part of this seduction as everything else.

She helplessly turned her face into the crook of his neck and her lips parted on instinct, tongue dabbing out to taste his skin.

The hand on her bottom clenched more possessively and a sound rattled in his chest that sent a heady sensation of power through her.

"You like that?"

"You can tell I do."

His briefs were struggling to contain him. She drew back enough to run her hands over his chest and the ripples of his ribs and down to the flat stomach that had called to her a moment ago. He was firm and warm and her thumb followed the trail of flat hairs to his navel.

When her fingertips splayed to the waistband of his briefs, she glanced up at him.

He lifted a brow in laconic invitation to continue.

She swallowed and let her touch stray into his waistband, discovering more heat, velvet and steel, aggressive strength and a power to make him hiss as she explored.

She couldn't believe she was doing this, touching any man like this, let alone Leander. He hated her, didn't he?

Not in this moment. His gray eyes glittered like sunlight on a lake. His mouth was relaxed and each of his exhales was a near purr of enjoyment.

"Like this," he rumbled, pushing his briefs down his thighs.

She was confronted by the sight of his erection, dark with arousal, intimidating yet compelling. She had another impulsive fantasy of taking him into her mouth, wondering what that would feel like, taste like. Wondering if he would like it.

He showed her how he liked to be stroked, guiding her, watching her, then he cupped the side of her neck and kissed her. At the same time, his hand plunged into the front of her underwear and he claimed the slick flesh he found, sending a sharp spike of pleasure through her, wiping her brain.

"Am I doing it right, *glykiá mou*?" he mocked against her gasping mouth. "Show me."

She couldn't speak. She lost her grip on him and her own control as he stroked his two fingers through her folds, returning again and again to tease the knot of nerves in the small vise of his touch.

"Did you think you weren't having this effect on me?" he asked as she pressed her forehead into his collarbone. "How close are you?"

Close. She held herself still for his touch, breath stalled as she chased the pinnacle that his teasing touch kept just out of reach.

She sobbed when he withdrew. She half expected a smug smile at denying her, but he only promised, "Soon."

There was nothing in his face except lust. Unadulterated lust as he finished removing his underwear and dispatched hers as adeptly. He pressed her onto her back.

This was it. She apprehensively parted her legs as he loomed atop her, but after one brief kiss, he began working his way down.

Oh, no. That would be too intimate.

"We can just…do it," she said, playing her fingers through his hair as his mouth went across the top of her chest. He was ready; she was ready. "Don't you want to?"

"I want to do many things, *ateleíoti gynaíka mou*." My endless woman. "Many."

He cupped her breast and licked at her nipple. Blew across the dampness so it tightened hard enough to ache, then enclosed it in the heat of his mouth. Bizarrely, the pull of his mouth sent electric heat into her loins, flooding her with a fresh response of damp arousal.

She found herself writhing beneath him as he anointed both her breasts this way. She slid her thighs against his hard ones, liking the scrape of his leg hair against the softness of her own limbs, arching so he would take her nipple deeper into his mouth.

At one point, he hissed something in a voice that wasn't quite steady and his teeth scraped the side of her breast. Then he was taking his kisses down and down, before parting her and then tasting her and leaving her with no secrets left undiscovered.

He didn't need her to show him anything. Before she could dream of being self-conscious, she was sobbing in the acute pleasure of climax.

That did make her feel abashed, tipping so quickly and easily into her own enjoyment. She felt selfish, but he didn't stop. He stayed exactly where he was, tenderly teasing her back into restless arousal, then growing more determined to make her moan.

When she began lifting her hips into his caress, he slowly made his way back up her body, reacquainting one kiss at a time with all the places he'd already visited.

"What are you doing to me?" she asked, baffled by how much care he seemed to be taking. By how much pleasure he was bestowing upon her with such generosity.

"Enjoying you. Enjoying what we do to each other. I love the way you're giving yourself over to me, letting me claim all of you as mine."

Her overheated brain tripped on his *I love*, but she didn't have time to become despondent that it wasn't a more profound declaration. He swept his hand down between them, before plunging a finger into the molten core of her, making her shake.

They kissed passionately and when she lifted her hips into his touch, he shifted to settle over her.

"I'm not wearing a condom," he reminded against her lips, guiding the blunt tip of his erection against her entrance.

"I know," she whispered, legs helplessly falling open even farther.

He watched her as he pressed into her. It was too much. She wanted to close her eyes against that intense look of his, but she couldn't make herself do it. She gripped his upper arms and bit her bottom lip and tried not to wince at the sting that grew to a white-hot warning of true pain. A small sound of alarm throbbed in her throat.

He froze. Tension pulled across his cheekbones. His nostrils twitched and his lips thinned against his teeth.

"Keep going," she pleaded. It hurt, but beneath the sting was a sweet stimulation that called to her.

He forged in, the pressure and stretch becoming insistent. Just when she thought she couldn't take it, his hips sealed themselves to hers. He let out a shaken breath and cupped his hand against the side of her head, one thumb playing at the corner of her mouth.

"All right?"

His throbbing flesh was inside her. She could feel him twitching within her in the most astonishing sensation. His hard legs kept hers open for his invasion and the rest of him was a heavy weight upon her.

In every way she was at his mercy. Helpless. But when he nibbled at the edge of her jaw and breathed, "You feel so good," she felt precious. Like she was giving him something merely by allowing this.

Her eyes stung then and he noticed the dampness gathering there. His brows came together. "Hurt?"

"A little. It's okay, it's just…" She almost said "big." *Not that, Ilona. He'll laugh.* "I didn't know it would feel like this. It's just sex. Everyone does it." But it was overwhelming.

A shadow might have passed within his arousal-fogged gaze, but he touched his mouth to hers and murmured, "No one does it like this. We're special. Move when you're ready. Find out what you like."

Curious, she shifted a little, arched and rubbed. Little fires restarted within her. An enticing promise called to her, keeping her searching for those sparks and swirls of pleasure. Her sensitized skin grew a fresh batch of goose bumps and her hands *required* knowledge of his back and shoulders and buttocks. Her mouth sought each place she could reach, opening against his upper arm and throat and chin, learning his textures and taste.

As she moved her hips, she discovered pressure and stimulation in some places that overcame the sting in others. In fact, when her knees bent against his hips, he slid a fraction deeper and the nudge of his pubic bone grinding against her mound brought a fresh spark of need to where they were joined.

She instinctually found a rhythm that built those deep, delicious sensations and realized after a moment that he was moving with her in this dance, meeting and matching her movements with perfect synchronicity. It was beautiful, really.

It was lovemaking. This was how it happened. She clung to the source of her pleasure—him and his flesh and the dream that they were one. He moved with more power, withdrawing and returning, reinforcing that he was strong enough to hurt her, but was taking care not to. He delivered that exquisite sting and the fiery ache that was becoming essential and she welcomed it. Welcomed him. *Come back come back. Again, again, again.*

She bit her lip and moaned with abandon, completely immersed in the ecstasy his body inflicted on hers. She surrendered to it. Surrendered to him and his ragged breaths and the way he caught a hand under her tailbone and tilted her hips and drove even deeper.

There it was, the pinnacle bathed in light and the chasm beyond.

This was how love happened. In this moment of joy and trust and feeling deeply attuned. Right here, she believed Leander had the power to make everything right in her world. She believed he would be bound to her always and she would never be alone again.

In this moment, as another climax swept up to suffuse her, her heart opened to let him in. She felt her love for him encompass her and believed he loved her back.

He must. He was shouting her name and they were tumbling through the unknown together, knitted and knotted and *one*.

It would be hours before she saw sex as the false promise it really was.

CHAPTER TWELVE

"YOU'VE MISTAKEN ME for someone who forgives easily. I'm not," were Leander's last words before he closed her into her car in the underground parking lot of the penthouse.

Ilona sputtered with laughter, besotted as she turned her head to watch him while her car pulled away and he moved across to his own. She was giddy with sex hormones and wedding excitement and stupid, cupid love. She closed her eyes as she came into the light, holding onto the image of his stern, unsmiling profile, adoring him.

At the rehearsal dinner last night, Susan had cornered Leander into picking her up this morning to bring her to the wedding, suggesting he breakfast with her since Ilona was going to the house early, meeting the team who would help her dress.

You're not supposed to see your bride until the wedding anyway. It's bad luck, Susan had scolded him.

They still hadn't told anyone they were already married. They were also the only ones who knew they had consummated that marriage. Three torrid times. Those memories from yesterday afternoon, from last night before they fell asleep, then again this morning were delicious secrets Ilona held close inside herself where they warmed her all the way until she arrived at the house.

Feodor met her, already run off his feet. "The WiFi is

spotty and of course the florist hasn't arrived yet," he muttered. "Hercules texted best wishes and said he's still willing to give you away."

If things had been different, she might have asked him to.

"Tell him Leander's mother will walk me up the aisle." Originally, she and Leander had planned to walk in together, but Susan had asked for the honor last night. Ilona couldn't refuse her, not when it made her feel as though she was being accepted into his life.

She went upstairs where she spent the next two hours being primped and pampered and polished. When her makeup was flawless and flowers intricately woven into her gathered locks and she had nibbled enough of an omelet to tide her over through the next hours, she was laced into her gown.

It was fitted through the bodice and hips then flared midthigh. Its long bell sleeves were made of pure lace. Diamanté crystals were strategically woven throughout to create flashes of rainbow brilliance. Like the sleeves, her back was bare skin beneath fine, netted lace with delicate floral patterns and two dozen tiny pearl buttons down her spine.

She felt more beautiful than she ever had in her life.

What would Leander think, she wondered?

"Is Leander here?" she asked. The sound of musicians tuning their instruments had become soothing background melodies while the din of gathering voices had grown.

"He might be having trouble getting in," someone said. "The drive is clogged by cars dropping guests."

"I suppose," Ilona said, but her stomach curdled.

Midas, she thought. If anything went wrong today, he would be to blame. But for some reason, her mind went back to what Leander had said as they had parted this morning.

You've mistaken me for someone who forgives easily.

She had thought he meant he wasn't prepared to forgive his mother.

Now, as she moved so she could see the growing crowd assembling on the lawn, she wondered if he had meant her. A Pagonis.

Her stomach cramped again.

Two hundred people had been invited. They spilled onto the grounds, eating hors d'oeuvres and drinking champagne, waiting to convene in the rows of chairs on either side of the white-carpeted aisle before an arbor that had been built for the occasion.

He already married me, she reassured herself. There would be no point in leaving her at the altar.

Except to humiliate her.

Her stomach kept taking dizzying swoops of grim premonition.

"Ilona?" Feodor came into the lounge where she was hovering. He looked pale. Two men stood behind him, both wearing police uniforms.

Her heart nearly came out her throat. "Is Leander here?" she asked, hearing the desperation in her own voice.

"No. And, um…"

"Ilona Callas?" One man introduced himself as a lieutenant inspector. "You have to come with us. You're under arrest for trafficking narcotics."

Midas has done this. That's what Ilona told herself for the first two hours, while she waited for her lawyer to appear.

The police hadn't even let her change from her gown. They had put her in handcuffs and forced her to endure the humiliation of being loaded into their car before the shocked audience of her wedding guests.

Then she was left in a cell with two other women who

were less extravagantly dressed, but equally miserable and quietly distressed.

Her flustered lawyer appeared, mumbling about unforeseen delays before he explained that the police had received evidence that drugs were being smuggled in shipments from Callas Cosmetics. Ilona had been implicated by a photo and a signature.

"That's doctored evidence!" she cried.

"It's flimsy, I know," her lawyer said grimly. "It's not even due process. The police have forty-eight hours to make an arrest without a warrant if they catch someone in the act of commiting a crime. They're claiming they had to act because you're about to leave on your honeymoon. I'll be filing for a dismissal and they will eventually face a disciplinary investigation, but that doesn't help you in this moment. I have to secure your release through normal channels which will take time. Hours. Not days," he assured her, but she was losing heart by the minute.

"Has…" She was afraid to ask, afraid of the answer. "Has Leander been informed?" *Why isn't he here?*

"He's not answering his phone and—" Her lawyer's face tightened. "There's a report his yacht left port with him on it."

You've mistaken me for someone who forgives easily.

If there had been anything substantial in her stomach, she would have thrown it up.

"It shouldn't be much longer," her lawyer promised and she was shown back to her cell.

When she was finally released, it was because her bail had been posted by Hercules. She went home with him.

A woman's startled cry opened Leander's eyes, but nothing about what he saw made sense. Was that a bed leg? Why was he drunk? *Where was he?*

"Help, help!" the woman cried.

"Is he dead?" another voice asked with alarm.

"I don't know."

They sounded like they were in another room. He heard the rush of feet coming toward him and pushed himself up enough to prop his back on the side of the mattress.

Was that his mother on the bed? He reached for her wrist and she moaned slightly, twitching. Alive, at least. *What the hell had happened?*

He swore, recalling helping her to the bed because she had suddenly felt ill. One minute they'd been sharing coffee, the next they'd both been nauseous and dizzy. Leander had staggered her to the bed and…must have blacked out because he couldn't remember anything after that.

"I was drugged," he told the women in housekeeping uniforms, both blinking with astonishment at him. It was the only explanation. "What time is it?"

He turned his head to the clock on the nightstand and swore again. *The wedding.*

"Ilona." Her name was a bitter pang of regret in the back of his throat.

He patted his jacket until he found his phone. Another string of curses came out of him as he saw dozens of texts and attempts to call, most of them from Androu, but others, too. His lawyer, guests from the wedding. All were asking some version of, Where are you? What do you want me to do?

"Get my mother a doctor," he said to the housekeeper as he forced himself onto his feet. His whole body felt a thousand times heavier than it should.

"Did I miss the wedding?" his mother asked on a sob of anguish. "I didn't mean to let her down. I swear, Leander." Tears dampened her fluttering lashes.

He squeezed her hand. "It's not your fault." It was his.

"But I have to find Ilona. A doctor is coming," he promised and dialed Dino as he bounced off the door frame into the hall. "Bring the car around."

"I'm having new tires put on. I stepped away for a cigarette and they were all slashed."

Of course they were. Leander could have smashed his phone to pieces at that moment, he was so furious. He ended his call and hit the speed dial for Androu.

"Finally!" Androu said in a choked voice. "I couldn't reach you—"

"Is she okay? Hurt?" His heart was clenched into a hard fist inside his chest. "Where is she?"

A beat of surprise, then, "Still with her brother, I think."

"Midas?" Again, he nearly battered his phone to pieces on the elevator wall. Had she somehow been part of this? Tricking him into going to his mother and risking both their lives with whatever sedative had been slipped into their food?

"The other one," Androu said. "I think. Feodor stopped responding to my texts, but the last I heard, Hercules was bailing her out."

"She was *arrested*?"

Hercules had brought her a clean set of clothes to change into—men's drawstring pants and a T-shirt that was likely tight on him and hung loose on her. Ilona changed into them for the drive to his place where he made her one of his fancy coffees from his espresso maker.

He took his phone into his bedroom when Odessa began ranting over video chat about the scandal Ilona had brought to the family name today.

Ilona could still hear both sides of the conversation. Hercules occupied an upper-level floor of an industrial building. His bedroom was behind a partition made of glass cubes. The only door in the place was on the toilet. The rest was open concept with easels and canvases before the tall windows. Brushes and rags were littered everywhere, all emitting the chemical scent of paint and turpentine.

When there was a buzz for the service elevator, Ilona reached to press the button, but paused. Feodor was bringing her phone and purse, but she had been burned too many times lately.

She opened the call to the speaker below. "Feodor?"

"It's me," Leander said. "Midas drugged me. I just woke up."

"I don't care."

"What do you mean you don't care?" he thundered. "I would have been there, Ilona. I wouldn't have let that happen to you."

"But you *did*." For the first time since the cold handcuffs had encircled her wrists, her eyes grew hot and her throat began to ache with a pressure she wasn't sure she could withstand. "I told you I didn't want to be in the middle of this war of yours. I told you I didn't want to trust you because you would only let me down."

"I'm here now. *Let me up.*"

"Don't," Hercules said, appearing from behind the partition.

"Is she there with you?" Odessa cried.

"Don't tell Midas," Hercules warned his mother, but they both knew she absolutely would.

The threat of having to face Midas was horrible enough Ilona knew she had to leave. She pressed the button to allow Leander up.

Hercules told Odessa he would call her back, then glared at Ilona. "Why did you do that?"

She didn't get a chance to reply. Leander appeared in the cage of the elevator like an angry god. He raked back the grill with a clatter, stepped in, then halted to stare at her.

She didn't move, but the shock was wearing off and hatred was seeping in to take its place.

"Get the hell out," Hercules told him. "Leave her alone."

"You're the hero now? When you're letting your brother assault her and manufacture drug charges against her? You and I will settle our differences in due course. Right now, I'm taking Ilona home."

"*You* think you're on the high ground?" Hercules scoffed. "You only tried to marry her to get your hands on our company! Do you realize that, Ilona?"

Leander transferred his sharp gaze from Hercules to her. "You haven't told him?"

"Told me what?"

"I'm too ashamed," Ilona said, purely out of malice.

Leander flinched and she immediately felt small, but Leander told Hercules, "We're already married."

"Ilona," Hercules breathed in horror. "You didn't."

"Tell your brother his attempt to stop our wedding didn't work. Let him know that investigators are already looking for the attendant who poisoned my mother and me as well as any connection he has to Ilona's arrest. You should be asking yourself how much longer you're willing to cover for him because I am very, very angry and I will not stop until *everyone* who played a part in this is extremely sorry."

"I—" Hercules was shooting his gaze back and forth between them, the helplessness in him breaking her heart. He was still there on the inside, caring for her, but not enough. Not even enough to save himself.

"Come." Leander's voice gentled as he crouched beside her. "I promised I would take you away from them and I will."

Leander had been blind with rage since leaving the hotel, but he had arrived below as Feodor was stepping from Ilona's car, her bag and other belongings in hand.

"Wait here," Leander had ordered the PA. "We won't be long."

Feodor had tried to stare him down and Leander had spared one moment to appreciate the man's loyalty to Ilona, but Leander was collecting his wife and that was that.

He physically gathered her up, ignoring her half-hearted attempt to be set on her feet.

"I don't want to go home with you," she said, voice filled with the ache of her disappointment in him.

"The yacht is waiting." To take them on their honeymoon. He'd been looking forward to it and she seemed to have been, too. Before.

What a bloody mess.

"They said it was gone. That you *left*."

He could hear the knife that had been to her heart. He paused to absorb how badly he'd failed her today. He hated failure. *Hated it.*

"That was a lie told to distress you." It had worked. She was insubstantial in his arms. The corners of her mouth dragged down, her sadness profound enough to send a fracture across his chest. "Do you have anything here that you want to take?"

"No."

Hercules turned his head, sending Leander's gaze into the corner. Her wedding gown was draped over a chair, it's white layers like a snowdrift blown into a corner, but the kind that had weathered winter and was melting in spring, streaked by dirt and stains, no longer pure and pretty.

She had been excited to wear that gown. Leander had seen it when she had told his mother about it. He was so sorry in that moment. So sorry that all his precautions had been against infiltrators and criminals. No one was supposed to be able to get to her today. It hadn't occurred to him that Midas would send the *police* after her.

With one final look of contempt toward Hercules, he made the lethal promise, "I'll see you at the next board meeting."

CHAPTER THIRTEEN

Ilona woke to darkness, eyes and throat still raw from the storm of tears that had taken her once she had come aboard the yacht. She had cried and shouted and said awful things to Leander.

"I *hate* you," she had screamed. The words had rasped from the very depth of her being.

"I know."

He hadn't offered any excuses. He hadn't reminded her that he'd been unconscious the whole time. *He* wasn't the one who had set her up to be arrested, but he had let her berate him as though he was.

It wasn't him she hated. It wasn't him she wanted to shout at, but he took it and held her when she fell apart. He tucked her into bed when she was reduced to a few stray sniffles and a desire to forget everything in the amnesia of sleep.

And now he rolled toward her in the bed and rubbed her arm. "Shhh. You're safe. Go back to sleep."

She couldn't, not until she said, "I'm sorry."

"Don't." His hand paused to squeeze. "I knew he would try to disrupt the wedding, but your bodyguards couldn't stop actual police. I expected an attack on *me*, not my mother."

"I'm apologizing for making you think that I blame you. I don't. It's not your fault that he's a terrible human being."

"But I should have expected—"

"Leander." She slithered near and something eased in her when he adjusted his position and gathered her close, aligned along his front. It was deeply reassuring and everything she needed when she felt so disjointed and broken.

"We agreed that he doesn't come to bed with us," she reminded.

His chest expanded and she thought he was about to argue, but he only let out his breath in a resigned sigh.

"All right. We'll talk in the morning. Good night." He pressed a kiss to her forehead.

She was still wearing Hercules's clothes, but Leander wore only briefs. She slid her hands across the warm planes of his body, rubbing her feet on the tops of his.

"Angele mou." He caught her hand.

"You don't want to kiss and make up?" She extracted her hand and caressed his shape through his briefs. Squeezed in the way that made his breath hiss. "It feels like you do."

He laughed softly and his nose bumped her cheek. His mouth found the corner of hers. "If it will make you feel better, then yes. I do." He was smiling; she could feel it.

"You'll make that great sacrifice for me?" This too was love, she realized, as softness and light crept back into her, edging out the day's darkness of anguish and resentment. It was soft caresses in the night, quiet words and help removing her clothes. It was tenderness and forgiveness and being both hurried, yet not, kissing and caressing and building something beyond tension and arousal. Trust and care and *need*.

They both gasped as he thrust into her and he held her tight, saying against her ear, "I thought I might never feel you like this again. Your lips still taste of salt."

From her tears. But his kiss dissolved those lingering traces and they moved and rolled and made so much love. When he brought her atop him, she threw off the blankets and straddled him and ran her hands over his chest, thinking, *I love you. I love you.*

"Ilona." He cupped her head and brought her down for a long kiss. Then he rolled her beneath him again, thrusting and thrusting until she was lost to a long, intense orgasm.

His teeth scraped her chin and he coaxed, "Again."

And that was how the night passed, in a blur of connection and closeness and endless pleasure.

I love you. I love you.

Did she realize she had said it aloud? If she did, was she wondering why he hadn't said it in return? Had she even been telling the truth? How could she love him when he'd failed her so spectacularly?

He didn't even know what love was. Not really. Oh, he had loved his parents as a child, but his mother had broken his heart and his father had been, well, a functioning adult, but there had been a certain amount of parenting the parent in their relationship.

To Leander's mind, love was responsibility. It was duty. It was suffering rejection and accepting their failings. Of missing them and not being there when they had needed him most. Love was intertwined with inadequacy and loss.

Even his most recent conversation with his mother, when they had unknowingly shared her laced coffee, had left him tasting the bitterness of being in the wrong. She had reminded him of the times she had invited him to come for Christmas and other events. *Come see my show.*

His father had always grown too anxious over his impending departure. Leander was the one who had canceled and stayed home, but he'd been a child, oblivious to what he was doing to her and their relationship. Oblivious to how limited time really was.

So, to have Ilona's love was to feel a weight on him. But when he looked on her as she came to the rail at the bow, her expression glowing with delight, the weight was only that of a little bird on his heart. An iridescent hummingbird that zoomed in, piercing into his tenderest flesh with her tiny claws.

"That's Paxos! How did you know?" She beamed up at him.

"How do you think? I asked Feodor where he thought you would most like to go. I don't think he'll be so forthcoming in future. Do you know if he's speaking to Androu yet?"

"Leander." She touched her chest in mock shock. "Are you matchmaking?" She accompanied her accusation with a skim of her fingers down his spine.

Her touch might as well be a bell pull, tugging and ringing all his nerve endings to life despite the fact they'd only left their wrecked bed an hour ago.

"Hardly. Our PAs need to communicate." He scooped her under his arm and gave her a squeeze. "How else will I know where to meet you for lunch?"

"Issue them a memo explaining the benefits of kissing and making up," she suggested with a bat of her lashes at him.

"You're in a cheeky mood." He liked it.

"I'm floating up there somewhere." She waved at the cloudless sky above the island of her birth, then wrapped both her arms around his waist, gazing up at him with eyes of inky wonder. "You brought me *home*."

The emotion in her voice sent a piercing sensation into his throat and vibrations rolled in his chest like thunder. Pride, he thought with irony. He was pleased he had given her something that made her smile so unreservedly, but there was also humility in how little it took to please her.

"You're not wishing I'd taken you to Paris for shopping?"

"Oh, I'll be shopping," she assured him. "This small island can't produce enough soap and olive oil for Callas, but I order for my own use several times a year. The fragrances are pure nostalgia triggers."

Her elation was so beautiful, she stole his breath.

Her resilience awed him, actually. He didn't know how she was so good at catching at a moment like this, of grasping the happiness and erasing everything else. His anger was still a cold wraith inside him, swirling and darkening his vision even as the affectionate way she rested her head on his chest filled him with softness and light.

He wouldn't spoil her mood, though. He rubbed her arm and kissed her temple and said, "I need to make one call, then we'll jump on the tender and go ashore."

His one call was to Androu. He issued a dozen orders, some to release his various hounds against Midas. Others were PR related, countering the headlines about Ilona's arrest. Each time Leander saw the photos of her being arrested in her wedding gown, he tasted blood. Midas would pay for that if it was the last thing he ever did.

"Your mother is safely on her way home," Androu informed him as they wrapped up. "Once the hotel identified him, the room service attendant turned himself in. He claims he only meant to drug your mother, not you. It was meant to draw you from the wedding to her side. He gave up the name of the intermediary who hired him. Investigators are trying to tie him to Midas. They *have* found a connection between one of the arresting inspectors and Midas."

Leander fought back a rush of *I knew it* rage.

"Keep me informed. And..." Was he losing his edge?

"If you need me to speak to Feodor, to explain that you weren't to blame for my absence yesterday, I can do that."

There was such a lengthy silence, Leander thought the connection had been lost.

Then, "Thank you, but we're both professionals. Any personal issues will be handled between us and won't affect our work."

That wasn't entirely what Leander was worried about. He appreciated both men. Androu had put out a thousand fires while trying to find Leander yesterday. Feodor would die for Ilona. They were too valuable to lose, but Leander didn't want either of them to be uncomfortable in their work life.

He *was* losing his edge, growing invested in the private lives of not only his own employee, but his wife's.

He donned his usual air of detachment and ended the call, heading outside to take Ilona to shore.

Paxos was a bustling tourist destination in the high season, as all Greek islands were, but it was inconvenient enough to reach that it wasn't as overrun as most others. Antipaxos, its smaller, modest sister, was even more serene, especially now as they explored the pair of islands in the waning shoulder season.

For the first few days, they sailed between Gaios, Loggos and Lakka, walking the narrow streets of each, stopping for iced coffee, eating in the main square and poking in shops for small treasures. When they reached the isolated west side, they went ashore to visit hidden coves and empty beaches and swam into the famed blue caves.

"I've always wanted to do this," Ilona said as they were treading water in one cool, shadowy cave, the water glowing dark blue around them. Her hushed voice echoed off the dripping ceiling.

"Why haven't you?" Leander asked.

"Fear." It was still there, but she was beginning to see that it was in her power to decide how much power that emotion had over her.

For instance, she kept holding back the words, those terrifyingly revealing words that were on her tongue and in her throat and pulsing in her heart every moment she was near him.

Why didn't she want to say them? Fear. Fear that he would reject her. Fear that he wouldn't feel the same. Fear that speaking her love aloud would break a spell and change all that was good between them.

But how he reacted was not in her control. If he didn't feel the same, that was his loss. She would rather allow her love to imbue her whole soul and flow freely from her heart than keep it boxed and dammed and compressed inside her like a miser hoarding gold.

"I love you, you know," she told him, and as she did, a glorious weight lifted off her. She became part of the air and salt and water, buoyant and whole. Universal.

"I do know," he said gravely. "I never want to hurt you. I hope you know that."

It did hurt to hear him say that, but the hurt was for him, for his inability to release himself to this thing that was expansive and healing and terrifying, yet so very right.

With a sway of her arms and a low, lazy kick, she moved across to him. He caught her and cradled her, holding her up as she wound her legs around his waist and cupped his jaw in her wet hands.

"Don't look at me with regret," she scolded gently. "Not ever. You've given me things I never thought I'd have. Courage." Her smile wobbled with self-deprecation. "Freedom." And maybe...

The timing was wrong. Her cycle was due in a day or

two. She wouldn't get her hopes up, but maybe, someday, he would give her love in its purest form.

"I don't ever want you to be afraid again. But I'm afraid for you when you're this unguarded. I will protect you in every way I can, Ilona, but I need you to protect yourself. Even from me. Especially from me. Can you do that?"

"No. It's too late," she said wryly and tried to kiss him.

He balked briefly, then kissed her back. Hard. As if he couldn't help himself. As if she was the source of his oxygen.

Then he drew back and released her completely. The seawater felt cold against skin that had been warmed by his body. His shadowed profile searched the darkest corners of the cave.

"We can't make love here," she said. "We might get crabs."

His crack of laughter bounced off the ceiling. "True." He shook his head at her, then sobered. "That's not what I was looking for."

She knew. He was looking for some way to let her down easy or put distance between them. He didn't want to hurt her, but he wanted to protect himself. She understood that. All too well.

"I've had to take care of myself for a long time, Leander. I know how." She dipped under and swam toward the sunlight, surfacing to say, "Let's go back to the yacht. I'm hungry."

Leander felt trapped in one of those medieval devices, the kind that was attempting to tear him apart.

One half of himself was firmly affixed in the heaven that was his wife. They made love and shared inside jokes and talked of what they wanted to accomplish in the future. She was fascinating in her approach to her work, smart and ambitious, yet driven by empathy and a desire to make the world a better place. If she wasn't so devoted to her own business, he would have lured her to a lead position in his own.

The other part of him was dragged down by the grim hatred and thirst for revenge that had governed his life for so long. He couldn't forget that soiled wedding gown or her absolute loss of faith in him. He *had* to make good on his promise to avenge her. It was as important to him as righting the wrong his father had suffered.

Leander began making headway once he was no longer giving in to the lazy bliss of sailing and lovemaking. They returned to Athens where they both became busy with work demands and, as Ilona had predicted that long-ago day, with social obligations. For some reason, being married meant invitations had increased exponentially.

Perhaps it was their notoriety. The headlines after the ruined wedding had shouted, Married in Secret! False Arrest Fails to Halt True Love, and More Family Twists than a Greek Tragedy.

The stock value in Pagonis had dropped shortly after, when an enterprising reporter, aided by Leander, had dug up his father's original lawsuit over the stolen technology. Midas disappeared from the public eye once he was identified by someone in Ilona's building from the night he had attacked her. He was quietly divesting some of his lesser, overseas properties, likely to pay his PR and legal teams.

Leander doubled the security presence that dogged him and Ilona. It was inconvenient, but he was especially concerned when she was at work.

"Half a floor may come open in my building," he told her one morning. He was actually considering not renewing the existing lease to vacate it. "You could move your headquarters there, leave the lab to do its work where it is."

"And meet you in a broom closet during coffee break?" she teased. "Delightful as that sounds, I'm in the middle of restructuring. Now that I have full control, I want to be on-site."

He didn't love that answer, but he let it drop since they were arriving at tonight's gala and always caused a stir when they walked a carpet.

Leander liked to believe it was because Ilona had finally embraced all that she'd naturally been given. She was an absolute vision wherever she went. Tonight, she wore a figure-hugging black gown with intricate silver beading decorating its waist and hem. The feature that had him biting his lip, however, was the sleeveless style that lovingly accentuated the fullness of her breasts. The way three very thin straps ran down her otherwise naked back made him want to keep her in this car and kiss every inch of skin he could find.

But he helped her rise and offered a steady arm as they made their way toward the entrance of the hotel.

"Who are you wearing? Tell us about your gown!" photographers shouted.

Ilona always paused to tell them, having accepted her infamy. In fact, she had turned it into a strength when these hounds had made their first appearance after their honeymoon. Facing a gauntlet of paparazzi and speculation, she had answered the question about her gown, then joked, "I wanted to look my best, in case I'm arrested again."

"Look your best for your arrest" had become a meme overnight and was regularly pasted over her photo in whichever glamorous gown was her latest. Anticipation and mystique had grown over what she would wear next, the furor so intense that top designers were now sending her gowns in hopes of gaining exposure.

This evening would have been yet another rousing success if two things hadn't happened. The first was that Odessa was intending to be here. Leander had learned she was on the guest list and would have had her removed—or would have refused to attend—but Ilona pushed his concerns aside.

"We have to cross paths at some point."

Leander still would have kept Ilona on the far side of the ballroom, but it happened that Odessa came onto the dance floor as he was circling with Ilona. It was a deliberate ambush, he suspected, since Odessa spoke loud enough to turn heads.

"That slut."

Leander instinctually angled his body to shield Ilona while glaring a warning at the woman, but Ilona brushed him off and turned to confront her stepmother.

"You raised three children, Odessa. At least one of them turned out very poorly. Any blame for that child's behavior lies with you."

An amused murmur went through the crowd and someone guffawed. Leander was pretty damned impressed himself.

"Would you excuse me?" Ilona asked Leander and disappeared to the powder room.

He waited near the entrance for her return to the ballroom, worried the confrontation had taken more out of her than she had let on, especially when she appeared only to say she would rather leave.

"I should have told them to remove her from the list," Leander said in the car.

"Hmm? Oh, I don't care about her." Ilona flicked her wrist in dismissal.

"But you're upset."

The corners of her mouth went down. "I had a backache earlier and hoped I was wrong, but... I'm not pregnant."

"Oh. I'm sorry." He was, but the words were stupidly in-adequate, especially because this was the second time she was disappointed on that front. The first had been while they'd still been sailing. She'd been philosophical, saying the timing wasn't right, but this time he could see she was genuinely saddened.

So was he, more sharply than he expected, but he didn't say so. He reached for her instead, drawing her across and into his lap.

But as he held her, the ache of something lost or a chance missed became so unbearable, he did what he always did, rather than dwell on the pain of everyday life. He turned his mind to his revenge.

The board meeting was two weeks away. Soon, he kept promising himself. All the pieces were coming together and soon he would swing his final death blow and every-thing would feel right again.

Ilona had begun to believe happily-ever-after was real and that she was living it.

After steeping in the harmony of their honeymoon, they had returned to Athens where she took full custody of her company. It was thrilling! No more Midas poking his nose in, questioning her decisions. She didn't even have to take his calls, not that he tried to reach out. He seemed preoc-cupied with keeping his name out of unfavorable headlines which suited her beautifully.

Ilona had half expected a call from Odessa after her performance at the gala the other night, but according to Feodor, Leander and Ilona were more coveted guests than Odessa was. The word was out that Odessa had seriously misbehaved. Her invitations had dried up overnight.

Ilona was neither pleased nor sorry. She was indiffer-ent and that, too, was thrilling. She and Leander rarely spoke of any of that old, painful business. He had told her he was keeping a wall between her and his actions as a sort of protection against Midas retaliating, but she had actually started to believe they were both putting all of it behind them.

Not so, apparently.

"I had lunch with Hercules today," she told Leander with concern when they were sitting down for a rare dinner at home. She had served the meal the housekeeper had prepared and had sent the woman home early so they could have some privacy for their discussion.

"Why?" Leander's shoulders tensed and his voice became lethal.

"Because he invited me." She poured the wine because he was only sitting very still, staring at her through narrowed eyes. "Have you really stolen his entire show?"

"No." He picked up the glass she filled and took a healthy swallow. "I stalled it."

"Leander—"

"Do not defend him," he warned. "He has benefited off my father's work, same as the rest of them. He has to pay."

"And he sees that. It's fair for you to go after his job at Pagonis. Go after the profits from his shares. But going after his paintings isn't right."

"Why not? How did he afford that studio and all the time and supplies to paint? Hmm?"

"The value isn't in the canvases and tubes of paint. It's what he did with it. He's an artist. A creator. What you're doing *hurts* him, Leander." Like her, Hercules didn't know how to be happy. He was afraid of it. But when it was only him and his brush, he poured out his soul. He had been in tears when he'd told Ilona what Leander had done.

"Good," Leander said flatly.

"Really? You have no empathy, no regard for him at all? He bailed me out of jail when you couldn't," she reminded.

"And remains complicit in all the things Midas has done to you," he shot back. "How can you accept that?"

"I'm not asking you to retaliate for *me*. Do you realize that? You deserve recompense for what Midas did. You do," she assured him. "But this…blind determination of yours to inflict pain is not healthy. Especially if you think you're doing it for my sake. I don't want you to do that, Leander. It makes you no better than Midas if you enjoy hurting people."

"I'm righting the scales of justice."

"No. What you're doing to Hercules is *punishment*." It was the twist in Leander's psyche she had feared could happen.

"You're really taking his side over ours?" He was more than affronted. Astounded.

"How is it 'our' side? You're not including me in any of this. Remember?" For her protection, he had said, but she suspected it was yet again a trust issue. She had been feeling so close to him. She *loved* him. But he was stuck in the past, still allowing Midas to dictate who he was and what he did and how he felt.

"Fine," he snapped. "It's not our side. It's mine. So pick which one you're on and it better be mine."

A tearing sensation went through her middle. She looked down at her fragrant lamb and roasted potato, appetite gone.

Tragically, she wasn't as surprised as she ought to be. She had always expected it could come to this. Leander was so fixated on his need for vengeance, he would push aside everything she offered him. Everything they'd made together.

But what had they made? If his revenge was still more

important than she was, if it was his everything, then they didn't have anything.

"I know you can't see it, but I'm not fighting for Hercules. I'm fighting for you," she told him shakily, throat going tight. "For *us*."

"You're fighting *me*. You're asking me to give up."

"To give in. A *little*."

"No!" He rose and left the table so abruptly, the wine sloshed in their glasses. "And the fact you're pushing me on this makes me wonder if you've *ever* been on my side. Is all of this a smokescreen?" He waved at their house, the one that had begun to feel like a home. "Because it won't work. I won't let you derail me from seeing this through."

A searing line sat like a spear from her throat into her chest, holding her still as she absorbed how painful it was to watch him lose faith in her so completely. To question her love for him.

"Do you remember what I said I would do if things came down to you or me?" she asked, voice thick with the anguish spreading through her.

She heard him swallow, but she couldn't seem to raise her eyes to look at him. She couldn't bear to see how little he valued the heart she had given him.

"I'm not cutting you loose," he said through clenched teeth.

"You're asking me to look the other way while you hurt someone I care about."

"I thought you cared about *me*," he shot back ferociously. "I thought you *loved* me."

His bitter taunt was the final straw. She felt the break inside her, but she had always known he would break her heart. She hadn't known it would be an actual shattering sensation in her chest, the resulting pain exploding like a hive of wasps, all determined to sting her to death.

"I do love you. But you don't love me." She could survive that, she could. But, "It's obvious you don't even care enough to recognize that what you're asking me to do will damage something in me that won't be repaired. I can't be part of this blood feud any longer, Leander. I can't side with you. For my own self-preservation, I have to side with *myself.*"

He let her go. She promised to keep her guard detail, but those were the last words they exchanged. She packed and hovered an extra minute, perhaps waiting for him to say more, to give in and beg her to stay, but he had nothing to say. He had come too far to give up now. How could she not see that?

He was furious with her. Forsaken. She had known who she was marrying! How could she desert him when he was on the cusp of vanquishing his enemy for good?

Hercules had come begging her to persuade him to show mercy. Odessa was rumored to be preparing for an extended stay in New York, having become deeply unpopular. Midas, that vile maggot of a man, was gasping for financial air. His reputation was tarnished, associated with Ilona's false arrest and other corrupt deeds. Leander hadn't leaked the restraining order for Midas to the press, but that too was being reported as an "unconfirmed rumor." Even the patent question on Leander's father's technology had been resurrected, proving Midas had feet of clay.

Leander *had* to seize his day when the board meeting arrived, but felt curiously flat when it did. He climbed into the back of his SUV, aware that he would push Midas off his pedestal once and for all today, but there was no excitement for the other man's downfall. All he could think about was Ilona.

Leander had already made enough compromises for her

Hadn't he? Did she not recall that he had agreed to run the company in good faith? Rather than level it? Why was that not enough for her? What more did she need to hear before she would stand behind him? Stand *beside* him?

God, her absence hurt. He had moved through these last days in a zombielike trance, making his final calls, ensuring the various board members would support him. They had all agreed to back his bid for the chair, but there was no satisfaction in it.

He, the man who had preferred for years to walk alone and eat alone and sleep alone was...alone. Desolate.

He couldn't stop thinking reliving those intimate moments when she had brightened and softened and exploded. Was it the sex? Did she not enjoy it the way he did? Because it nearly killed him in the most deliciously satisfying ways. Every time. She was fierce and uninhibited and they always seemed to arrive at culmination together, bodies shaking and hearts crashing and ecstatic cries filling the room.

He didn't want to lose that. How could she let it go so easily?

Was it his desire for children? The fact it hadn't happened? Did she blame him?

Was it *him*?

Here was the deepest bruise, the darkest fear, the rawest worry. Was there some flaw in himself that he didn't see? One that caused the people he loved to disappear when he needed them most?

Oh, hell. He closed his eyes and the breath he sucked in seemed filled with powdered glass, expanding in his lungs with fiery tingles, leaving him without oxygen. Lightheaded.

He loved her.

The poignant arrow of love was lodged so deeply in his heart, it had become a part of him without his realizing it.

He loved her. He loved her beyond what he thought was possible. Beyond what any one person had felt for another in the history of time. His love was epic and terrifying and so bright and *right*, it caused a hot pressure behind his eyes and in his throat.

That's why his chest was a hollow, cavernous, windy space. That's why his bed was, too. And their new home. Ilona could have moved into her unused bedroom, but instead she had left him completely. He couldn't bear it. Not for another second.

He turned his head. "Call Feodor and find out where she's staying."

Androu didn't ask who he meant. He placed the call and his mouth went flat. "Feodor can't say," he relayed.

"Give me that," Leander snarled, holding out his palm "Tell me where she is, Feodor." He *needed* her.

"I genuinely don't know. I swear. She asked me to get our new CEO organized—"

"Your new—? She stepped down from running Callas?" Leander sat up and clamped a hand on Dino's shoulder, ensuring his driver knew a sudden change in route might be necessary. "Is she even in Athens? Is she *accounted* for?"

"She texted twenty minutes ago, reminding me the plant in her office shouldn't be overwatered."

A ridiculously innocuous message, yet jealousy overwhelmed him that she continued to communicate with Feodor and wanted nothing to do with him. Because he had hurt her. He had asked her to compromise her principle to prove her love, which wasn't love at all.

He handed the phone back to Androu and stared at the back of Dino's head.

"She's on Paxos. She must be," Leander muttered.

"Would you…like me to have the yacht prepared?" Androu asked tentatively.

Dino was looking at him in the rearview mirror. Both were awaiting his decision.

The helicopter would be faster, but what if she wasn't there? What if he went all that way and missed this meeting only to miss her?

Or worse, what if she was there and he went all that way only to have his love thrown back in his face?

He pinched the bridge of his nose, head tilted back, filled with despair because he was about to get everything he wanted—

No. He had *had* everything he wanted. Everything he needed. Ilona filled his life with meaning. She made him laugh, made every moment of every day more enjoyable. She consistently took him to the heights of profound pleasure. She made him *happy.*

She made all that had happened in his past bearable. She pushed it into the past so he could look forward to his future with her.

Yet here he was, chasing destruction. Returning to the rotten tooth, rather than pulling it. He was reveling in pain and wanted to inflict it on others, purely to satisfy some demon inside him. He *was* no better than Midas.

"Dino—" he started to say, but Dino was halting at the curb outside the Pagonis International building, the citadel Leander had spent half a lifetime plotting to conquer.

How had he thought crushing someone would fill the void inside him? Ilona filled that void. *Love* did.

"Sir—" Androu was looking toward the building.

"Find out if she's on Paxos," he told Androu without moving. "Ready the helicopter if she is."

"She's, um, here." Androu pushed from the vehicle and pointed. "I can see her through the window, looking at us." He lifted his hand in a wave.

Leander thrust himself from the car, heart following a

second later and crashing into its place inside his chest, then filling his throat with a hammering pulse.

There she was, standing at the lobby window, solemn as she looked at him. Her hair was gathered in a single dark line against the front of her fitted navy blue dress. Always so beautiful and patient.

Patient enough to wait for a man who hadn't seen what he had? Was he too late to tell her how he felt?

Her expression didn't change as he strode into the building, but she turned to face him as he approached her.

"You're here." He opened his hands, wanting to grab her close. Wanting to *hold* her. Claim her. He wanted to kneel and beg her to never leave him again.

Her grave expression held him off. Her words about a blood feud were still ringing in his head.

"You don't have to be," he told her. "*We* don't have to be here. We can go anywhere."

Her eyes flared wider briefly before she said, "No. This is important. To both of us."

"*You* are important to me." He stepped forward and caught her cold hands. "I was going to come find you. Were you on Paxos?"

"I was, but—" Her face flexed with conflict, then her expression darkened as she looked past him.

Leander looked over his shoulder in time to see Midas pause as he spotted them. His face twisted and he continued on into the elevators.

Leander closed his hand more securely over Ilona's and felt her nails dig into his skin. When he looked at her, she wasn't showing signs of fear. Only anger. Steely determination.

"Let's go up," she said.

"You're sure?"

She nodded.

His heart lifted. He really was getting all he'd ever wanted.

They rose to the executive floor where the board of directors was assembling. As they entered, Leander overheard Midas arguing with Hercules.

"*I* vote Mother's share when she's out of town."

"Not this time." Hercules handed a piece of paper to someone stationed behind a laptop. "She gave me her proxy last night."

Midas narrowed his eyes. "Don't do anything stupid, Hercules. And why is *he* here, if you are?" Midas demanded as he transferred his glower to Ilona.

"Leander is my proxy. I'm here for other reasons," Ilona said with unruffled composure.

"She's a material witness," Leander clarified.

"To *what*? She's the one who was recently arrested. Not me."

"To the fact you're unfit to run Pagonis International," Leander said firmly. "Is everyone here? If so, I've added a leadership review to the top of the agenda."

"You're not in charge," Midas said. "So pipe down and get lost."

"I'm about to be in charge," Leander assured him, still holding Ilona's hand tight in his own. "Ladies and gentlemen, your current president is not only a walking disgrace, he'll soon be arrested on charges of assault and making false reports to the police. The things you've read online are not a PR smear as he would like you to believe. They're true and I've brought a presentation and documents to prove it." He nodded at Androu to start the projector.

"And embezzlement," Ilona interjected.

The room went silent. Everyone swiveled their attention to her. If a pin had dropped on the carpet, it would have struck with the force of a gong.

"That doesn't surprise me," Leander said to her. "But I don't have evidence of that. Do you?"

Midas snorted. "No. Because it's not true."

"I went to Paxos," she said. "I tried to buy the restaurant my mother once worked at, but learned it was already a Pagonis property. The proceeds are supposed to accrue for my use, but somehow the funds have been going into an account that eventually benefits Midas. And it's *empty*."

All the heads swung back to Midas.

"Accounting error," he said with an unbothered blink. "I'm sure we can clear that up."

"Indeed. A full audit will be my first priority," Leander said with deadly assurance.

"You don't have the votes to take over," Midas said with a scathing chuckle. "I *know* you don't." He sent a glare of intimidation around the table.

Several people dropped their gazes and shifted in their seats.

"Did dear Mitéra instruct you to vote for him? Or me?" Midas asked Hercules as if he already knew the answer.

"She wanted me to vote for you," Hercules admitted then sent a glance toward Ilona as though looking for her reaction to that.

Midas sat back, releasing a snort that said, *See?*

"Until I explained that I spoke to the police and reported *I* was with her the night Ilona was assaulted in her apartment. And that you weren't with us." Hercules darted a glance at the gathering thunder in his brother's expression. He slouched protectively, but continued. "Once she realized she might be charged with providing a false alibi, she told me to vote with my conscience and left for New York. She'll remain there indefinitely."

Leander lifted a brow at Midas. *Your move.*

Midas ground his teeth so hard there should have been

an audible crack. "That doesn't prove I was anywhere near Ilona."

"No," Ilona agreed with quiet dignity. "But the florist receipt for the roses and vase does imply you had them brought to my door. And my neighbor heard your voice. He and his partner both reported that I said it was you outside the door."

"Why are you still here?" Midas demanded hotly. "Only one of you should be in this room. You said he's here to vote your share so get out."

"The one who is leaving is you," Leander said with grim satisfaction. "Let's proceed with the vote."

Leander looked around the table, ending with Hercules. He felt a pinch of guilt for stalling the man's gallery showing. He had meant it to be further pressure against Midas, but Ilona was right. It had taken on a more personal element that wasn't right.

"Are you prepared to support me?" Leander asked, accepting that Hercules might refuse.

Hercules licked his lips and looked to Ilona again. "I can't. Keep my paintings. Get whatever you can for them. Ilona has explained you're due compensation from our family. Let that be mine to you."

Leander didn't want *paintings*.

"Forget what ought to come to me," he said impatiently. "Are you really not prepared to depose the man who is responsible for all of these scandals? For harming your *sister*?" Leander shook his head in disbelief. Outrage. "I'm not here for payback." Not anymore. "He has to be stopped. Surely you can see that! I do have the votes, by the way," he told Midas as the other man made a dismissive noise. "Even without Hercules or your mother."

This time, however, when Leander looked around for confirmation, gazes dropped. Men and women he had spoken to himself, people who had assured him he had their support, couldn't meet his eyes.

A cold fist wrapped itself around his heart when even Rideaux winced and opened his mouth, seeming to search for words as he looked to Ilona.

"Leander." Her voice was apologetic, her touch on his arm light. Tentative.

And he knew. He knew that she had interfered. She was preventing him from taking over. She was *stealing* his moment when he should be exacting the revenge he had poured his heart and soul and blood and sweat into achieving.

She had warned him from the beginning she wouldn't be used as a pawn.

Apparently, she would rather be a queen.

Ilona had gone to Paxos determined to flip the script on her life. For most of her life, the dream of starting over there had been her mental refuge from heartache, the place she believed would be there for her when existence became too much to bear.

Leaving Leander had been excruciating, but staying hadn't been an option. She had really thought she was saving herself by seeking that simple life she'd always dreamed of.

It hadn't worked. Leander had been there, imbuing every inch of beach and rocky hill and placid cove with memories of their honeymoon. And when she had tried to find solace in that whimsical connection to her mother's memory, she had only confronted more of Midas's treachery.

Hatred had nearly consumed her, then. In those moments, she had understood why Leander was so bent on destroying Midas. It had felt as though Midas had ruined *them* and she had wanted to make him pay for all she had lost.

If Midas did tear them apart, however, it would be because she had let it happen. Whether Leander loved her back wasn't important. Leander had helped her believe that she mattered. He had taught her to have courage and strength and had shown her how to stand up for herself. For that, he deserved her love. She would *always* love him.

And in loving him, she held a force more powerful than destructive hate. Love infused her with hope. Love *healed*. Love made her brave enough to pull the things she loved from the fire. And that's where Leander was right now. He was burning up in the flames of hate.

She wanted to lift him out, but would he see it that way?

"They're voting for you. Aren't they?" He was putting it together very quickly. "That's why you brought in a new CEO at Callas."

She held her breath, waiting for the lash of betrayal to strike behind his eyes.

"I was hoping you would support me, too." Her voice was a near whisper. "Justice will be served, Leander. I'll go back as far as I need to ensure it." She clenched her fist on his sleeve. "You don't have to keep fighting to take what you think should be yours." She couldn't interpret what he was thinking as emotions shifted like storm clouds in his gray eyes. "You can put down your weapons and let me give it to you. If you'll trust me to do it?"

Her own eyes were growing damp with distress. He seemed to be growing bigger before her, swelling with something...

Pride? Wonder?

A hot lump of emotion, of optimism, formed behind her breastbone.

"I would trust you with my life, Ilona. With my future. My children. My heart." His warm hand cupped the side of her neck. His smile grew with the fullness that was expanding in her chest. "Of course, I trust you to make things right for me. You already do."

She blinked fast, trying to see him through her gathering tears, smile wobbling all over the place.

Midas swore disparagingly, saying, "Get a room."

Leander sighed with annoyance. "I move that Midas be removed from his position as president and Ilona appointed in his place effective immediately."

"Second," Hercules said promptly.

Every hand went up except Midas's.

"Motion carried," Hercules noted to the meeting secretary. "I also move that any profit going to Midas from Pagonis International be held in trust pending an investigation into the technology in question. Those funds will be paid to Leander as part of his settlement if wrongdoing is found. It will be," Hercules said with distaste. "Mama left the safe open after collecting her jewelry. I turned over some very interesting documents to Leander's lawyer that our father had kept from that time."

"Second," someone else murmured.

Midas grew more agitated as votes returned a unanimous affirmative.

"You can't *do* this," he insisted.

"Notify Security to escort him out," Leander said to Androu.

"You'll be sorry," Midas said to Ilona as he thrust himself to his feet. "I'll make you pay for this."

"You're making threats in front of witnesses," Leander pointed out and tried to place himself protectively between Midas and her, but Ilona leaned forward against the table, staring down the man she had once feared. He seemed utterly pathetic now. Weak and small.

"Your threat will go in the *minutes*," she told him. "And I'll add it to the evidence of your assault. I advise you to retain good counsel for the plethora of legal problems you are about to encounter."

As Androu let in a security guard, Ilona flicked her tail of hair behind her shoulder.

"*Your* presence is no longer required," she told Midas. "*Get lost.*"

Midas left with a kick of a chair toward a window, leaving a web of cracks where it struck. He jerked his arm from the security guard's attempt to hold on to it, but he left.

The whole room exhaled. Everyone looked to each other with mixtures of shock and astonishment.

They had done it!

Light-headed with triumph, Ilona tried to gather some semblance of order.

"Has everyone met my husband?" she asked, hand shaking as she indicated him, unable to resist a proprietary sweep of her hand down his silk tie. "Leander will be voting my shares for the foreseeable future. He'll recuse when we negotiate my salary, obviously. Let's finish this as quickly as possible." She wanted him to herself. She wanted to go *home*.

She started to walk around to where Hercules was righting the chair Midas had vacated, but Leander caught her hand to draw her back.

"Do you know how incredible you are?" He stood her right in front of him and looked deep into her eyes, not seeming to care they had all these witnesses. "Do you understand how much I admire and love you? Because I love you more than I can express. *Nothing* matters if you're not in my life."

She had to swallow her heart back into place. His words shook her to her core. She was hardly able to bear the naked emotion in his eyes. He could have turned on her, but he loved her. She felt it soaking into her cells and membranes and soul. She might burst with the sheer volume of the seemingly endless pouring of joy into her being.

"I love you, too," she assured him shakily.

His arm looped behind her back and he lightly crushed her into his front.

As his mouth settled on hers, she heard Hercules say with amusement, "That goes in the minutes, too, that they love each other. In case there's any doubt in future."

There wouldn't be.

EPILOGUE

London, two years later...

"SHE'LL BE FINE," Leander's mother assured Ilona. "The nanny is here. We'll have a little play time, a bath, a story and a song... She'll wake in the morning and not even know you weren't here until you're back."

"*I'll* notice," Ilona said plaintively.

Leander didn't admit it, but he suffered hints of separation anxiety, too. It was hard enough to leave Delphine, named for Ilona's mother, for a few hours when they went to work. Leaving her overnight, even with his mother, was a big step.

It was also something Ilona had told him a dozen times was necessary for him to repair his relationship with his mother. *It's a sign of your forgiveness. She needs to know you trust her. She needs a chance to bond with Delphine, too. This is good for all of us.*

He had succumbed to her logic and, truth be told, was already fantasizing about having his wife to himself for a night in a very private and well-appointed hotel room.

First, they had to visit a gallery that was showing Hercules's latest works, though.

"The car is waiting," he reminded her. "We'll leave extra security here if that will make you feel better."

They didn't need security the way they used to. Midas

had used his last resources to flee to his mother's New York apartment. He was awaiting extradition to face charges in Athens. He also had various accusations working through courts in a number of other countries, many having come to light as his power to intimidate and retaliate had waned. He would always be a small concern, but Midas had become something unpleasant they only thought about so they could be sure they caught it early, like prostate cancer.

Ilona stole one more pet of Delphine's fine black hair and kissed her little wrinkle-nosed smile and they were away.

"Finally, I have you to myself." He picked up Ilona's hand and kissed her knuckles, noting the coiled ivy climbing toward the knuckle of her index finger. "What's this? Going somewhere?"

"No. I have two things I've been meaning to tell you. First, we have to work out a stretch of time where we can give up both Feodor and Androu."

"Feodor finally proposed?"

"He did." She cocked her head and made a face of sweet sentiment.

"Good for them. Tell them to book whatever works. Androu will figure out how to keep us from imploding in their absence. What else?" He gave the ring a small twist.

"Oh. Um. I thought you'd want to know that I, um…" She glanced at the closed privacy screen and whispered, "I had the doctor remove my IUD."

"You thought you would forget to tell me that?" he asked with amusement and another emotion that was bright and warm. He loved Delphine. Loved her to the moon and back. He and Ilona had talked about more children and he had made it clear he would have a dozen if Ilona was up for it, but he'd left it to her to decide when to try again.

"Sometimes we get carried away." She rolled her shoulder. "I thought you should be fully informed."

"We do get carried away," he acknowledged, tugging

her into leaning close enough he could nibble at the edge of her jaw. "Let's get carried away right now. We don't *really* have to see Hercules, do we?"

"I want to make an appearance so there aren't any hard feelings. Don't," she quickly added, holding up her finger between them. "I heard it as I said it."

A hard feeling was definitely liable to happen. He grinned and snapped his teeth at her finger, so enamored, he was stupid with it. And yes, he was impatient to get her alone, but anticipation had its attractions.

"Do you remember, a long time ago, that you told me the best revenge is to be happy?" he reminded her. "I didn't know I could *be* this happy until you came into my life." Until he had put down his anger and hatred and all the baggage he had carried, and allowed her love to surround him and fill him with this unrelenting contentment. "I'm smug as hell these days."

She blinked and bit a lip that had begun to tremble with emotion. "We're a good pair then, because I'm completely insufferable, too."

"I'm doing it right?" He touched his thumb to the dampness in the corner of her eye. "Loving you?"

"You really are." She offered her mouth for a soft, lingering kiss that could have turned into more. He couldn't help trailing his fingertips along her bare shoulder and she sighed a small encouragement as he did, but the car halted outside the gallery.

Ilona drew back and moved her ring to her thumb.

"That's to remind me we're only staying a few minutes. We have somewhere important to be. Bed," she mouthed, as if he wasn't already on that page with her.

He helped her from the car, so pleased he was obnoxious with it.

* * * * *

COMING SOON!

We really hope you enjoyed reading this book.
If you're looking for more romance, be sure to
head to the shops when new books are
available on

Thursday 18th August

MILLS & BOON®

Coming next month

INNOCENT UNTIL HIS FORBIDDEN TOUCH
Carol Marinelli

"Seriously?" His deep Italian voice entered the room before he even walked in. "I do not need a PR strategist?"

"A Liason Aide, Sir," his Aide murmured.

Beatrice stood as she'd been instructed earlier, but as he entered, every assumption she'd made about him was wiped away.

Prince Julius brimmed, not just with authority but with health and energy. It was as if a forcefield had entered the room.

She had dealt with alpha males and females at the top of their game – or rather – usually when they crashing from the top.

Not he.

He was, quite literally, stunning.

He stunned.

"It's a pleasure to meet you," she said and then added. "Sir."

"Likewise," he said, even if his eyes said otherwise.

God, he was tall, Beatrice thought, it was more than just his height, he was the most immaculate man she had ever seen.

Beatrice swallowed, not wanting to pursue that line of thought. The issue was that at most interviews she had found most people were less in the flesh.

He was so, so much more.

Continue reading
INNOCENT UNTIL HIS FORBIDDEN TOUCH
Carol Marinelli

Available next month
www.millsandboon.co.uk

MILLS & BOON

THE HEART OF ROMANCE

A ROMANCE FOR EVERY READER

ODERN

Prepare to be swept off your feet by sophisticated, sexy and seductive heroes, in some of the world's most glamourous and romantic locations, where power and passion collide.

STORICAL

Escape with historical heroes from time gone by. Whether your passion is for wicked Regency Rakes, muscled Vikings or rugged Highlanders, awaken the romance of the past.

EDICAL

Set your pulse racing with dedicated, delectable doctors in the high-pressure world of medicine, where emotions run high and passion, comfort and love are the best medicine.

ue Love

Celebrate true love with tender stories of heartfelt romance, from the rush of falling in love to the joy a new baby can bring, and a focus on the emotional heart of a relationship.

Desire

Indulge in secrets and scandal, intense drama and plenty of sizzling hot action with powerful and passionate heroes who have it all: wealth, status, good looks…everything but the right woman.

EROES

Experience all the excitement of a gripping thriller, with an intense romance at its heart. Resourceful, true-to-life women and strong, fearless men face danger and desire - a killer combination!

To see which titles are coming soon, please visit

millsandboon.co.uk/nextmonth